REDEEMING THE DEAD

Also by Steven Kerry Brown

The Complete Idiot's Guide to Private Investigating
5 Things Women Need to Know About the Men They Date
Redeeming the Dead

REDEEMING THE DEAD

A MORMON MURDER MYSTERY

BY

STEVEN KERRY BROWN

Hard Row Publishing Inc.

PREFACE

This book is a work of fiction. The settings are real but any likeness to any person living or dead is totally coincidental and not intended by the author.

REDEEMING THE DEAD

First Edition: October 2014
Hard Row Publishing Inc.
ISBN: -13: 978-0-9892054-2-9

First Edition
987654321

ONE

AUGUST 1990

The phone rang again. Patricia stared at the Sheriff's office switchboard and inwardly groaned. A quick glance around the communications center showed she was alone.

She'd hoped to get a head start on her math homework between phone calls but the thing was ringing non-stop. Not to mention the deputies radioing in, requesting 10-27s and 10-28s, thinking every person they stopped was a Top Ten FBI fugitive. And now that it was noon, half of the deputies were 10-7 for lunch.

"St. Johns County Sheriff's office. May I help you?"

"Pete Bagger here. Punk kids broke into my potato shed again. Hard enough to make a living growing tubers without fighting thieves. Can you send Dick Sharp out?"

The voice was not Pete Bagger. Gravelly and obscured like the caller held a kerchief over the mouthpiece. She still recognized the voice. Afraid to do what he asked, but more afraid not to. "I can have a unit there in about an hour."

"Dick Sharp said he'd come himself next time this happened. Wanted to be the first to look the scene over real good before anybody else tramped around. Messed up the evidence, you know? And no marked units. The neighbors'll see, and I think one of them done it."

"Let me see if I can reach the detective on the radio. Can you hold?"

In a minute she'd contacted the detective and he agreed to meet the man at his potato bagging shed, just a toad jump south of Molasses Junction.

* * * *

Dick Sharp drove west on County Road 214 out of St. Augustine. The land was smooth as a snapping turtle's shell. Most of the fields were fallow. The potato and sweet onion crops already harvested. Bank loans paid and farmers' accounts fattened. He figured after he finished taking the burglary report from Pete Bagger he'd stop at the country store at Molasses Junction and pick up a gallon of wild flower honey that his wife loved so much. Surprise her with it.

The afternoon summer storms would begin around 4 pm. But right now the sky was clear. The area around Bagger's shed was ankle high in weeds. A creek ran behind this section of property and a copse of broad-leafed maples thrived in the higher drier land. Not low lying and swampy like most of St. Johns County.

Sharp exited the asphalt and drove through the open gate, navigating in muddy tractor ruts, hoping he wouldn't high-center and tear out the oil pan of the unmarked. A shiny new padlock secured the main rollup door to the barn-like building but the tin walk-through door stood open and swung on its hinges in the slight breeze. Another new padlock lay on the ground, shackle cut through. He bent to examine it. Looked like bolt cutters cut it not a hacksaw. An open-aired high-roofed building, where the actual picking and bagging took place, stood next to the shed. Nobody there.

He stuck his head into the barn. "Pete?" He smelled the heavy scent of diesel farm equipment, old oil spilled on concrete, and dry tilled soil.

"Back here," a gravelly voice said.

Didn't sound like Pete. He must be coming down with a case of bronchitis. He couldn't see squat in the dark, but shuffled deeper into the barn toward the sound.

When he'd stepped well into the shed, something like a two-by-four whacked him across the head and he fell to his knees.

"Teach you a lesson, didn't I?"

He raised himself to his knees, reached for his .357 revolver. Gone. He must have been out for a few seconds. A flashlight lay on a bench, its beam illuminating the man standing over him.

"You," Sharp said. "I should have known."

"I got two shots for you. One for my wife and one for nosing around my property."

Sharp saw the hollow points of the magnum rounds glisten in the light as the cylinder began its rotation and knew his wife would never get her honey.

TWO

DAY ONE

TWENTY-FIVE YEARS LATER

Winchester Young left his home, the fiberglass-over wood motor-cruiser docked at the Conch House Marina, ready for the day's surveillance. He drove across the narrow two-lane Bridge of Lions, which connects the shifting sands of Anastasia Island to the ancient city of St. Augustine. He passed the Spanish-built fort, Castillo de San Marcos.

Lots of blood shed on both sides of that fort's three hundred year-old walls. What is it about the letting of blood that encourages men to glorify battlefields?

A few miles farther south on the river is the federal park, Fort Matanzas. In 1565 two hundred and sixty-one shipwrecked French Huguenots surrendered to the Spanish who summarily dispatched them to the Spirit World. For four hundred and fifty years that little inlet to the ocean has borne the name *Matanzas*, Spanish for "slaughter."

He began his surveillance of Lisa Chambers a bed-hopping wife according to his client Rudy Chambers. The day before, her husband brought Winch her La Perla underwear. The two-step test kit he kept in his office showed positive for zinc. The second step confirmed the presence of acid phosphatase enzyme. The one-two punch, positive for somebody's DNA. Rudy Chambers swore the DNA did not belong to him.

Lisa had a three-day window of opportunity while her husband traveled to Belle Glade. But any rendezvous needed to be between 8:30 a.m. when their last kid departed home and 2 p.m. when the first school bus returned.

Some private investigators turn up their nose at family law cases. But Chambers's money paid his alimony obligations just as well as any corporate check and came as a cash retainer in advance. Saved him from chasing some cheap insurance company ninety days later. Insurance companies and attorneys are the slowest paying clients in the PI business.

Outside the mall entrance she sat in the Expedition applying fresh pink lipstick. One of the accouterments of war that women use to capture "their man." Capture being the operative word, and as in any victor-vanquished relationship, to the victor belonged the spoils. Which pretty well explained why he drove an eight-year-old Jeep with a hundred and fifty-thousand miles and lived on his beat-up boat while his ex lived in the house across the street from the beach and tootled around town in her Prius.

Winch pulled out his cell phone and spoke: "Call Woody." In a moment a female voice said, "Calling Woody." Woody, short for Woodrow "Eagle Feather" Copeland, as full-blooded Seminole as one could still find. Woody described himself as a direct descendant of the Timucuan Indians who hunted and fished the Florida peninsula for ten thousand years before the Spaniards arrived. But history argued with Woody, claiming the last of the Timucuans sailed to Cuba with the Spaniards when they ceded the flower state to the British in 1763. His cell made the connection.

"Security," Woody answered.

"Tonto?" Young said.

"Screw you, Winch. How many times I got to tell you not to call me Tonto?"

"Lighten up, I need a favor."

"Pretty stupid to be calling me then."

He sighed. "There's a lady coming into the mall entrance right now. Five feet, red hair."

"And I care why, exactly?"

It delighted Winch to get a look at his subject walking. Each person has her own distinct body language and range of motion. Once you've seen the subject walk they are easier to identify.

"Do you see her or not, man?"

"Okay," Woody said. "Tagged her with the front door camera. Now what?"

"I'll be right there."

Winch parked around the west side, knocked three times on the back door to the security office. Come on, Woody. He hit redial.

"Security," Woody said.

"I'm at the back door. Let me in."

"No can do. I'll get fired."

"What's it going to cost me, Woody?"

"Let's see, you got a beat-up, broke-down boat that can't get out of her slip. Two ex-wives–"

"Two? Depends upon how you count. Take over the payments, and she's yours."

But Winch would never give away Tracy, his first and last. Losing her pained him to the deepest levels of his being. They both cried when the judge granted their second divorce. She'd wanted it, not him. His steadfast belief in the Mormon Church and her carpe diem approach to life just weren't compatible.

"You win. I'll give you my copy of James Hall's *Tropical Freeze.* First edition, first printing." Sometimes he and Woody spent a Saturday morning cruising garage sales for rare books.

The security door opened. Woody, an olive skinned man of forty-three, black hair with a grey streak down the center of his pony tail stood in the opened doorway wearing his blue security uniform, a silver badge and a logo on his shoulder that read "Serve and Protect."

"You've got two of them," Woody said.

Winch snapped his phone shut and looked at his friend. "I'll give you the signed one." Woody glanced over his shoulder toward the darkened room and waved him in. Winch had been inside the security office more times than he could count and couldn't understand Woody's sudden hesitancy.

The room smelled of perfume. Orange and vanilla, maybe. Fruity. Or perhaps it was an air freshener. On Woody's desk lay a map of St. Johns County with a large area outlined in red marker.

"What's this?" Winch said.

"Thirty thousand acres of sacred Timucuan ground. You watch me, Bro, I'm going to stop those developers."

"It can't all be sacred." He turned his attention to a bank of sixteen color monitors which covered one wall of the room. He scanned for Lisa Chambers. "There weren't that many Timucuan Indians altogether."

"They're gone. Someone has to watch their backs."

"Stop them how?"

Woody pointed to an area on the map. "See this swamp. Originally it was wetlands. A hundred years ago they dammed it up and dewatered the acreage surrounding it so they could plant pine trees for the pulp mills. Now it's been sold to developers who are going to flood part of the pine tree land and make lakes for the golf courses."

Winch had more interest in where the Chambers woman had gone. "Where is she?"

Woody pointed to a smaller piece. "There are a couple of Timucuan mounds right in the middle of all that. One of those mounds will become the seventeenth green. A seven iron shot across the lake from the tee. I'm not going to let it happen. I'll sabotage the damn bulldozers so they can't breach the dam."

Winch shook his head. "They'll put you in jail."

Woody looked at one of the monitors and tapped it with the eraser end of a yellow pencil. "She's there."

They both studied the flickering screen. "Get arrested, you'll lose your job."

"You have to make a stand, sometimes." Woody adjusted a knob and the flicker ceased. "I know I can't stop them, but I can make a stand. You, a Mormon, of all people should understand that."

He was right. Choosing a course and staying firm even in the face of overwhelming odds was more important sometimes than winning.

On the monitor the short little redhead checked her watch. "Shopping?" Woody said.

"She's on a schedule."

"Aren't we all?" Woody turned his gaze away from the screens.

"Woody, you need to change your view on life from day-by-day to an eternal Mormon perspective like mine. What's a few years one way or the other in the face of eternity?"

His friend lifted the ponytail off his neck. Fanned the air. "You know what Einstein said about marriage and divorce?"

"I must have cut science class that day."

"He said insanity is repeating the same action over and over and expecting different results. Twice man. Same result." Woody made a gun out of his hand and shot him. Then blew across the tip of his index finger.

Winch studied the Chambers woman, wondering if Woody was right. He'd tried it twice with Tracy and even though they couldn't make it work his heart still belonged to her.

His subject walked into the food court, looked around and gave a little finger wave to a man sitting at a table drinking coffee alone. She bought a cup and sat across from him.

"Whoa," Woody said.

"You know the dude?"

"Vincent Renfro. First chief deputy at the Sheriff's office. Right hand man to the Sheriff himself." Woody ran his hand through his hair. "And a major player with the women in Ponte Vedra."

Ponte Vedra: the ritzy beach area of St. Johns County, where the number of trophy brides was surpassed only by the number of rich widows. Winch thought he saw movement under the table. "Can we get a better view of what's going on down there?"

Woody moved a joystick. "Your woman there, she ever come home with bruises?" The camera zoomed and the auto iris opened. Lisa rubbed her foot over Renfro's calf.

"I'd have to ask my client."

"Renfro's known for playing rough. There's more than one complaint at the Sheriff's office."

"Is he married?"

"His wife thinks so."

Winch looked around the security room. "I need a jacket, a coat."

Woody gave him a questioning look.

"Like the food service people, or the cleaning folks wear."

Woody nodded toward a closet. "Over there."

He picked one that looked to be about his size. “A baggie—a plastic bag? You got one?”

Woody pointed to the trashcan.

Winch sifted through the garbage can. He reached for a sandwich bag, pulled it out of the trash. Opened it, and blew breadcrumbs out. “This’ll do.”

He stepped into the mall, wearing the coat, baggie in his pocket and headed to the food court. Vincent Renfro stood and whispered something in Lisa’s ear. She smiled. Renfro trailed his fingers across her shoulders as he departed, a Glock strapped to his hip.

As Lisa rose, he approached the table. “Here ma’am.” He reached for the two coffee cups. “I’ll get those for you.” That air freshener scent again. The mall must pipe it in with the air conditioning. When she turned her back he poured the dregs from Renfro’s cup into the trash, careful to pour it away from where Renfro’s lips touched the rim. Then he slipped it into the baggie. With any luck he’d have some of Renfro’s lip cells on the cup. A private DNA lab would match them with the sample from the La Perla underwear.

He left the coat with Woody and slipped out the security door to where he’d left his car.

Renfro leaned casually against his jeep.

What the crap? How did Renfro know he’d parked out here?

He grabbed Winch’s bicep and squeezed. “You got any ID on you?”

“Let go of my arm and I’ll show it to you.” He pulled his PI license out of his wallet.

Renfro wrote his name and license number on a small pad of paper. Handed it back to him. “She’s a friend of mine. You need to leave her alone.”

“I have a perfect right to be here.”

“Your little surveillance gig is blown. Trust me, following her is a waste of time.”

Renfro sauntered up the backside of the buildings and disappeared around the corner.

Winchester couldn’t figure out how Lisa Chambers made the surveillance? Someone must have tipped her off. But who?

THREE

The day's surveillance troubled Winch. He sat on a deck chair of the *Dos XX,* his almost rebuilt 38-foot Chris-Craft cabin cruiser, with a cold can of Diet Coke in his hand. He'd been thumbing through the Field Guide to Florida Dunes, learning he could make root beer from the smilax vine. A cousin to the sarsaparilla.

As troubled as he was at being made by Renfro and certainly Lisa, he also felt sort of smug since he'd probably obtained DNA from Lisa Chambers' lover, Detective Vincent Renfro. He figured he'd botched the surveillance in the morning by losing her, but then heroed out by finding her again at the outlet mall. And snagging the DNA? An act that would have impressed even his Uncle Benjamin, who'd willed him the P.I. agency.

Smug, yes, until he eyed the woman walking determinedly down the dock toward his wooden motor cruiser. Blond hair. Tailored and pressed blue jeans. She filled out a red sleeveless silk blouse and wore black flat shoes. From a distance this one looked to be in her early thirties. He was good at ages. She carried some sort of satchel or attaché case. Process server? Wouldn't be the first time he'd been served.

Keeping an eye on the approaching woman, he hefted the unopened envelope from a literary agency. It was thicker and heavier than the typical rejection letter. Probably contained the agent's uneaten tuna fish sandwich. He sniffed. Didn't smell like tuna fish. He stood, leaned it against the outboard side of the galley window and waited.

The woman in the pressed jeans looked left, then right, checking the names on each boat as she continued down the dock towards him. Barely five feet tall and a tiny waist. If the body is a tabernacle for the spirit then this was one well tabernacled spirit. Finally she came to his boat, looked at the name painted on the stern, *The DOS XX*.

"Dos Equis," she said. "Like in the beer?"

"Dos exes," he said. "As in wives."

"You proud of that?" She tilted her head. "A badge of honor or something?"

Having an ex-wife did not make him proud. Never, ever, thought he'd be divorced even once, much less twice. "More like a purple heart. Think I should just put hash marks on the stern. Save on paint."

"You think changing the name of your boat will change your luck with women?"

She looked maybe five years younger than he was. Thirty seemed about right. A very attractive face, slightly upturned nose.

"You hiked clear to the end of the dock just to insult me?"

"May I come aboard?" She kicked off her shoes, a sign that she knew some boat etiquette. She stretched out her hand. "I'm Carla Fox."

The name bounced around in his head, but he couldn't place it. He opened the boarding door and motioned toward one of the webbed beach chairs he used on the aft deck.

She gave him an appraising look. "I'd like to retain you."

"I'm a little picky about the cases I take." Which, of course, was about as true as calling his boat a yacht. The bilge pumps could barely keep the waterline below deck where it belonged.

"I'm picky about whom I hire. If I'm wasting my time. . . . "

He could use another case to work. "Something to drink?"

"Scotch," she said.

He held up his can. "How about a Diet Coke?"

"You don't drink?"

He shook his head. A charter sport-fishing boat passed, four guests toasting with cans of beer. The twin diesels, at idle, exhaust bubbles gurgling to the surface.

Carla watched the boat pass and then said, "I dated a guy who said he never trusted a man who didn't drink."

"Sounds like a wonderful judge of character. You ever been married to an alcoholic?"

"People told me you are a Mormon. In fact, that's partly why I'm here." She sat in the chair he'd indicated. "No iced tea?"

"Sorry." A faint scent of some flower blossom in her perfume drifted over him. Light and airy. Nice. No wedding band. Very nice. Maybe very unmarried.

"We southern girls need our sweet tea." She smiled. "But I guess I'll have to settle for a Coke." She looked at his Diet Coke. "I thought caffeine was a no-no for Mormons."

He reached into the deck refrigerator. "Popular misconception. Mormon's can drink caffeine and eat chocolate, thank heavens. But coffee and tea, tobacco, and alcohol are no-no's." He took a look at her manicured fingernails and popped the tab on the can of cola for her.

He recognized the name now. Carla Fox, some sort of chick-lit author. He'd never read her but he'd seen her books at Barnes and Noble. A motorboat putted past and the *Dos XX* rocked. Rose slightly. The swell of the passing wake slapped the floating dock.

"You're an author," he said. "What can I do for you?"

She put her hand into her satchel and pulled out a paperback, *Until Death Do Us Part.* "I'm looking for my sister. She disappeared here in Saint Augustine."

"Missing persons, skip tracing. Not my specialty, but I am pretty good at it."

She paused, seemed to be thinking. "She's been missing twenty-five years."

"And . . .you just now realized she's missing?"

"Not funny, Mister Young." She shook her head. "I was twelve when Sarah, who was eighteen, disappeared." She fanned the book. "I hit it big with this one. My father had already left us. Depression settled over Mom after Sarah disappeared. She got drunk and drove into a bridge abutment in South Carolina, killing herself. I'm selling a lot of books," she fished through her case again and held out a newspaper clipping, "I thought maybe I could put Sarah to rest."

He read the clipping:

Woman disappears, authorities baffled

Eighteen-year-old Sarah Fox of Athens Georgia disappeared this week. Relatives said she'd been in route to Daytona for spring break with three young men. The woman went missing after a visit to the Castillo de San Marcos and a stop for gas on US 1 South. When the trio readied to leave the convenience market Ms. Fox had disappeared.

Fox left the store to use the restroom. After gassing the car the boys found the restroom door locked. When opened by the manager the restroom was empty.

"She just vanished," one of Fox's traveling companions said. "One minute she was here, the next she was gone."

"There was no way she could have gotten out of there without us seeing her," another said. "We were, like here the whole time. And where would she have gone? There's no window in there. It's a mystery."

"Twilight Zone stuff," said another.

Fox hasn't been heard from since. A spokesperson for the Sheriff's office indicated no evidence of foul play had been found.

Fox was last seen wearing blue jeans, a hibiscus print flowered top, and hiking boots. Her backpack with clothing and personal items is also missing. St. Johns County Sheriff's office is asking for anyone with information concerning Ms. Fox's whereabouts to please call.

"Must be tough having a sister missing for twenty-five years. Anything else?" he said.

"Just the clipping. That's all I've got." From a side pocket of the satchel she pulled out a checkbook. "I'll give you a retainer."

Winch shook his head. "Ms. Fox, really, I couldn't do you any good. I'm a window peeper. I do surveillance, not murders." He pulled out his cell phone, began scrolling through his contact list. "I can refer you to another private investigator." He stopped scrolling. "You know that whatever you uncover now is not going to help your sister."

"I want you to dig into this," she said. "She's my sister. I'm going to find out what happened to her." As she slid her checkbook back into her satchel, a moment of regret passed through his mind.

He watched her eyes drift to the envelope from the literary agency. Cocked her head slightly, reading the return address label. "You have a manuscript? An agent?"

"I need a better boat." The bilge pump whirred. A stream splashed water over the side.

She looked around at the *Dos XX*. "Of course you do." She motioned toward the letter with her chin. "May I?"

"You may, but you don't need to. You know better than I, that in the publishing business, good news comes by telephone or email, bad news arrives with a postmark."

She nodded, opened the envelope. A quizzical look came over her face. She turned the envelope upside down. Several dozen inch-square pieces of paper floated to the deck. "Looks like a rejection."

She read from a white sheet.

Dear Mr. Winchester Young,

We are returning your first chapter. Please do not contact us with any additional materials until you graduate from high school.

Sincerely,
James Ivey

"Jerks," Carla said. "That's about the rudest rejection I've ever seen." Carla refolded the letter and drummed it against her chin.

He'd received plenty of rejection letters, but the confettied manuscript—that sunk to a new low. Then realization flashed in his head. He knew she was going to offer him the one thing most aspiring authors would slit throats for.

"I, of course, have an agent. My agent makes a lot of money off of me. If you'd be willing to work this case—"

He held up his hands. "Don't say it."

"I'm sure my agent would give your work a good read." She raised her eyebrows expectantly.

He stood. "I can't help you with a twenty-five-year-old murder. I follow cheating husbands and wives. That's about it."

"I need somebody I can trust, Winch. "I've talked to three other PIs," she shook her head. "I wouldn't trust them with an empty wallet."

"So I was fourth on your list?"

"Sixth. Two didn't answer their phones."

He shook his head.

"But one of them said some nice things about you."

He brightened. Maybe he was beginning to develop a reputation among his peers. "Oh?"

"Said you carried a big ego, but it was probably deserved. He also said you're honest. Ethical, even. A good Mormon boy. That's when I knew you were the private investigator I wanted."

"You looking for religion, are you? I can send a couple of missionaries on bicycles over to see you."

She reached into her purse and handed him a photo. Two girls and a boy.

He flipped it over. On the back was written, "March 1986 Carla-8, Rusty-12, Sarah-17."

He stared at the photo. In 1986 he was ten. He compared "little Carla's" face to the attractive woman sitting on his boat and could see it was the same person.

Seventeen-year-old Sarah: curled hair to the tops of her shoulders, a simple spring frock, sandals, and a crooked smile that said she was full of life, mischief, and fun. Three siblings, the oldest missing, presumed dead. He knew how it felt to have loved ones disappear. His own parents disappeared when he was ten. Only a photo for remembrance. Not even a grave for flowers.

His Uncle Benjamin, the great FBI agent, couldn't find them even with all of the agency's resources at his disposal. Here today. Poof. Gone the next.

"Sarah deserves a decent burial," she said. "Not some shallow grave in the sea oats and sand dunes. She deserves justice. Somebody killed her. Who's to say he hasn't killed others? He needs to be caught."

"Carla, I'm flattered, but you've got the wrong man. I won't take someone's money if I don't think I can help."

"Mr. Young–"

"Winch."

"Winch, you're. . . ." She ceased speaking. Her brow furrowed and her eyes wetted. "I need someone I can trust unconditionally. Someone who can't be bought or scared off." She stood and put her hand on his forearm. He felt heat from the palm of her hand. A shiver passed down him.

"I know your reputation. You may not be an experienced homicide investigator, but even your peers tell me you're clever. And resourceful too. I need you. But more than me, Sarah needs you. She's waited twenty-five years for you to find her killer. For me to come and pay the price that is needed to pull her out from whatever unmarked grave this killer put her in. Maybe find a little justice in the process. She deserves that, Winch."

"Are you sure she's dead? Maybe she ran away."

"Our home life seemed pretty decent. Our father the idiot skipped out but I don't think…well, you know. Sarah was an adult. She was in college. She could have just moved out if she'd wanted to. But then you can't ever be sure without a body."

He took a deep breath to buy himself a moment to think about innocence and justice and redemption. A clutch of gulls, cawing and screeching, fighting for scraps, hovered over the fish-cleaning station while a charter boat mate gutted a catch of snapper and trigger fish.

He made his living helping people who'd been wronged. And there's no greater wrong than the shedding of innocent blood. Was he up to this kind of case? He followed people. He'd never been schooled in police procedure and certainly not in the investigation of a murder.

Was he up to the task? He wasn't sure. Maybe he could get one of the other private investigators in St. Augustine to partner up with him. But he already had two interns working for him—Brandy and Woody. Did he need another who had experience with homicides?

"No," he said out loud, answering his own question.

"No?" Carla Fox said. "You're not going to help me?"

"No," he said. "That's not what I meant. Sorry." he said."

She opened the leather satchel and pulled out another sheet of paper.

Even looking at it upside down he could tell it was a fax.

“There’s one more thing you need to know, Winch. I have fifty thousand reasons why your honesty is important to me.” Carla handed him the fax.

Carla Fox,

I know where your sister is. Pay me $50,000 and I’ll lead you to her. You must do this within ten days from today or Sarah will be gone forever.

Check into the Casa Monica hotel in St. Augustine and wait for instructions. Bring the coin. You can call me Charon.

FOUR

The afternoon sun rested high in the sky. Plenty of daylight left. The double spreader mast on the sailboat next to the *Dos XX* cast a short shadow like a two-armed cross over the floating dock. Carla Fox sipped at her Coke.

He examined the header on Carla's fax. No sender's phone number. The received date was the day before yesterday. With sufficient time and proper warrants, law enforcement could eventually force the phone company to cough up the incoming number. But not a private investigator.

"Caller ID on your fax line?" he said.

She shrugged.

"Well, when you checked into the Casa Monica—?"

"Last night." She shook her head. "No messages yet. I told the desk to call my cell if I get any."

Winch reread the note. "He's a literate fellow. Probably smart. He'll want his money and he'll have some clever way of getting it from you."

"You can tell all of that from this one note?"

"I'm pretty clever too," he said. "But then sometimes my cleverness is obscured by my humility."

"And a wise guy too?" she said.

"That's one of the nicer things I've been called. But really, this request is very slick." She gave him a quizzical look. He pointed to the last word.

She shook her head. "Charon? You think that's his real name?"

“No way.”

“What am I missing? Bring the coin means bring the money, right?”

“Yes and yes. In Greek mythology, Charon ferries the dead across the river Styx. In your case it’s really the reverse, he’s taking the living to the dead.”

“Me to Sarah.”

He nodded, thinking.

“And bring the coin means for me to bring the money?”

“The Greeks would leave a coin in a dead person’s mouth to pay Charon his fee. No coin in the mouth and the dead person’s soul was forced to walk the river banks for a hundred years before Charon would give him passage.”

“What is this? A metaphor? Is this guy a writer?”

He gestured around the marina with his hand. “Lots of water here. But that may be too literal. He chose the name Charon for a reason. Consider the dual nature of man. Two parts, composed of a physical body and a spirit. Our earthly desires and our spiritual quests. The body and the spirit, or soul as some might call it. Two parts to our existence. And now Charon, carting souls from one side of the river to the infernal regions on the other.”

“My,” she said, “you cast your bait toward the deep end of the pond, don’t you?”

“English lit, 341.”

“I never finished college,” she said. “I think too much education can cloud a writer’s view of the human condition. But I understand the human heart enough to write a bestselling romance. I know what makes a woman cry. I know what gives her hope, causes despair.”

Carla sat her drink can on the boat’s rail, maybe considered it might leave a ring on the varnished mahogany, and picked it up. “I can write,” she said, “about women trapped by men dressed in Brooks Brothers, who are as cruel and draining as spiders. And other men who are thick, vulgar, and coarse as oak bark, but courageous, and strong as heart of pine. Men who love as tenderly as a hummingbird sucks nectar from a blossom. And their women who can blindly ignore the roughed-out exterior and love the gentle soul inside.”

Carla Fox didn't wade in the shallows either, he thought. There's something to this woman. "It might be he knows a little mythology and he's playing with us," he said.

"He's extorting fifty thousand dollars from me." She checked her watch. "Probably the murderer too."

"I'm not sure this is extortion. He's not forcing you to pay."

"If he's not the murderer, how else would he know?"

"Maybe he carried her there, like Charon. I don't know, Carla. I just know this guy is not stupid. If you're going to get into his game, you've got to be smart. Plan your moves."

"Your moves," she said. "You're my proxy."

Her proxy. Me instead of her. He calculated out loud. "If the body is going to disappear on the tenth day, then–"

"Today is the third day. It took most of the last two days to gather the cash and get down here. All I know is that not counting today, you have six days, Winch."

"Geeze, Carla. The Sheriff—?"

"I'm not taking it to the Sheriff. They've had plenty of time. You think they'll do any better in the next six days?"

"They have more resources."

She reached into her purse, pulled out her checkbook and waved it. "I have all the resources we need. How much do you want?" She wrote, tore off a check, and handed it to him.

Twenty-five thousand dollars. It'd make a fine down payment on an Island Packet 48. But it wasn't the money. Though he'd be lying if he said the money didn't interest him.

He studied the photo of Sarah, fresh, full of energy. Carla might be paying the bills but in his mind Sarah would be his client. A fleeting wish that his Uncle Benjamin was still alive to help him passed through his mind.

And then he wondered if Uncle Benjamin knew Sarah, met her in the Spirit World, where Mormons believe all people's spirits wait for the resurrection. Maybe they were both watching him at this very moment, urging him on. He would do it, he decided. He would take this case and find Sarah.

He looked over his shoulder, half expecting to see a split in the veil between the Spirit World and earth, his Uncle Benjamin and Sarah hovering in the air about the level of the first spreader on the sailboat in the next slip, smiling and nodding. But all he saw was a pair of Bonaparte gulls standing on the spreader. One let loose with a solid plop, splattering the blue canvas Bimini with white.

Carla waved her hand in front of his face. "Earth to Winchester." The citrus scent on her wrist swept him back.

"Carla," he folded the check and slid it into his pocket, "you've bought yourself a PI. The only promise I can make to you is that I'll do my best."

"Good enough, Winchester Young." She extended her hand and they shook. Her grip, firm and warm. Her hand, tan, with a sun bleached fuzz on her forearm. She stooped and picked pieces of his shredded manuscript off the deck, stuffing them into the envelope. "I'll have my agent call you. He'll want you to email your manuscript."

Winch leaned against the rail and admired her taut butt under her jeans. A jean-butt?

He knew he couldn't accept her offer. "I want an agent, Carla, that reads my work, loves it, and wants to sell it because he knows it's good. Not because his biggest client told him to sign me."

"Everybody needs a hand up in this business, Winch. I'm not pimping out my agent to you. I'll strongly suggest he read your material. He makes his own decisions."

Music drifted from the bar at the end of the dock. A puff of breeze made the boats uneasy at their lines, fittings rattled on masts. She faced him, cupped one of his hands in both of hers. An immediate warmth went to parts of his body that he ought not to be thinking with. "Sometimes, Winch, don't you find your ethics get in the way of your success?"

He smiled. "I think I succeed in spite of them. That's why you hired me, isn't it?" He checked his watch. Two P.M. He shut the slider into the boat and locked it. "You want to come? We've got six days and a few hours."

She hesitated. "If Charon is the killer this will be dangerous, won't it?"

"Fifty thousand dollars is a lot of cash to be carrying around."

"I would have paid more."

As he offered his hand to help her off the *Dos XX*, a ski boat, loaded with kids, roared into the marina, rocking the *Dos XX* and every other boat on the dock. Behind it were two sport fishers sedately making their way toward the cleaning tables.

"Hey," someone yelled. "Watch the wake."

The ski boat cut its single inboard/outboard suddenly. Two preteen girls standing on the engine cowling at the stern were dancing and goofing off. As the boat lurched to a near stop they lost their balance. One plopped to the top of the cushioned engine cover. The other wobbled on one foot and then the other.

The boat lost steerage, drifted toward the concrete bulkhead. The adult male at the wheel revved the engine, slammed it forward and the boat leapt. The last girl standing was flung backwards into the water with a scream.

The charter boats were a couple of dozen yards behind and Winch wasn't clear whether their captains had seen the girl. He ran to the bow of the *Dos XX* and pulled a braided nylon line from the anchor locker.

The girl in the water thrashed and screamed. "I can't swim." Someone on the ski boat got the driver's attention. A teenage boy tossed the towrope out of the boat. The driver rammed the shift lever into reverse and promptly backed over the line. The engine coughed and died. Ski rope wrapped around the prop.

The charter boats continued their movement forward. Now less than ten yards from the sinking girl.

The ski boat banged against other boats in their slips. People ran toward their bows, fending off the hapless skiers with boathooks, fish gaffs, deck-brushes, anything they could use to extend their reach.

Winch, with a practiced move, in a seemly single motion tossed a perfectly round loop over the girl. "Grab hold."

He pulled her along side the *Dos XX* to the finger-pier. Carla helped her up while he fetched a towel.

"I thought I was going to drown," she said and burst into tears.

After the girl was reunited with her friends, the ski boat tied to the fuel dock, calm returned to the Conch House marina.

"How did you do that?" Carla said.

"Do what?"

"What kind of knot thing did you tie in that rope that you tossed to that girl? It took you all of less than a second."

"It's a line. Not a rope." She raised her eyebrows. "A flying bowline. Much faster than the rabbit goes in the hole, out of the hole and around the tree, or whatever."

"I don't have a clue as to what you're talking about."

"Everybody should know how to tie a bowline," he said. "A flying bowline is just a very fast way to tie it. It's the one knot that they should teach in first grade."

She gave him a look.

"Really. It's a great knot. It can save your life."

FIVE

Winch walked down the dock with Carla. He pointed out the sport fishers, a compact motor-cruiser, and a really nice Baltic 48 sloop, with teak decks and a blue hull. He would have lingered more but now he was on a deadline. Six days and counting.

"Your wood work is better than any of those," Carla said.

Inwardly he smiled. While his boat was older and cost less than the others on his dock, he'd worked hard on her restoration. To be fair, his ex-wife Tracy worked just as hard. Until Tracy decided she "needed more space" and left him and the boat.

The *Dos XX*'s mahogany cap rails and teak window trim glistened in the afternoon sun. Positively sparkled from the six coats of varnish he'd layered on. Sanded by hand with one-hundred and eighty grit sandpaper and then varnished. Sand and varnish. Sand and varnish. Six times. Now with the sun just right he could lean over the rail and see his reflection peering up at him from a foot deep within the wood grain.

All he wanted was to sail off to the Bahamas. Make his living writing novels. Of course he hadn't sold one yet. So he now headed out on a case with a new client in tow and a $25,000 check in his pocket.

He'd taken the case not so much because of Carla, although he connected with her in some way he didn't understand. She brought an air with her, like the first winds of a new high pressure blowing out a stagnant low. A thought nagged at his mind. Some inner feeling that he was the right guy, at the right time, to match wits with Charon.

They climbed the aluminum ramp from the floating boat dock to the fixed concrete pier. Woody Copeland leaned against the railing next to the thatch-roofed bar, drinking from a bottle of Corona. Woody had shed his guard uniform from earlier in the day and dressed in blue jeans, sandals, and a gray T-shirt with an image of a traditionally garbed Timucuan Indian on the left breast of the shirt. Loin cloth, a round woven hat topped with feathers, and a heavily tattooed body. Winch knew the back of the T-shirt was silk screened with "Save our land. Save our heritage."

Brandy, one of the bartenders, stood next to Woody. He'd known her for the two years he'd been docked here. Twenty-four and working on her MBA during her few spare nighttime hours. Blonde hair under a billed fishing cap, sun streaked ponytail stuck through the hole in the back of the cap, making it bounce. Today she wore a blue pinstriped man's shirt, tails tied in a knot above her belly button and sleeves cut off at the shoulders. Gym-hardened body. Barbell biceps. Tan abs that rippled like a spool of braided rope. Brandy's cleavage, so famous at the Conch House bar that a drink was named after it. Ask for a Brandy here and you'd get something similar to a tequila sunrise with two wedges of a naval orange on the rim nestled side by side. Both Brandy and Woody held intern PI licenses and worked the occasional case for him. Woody waggled the bottle of Corona at him.

Winch turned to Carla. "These two scallywags help me from time to time. Might use them on your case."

Carla gave him a "what are you kidding me?" look.

"They get into places that might not be so easy for me." He made the introductions to Carla. They left Woody and Brandy and walked up the dock, standing for a moment at a pit where two alligators, as long as a man's leg, languished in a mud hole for tourists to gawk at.

Winch unlocked the passenger door to the Jeep and opened it for Carla.

He headed west across the Bridge of Lions, out of the old town district and its cobblestone paving. "Where are we going?" Carla asked.

“Someone called. She needs to see me. It’ll only take a minute and then I’ll take you to your hotel.’

The drove past Riberia Street and the boatyards and onto US 1 South. At the corner sat a large vacant lot. His buddy, former Sheriff Deputy and now fellow PI Glenn Lightsey sells pumpkins on that lot in October and Christmas trees in December. South of King Street women dressed in vinyl micro skirts and platform shoes and stood in shadowed doorways. St. Augustine had its tenderloin like every other town.

He glanced over at Carla. Tanned and thin-limbed. Thirty-six years old and hitting it big in the publishing world. No ring on her finger. But she must be thinking about that biological clock thing.

He wondered for a moment what life would be like with her. The two of them both bestselling novelists, sailing around the world, writing their books. His fantasy, he realized. She’d achieved hers.

After he passed Lightsey’s lot a platinum-blonde woman wearing a net top over a low-cut flesh-colored body stocking stepped away from a tree and gave a little wave wiggling her fingers at him. He drove over the curb and the sidewalk and rolled down his window.

Carla looked at him. “A little early for her to be out, isn’t it?”

“You know the saying, ‘The early bird gets—’”

She put three fingertips on his elbow. “Hush, don’t say it.”

The woman came up to the car and leaned in showing enough cleavage to get him interested. “Winch,” she said, eyeing Carla. “Consorting with the competition?”

“We all sell ourselves one way or another. Summer Dawn, this is my client, Carla Fox.”

Summer Dawn extended her arm across his chest and Carla shook her hand. The scent of peaches perhaps, and something else, maybe apricots washed across him and snuffed the life out of Carla’s perfume. “You’ve never given me that ride you promised.” She winked at Carla. “On your boat.”

“The boat still floats,” he said. “Come over sometime. Anything new on the street?”

“Same old bump and grind for me, honey. But I understand you’ve got something new.”

“You lost me, Summer.”

She spoke to him but kept her eyes on the street. “I heard about your client there.” She gestured toward Carla with her chin. “It’s why I called you.”

“What have you heard?”

Her eyes moved, watching the traffic. “Looking for her lost sister or something like that.”

“How could you possibly hear that?”

“Valene. You know Valene?”

He shook his head.

“Works the corner, King and 18th. She met some guy last night. Big tipper, she said.”

He raised his eyebrows. “And?”

“He was bragging about it, like, maybe it was newsworthy or something.”

“Local dude?”

“Some guy with just one leg,” she said. A slow moving white Mercedes passed by. “That’s the second time that white German’s given me the look. I got to go honey. Do my duty.” She reached down and squeezed his thigh. “I’ll keep my ears open for you. I know where to find you.” She gave him a kiss on the cheek, leaned in a little further and to Carla said, “Love your books, sweetie.”

He eased off the curb and back into traffic.

Carla edged closer to the passenger door.

“Who else knows you’re here?”

“This Summer Dawn. She a friend of yours?”

“She helps me out once in awhile.”

“I bet.” Carla eyed him.

“Charon,” he said, “wouldn’t be bragging to a street walker. He’d be too clever to mention his demand to anybody.” He glanced at Carla.

“Nobody knows I’m here. I checked into the Casa Monica last night. Maybe one of the other investigators I talked to?”

Winch knew most of the PIs in town. None of them were missing a leg. “Your brother? Where’s he?”

“Military. In the middle east.” Carla slid back toward the center consol, laid her hand on his thigh. “Probably one of those other investigators told someone, who told someone. Something like that.”

“Yeah, probably,” he said, but didn’t believe it.

Carla ran her hand through her hair. “Summer Dawn is beautiful, what’s she doing on the street?”

He shrugged. “Building up her IRA?”

“Summer Dawn? Is that her real name?”

He shook his head. “Her real name is Barbara Jean Quintero.”

“You know her pretty well then?”

He could see Carla evaluating. Wondering if he’d ever had a thing with Summer Dawn. “She’s a former client, I worked her divorce.”

“And what, her alimony gave out so she’s working the street? You should have done a better job. Gotten more from her ex.”

“She’s a deputy, works for the Sheriff’s office. Undercover-vice. Yankee tourists offer her twenty bucks for her attention. She talks them up to thirty and then pops them.”

“They ought to be arrested.”

“Yeah,” he said. “Ought to be arrested for being so cheap. She’s worth a hundred at least.”

Carla slugged him on the shoulder. In a few minutes he pulled up in front of the Casa Monica Hotel. “Call me if you hear from Charon. I’m headed to the Sheriff’s office to see who has the case on your dead sister.”

“I don’t like to think of her as dead,” Carla said.

If Carla wanted to cling to some forlorn hope that Sarah was alive, who was he to deny her that? But why was she murdered? Most murders occurred because of sex, jealousy, drugs and alcohol, money, or fear of exposure. The Sheriff’s office probably worked it backwards. Looking for clues to the unsub first and then counting on getting the confession as to how it went down.

Unsub, his Uncle Benjamin taught him. Bureau speak for “unknown subject.” This case was too old for that approach. Any evidence that might point to the subject would be long gone. He’d go the other direction. Figure out the motive first. Look for why she was killed. Then find the killer. And somewhere, Charon and the fifty thousand dollars would fit in.

SIX

Winch swung by the post office and found two envelopes in the box, and a key to a parcel locker. Each bore a different literary agent's name. Of the hundred he'd queried, he'd sent most of them a letter and the first three chapters of his book. Would one of these two be a request to see the entire manuscript? He fingered the envelopes. They'd keep. He needed to make it to the Sheriff's office and frankly, he enjoyed the anticipation of opening them more than reading the rejections that would surely be inside.

He opened the parcel locker and pulled out a package. Hefted it. Felt like a book. With his mail on the seat next to him, the air conditioning whistling full blast, he hustled up US 1.

He slid the Jeep into the lot in front of the Sheriff's office and parked in an unpaved slot under a water oak. The building itself the color of white-bread crust. Unimaginative. The jail, a four-story angular concoction of concrete and double-stranded barbed wire sat next door. Pink concrete benches in front of the jail, worn to a smooth polish, were crowded mostly by women with plump butts, smoking cigarettes, checking their watches.

He'd been here a hundred times pulling case files, logs of 911 calls, and incident reports. Inside he went directly to the records section, the public area about as large as a walk-in closet. Bullet proof glass separated him from the clerks. One of the records clerks, Patti Reynolds, a thin woman with shortcut auburn hair, glasses, and freckles came to the window and smiled at him through the glass partition.

"Winch, what brings you slumming today?" Her voice sounded metallic.

"You know me, Patti. Any day I can find some air conditioning and bill my client at the same time is a good day."

He'd written on a piece of paper Sarah Fox's name and date of birth and slipped it under the bullet-proof partition.

"Background check?" she said. She read it. Her head snapped up and a look passed across her eyes. She turned away from him for just a second and then faced him.

"You recognize the name don't you?"

"Anybody who was here then would."

"But you're too young. You were–"

"Her age more or less. Eighteen. I started part time at sixteen. My dad and the Sheriff were. . . . " She held two fingers up tightly together. "I worked in dispatching after school."

She glanced around the office to see if anybody was listening. "Why are you here, Winch?"

"I'm working for her sister. We're looking into the murder."

"Disappearance," she said. "She ran away."

He waved dismissively with his hand. "Do you read romances?"

Her faced blanched. "Oh, no kidding." She opened a drawer in her desk and held up a copy of *Until Death Do Us Part.* "You're telling me Carla Fox is Sarah Fox's sister?" She whispered, "No way."

A deputy in uniform approached Patti and gave Winch a stern look. "Everything okay here, girl? You sort of lost your color."

"Fine, Jonesy." She shushed him away, waving her fingers at him.

"Carla is my client."

"Big bucks equals a big retainer? Good for you. She staying at some expensive condo on the island?" Locals referred to Anastasia Island as "the island," a barrier of sand dunes and sea oats that has protected St. Augustine from hurricanes and foreign invaders.

He shook his head. "The Casa Monica."

"Whoopee," she said and fanned her face. "Five star."

He knew the hotel, of course, and some of its history. Built in the 1880s by the same man that founded the YMCA. In the mid 1900s, the hotel served as the county's courthouse before being returned to her grandeur as a class hotel. Sort of a painted lady past, with crooks and scoundrels, the very rich and the very poor, walking down its hallways in both of its lives.

"You know," Patti said. "I bet that file is still marked as active."

He gave her a look. "Some hot-shot detective reheating cold leads?"

"Winch, I've known you, what—for six years? More even. I'll see what I can do. I'll put a call into the detective that it's assigned to. Maybe he'll talk to you as a favor for me." Patti stood.

She left the counter saying, "I'll be back in a minute." She walked to a corner out of his sight.

Across the room a half dozen women sat at various desks typing on keyboards, answering phones, and chatting with the occasional deputy that swaggered by.

"Vincent Renfro," Patti said. "The case *is* still active and assigned to him. He'll be out in a minute."

Oh crap. He didn't need another confrontation. Renfro, of course, would remember him from this morning's surveillance at the mall. Crap, crap, crap.

"Problem with Renfro, Winch? You look sort of, oh, I don't know, sort of screwed, if you know what I mean?

"No problem." He shook his head. Liar. There was a huge problem. Renfro hadn't arrested him this morning, still . . . what leverage could he have over Renfro?

"Patti, this Vincent Renfro, is he married?"

Patti gave a conspiratorial look around the records section, said, "Very much so. Married a former detective's wife. He's got a bit of a reputation though, well, how can I put this? Okay here, sometimes he gets phone calls from women and it's not Sheriff's office business. Know what I mean?"

"You're not seeing him, are you?"

She stepped back from the window. "Oh heaven's no." She held up her ring finger. A white circle of flesh showed where her wedding band used to be. "I'm not seeing anyone yet."

He wondered about her. Certainly attractive enough. He could go across the street to the clerk of the court and pull her divorce file. See who was doing what to whom. Divorce files made interesting reading.

His cell phone rang. He motioned toward the front door. "I'll wait out there." He gave Patti a wave, walked toward the exit, and looked at the calling number before he answered. Ex-wife Tracy.

"Winch," she said, "I think we should talk some. Would you like to come over later? Maybe have some dinner?"

Strange, that Tracy, who'd left him, now wanted to talk. In his mind, Tracy was the one that got away. Whenever he thought about her his pulse raced. From behind him he heard, "Young. I want to talk to you."

He turned and saw Detective Vincent Renfro. "Trace, can I call you back on that? Something just came up I have to deal with." He hung up and faced Renfro.

Over Renfro's shoulder he noticed Patti watching them from behind the glass. She gave a little helpless shrug. "Where'd you park, Mr. Young? I'll walk you to your car."

Winch turned and moved toward his Jeep. "Which gas station did she disappear from, Detective?"

"That old hunk of junk down there on U.S. 1, before I-95." Renfro kept pace with him. "It's not a secret, you can look it up. Why are you looking into my old cases?"

"I have a client in the Sarah Fox case."

Renfro shook his head. "Active investigation. You're not getting your hands on it."

"Active? When was the last bit of investigation done?"

"Sorry. Too bad."

"Look, you already screwed me over with one client today. You going for number two, now?"

"You screwed yourself this morning," Renfro said.

But he hadn't. He knew he'd done nothing to get made.

Renfro gave him a careful looking over. His jaw tightened. "You idiot. You stay away from Lisa Chambers. She's a friend. And stay away from the Fox case."

"No can do. I have paying clients on both cases. The Chambers case is a civil matter and you have no jurisdiction in it. If you screw me over with that case again, I'll make a complaint to the Sheriff."

"Think you're clever, don't you?"

"Oh, not as clever as you, I'm sure. At the mall, did you ever consider that maybe it was you I was following? I'm sure your wife would be interested in knowing that you were meeting with the Chambers woman."

"I catch you talking to my wife . . . and so help me . . . you'll pay."

"Why do you care who looks at a twenty-five-year-old file?"

Renfro dropped his hand, let it rest on the black handle of the Glock strapped on his hip.

"Threatening me?" Winch said. "I wonder how the Sheriff would feel about that?"

"Watch yourself, Young." Renfro clenched his hands into fists. "If I catch you talking to the Sheriff—"

Winch seethed. There was a line he couldn't cross with this guy. He needed the Sheriff's cooperation or he'd get nowhere. "Look, I understand your desire to keep your little rendezvous with Lisa Chambers a secret. But I have a duty to my client."

Renfro was nodding his head now. "Trying to extort me?"

"It's not extortion. More like blackmail. There's a difference. You really ought to study the law."

"You've really stepped in it this time, Young."

"Tell you what, Detective Renfro. I have an appointment with the Sheriff in the morning. I'm bringing my client, Sarah Fox's sister, Carla." Winch put his sunglasses on. "You'll have until then to decide if I can see the Sarah Fox file. If not, then Lisa Chambers' name will probably surface in our conversation. And Rudy Chambers just might give your wife a call. Wouldn't you like to eavesdrop on that?"

Renfro moved right up to Winch. Put his chest against his. The Kevlar vest unyielding under Renfro's uniform. "You low-life window-peeper."

"I may be that, but at least I'm not a steroidal freaked-out misogynist."

Renfro shook his head. "What did you call me?"

He unlocked the Jeep's door. "You've got a dictionary in there somewhere. Look it up." He flipped one of his business cards at Renfro. It bounced off his chest and landed at the man's feet. "Call me if you have a change of heart."

Renfro slapped his hand on the quarter panel of the Jeep, sounding like a .38 at the range. "Yep, what is this car, twelve years old? You're doing really good for yourself, Young." Then he took a step and ground his heel on the business card.

Renfro sauntered into the Sheriff's office. Winch tilted his back against the headrest, closed his eyes, and took a deep breath. He didn't like confrontations. But Renfro had his back up for no reason. He'd lay odds that nothing significant had been done on Sarah's case in fifteen years.

The article from The Record rested in his pocket. He knew the little country gas station where Sarah vanished. Way out in the boonies south of St. Augustine. He wondered what the chances were of the same owner being there. Not good. He could check the property appraiser's records, see who owned it now and when they bought it. But a ride down the road might do him some good. Give him a chance to calm down.

He thumbed the two envelopes on the seat. One return address read ARC Literary Agency New York and the other said Washburn and Stevens Literary. Neither of the evenopes was thick. One page only inside. Probably bad news. It could wait. First the book parcel.

He pulled out of the parking lot and headed south. Inside the priority mail box was a copy of John Dunning's *Booked to Die*. A terrific murder mystery that educated the public about book scouts and the value of first editions. He flipped it open to the copyright page. Yes! Copyright 1992, and near the bottom of the page was the number line. A series of numbers that began with ten and counted down to one establishing it as a first edition, first printing. This was an ex-library copy, but in fine condition except for a couple of faded stamps on the inside flap. Normally he wouldn't buy an ex-library. But this book was so rare he doubted he'd ever be able to afford one in pristine condition. Without the stamps it would be a two thousand dollar book. With the library stamps, about two-hundred and fifty. He'd scored it on EBay for fifty. He examined the book from every angle. Nearly perfect. Made his day.

His mind drifted back to Sarah Fox's disappearance. In a half-hour he'd visit the crime scene. What did he hope to see today, that the cops didn't see back then?

SEVEN

Winch drove south toward the gas station. Probably going to be a waste of time. Still, one never knew for sure. Sarah disappeared in 1986, before the FBI became involved in missing children cases so the county Sheriff caught the ticket. Maybe the Sheriff's detectives missed something —maybe not?

He glanced at the two letters from the literary agents, begging to be opened. He couldn't stand the suspense. He chose the envelope that said ARC Literary Agency, kept the highway's centerline in his peripheral vision, pulled his rigging knife out of the glove box and slit the envelope open. A photocopied piece of paper the size of a business card fell into his lap. A bad photocopy at that, top and bottom at screwy angles and hand cut by scissors.

Across the top was the name of the agency. Then: Thank you for sending us this material. We're sorry, but it doesn't meet our present needs.

That was it. A form rejection. Not even a whole page of paper.

Crap. Well, he'd open the other one later. Prolong the agony. Clearly a masochistic streak ran through the middle of his brain. Why else would he write? He'd mentioned that to another aspiring writer once and the other fellow simply said, "That's why writers drink and Hemingway killed himself. Writing is torment and the publishing business is torture."

Ten miles south of town he passed Moultrie Creek, a shallow meandering stream full of cattails, islands of savannah grass, and the heavy musk of spawning large mouth bass. Two hundred years ago the Seminole nation was established here with the treaty of 1823. For a thousand years before that, Timucuan Indians settled along the creek bed. They vanished leaving behind barn-sized earthen mounds. Most of their mounds were thousand-year-old garbage dumps of broken pottery and oyster shells. Some, however, were the burial grounds for their ancestral dead. This was Florida's aboriginal outback.

Down the road another couple of miles he came upon a single story wood-framed gas station. The wood siding streaked with rust. A tin-roofed portico ran between the front door and two gas pumps. Winch parked alongside the building so as not to block the pumps. A man, maybe seventy-five years old, with a green John Deere ball cap, wearing "Farmer-John" coveralls squeaked back and forth in a rocking chair. The name "Philip" was embroidered on his breast pocket.

Another rocking chair sat on the other side of the door. Winch gestured toward the empty rocker, "May I?"

"Don't see nobody's name writ on it."

They both rocked in silence for a few minutes until the man couldn't stand it any longer. "You come all the way out here just to rock in that chair?"

Winch pulled from his shirt pocket a copy of the *Record's* article on Sarah Fox's disappearance and handed it to the old man. "Mr. . . ?"

"Patch," the man said. He tapped the name on his chest. "My friends call me Phil. But I don't know you. You call me Mr. Patch." The man dipped his fingers into the breast pocket of his coveralls and slipped out a pair of bifocals. "That was a century ago. You expect me to remember anything about that?"

Winch reached for the article but the man didn't hand it back. "I'm surprised your place is still here."

"Not for much longer." Patch leaned forward and pointed to his left. "See that dirt road right there? Keep your eye on it."

Winch was in no hurry so he rocked a little in the chair and waited. The smell of land being cleared, pine branches burning drifted in the air. A low silver Lamborghini, like a sequined slipper from Frederick's of Hollywood, whizzed southbound down the paved highway. Sucking the Lamborghini's vapor trail, a purple VW convertible bug zipped along with four young women, halter-topped, sun-glassed, and hair blowing. Two of them waved and he waved back. The Lamborghini and the Bug. The Hare and the Tortoise. Motorboats and sailboats. Some folks hurry to their destinations. Others enjoy the journey.

A minute later a logging truck rumbled and coughed and poked the nose of its tractor out of the trees where the dirt road met the pavement. Its trailer was loaded with branchless pine trunks trussed to the bed with chains. "There," the old man said. A crack of a smile appeared on his face. "My daddy bought eight thousand acres of pine tree pulp back yonder behind us in '35."

Patch stared after the truck as it eased onto the highway and headed south. Pine bark blew from the trailer and speckled the asphalt. "He built this gas station and store. I grew up pumping gas and selling cigarettes. He died in '50 it was, and I've been running this place ever since. I sold it earlier this year. Got a pretty penny for it, too."

"Guess you can finally retire?"

The old man nodded, but not very enthusiastically. "Yeah, I guess, for maybe three or four months."

Winch didn't say anything. Finally Patch said, "I got the cancer. Doesn't that just beat all? I got millions in the bank and the doctors tell me I've got maybe six months. Or less."

"You look good."

"You can't see my liver. It don't look so good."

"You have family? Kids?"

"Got a daughter. Good girl, too. The wife, the first one passed thirty years ago. The second one ran out on me over twenty years back so I give up women."

"Married twice, huh?"

"What's with all of the questions?"

"I've been married a twice myself."

"Stupid, aren't you?"

"I'm looking into Sarah Fox's disappearance."

Patch set the news article on his lap, slapped his hands together and flicked a squashed mosquito from one palm. Wiped his hand on his thigh. "You some police type or something?"

"Private detective."

"Well, I think you ought to just get on out of here and do your detecting someplace else."

"I'd like to have a look at the restroom."

"It's just a piss-pot and sink. You think I got that girl still hid up in the john?"

Winch held up his hands. "No, sir I—"

"If you ain't going to buy something then move on along, son. Got no desire to spend the last few months of my life associating with bathroom perverts."

"Fine, I'll go—" He stood up.

"I'll call the cops and have them run you off."

Winch had been cited for trespassing before. The cops would give him a written warning, not arrest him. He wasn't about to leave without getting a peek inside that restroom. He'd buy something, make Patch happy. "I'll buy a soda. Do you want me to get it myself?"

Patch began reading and waved a dismissive hand. Winch eased the screen door shut behind him. "Don't steal nothing in there," Patch yelled.

Inside, a counter to his right held a cash register, a large jar of pickled pigs feet, and another jar of pickled eggs. Do people really eat that stuff?

Cigarettes were on shelves behind the counter. Along the back wall was a cooler with beer and soda. He took a Barqs Root Beer out of the cooler and laid a dollar bill next to the cash register.

Behind the counter the restroom keys hung on nails, both wired to blocks of wood. He took the ladies key.

The old man looked up at him as he came out to the porch. "Steal that soda did you?"

What do you say to a man who has millions in the bank and is going to die in six months? "Want to adopt a kid?" he said.

"You are weird." Patch sneered. "Hell no, I don't want to adopt nobody. Did that once, too. Worst mistake I ever made."

"You adopted your daughter?"

"No, she's mine from my first wife. My number two, she birthed a son before I met her. I never really adopted him, but I raised him. He's madder than hell I sold the property. Thinks I'm going to spend all of his inheritance. He hasn't seen the pictures of my liver."

He studied Winch's face. "You favor somebody I knew."

"My uncle, maybe? Benjamin Young?"

"I knew Ben Young. Fine fellow. Used to sit right where you are and drink a soda with me and sometimes he'd let me beat him at checkers. I'll be damned."

"Uncle Benjamin raised me."

"He said he was raising a no good scoundrel nephew."

Winch shrugged. "I'm afraid I caused him some trouble."

"Young was one of them Mormons. The ones with the golden bible. You one of them too?"

Winch never knew how to answer that question. When people asked about "the golden bible," the questions usually came in a sarcastic or derisive tone. But Patch was facing imminent death. He'd probably been contemplating his life and maybe was looking for a death bed repentance or maybe some idea of what waited for him on the other side. He could have told Patch his first wife or his parents would be there to help usher him through the veil that separated mortality from the Spirit World. The idea that he would be with his loved ones again could be consoling for someone with no understanding of the next life. He should take a minute to help him understand. "You know who's waiting for you on the other side?"

"I'm not interested in your preaching," Patch said. "Your Uncle Benjamin tried that with me. I flat told him not to be dragging his Sunday school clear down here and bother me with it. Leave church at the church building."

Patch stroked the side of his nose. His hand trembled as he held up the news article. "Them's my words right on the paper. Just as that paper man writ them down. Can't remember his name but that detective, called himself Sharp. Detective Dick Sharp." A smile came to his face. "That detective was coming back here every week. Like a dog pissing the same light pole."

Winch didn't recognize Sharp's name. He must have retired.

Patch nodded. "Okay, Ben's boy, you didn't come here to play checkers. What do you want?"

"Tell me about the day Sarah Fox disappeared."

"I remember everything fine. That girl ran off with the key to my restroom." He related what he remembered and it pretty much followed the lines of the newspaper article he'd just read.

Winch stood. "Mind if I look around?"

"You already got the key." Patch waved his hand toward the south side of the building. "Nothing to see but you're going to look anyway. Don't piss on the floor."

His uncle taught him when performing a search, not to search for a particular missing item, thinking, "Oh, it could be behind the couch. Or, "maybe it fell behind the dresser," but to consider the space as a whole, section it off and search methodically.

Two doors, side by side. The one toward the rear held a large alligator's head nailed to it with a sign above in blue paint that read "Bull Gators." He put his nose next to the gator head, smelled like varnish. His finger ran over its teeth, sharp as a shark's tooth.

The other door—a smaller alligator's head on it. In pink it read "Gator Tail." He inserted the key into the "Gator Tail's" door and entered. The room had a toilet, sink, and small vanity counter with a mirror on the wall. Smelled like Pine Sol. Rust streaks coppered the bottom of the washbasin. Stains of some indeterminable origin coated the vanity. In the yellowed plaster ceiling an exhaust fan clanked when he flipped the light switch, but the hole for the fan was the size of a salad plate. Absolutely no place to hide in this room. No way in or out except for the door.

He stood not knowing what to do. Sometimes on surveillance cases he'd lose a subject and go back to where he'd lost him, pull off the side of the road, blank his mind and occasionally an impulse would head him in a specific direction. And bam he'd run into his subject. Nothing supernatural about it. Usually the impulse followed along the lines of something he knew about his subject and his subconscious batted it out to center field. He waited now, but the only thing that came to him here were smells of urine and vomit percolating through the Pine Sol. What did he expect? A hot lead after twenty-five years?

Outside, under the roof soffits, carpenter bees buzzed, drilling perfect dime-sized holes. Granules of sawdust sprinkled the ground. He walked past the "Bull Gator" door and looked at the building's rear. A blacked-out window in the wall probably opened to the men's room. A cleared area as wide as an eighteen-wheeler ran the length of the structure. Beyond was a wild overgrowth of sawgrass, wax myrtle trees, and thickets of palmettos. Visually impenetrable.

He tried the door handle to the men's room. Locked. Footsteps behind startled him and he whirled.

Patch stood there. "See, no place to hide in there."

He heard the crunch of tires and walked to the front. A vintage British racing green Jaguar XKE ragtop pulled into the lot. Strips of roof shingle layered over the drive area like spilled dominos and crackled as the black-walled tires rolled over them.

"Louie, my step-son the golfer," Patch said. "He don't know about my liver, and don't you go telling him neither. You hear me now?"

Louie, lean and tan climbed out of the convertible. He smiled with a set of perfectly white orthodontically even teeth.

Winch nodded. He wondered why Patch would tell him, a perfect stranger, he was about to die and not inform the boy he'd raised. What kind of bad blood flowed between the two of them?

EIGHT

Winch stepped to the Jaguar XKE and glanced through the windshield of the sports car. A white leather golf bag with lots of side pockets, blue leather covers over the woods, and polished irons was belted into the passenger seat.

He laid his head sideways to the hood, nearly touching it with his cheek, and admired the finish, smooth as cultured marble. The reflected gas pump, red and blue, looked six feet deep. Heat from the engine warmed his face and he smelled a little smoking oil. Probably needed a new head gasket. "You have her long?"

"About ten years," Patch's step-son said. The man's complexion was weathered and brown as pine bark. Hair, thinning with transplants across his forehead like rows of miniature ferns. Teeth white as catfish bones.

"Long enough to replace a clutch or two," Winch said.

"You know your XKEs, Mr.—"

"I owned a sixty-seven when I was younger. Then I began acquiring ex-wives instead of sports cars."

"You remember Benjamin Young, Louie?" Patch said. "That FBI fella' that come down here from time to time. This is his kid."

Winch stuck out his hand and they shook. "Winchester Young."

"Luther Calderone. My old man calls me Louie. Everybody else calls me Luther."

"Mr. Young here is a private investigator," Patch said. "He's looking for that girl that disappeared from the restroom."

Luther shook his head. Patch thrust the news clipping at him. He read it for a second and handed it back. “Oh yeah. It was big news for a day or two.”

Winch wondered, was that all Sarah’s life was worth? A day or two of news and then forgotten. Maybe if her mom had made more fuss, like Natalie Holloway, the girl that disappeared in Aruba. Somebody might have picked up the story and kept it alive. But then teenagers run away frequently. A big news story only on a slow news day.

“So what brings you down here. . . .” Luther took the news clipping from Patch and examined it again. “So many years after the fact? A little late, aren’t you?” His face bore a wary look like that of a feral cat approaching a food bowl. Hungry, but not wanting to be captured.

“Were you here when she disappeared?” Winch said.

Some look passed between Luther and Patch but he couldn’t decipher it.

“Am I under some suspicion, Winchester?”

“You lived here then?” Winch said.

“Athens, Georgia.” Luther started to run his hand through his wavy black hair, fixed solid with hair spray, thought better of it and dropped it to his side.

“In a frat house?”

“I don’t see where my fraternity has any relevance to Sarah’s disappearance.”

“It was spring break,” Patch said. “Louie came home later that afternoon. You can ask the cops. They were here.”

“What do you need, Louie?” Patch said.

Just then another flatbed of pine trees headed to the pulp mill pulled out of the dirt road on to the pavement. Luther shook his head. “I’m just getting some of my stuff out back.”

“Louie’s got himself a new girlfriend. Out of here and in with her. Forty-five years old. ‘Bout time, don’t you think?”

“Considering your luck and mine, with wives, maybe he’s the smart one,” Winch said.

“My first wife was a good one.” Patch stroked his chin. “Louie’s mom though. She was one slick bitch.”

“Pops, I wish you wouldn’t say things like that.”

“When’s the last time you heard from her, Louie?”

"Same as you, Pops." Luther turned to Winch. "She left us a note on the kitchen table the night she ran off. We haven't heard word one since."

Winch wondered if she'd been declared dead but he wasn't going to ask. He could look it up at the clerk of the court if he really wanted to know.

Patch waved his hand toward the dirt road. "Just go on, Louie. Get your stuff. Leave your old man to fend for himself when he gets old."

"You sold the place, Pops. You're leaving me."

Patch turned his back to Luther and trudged up the steps to the front porch. Took his place in the rocking chair. Back and forth. Back and forth.

The XKE disappeared down the dirt road, behind rows of palmettos and hillocks of sawgrass.

Patch stood and went into the store. Winch followed. The old man picked a beer out of the cooler and offered one to Winch.

He declined. "Any other customers around that day when Sarah disappeared?"

"Stupid question. How long have you been a detective? 'Course we had customers. A long time after she disappeared that detective Sharp asked me to go through my receipts for that day and make him a copy of all of the charge cards and IOUs. I did, but he never come for it. He was shot and nobody ever snooped here again. Until you come today."

So Sharp was killed. No wonder he didn't know him. And this was no open case. Nobody was working this thing. Not Renfro. Not anybody. Then he wondered if snooping around here might be a dangerous occupation. First, Patch's wife disappears. Then Sarah. Then Detective Sharp is shot. Enough to make one wonder.

He thought about the IOUs. "Give a lot of credit to your regulars?"

Patch pointed to a faded black and yellow sign by the cash register. It read NO CREDIT-SO DON'T ASK.

"But you said IOUs?"

"I take some IOUs from my kids and friends. But they have to work the gas off. No free ride here."

"You still have those receipts?" Winch pointed in a backroom where he could see file boxes stacked along one wall.

"Them boxes are my taxes."

"It'd maybe be in your tax box from nineteen eighty-six?"

Patch shook his head, huffed, and mumbled something that sounded like a swear word as he walked into the back room. One box fell and he could hear envelopes or folders slide across the cracked linoleum. In a few minutes he came out holding a yellowed number ten envelope. "Want it?"

Winch took it. A silverfish ran the inside length of the envelope. He squeezed the paper with his thumbnail and index finger, squashing the insect. He thumbed through faded old copies of charge tickets with barely readable names and credit card numbers. And some copies of IOUs with cash register receipts stapled to them. Would they be of any help now? Probably not. "Thanks," he said. "You never know."

"Isn't that the truth. You think you know but you never know nothing."

He folded the envelope in half and stuck it in his back pocket. "Anybody unusual around here that day?"

The man shook his head. "Mostly regulars."

"Your step-son pump gas?"

"When he was in town. But he was off to college like he said."

Winch pointed in the direction of the dirt road. "Your house down that road?"

"A half mile or so. Why, you want to go see my john too?"

"Just trying to get the lay of the land." He walked out of the store and to the gas pumps. Patch followed. He looked at the restroom doors. From the north pump he couldn't see the doors. A clear view from the south pump. He placed his hand on the south pump. "This the one they used that day?"

"That's the one," Patch said. "Cops were all over it. Figuring angles and all. One of them boys stood out by the car the whole time."

Why would they do that? "Was somebody after them?" he said.

Patch rubbed the toe of his shoe back and forth in the dust. "Don't know exactly. I recollect some talk about a run in with some fellow at the beach the night before. Tried to pick the girl up or something. I just heard pieces of it. You got what you need Mr. PI?"

"I might be back in a few days, if you don't mind."

"This place ain't going to be here more than a week or two."

Winch cranked up the Jeep. Put the air on high. He'd have to track those three boys down. Boys? They'd be Luther's age? Still, he wondered why they kept an eye on her while she was in the restroom.

NINE

Winch sped northbound, contemplating how Sarah disappeared. The witnesses were unanimous, she'd entered and not exited. Yet she was gone. A dragonfly, black-tipped wings and a body the size of a mechanical pencil, whacked the Jeep's antenna and stuck there, transparent-wings fluttering in the sixty-mile-per-hour wind. He wondered who was to blame for this creature's premature death? Him? The car? The wind? The dragonfly?

Was Sarah Fox's death really any different? An accident in timing. If she and her companions had lingered over lunch another fifteen minutes, would she still be alive? Could it have been a planned abduction? Did they know they were going to stop at Patch's gas station? He wondered if the cops thought to look for a preexisting connection between Sarah and the gas station. It couldn't have been a coincidence, Patch's stepson arrived from University of Georgia and Sarah and the three boys also were from there. Had the Sheriff's investigator even made that connection? He took his pen and jotted a note to himself to check on it.

He couldn't see Patch being involved in Sarah's disappearance, but he couldn't eliminate him either. Who else was at the gas station when she disappeared? Patch and the boys were it, as far as he knew.

He hit the speed dial on his cell phone for Tracy's number and wondered why he still had her in the phone's memory. He'd married and divorced her twice. Was he foolish enough to think they should take a third shot?

When she answered he said, "Trace, sorry it's taken me so long to get back to you."

"Are you coming over, Winch? I could still throw some food together."

"I'm having dinner with a client. But I would like to drop by, if that's okay." He looked at his watch. "I can be there in a half hour."

There was a pause, long enough that he thought maybe his cell dropped the connection. Then she said, "So tell me again why you're coming?"

"You asked me to, remember? To talk or something."

"But you're not coming to talk." He could hear the resignation in her voice. "What do you need, Winch, your tools?"

Tools were as good as an excuse as any. Somewhere in the back of his brain, he'd the thought that he and Tracy might try it one more time. "Tools," he said. "Right." And punched off.

He kept a small toolbox in the back of the Jeep, some on the *Dos XX*, but most of his tools still sat on shelves in his . . . Tracy's garage.

He lowered the windows and enjoyed the scent of wild flowers, the sun shining off the false goldenrods growing in the roadside ditches. Foot high spikes of yellow blossoms whose flowers open first from the top of the spike to attract the pollinator bees and then proceed opening one by one down the spike. He wondered how such beautiful flowers could materialize out of such muck.

* * * *

Winch zipped across the Vilano Bridge and cruised up the two-lane strip of asphalt, highway A1A, catching glimpses of the long ocean swells pushed by tropical storm Florence five-hundred miles out to sea. A set of high dunes kept the pounding surf in check. A wedge of airborne pelicans coasted slowly southward on a steady westward breeze. The wind held the curl in the waves, making surfers happy.

After the divorce, Winch moved aboard the *Dos XX* and Tracy stayed in the house. He admitted he still held feelings for Tracy. Possibly he still loved her. Or perhaps now that he didn't have her, she'd become more desirable. The law of supply and demand. She dumped him. He was the dumpee and she the dumper. He didn't like to think she'd dumped him. Dumped has bad connotations. You dump the trash.

He pulled into Tracy's driveway.

His and Tracy's house, a single story seashell stuccoed home across the street from the beach. He still owned half of the residence, joint tenants with right of survivorship. Only they weren't joint tenants anymore.

"Miss it?" Tracy said. She stood on the front stoop, hands on her hips, wearing blue jeans, a white ribbed T-shirt, sandals on her bare feet. A splay of freckles ran across the bridge of her nose and spread to the width of a dollar bill on each cheek. Her exposed skin burnished to a mahogany brown by the sun and sea breeze. Her auburn hair was cut to the bottom of her cheeks. Short and beachy.

He inhaled the salt air and then noticed the deterioration of the aluminum window screens he'd replaced three years ago. Everything this close to the beach corroded. Marriages too. "Yeah," he said. "I do miss it."

"Want to come in?"

"What did you have in mind?"

"Us."

"I didn't think there was any 'us.'"

She stepped inside and he followed.

"How is the *Dos Equis*? Geeze, I miss sleeping on her."

He thought he'd say something clever but he didn't. Instead he said, "I'm sure she misses you too."

Tracy shook her head. "Oh, the bright work needs sanding, does it?"

He sighed.

Tracy sat on the couch. His couch from before he married her the first time. She patted the cushion next to her. "Here, sit."

"I'm not a dog." But he sat.

She pushed her knee casually against his. "Says who?"

Her body heat passed right through her jeans, warm against his leg. She'd always turned him on. "You shouldn't have left, Trace."

She waved her hand in dismissal. "History lessons." She put her hand on his shoulder. He shifted slightly to face her more directly. One of her hands went to his thigh and she drummed her fingers there.

"Do you still love me, Winch?"

He'd been asking himself that same question less than a half-hour ago. "Maybe." He said it cautiously, not willing to leave himself fully exposed.

She smoothed the back of her other hand down his cheek. Her fingers still drummed his thigh, messaging she wanted more than just talk. "Winchester Young, my poor Winch. I didn't treat you very well. I'm really very truly sorry about that."

She stood and took his hand. "Let me show you the new print I put up."

Tracy made a good living as a photographer. Selling prints of local scenes to the million tourists a year that walked down St. George's Street in St. Augustine, past the oldest school house in the country. She led him into the bedroom. On the wall was a black and white of the two of them on the bow of the *Dos XX*.

"I turned thirty-one last month," she said.

"I didn't get an invite to the party."

"You didn't send roses either." She ran her fingers through her hair. "I've been thinking," she said. She stepped between him and the photograph. Put her arms around his waist and pulled him to her. She unbuttoned three buttons on his shirt and pressed her nose to his chest. Inhaled.

She pressed into him. "Trace, what are you doing?" His hands involuntarily went under her shirt and rubbed her back. His mouth went to hers and his hands wanted to move to her breasts. He knew how they would feel—skin, soft and smooth like slipping a hand into warm sudsy water. But he held them back.

"I thought maybe," she got the words out between kisses, "if we were still good, you know what I mean, then. . . . "

He pulled his lips from hers. "Tracy, I may still love you. But I don't want just a fling." She peeled her T-shirt over her head. Just jeans and a sports bra. No tan lines. Dark brown all over. Around her waist she wore a thin gold chain. Something new he'd never seen before.

She put her arms around his waist. She smelled of soap and a light hint of citrus from behind her ears. "New perfume?" He wanted her, in the worst way.

"A new me," she said.

His hands ran around the chain feeling for a clasp. "You want me to unhook you?"

"You can't. It's soldered on. A never ending chain."

"Permanent huh?"

"Nothing's permanent," she said. He knew she was right. Not life, not even death.

He kissed her. It'd been so long. He shouldn't be doing this. In his mind he knew he should leave. Even though he'd been married to her twice, he wasn't married to her now. He shouldn't be having sex with her if he wasn't married to her.

She pushed him onto the bed and pulled off his shoes. His eye glimpsed the nightstand, an empty glass with a thermometer in it.

He sat up. "Wait."

"I don't want to wait." She stepped out of her jeans.

She kissed his chest and pushed him back on the bed.

"No, I mean it." He pushed her back. "Wait a minute." Her feet still on the floor, she stood. Her eyes followed his to the nightstand.

"Thinking of getting pregnant, were you?"

She went to work on his belt. He grabbed her shoulders and slid her up so they were face to face.

"Trace, what's going on here?"

She sighed, rolled over and sat next to him. "You have good genes, Winch."

"You don't want me." He sat up. "You just want a DNA donor. I guess I should be flattered."

"What a cute baby we'd have. Your good looks and my brains."

Was that a compliment or a slam? He wasn't sure. Of course he too would like to have a child. A little Winch running around is exactly what he wanted. Traditional families are the divine building blocks of the universe. But the last thing *he* wanted was his child being raised and him not having parental rights. Tracy would be a good mother. And he would be a good father. But their child, any child, deserved to have both.

"Trace, our marriage didn't work the first time. Or the second. What will have changed to make it work now?"

"I wasn't really thinking marriage, Winch. But sure, maybe . . . we could talk about that. The baby would change everything. We could be a family." She pushed him back on the bed. Climbed on top of him.

He turned his head away. "Yeah, that would certainly change things. Until you decided that now with a baby you felt really tied down. Needed more space than ever. And ol' Winchester would be sleeping on the *Dos XX* by himself and little Winch would have . . . what? Mommy here? Daddy there? Mommy's boyfriends in and out? What kind of home-life would little Winch have, Trace?" He stood and buttoned his shirt.

"Wait," she said.

"No, you wait. You think you can outsmart me. Think I'll jump into bed with you because I may still love you. Well, you're right. I might still love you. And you know you turn me on. But I won't have sex with you, Tracy."

She'd picked up her own shirt, stretched it over her head and down her torso. "I guess it wasn't meant to be, Winchester. Go work your stupid case or whatever. You've ruined it now."

"No Tracy, you ruined it when you left. When you couldn't commit. Before that it was good."

"You make me so mad, Winch. Always blaming me."

"Maybe I wasn't the best husband. I don't know. I do know it only takes one to wreck a marriage, Trace. But it takes two to make it work."

She stomped her foot. "This is my house now. Get out."

TEN

Winch sat on the stairs leading to his office, listening to music from a local group playing at O.C. Whites restaurant.

For two hundred years the Spaniards sailed their treasure fleets from Havana right past this spot, riding the two-and-a-half knot Gulf Stream current to Europe. When the 1715 Flotilla was wrecked with a gazillon dollars worth of silver, south near Ft. Pierce, an area still known as "the treasure coast," some survivors made their way to St. Augustine to report the disaster. Pirates based in the Bahamas stole thousands of pounds of pieces of eight. Eventually the wreck sites were forgotten until the 1960s, when modern treasure salvors harvested the wrecks.

He'd bought Tracy a piece of eight from the wreck of the Atocha, found by Mel Fisher, southwest of Key West, as an anniversary present during their first marriage. During the second round he'd had a gold bracket custom made for it and gave her a gold chain to wear it on. Sheesh, was he really considering round number three?

Brandy and Woody arrived in Woody's Chevy pickup. The rocker panels on the driver's side were pin-holed with rust and Winch could see the grey cobblestone of the road under the truck. Woody had Bondoed both rear quarter panels but hadn't yet sanded them, leaving them looking like an albino alligator hide. The floorboards were rusted through and if a passenger picked up his foot and moved the piece of shag carpet he could see asphalt whiz by at fifty miles-per-hour which speed pretty much top-ended the truck.

Although it was an eight-cylinder engine, only six-cylinders fired. Drips of non-combusted gasoline would occasionally pass over a hot spot in the exhaust and explode, startling adults on the sidewalk, making children in strollers cry and dogs on leashes bark. Loose dogs were reluctant to chase the truck, preferring vehicles that didn't bark back at them.

They stepped out of the truck. Woody still in his Save Our Land–Save Our Heritage T-shirt and Brandy with her blond hair piled on top of her head, held by two combs. She wore what he liked to call a "Brandy t-shirt." The front bore a dollar sign over each breast. The back read, *Madoff didn't steal my assets*. As good as she looked, his heart belonged to Tracy. Now wasn't that a heck of fix? Still in love with the ex.

Winch handed Brandy the envelope of IOUs and credit card charge slips Patch gave him. Explained what they were.

Brandy flipped through them. "Why would he give these to you? You know what I mean?"

"He has nothing to hide," Woody said.

"Or," Winch said, "he knows there's nothing incriminating in there. Spreadsheet them will you, Brandy? There might be something there. Probably not, but as I told Patch, you never know."

"Woody," he said. "I need you to find a hooker."

Woody's eyebrows went up. "You paying?"

"Only for information." He proceeded to explain about Valene, the hooker whose john gossiped about Carla's search for her sister. "See if you can find her and—"

"Right," Woody said.

"Call me later and let me know how it goes. Track your expenses, time, and mileage so I can bill for it."

A grin spread Woody's face. "You mean I get to see a hooker and the three of us make money on the deal? Heck of world you live in, Winch."

Winch shook his head. He'd call Carla and tell her to pick him up at the marina.

"That's not fair." Brandy huffed. "I do spreadsheets while Woody is out doing real PI work."

Woody smirked.

"Putting together and analyzing a spreadsheet is real PI work," Winch said. "It might break the case."

"I can talk to a hooker just as well as Woody, maybe better. A woman-to-woman thing."

She was right. It might be better to send Brandy to find Valene. "I expect that Valene would be jealous of your good looks," he said. "You're the MBA and Woody doesn't know how to do a spreadsheet. Do you?"

"I can do a spreadsheet," Woody said. "What program do I use for that?"

"All right" Brandy adjusted the combs in her hair. "I'll do the spreadsheet, but I get the next street assignment."

Woody looked at him. "You think that old man had something to do with your case?"

"He was there when Sarah disappeared so I don't see how he could have spirited her away. She left, he didn't."

Brandy stepped close to Winch. "Could Patch be Charon?"

"He barely speaks English. I doubt he's well read in Greek classics."

His gaze shifted to Brandy's face. Dark eyebrows. A Hapsburg bottom lip that she chewed on, giving her a pensive sultry look without collagen. "Patch's step-son, Luther, still lives at home. Has a boat at the Conch House. You know him, Brandy?"

"Not by name," she said. "What's he drink?"

"Luther Calderon," Woody said. "Golf pro, no, assistant pro, at Sawgrass. Real popular with the club members. Three businessmen sponsored him on tour for a couple of years, but he almost never finished in the money."

Interesting. Not sure how that fit in, if at all. He checked his watch, five-thirty. "Woody, good hunting."

"I have the six-till-close shift," Brandy said. "If we don't leave now I'll be late. I'll do the spreadsheet in the morning."

"I'll drive you to the marina," Winch said. "Carla is meeting me there."

In the Jeep, Brandy lifted the envelope from the literary agency off the center console.

"Good news?" Brandy said. "Come on. Let me open it. Let's read it. You're going to be rich and famous, Winch. I just know it."

He shrugged. The envelope was from the Oscar Parkinson Agency. Thicker than the last one. Maybe they'd want to read his manuscript and represent him. "There's a rigging knife in the glove box. Use that."

Brandy ignored his suggestion and ripped the end off of the envelope.

ELEVEN

Winch tried to act nonchalant as Brandy slid a letter partway out of the envelope while he hummed the Jeopardy theme song. Maybe this one would represent him.

"Before I read this, Winch, tell me, why do you write? It seems to bring you so much misery. You seem so depressed when you receive these rejection letters."

He nodded. A good question. One that he'd asked himself while he sat alone in his car, on a boring surveillance, thunderstorm pounding on the roof, pen in hand, scribbling scenes of his novel onto a yellow legal pad. Rain or shine, daylight or darkness, he either wrote his novel, or thought through scenes in his head before committing them to paper. He wrote because he couldn't not write. "It'd be easier for sure, to lead a long and happy life than to write well," he said.

Brandy pulled the two combs from her hair. She shook her head and blonde tresses cascaded to her shoulders like water down a fall. "You're deep, Winchester Young. I didn't know you were that deep. You know what I mean?"

"Just read the damn thing."

Dear Mr. Young,

Thank you for allowing us to review the first three chapters of your novel, <u>Murder in the Conch House</u>. The beginning is great. You write of a world that you clearly know inside out. Your narrative is very fast paced, and your characters all ring true.

If the manuscript is still available I'd like to read the rest of it. You may send it to me electronically at the email address below. However you should be aware that if we're going to invest the time in reading the complete manuscript we'll want an exclusive until we're finished.

You can expect an answer from us within three to six months.

Sincerely,

Jeremiah Snow

Editorial Assistant to Oscar Parkinson

"Yes," he shouted. Finally someone took him seriously as a writer and even better, wanted to read his work.

"That's great, Winch." Brandy paused, a frown creased her forehead. "Isn't it?"

He wasn't exactly sure, though. "I think it is. Maybe . . . I don't know."

"Of course it is," she said.

"Six months is a long time to wait for an answer."

"Some people wait a lifetime," Brandy said.

Upbeat Brandy. One of the qualities he liked about her. "Now who's being deep, Miss Philosopher?"

Others wait an eternity, he thought, but didn't say it. Our mortal existence is but a speck of time in our eternal existence. But perhaps the most important speck, because everything that follows in the next life is dependent upon our actions here, on this earth. But it's hard in this life to have an eternal perspective when you've got to deal with the ex-wives, mortgages, boats, and car payments. Rent and electricity. But the joys in life are commensurate with the sacrifices: Sailing on a steady breeze and flat seas. Sunrises. Hale-Bopp's comet viewed from clear skies thirty miles offshore. A positive letter from a literary agent.

"You heard what she said. The part about your characters. I'm going to read it again."

And she did. And it sounded very good to him.

* * * *

Winch looked across Salt Run, the dredged tidal creek where the Conch House Marina sat. He stepped aboard the *Dos XX*. A slight swell was running from the north and she strained at her starboard lines. He checked for chafe. The lines looked good.

In June of 1740, Salt Run was an insect-infested creek. It was about here that Oglethorpe, from the Carolinas, commanding his siege of St. Augustine, unloaded cannon onto the shore. With the batteries set, day in and out his cannon balls rained over St. Augustine, bursting overhead and dropping into the city. Killing and maiming Spaniards. But the Carolinians themselves didn't fare so well. The troops hadn't learned from the Timucuan Indians to build their bunks more than a yard off the ground, higher than fleas can jump. Consequently, the unrelenting hordes of noxious insects inflicted more damage on them then the occasional return fire from the Spanish fort, Castillo de San Marcos.

He stepped inside the *Dos XX* and paused to examine the photograph of the Island Packet 48 center-cockpit sloop. When his book sold, he'd leave the PI business and go sailing. Writing books as he cruised throughout the Bahamas. Between the diving and sailing he could squeeze out a novel per year. He held the framed photo for a minute and his mind drifted to the warm shallow waters of the Bahamas, spearing fish and grabbing lobster.

His cell phone rang. Carla Fox.

"I'm leaving the hotel headed your way."

"Everything okay?"

"I'm anxious to hear what results you have for me."

Sheesh, he'd only had the case a few hours. She expected miracles. But he wondered about the guy who'd been with Valene, the hooker. It was unexpected, unexplained, and worried him. How had this stranger known about Carla Fox and her money before he did? Maybe she was being followed. Somebody in Atlanta who knew she'd withdrawn the fifty K and was now out to get it?

His fingers played down the side of the picture frame. Thinking. Was he just paranoid? Usually it was his clients who were paranoid. But Summer Dawn was a cop, and he could count on what she'd related.

"Drive on over. If I'm not in the lot, walk down to the boat."

He left the boat and headed for a spot across the street and down from the marina parking lot where he could set up a counter-surveillance on Carla. Catch her coming in and see if anybody bumper-locked her to the marina. If they were very competent it'd be tough for most investigators to make them. Too much traffic at the dinner hour. But having completed a gazillion miles of following people, knowing what to look for, he could run a counter-surveillance with his eyes closed.

Winch stood in the garage of an empty gas station. Carla's Porsche made the turn onto Comares Avenue and drove right into the marina parking lot. No other car came directly behind her, but a black Lexus, with Georgia plates, slowed at the intersection of A1A and Comares, moved into the left turn lane, hesitated, and then sped back into the fast lane of A1A.

Carla would walk down to the *Dos XX*, probably put out a bit that he wasn't waiting for her in the lot. Too bad. In a couple of minutes the same Lexus came from the other direction and drove down the road, slowing as it passed the marina. Then moved on to A1A. Coincidence? He couldn't tell but he wrote the tag number onto the palm of his hand in blue ink.

He made his way to the Conch House, entering the property near the motel office on the other side of the parking lot. Then he headed for his boat when his cell phone rang. Carla, wondering where he was.

"Make yourself at home, I'll be right there."

Should he tell her about the Lexus? If he did, her paranoia would riot like a Chattahoochee lock-down ward on LSD. It was probably nothing. Winch could run Florida and twenty-two other state tags instantly from his office computer. Georgia was not one of the them. Law enforcement could get it no problem. But for a PI, Georgia tag info was harder to get than fresh water out of Salt Run.

TWELVE

The micro-brewery A1A Ale Works bustled with activity. The wait staff trotting out food. Busboys clearing tables. Winch sat opposite from Carla. She'd downed two vodka collins and was lavishing attention on her third. As relaxed as she seemed, he sensed an edge behind the curtain of alcohol. The sea breeze carried Carla's perfume across the table. Something with watermelon and apples, maybe.

"I hope this is okay," Carla said. "Instead of eating at the Casa Monica."

Cordova 95, at the hotel, was a five-star restaurant. But the food here was good, and it came with a view of the boats moored in the bay, anchor-lights atop their masts arcing back and forth like restless stars tethered to Earth.

A handsome man in his late thirties stepped to their table. "Winch, how are you?"

"Phillip? Good to see you." He gestured toward Carla. "Phillip, this is a client of mine, Carla Fox. Carla, Phillip Maddox. He's the general manager here."

He could see Phillip's mind racing. "Carla Fox, Carla Fox." Then his face brightened. "Yes, of course, the writer. Well, how nice to have you in our restaurant. I think my wife Karen has several of your books at home. I wonder—"

"Bring them to the office tomorrow. I'm sure Carla would be glad to sign them."

“If there’s—”

Winch waved him off. “We’ll talk later Phillip.”

Phillip wandered toward the kitchen area barking orders. Carla stroked her fingertip down her glass and wiped moisture onto a napkin. “After what you said earlier about that gas station. . . . For gosh sakes why did they stop at that place? Some broken-down single-pump hayseed joint alongside the road.”

He examined the photo of Sarah taken the day she’d left Georgia. There was something in the picture, but he didn’t know what it was. Just the two sisters and the little brother. The three of them smiling. He turned it over, read again the inscription on the reverse. Looked at it upside down. Then he saw a chain hanging from Sarah’s neck with a pendant. No, it looked like a— “Is that a gold nugget?”

“Daddy gave each of us one when he walked out on mom. Sarah never took hers off.”

“You don’t wear yours?”

“Rusty and I lost ours, or they were stolen, when we were in foster care.”

“Sorry,” he said. But he knew a simple sorry couldn’t make up for a childhood deprived of parents. “What about boyfriends? Did Sarah have anyone?”

“She dated a frat boy, Andrew, Andrew something. I can’t remember his name.”

He spoke out loud as he thought. “Andrew, the boyfriend, met her down here and they took off together?” He sipped from his water glass. “Only something went wrong. Maybe Sarah changed her mind. They fought and Andy hurt Sarah and he covered it up.” No, that didn’t seem quite right to him. In those days young kids ran north across the Florida state line *to* Georgia. No waiting period to get married. Not south from Georgia to Florida.

Carla brushed a stray twist of hair off her forehead. “Andrew was in Georgia, with us. He was at the house when Sarah and his three fraternity brothers left. In fact, he took that picture with my camera. Sarah, Russell, and me.”

“So they all were students at the University of Georgia?” Thinking out loud again he said, “Andrew and his frat brothers maybe concocted the whole thing?”

Carla shook her head. "Andrew was fraternity president or something. When the boys called up and told mom that Sarah disappeared, she called Andrew and he came right over. So I know he wasn't in St. Augustine. He stayed at our house the whole of spring break while we waited for word."

Carla used her napkin to dab at the sheen of sweat on her forehead. "Maybe they never even stopped at that gas station."

"Phil Patch, the owner, says they bought gas. Remembers Sarah. She was there. . . and then she wasn't. The women's restroom has no windows. No dropped ceiling. Just the single door. No way she could have sneaked out. Patch said the boy pumping gas kept the bathroom in view the whole time. No question she went in. Then she vanished."

Carla furrowed her eyebrows and seemed to be thinking. His own mind raced. How did the girl vanish? He didn't know. More importantly, what happened to her afterwards?

He eyed Carla. He liked her. Flip, what wasn't there to like? A Porsche, money, good looks, and literate too. Still, this was business. He put his hands flat on the table and leaned toward her. "What was the name of their fraternity?"

She shrugged and gave him a loopy half-grin. Too much Stoli.

"Patch said the detective, Dick Sharp, was persistent. I think Sharp's murder might be tied into your sister's disappearance."

Carla sat upright. "Why would you think that?"

"Sharp kept poking at this case. Maybe he was making progress and someone couldn't have that. So they killed him."

Carla leaned back in her chair. Drank some from her glass. His mind flashed on Tracy and the gold chain around her waist. Tracy, with her sun bleached hair and freckles. And why would he be thinking about Tracy when across from him sat a woman every bit as beautiful as Tracy was cute? Plus she was a talented bestselling author with an agent who would actually read his manuscript if he'd just give the nod. His stubbornness, or was it pride, forcing him to wait, how long did that letter say? Three to six months before they'd respond. As a little kid his mother once told him he was so stubborn, trying to get him to change his mind was like towing a back-hoe with its bucket down.

Carla reached out and touched his hand. "Where'd you go Winchester? You weren't listening." She thinned her lips. "Why can't men just sit on their hands, open their damn ears, and focus when a woman talks. Is that asking too much? You know I'm paying you to listen."

He flinched at that. She'd said something, but his mind wasn't on her. "I didn't know I was on the clock. I thought, you know, you and me—this was pleasure, not. . . . " He waved his hand.

"It is pleasure," she said. "I shouldn't have said that. I'm really glad we have this evening together. I'm just stressing over this whole Charon thing."

She fanned her face. "I never drink this much."

He wondered if that were true. In fact, his clients seldom told him the entire truth. They'd give him their version and never relate facts that might damage their own standing. But did he really expect clients to wave their hands and say, "Oh, by the way. I have a drinking problem and it has no bearing on my case and my husband left me, the kids won't talk to me and I pass out on the couch every night, but not to worry."

"Go on, I must have fogged out for a moment. What was it you said?"

"I asked you where you were when I got to the marina." She said the words much louder than necessary.

He glanced at his hand where he'd written the Lexus's license plate.

Carla caught his glance and grabbed his wrist. "What's that?" She tried to force his hand over, palm up but her grip slipped, her hand whipped across the table, her elbow knocking a water glass to the floor, shattering.

He lowered his voice. "Let's go back to the hotel. We can talk there. More private." The waitress watched them, probably wondering how much of a scene they were going to make, then came over and picked up the larger chunks of glass. "I'm so sorry," Carla gushed.

Winch laid four twenties on the table, enough to cover the check and a generous tip. He'd worked as a waiter in college and understood tips. Carla downed the last half of her vodka collins and stood. Then plumped back into her seat.

"Whoa," she said. "Who's moving the floor?"

He moved behind her chair and helped her to her feet. His mind running. First: Andrew and his fraternity. Second: Luther Calderone,

Patch's stepson coming home from UGA. Third: Too many Fraternity brothers. There has to be a connection but he didn't have enough facts.

Then there was the nugget on a chain around Sarah's neck. It would play in here somehow.

And how did detective Sharp's murder figure into this? What did he hope to learn by visiting the crime scene, long after the crime? Like Patch said, Sharp, a dog pissing the same pole over and over.

He guessed now he'd soon be dog number two.

THIRTEEN

Winch released Carla's hand as they entered the Casa Monica, walking under the draped arches and through the smells of garlic and coffee from the Cordova 95 restaurant and the clink of ice and fluted glasses from the Cobalt Lounge.

Carla stopped in front of the elevators and grasped Winch's shirt with both hands, pulling him to her. He thought she was going to kiss him and a debate flashed through his mind about the propriety of involvement with a client. He could argue the case effectively either way, and he didn't know what to do. They were both single, unattached, and eligible. Still, Carla was a client.

She stood on her toes and leaned in, her lips close to his. Instead of kissing him she said in a whisper, "Meet me upstairs."

He barely nodded but it was enough for his lips to brush hers. He smelled the sweet grapefruit of the vodka collins on her breath. He left his lips on hers. She didn't pull back and he didn't press forward. He'd walk her to her room. Make sure she got there okay. In her state, who knew what might happen between the elevators and her door?

She handed him a room key. "Be a dear and go into the bar and get me another drink. Then come up."

The elevator dinged and she stepped in. "Three-oh-eight."

As the doors closed he wondered what he was getting himself into. He wasn't going to sleep with her. But it's not like he was a mid-life virgin either. He was an adult in his mid-thirties. Not some teenager groping around in the back seat of a car.

And now he'd gotten himself in a heck of a fix. Upstairs waiting for him in her hotel room, probably "freshening up" was this thirty-two-year-old female hot enough to melt the rubber off his soles.

* * * *

Carla stepped out of the elevator on the third floor and slipped off her shoes. She held them by their straps over her shoulder, enjoying the feel of carpet on her bare feet. She'd have to hurry. Winch would be up in a moment. She ran the fingertips of her hand down the wall and over each doorframe, looking at the numbers. Now let's see, 308. The thought of Winch made her giddy.

They hadn't kissed but almost. She wondered about Winch. He wasn't some boring accountant whose conversation centered on overdrafts and IRS loopholes. Winch lived real life. Adultery. Missing persons. Murder. Death. And life. Not to mention his cute butt.

FOURTEEN

Winch held the vodka collins in one hand, feeling something like a golden retriever fetching for his master. He pushed the feeling aside. He couldn't suppress the excitement he felt. Was she not everything he wanted in a companion? Cute, smart, successful, and independent.

He sniffed the drink and liked the grape-fruity smell of it. For a non-drinker he had to admit it smelled pretty good. He was clear on what Carla had on her mind. Who was he kidding? It was at the forefront of his mind, too. Still, he wouldn't have sex with her. He knew that. Not that he didn't want it. She was a client, and he wouldn't date clients. But in the Mormon Church, he'd made certain covenants. Probably the most difficult for an adult single Mormon male, was the covenant, the promise, not to have sexual relations with anyone unless he was married to her. Old fashioned by today's standards, he knew.

Most of his single friends engaged in sex on the second or third date. On the first date, they told him, if a lot of drinking was involved. Ogden Nash's poem, *Candy is dandy, but liquor is quicker* apparently was true. And Carla drank plenty of Vodka this evening.

Old fashioned or not, he'd keep his covenants. They were more important to him than his client's feelings. Clients come and go. But the promises he'd made were eternal.

He turned and walked to the elevators. The door opened and he slid the room card through the reader by the buttons and punched three.

At room 308 he knocked three times and was about to put the card in the lock when his cell phone rang. Rudolph Chambers. He set the drink on the floor and leaned against the wall. "Rudy," Winch said.

"I took an early flight and just got home, Winchester." He didn't sound happy. "Guess what I found?"

"New locks on the door?"

"No, our babysitter and her boyfriend making out on my couch."

Winch stepped away from the wall, careful not to kick Carla's drink. "Any chance the underwear you brought me belonged to the babysitter and not your wife?"

"Young, you're being funny aren't you? You don't get it?"

"Of course I get it, Rudy. You're frustrated. Your wife is stepping out on you. She's meeting with strange men at shopping malls, and the cute babysitter you've been lusting after has the hots for high school jocks and you're pissed because she's too young for you and you don't want to go to jail. How'd I do?"

There was silence on the phone and he checked the signal strength. Plenty of bars. Then Rudy said, "What do you mean meeting with strange men at the mall?"

Winch told him how he'd followed Lisa Chambers to an outlet mall in the morning and her foot play with Renfro under the table. "I'm pretty sure he's your guy. But he carries a gun so watch your step." He didn't tell him he'd been busted. Now wasn't the time for that.

"That's all fine, Young. But you didn't catch them in a motel, so maybe he is the guy or maybe he isn't. The question I have is where the hell is she right now Mister-I'm-the-best-PI-in-town? And what's more, I want to know who she's with."

"Listen, Rudy, you're not paying for twenty-four hour surveillance. If you wanted me on her tonight you should have said so. Or let me put the GPS on her car."

"I'm paying you to find out who's having an affair with my wife. And you're what, out on the town?"

He looked at the door and wondered why Carla hadn't answered his knock.

"I'm on another case. I'll run the DNA up tomorrow," Winch said. "They'll compare what we got off her panties and with some skin cells from the coffee cup. It'll take a week, maybe ten days, to get a verbal on the results. Come by in the morning and we'll talk."

"After your screw-up tonight I'll probably have more underwear to give you in the morning. And not the damn babysitter's either. I know who *she's* lusting after. I'm telling you this, Young—that DNA better match or with what all I've paid you we'll have a 'come to Jesus meeting' with the licensing board before we get done."

"I can't promise you anything, Rudy. Here's a plan though. You check out your wife's underwear in the morning and then call me." Winch held the phone away from his ear as Chambers yelled at him. He looked at the phone's display and powered the phone down. Screw Chambers. He'd solved the Lisa Chambers case and the DNA results would prove it.

He took a deep breath, closed his eyes and went back to leaning against the wall. Is this what he wanted? To cut crotches out of client's underwear for the rest of his life? Follow miscreants from one rendezvous to the next? No. He knew what he wanted. He wanted to sell the novel he'd written. And then he wanted to write another and another after that. Build a readership and live the life of a writer. He looked at room 308. Through that door might be the key to the life he wanted. Maybe he ought to forget his pride and accept the offer of her agent.

He was torn over this decision. He wanted an agent who loved his book. But he also wanted an agent who could sell his book. Did one require the other or were they mutually exclusive? So maybe he'd let Carla send his manuscript to her agent and see what he thought. But he didn't want to be indebted to her. Crap, he was already fetching her drinks. What would he do if she lined him up with her agent?

FIFTEEN

He rapped on Carla's door, wondering what he would face on the other side. He'd give her a quick hug and kiss on the cheek and be gone. Okay, he was good with that plan. He slid the key through the lock, the light turned green and he went in.

Her voice called out from the bathroom. "Be right out."

The room smelled like her. Light and airy. Gosh, he hoped she didn't come out in a negligee or something. That would be awkward. He pawed through some bottles on the dressing counter. Juicy Couture Parfum. Had to be expensive.

She stepped out of the bathroom wearing jeans, sleeveless pink cotton blouse, tennis shoes and carrying a make-up bag. "Don't drop that," she said.

He removed the lid, smelled the bottle. "Very nice. Smells like you. How much an ounce does this go for?"

She waved off the question. "Let's go."

He held up the glass of Vodka Collins.

"I think I've had enough." She took the glass and poured it down the sink at the wet bar.

"Where're we going?" he said.

"I've never slept on a boat before. I can use it in my next book."

He didn't know what that meant. Did she expect to sleep with him or was this really research for her writing? "You can have the master cabin. I'll take the crew quarters."

"Fine," she said, and they were off.

As they pulled into the marina, Winch scanned the parking lot. Well after midnight and still there were more than two dozen cars. Some belonged to live-a-boards. Others to a few hardy souls drinking at the thatched hut bar. No Lexus with Georgia plates. He glanced at the palm of his left hand. He'd write it down when he got on board.

"Tell me about your next book," Carla said.

"I'm working it out in my head."

A lock of hair fell across the middle of her face. She blew at it and it fluttered as if it had wings and settled again across her forehead and over her nose. He reached up and tucked it behind her ear. His fingers lingered on her neck, sweaty in the summer evening heat, and he wanted to pull her face to his, but the timing wasn't right.

Her cell phone rang. She unslung the purse from her shoulder and peered at the phone, then stuffed it back into her purse.

"Will I get seasick?"

"Some people become nauseated standing on the dock."

"Very good, Winchester."

He gave her a look. "What do you mean?"

"Most people misuse the word nauseated. Substitute nauseous. Maybe there's hope for you yet."

He gave her a slight grin and helped her through the boarding gate.

She held his hand as they boarded. "As a writer I mean."

A slight breeze blew across the barrier island toward the shore, ruffling the water, sending a slap-slap against the boat's hull. She turned her face into the wind, lifted the hair from off the back of her neck.

"Sea breeze," he said. "The land cools faster than the water making a low pressure area. The warm ocean air flows toward the low. Nature abhors a vacuum."

"My, aren't we the scientist?"

"The sailor," he corrected.

"I need to use the bathroom," she said. "I want to shower."

"The head," he said.

The *Dos XX* had the familiar smell of boat. It was not stuffy with the air conditioner running. More like stepping into a walk-in-closet.

He showed her how to pump the marine head, moving the levers from flush to dry bowl. And how to pump the shower sump.

"Where does it go? Certainly not just into the water out there, does it?"

"Fish poop in the sea, don't they?" he said.

"Disgusting. I hope I never fall overboard in this marina."

"Good idea," he said. "Not to worry. There's a holding tank." He gave her his usual quarters, the master stateroom, with its centerline queen berth and lots of room. He'd sleep in the aft stateroom. A misnomer. Really more like a double-bed mattress stuffed into a cubbyhole with a ceiling so low you had to hunch your shoulders before turning over.

Carla came out twenty minutes later, hair wet, wearing one of his T-shirts which dropped to her knees. Her fingers ran lightly over the books on his shelves. She held up the Plexiglas easel frame of the center-cockpit Island Packet 48, his dream boat. "I thought you liked motorboats."

"I'm a sailor at heart. You know, fool enough to stay out in bad weather and get beat to death, and drowned at the same time."

She admired the cutter-rigged boat. "And this is. . . ?"

"My motivation."

"Everybody needs a dream."

"I'll never make enough in the PI business to afford that boat. But maybe—"

"If you write one of these?" She set the photo down and her fingers ran lightly across the spines of the books on the shelf, pulling one off. "*Cool Breeze on the Underground.* Don Winslow." She flipped it open. "Signed?"

"First edition, first printing."

"I'm not familiar with him," she said. "Is it rare?"

"That one will go from two hundred to three-fifty."

"Three hundred and fifty dollars? Mine sell for six-ninety-five."

He reached over her shoulder, smelling soap. "This one is better. *California Fire and Life.* A stand-alone by Winslow but it's terrific. And you can find it in used bookstores for twenty bucks."

She flipped it open. "Signed, too." Her fingers ran across the other Winslow books on the shelf. *While Drowning in the Desert. Way Down on the High Lonely. A Long Walk Up the Waterslide.* "You must like him."

"His titles are very good. He's not perfect. If he'd study the craft a bit, he could be great."

"And your craft is better than his?"

"His 'voice' is better than mine."

She pulled another book out. "*The Blue Max*."

"Jack Hunter," he said. "He lived here in St. Augustine. Died recently. Signed copies have quadrupled in value since his death, if you can even find one. I have two."

She nodded. "Right, the movie, with –"

"George Peppard and Ursula Andress."

"It's easier to collect books than to write them," she said. "Easier to critique other's writing than sweat out the pages yourself."

"I can write," he said.

"Ah," she said, "But can you publish?"

That steamed him a little. "I write for myself. I don't write for publication."

"Oh, you're an artist? A purist, I suppose? Not willing to prostitute your writing for the enjoyment of the masses."

"My book deals with good versus evil, and man's struggle between the two."

She pulled *The Blue Max* from off the shelf and held it out. "And this doesn't?"

"Sure it does, but–"

"But does your book tell a really good story like this one? Story is the key to fiction writing. If you don't tell a good story then it's just self-indulgent prattle."

"*You're* telling *me I* prattle and *you* write romance?"

"You're saying your hardboiled PI is more literary than my romance?"

"Writing romance is closer to prostitution than the PI genre."

"Get your nose out of the air, buddy." She reshelved *The Blue Max*. "And if your fantasy is not to be a 'rich and famous' author then tell me, please, why you're trying to find an agent?"

She'd trapped him. Of course he wanted to publish. Still, that's not why he wrote. He wrote because he had a story to tell. But it might be more satisfying if he had an audience. Some validation that he'd mastered the craft of writing.

"Agents are prostitutes," he said.

"No." She turned to face him. "Agents are pimps. Writers are the prostitutes. Now, do you have your manuscript here? Let me read your first chapter."

His eyes flicked to the envelope on the counter that held the pieces of his first three chapters shredded by that rude agent.

She glanced to where he looked. "Maybe a copy we don't have to glue back together."

"It's late. We should get some sleep."

"Afraid?"

"I don't let friends read my work."

"I'm a professional."

He knew she was too. A novel a year. A *Times* bestseller.

From under the chart table he pulled out a stationery box. Extended it to her.

She took it. Hefted it. "How many words?"

"Ninety-six thousand."

She read the title page. "*Murder at the Conch House*. It's set here at this marina?"

"The protagonist is a PI. The setting is St. Augustine."

She tucked the manuscript under her arm. "It's not about some girl getting killed on a boat, is it?"

"You're safe tonight," he said. He stepped over to the sliding glass door, the only door to the outside, and locked it with a key. Somebody would have to break glass or jimmy the door to gain entry. He'd hear either.

She padded barefoot through the galley. Looked as good to him from the back as from the front and his heart tugged just a bit. She was difficult, but no doubt a connection existed between them.

Over her shoulder she said, "I'll read a bit before I go to sleep."

He didn't know if he could sleep while she read the manuscript. He wanted to watch her read. Examine the expressions on her face. See if she smiled at his humor, bit her lip at the danger. Would she laugh at the jokes and tear-up at the romance?

She shut the door to her cabin. He turned off the main salon lights and headed to the aft head where he showered. The boat lurched once, and he grabbed the handrail in the shower to keep from slipping on the teak grate. He heard the putta-putta of a passing motorboat over the sound of the rat-a-tat-tat of the fresh water pump.

Finished, he stepped into the main salon, drying his head with a towel. Light shown from under Carla's cabin door. He put his ear against the mahogany panel, cool to his warm face. The smell of wood oil. He listened. Nothing. The prospect of trying to sleep in that claustrophobic excuse for an aft stateroom with the deck a foot above his nose, condensation dripping like a cold rain in Seattle, made him wish for his own bed. He rested his hand on the doorknob. Curiosity as to her reaction to the first chapters of his book ran through his head. He knocked softly. "Carla?" He twisted the door handle.

The bulkhead reading-lamp spotlighted onto Carla. Mouth slightly open. Breathing heavy. Pages of his manuscript fanned across the sheet. He first thought the book put her to sleep. Not good.

She roused when he stepped into the room. As he gathered the papers together she smiled. "Pretty damn good, Mr. Young."

SIXTEEN

DAY TWO

A low-slung concrete building housed the Sheriff's office. An officer in a green uniform behind the high counter eyed Winch as he walked in. The deputy's biceps bulged, making his short sleeves look uncomfortably tight. His neck, or the area where his neck should have been, was corded with blunt-edged muscles running fan-shaped from the base of his skull to his shoulders. Like the bottom half of a pyramid with a peach of a head poised on top.

Carla, too hung over from last night's dinner, was still in bed on the *Dos XX* when Winch left. He glanced into the record section. Patti gave him a little wave with the back of her fingers. He smiled and nodded at her, but she'd already turned away. He approached the duty desk. "I'm Winchester Young to see Sheriff Osborn." He handed the deputy his card.

The deputy looked at the card, snorted, and slid it back across the counter to him. "You're a hot-shot PI, huh?"

"The Sheriff is expecting me."

"Yeah, you and that woman porno writer."

"Romance, not porno."

The deputy made a point of looking around the room. "Fiction. It's all the same isn't it? Mindless words just stringing sex scenes together."

Winch peered at the deputy's name badge. Wilson. "Deputy Wilson. You read a lot?"

Deputy Wilson stood and flexed his pectorals making his uniform ripple across his chest. "Nah, I mostly work out."

"Yeah, reading an entire book can be a lot of work. Make's your lips tired."

A confused look passed over the deputy's face as he silently mouthed the words, "Makes my lips tired."

He wondered about the deputy's literary IQ. "The steroids, they shrink more than just your nuts?"

The deputy's face flushed pink. Roid rage? He gripped the counter and leaned over, breathed a brassy metallic breath into Winch's face. "Don't say that around here. You never know who's listening."

Winch put one finger to his lips. "Oops, okay. Our little secret then." He made the motion of locking his lips and tossing away the key.

"You funning me?"

"I was one hundred percent serious."

The sound of clapping came from the hallway. Renfro. "Nice job, Young. You certainly know how to piss people off." He held a manila folder under one arm and beckoned Winch to follow. "Wilson may have peanuts for balls but if you need someone to back you up in a brawl, he's the guy I'd take."

"I prefer brains to peanuts."

"You got something against authority figures, Young?"

"I have a problem with law enforcement thinking they're above the law. Don't you guys drug test around here?"

"Yeah, well, I have a problem with PIs thinking they are law enforcement. Murder is against the law. It should be investigated by L.E. professionals, not PIs."

He wanted to respond with a smartass comment but he figured that he needed their cooperation.

He walked a half-step behind Renfro, who wore short sleeves, blue jeans, a set of handcuffs tucked behind his belt at the middle of his back, and a black plastic-gripped Glock on his hip. The hallway felt sterile. No posters on the walls. No bulletin boards. Tiled floors. Renfro was built so solidly he wondered if he too used steroids.

Winch was determined to solve this case and Carla would thank him for it. "I am a professional too, Detective Renfro. Nothing wrong with approaching a problem from a different angle. We both want the same thing."

"I don't know, Young. We may not want the same thing. What's important to me is what the Sheriff wants."

"I think the Sheriff will want what I have to offer."

The Sheriff stood and extended his hand as they entered his office. "Miss Fox isn't with you this morning?"

"She asked me to make her apologies."

The Sheriff looked at a short stack of paperbacks on the corner of his desk. Carla's novels. "Oh, my wife will be disappointed. She asked me to have these signed."

"I'll be seeing her later. If you want them signed. . . ."

The Sheriff picked up one of the books and fanned its pages. "You know, I've never read one of these romance books. Have either of you?"

Both he and Renfro shook their heads.

"Would you happen to know whether she's a Republican or Democrat?"

Winch didn't know. But he did know the Sheriff was a Democrat facing an election in the fall in a mostly Republican county. "I'm sure she's a registered Democrat."

The Sheriff nodded. "A couple of good men are lining up to run against me."

Renfro's eyes narrowed. He'd probably figured where things were headed. "Boss," he said. "Before we get too deep into this, you need to think how it might look in the fall. How the papers will play it when word is out we've resorted to using some PI to work our cases."

Renfro continued, "Not only a PI but one with no previous law enforcement experience. I mean, if he were a retired cop or something. . . ."

The Sheriff's face took on a thoughtful expression. He should have been an actor. Come to think of it, as a politician he was one.

"Yes, detective. I suppose Mr. Young's involvement could be viewed as you describe."

"Miss Fox," the palms of Winch's hands sweated and he wiped them on his trousers, "contributes heavily in political races where she has strong feelings for one of the candidates. Even though she's not a resident–"

"Mr. Young," the Sheriff said, "do you know what the penalty is for attempting to bribe a law enforcement officer?"

Winch shook his head, "I don't know where the line falls between bribery and campaign contributions, but I'd guess it's a pretty broad one."

"Sheriff," Renfro stepped forward. "He's trying to buy us."

The Sheriff stroked his chin then gazed at Renfro. "This office has investigated the Sarah Fox disappearance case for twenty-five years, Detective. You've been the lead detective on the case for ten. I reviewed the file this morning. Anything new in the last ten years?"

Renfro cast his eyes downward then glared at Winch. "The leads were all worked out when I took the case over. It's as cold as it gets."

"Then I think we have nothing to lose," the Sheriff said, "by letting Mr. Young take a swing at it. On two conditions, Mr. Young."

Winch nodded. Waited.

"You work closely with Detective Renfro here. Keep him apprised of your every move."

He nodded.

"There's a front page story above the fold in *The Record* today," the Sheriff said. To Renfro: "Did you see it?"

Winch hadn't seen it. How did *The Record* get on to the story? Carla must have done an interview with the paper after he dropped her off. He wondered if this whole case was just a way for her to get some press coverage? Was she just using him to sell copies of her book?

To Winch, the Sheriff said, "Does Ms. Fox know something about this case? Perhaps she has some information that we've not been privy to?"

Winch didn't know how much to tell the Sheriff. He couldn't tell him about Charon and the fifty-K demand note. Misprision of a felony, he thought. The overt act of concealing a felony was in itself a felony. This was like walking down the double yellow line in the middle of a highway. Cars whizzing past him from each direction. Buffeted by the crisp envelope of wind by the Sheriff's office on one side, Charon on the other. One misstep either way and he'd be slammed to the pavement. "I don't know what's in your file, so I don't know if I have any more info than you. I'd think not."

"I figured as much."

"You said there were two conditions," Winch said. "You've only given me one."

"Right." The Sheriff took a sip of coffee. "All media contacts are made through this office." He rapped *The Record* again. "None of this."

Winch scanned the article. He wanted to say, "None of this unless accompanied by your photo," but he didn't. Instead he said, "You got more publicity out of that article than I did."

"One more thing, Young."

He waited.

"Do you know why I'm being so generous?"

"Because you're expecting a big fat campaign contribution from Carla Fox?"

"Damn, you are impertinent, aren't you?"

"I might be." Winch scratched his head. "I've never been called that before. I've been called other things."

The Sheriff gave him a quizzical look.

"There was the retired Jewish lady I busted pinching twenties out of a cash drawer."

The Sheriff gave him a look.

"She called me a Philistine."

"A Philistine is—" Renfro said,

"I teach Sunday School. I damn well know what a Philistine is," the Sheriff said. He pointed to a photo on the wall. The man in uniform in front of a local Baptist church.

Winch nodded. "Yeah, I get called lots of things. And then there are your deputies . . ." the Sheriff raised an eyebrow, and Winch eyed Renfro, "they usually sneer and pencil me out a citation. But I'd be glad to let you call me 'impertinent' as long as there's no fine associated with it."

"See, I love guys like this." The Sheriff looked at Renfro. "I love him because nobody around here has the cojones to say things like that to me. When he's on something, he's committed. I love commitment. I love stand-up guys. I wish all of my deputies were just like you, Young. I think that even after twenty-five years that murdering son-of-a-whatever better watch out because you just might nail his butt."

Then the Sheriff turned reflexive, pursed his lips, eyebrows coming nearly together. "You'd better watch your own back, Winchester. If you get close to the guy who murdered Sarah Fox, he might not be so friendly."

"So you don't think she was a runaway?"

"I wasn't Sheriff back then. I didn't make that decision. But use some common sense, son. If she ran away, where's she been hiding for the last twenty-five years."

Winch nodded. "Exactly my thought."

The Sheriff stood, "Take him to your office, Vinnie. Give him a copy of the file and also those personal items that belonged to that poor girl. I don't think we need to keep them in evidence any longer, do we?" As an after thought the Sheriff said, "But make him sign for them."

As he and Renfro turned to leave, the Sheriff cleared his throat. "One more thing, Young."

Winch turned.

"I sense," the Sheriff said, "some animosity between you and Detective Renfro. You boys be nice. My guess is that you two are more alike than either of you suspect."

After the office door was closed, Renfro said, "We're not alike, you know."

Winch studied the man's face and wondered what Renfro's agenda was. "I hope not."

He trailed Renfro down the hall. "You have 'personal items' of Sarah's?"

Renfro motioned for him to follow.

SEVENTEEN

Winch and Renfro walked through the bullpen. Deputies eyed them. Handcuffs hung in pouches on their leather belts. Black Glocks were holstered on their hips. Once they were behind the blue Orlon covered cubicle Renfro reached into a drawer and plopped out a thick binder. Winch raised his eyebrows.

"A complete copy of the murder book. Photos and everything," Renfro said.

"How'd you know the Sheriff–?"

"I've been chief deputy for six years. I know the Sheriff. Is this an election year or what?"

Winch nodded toward the duffle. "The Lands' End bag. Anything there?"

"The bag was found on Vilano Beach, just above the high tide line." Renfro opened the murder book. Flipped through a few pages and then read, "In 1982 Lands' End shipped four thousand two hundred and twenty-four of this model bag. Twenty one hundred and sixteen were green. One of those was shipped to eighteen-twenty, Ridge Dr., Athens Georgia, to a Ms. Lydia Fox. A gift card was enclosed that said, 'Happy Birthday, Sarah.' Does that answer your question?"

"Good work." Winch reached for the copy of the murder book but Renfro kept his hand on it.

"You're not going to find squat, Young. Nothing to find. The work was all done. She's been gone years."

"I get paid for looking, not for finding."

"Is that it for you? Just another check to go into your bank account?"

"What's in the bag?"

"She's wasting her money, isn't she?"

Winch unzipped the duffle. Reached in and stopped. "Do you have gloves?"

Renfro shook his head. "It's all been processed. It's being released now to next of kin. You think we missed something? We're not idiots and we're not amateurs."

He reached into the bag and pulled out clothing. It smelled musty but appeared clean. Girls jockey underwear. Some T-shirts. A pair of jeans, a two piece swimsuit. One pair of cutoff jeans. A pair of gym shorts. A pair of sandals. "Do you have an inventory of this?" In the bottom he found a spiral notebook. He leafed through the pages. A girl's handwriting. Little circled smiley faces over each "I". He held up the book. "Anything good in here?"

"You're just a thief." Renfro shook his head. "Like a quack doctor. Taking money and handing out hope."

"I hand out facts, deputy. Not hope." He held up a pair of underwear, and looked at the crotch. Soiled with something. "Did your lab process all of this stuff?"

"We don't have a lab. And yes it was sent to the State's after we found it. We're not morons you know."

"Did they blood type this?"

"Let me see." Renfro held out his hand. "Doesn't look like blood to me."

It looked like DNA stains on the underwear to Winch. Even though he didn't like to admit it, it was the one thing in which he'd garnered a lot of experience. It could, of course, have just been twenty-five year old dirty underwear. At the office, he had the test kit which would tell him. But eighty percent of all people secrete their blood type in their body fluids. So even though they didn't have DNA back then, they could have determined if it was bodily fluids and if so, probably the blood type of the donor.

Winch nodded. "The bag was found how?"

"Three days after she disappeared, a tourist found it on the beach." Renfro slapped his hand on the binder. "It's all in there. Take it and do your homework."

"One more question and I'll get out of your hair." Renfro made an impatient waving motion with his hand. "Detective Richard Sharp? Did you guys ever consider that his murder was connected to Sarah Fox's?"

Renfro's head jerked up. "Stay away from Sharp's murder. It's none of your business."

Why the reaction? "Right. Thanks, Deputy. I'll call when I have something to report."

Renfro shook his head. "You can be sure we'll keep a line open for you, Young." He flicked a dismissive wave with the back of his hand.

The detective slid a printed form across the desk to him. "It's a receipt. You've worn out your welcome. Sign it and take the dirty underwear with you."

He'd take it all right. And he'd run it up, with Lisa Chambers' underwear, to the private lab he used in Jacksonville this afternoon. Pay for a rush and have the results back day after tomorrow. If it was DNA, what were the chances it belonged to the guy who took Sarah?

EIGHTEEN

Sarah's green nylon duffle lay on Winch's desk like a fat watermelon. He pursed his lips and considered the fact that this bag had been locked in the police evidence room for over two decades. Was he enough of an investigator to find something here . . . something the Sheriff's detectives missed . . . anything that might help him figure out how she disappeared?

On the far right corner of his desk sat a duplicate framed photo of the cutter-rigged sailboat. Next to that lay the photo of Sarah that Carla left with him. The happy seventeen-year-old girl with the mischievous smile in the simple frock.

Out the window, brake lights brightened as cars on the Bridge of Lions came to a stop. The bridge rose and a sharp-bowed, center-cockpit sloop, nose into the wind, sails fluttering, passed beneath. His eyes flicked back to the photograph of his dreamboat.

He picked up the photo of Sarah. He would solve this case. Prove he was just as good an investigator as his Uncle Benjamin. Better even than the detectives who'd delayed years in solving this case. He had five days and counting. He would do this for Carla. As soon as that thought flicked through his mind he knew it was a lie. He wasn't doing this for Carla. He liked her, for sure. Why then? For Sarah, a girl whose name he'd never heard of until a couple of days ago? Sarah, whose totality of worldly possessions lay before him in that bag. He found her photo enchanting. The innocent yet knowing smile, given when she had no reason to believe her life would snap short like a twig on a winter-dead tree.

That was it then. For Sarah. Not the flesh and blood Sarah. She wouldn't know, at least not in this life. But where she was now, in the Spirit World, she'd know. If the need arose, there could be some communication between the Spirit World and earth. It was something the Mormon Church didn't talk about openly, but it was there. It was one reason for Mormon temples. A place where the veil between the two worlds thinned. But the veil thinned at times of passing as well. At his Uncle Benjamin's viewing the night before the funeral he'd overheard two teenage girls talking. One asked who the viewing was for? The other said "Benjamin Young." The first said, "That can't be, I just saw him standing over there" she pointed, "in the corner."

Winch looked but didn't see his Uncle in the corner. But he felt sure he was there, staying close to the body until it was buried. For what reason, he didn't know. But this teenage girl was allowed to see his Uncle's spirit for some reason. Maybe for something that would become important in *her* life down the road.

When he, himself, arrived on the other side, he'd meet Sarah and tell her he'd done all he could to find her earthly body, gave it a proper burial, and sought justice for whoever sliced short her life.

The drawbridge lowered, and the sloop's captain hauled in the mainsheet. The boat caught the wind, heeled to port and slid through the water as slick as a shark fin past the old fort, Castillo de San Marcos. His eyes went from the fort to a rendition on his wall depicting the siege of 1702. Five hundred English Carolinians and 300 Indians laid siege to St. Augustine. Fourteen hundred inhabitants of the old town took cover within the walls of the fort. Anticipating the attack, the Spaniards ordered cattle and supplies brought into town from the western regions of the state. But the siege began before the supplies arrived. With the blockade already underway a handful of Spanish soldiers stampeded a hundred and sixty head of cattle through the Carolinians, scattering the foot soldiers and running the cattle into the boggy moat surrounding the fort. Throughout the two-month occupation, whenever one of the English musket balls would kill a steer, the Spaniards would drag the carcass into the fort and butcher it.

Winch moved to his worktable, a piece of beige countertop laid across a pair of two-drawer filing cabinets. He ran his hand over the canvas bag.

He opened a drawer and put on a pair of latex gloves. Probably no reason to do that since the Sheriff released her belongings. Still, prudence dictated. . . .

He took a deep breath, unzipped the duffle, and dumped the contents on the table. Two sandals. Leather soles and straps with a white plastic daisy where the straps met near the big toe. He held them to the light. Rotated them. Nothing there he could see. A pair of solid blue shorts, no belt. Surely the forensic people had gone over all of this. Nevertheless he'd check each item carefully.

A beach towel, red, white, and black, with the Georgia Bulldog in the center. The two-piece swimsuit. Next the make-up kit. He knew little about women's makeup. He'd have Brandy look it over, maybe she'd see something of importance there. A flowered print top. A pair of jeans. A pink T-shirt silk screened with "Pretty" across the chest. Two pair of beige women's Jockey bikini underwear. One clean, the other soiled. He separated the soiled pair, stuck as it was to itself.

Renfro told him the underwear hadn't been tested for blood type. Sloppy police work. Of course they'd need a suspect for matches, which they didn't have, so it didn't really make any difference back then. But now they could get the DNA and enter it into CODIS, the software program that allows law enforcement to enter DNA profiles into databases, and compare it to those of convicts, missing persons, and unsolved crimes. Maybe get a match with someone in the database.

And there was a spiral bound notebook. The name Sarah Fox written with a flourish in ballpoint ink on the inside front cover.

He flipped through the pages of the notebook. Four pages of writing and the rest were blank. In a girl's handwriting at the top of the first page it read, "My Spring Break" Then began a diary of sorts detailing her trip. She'd left Athens, Georgia with Kevin, Tony, and Trey in route to Daytona. Andrew couldn't come because he had a big project due the day after spring break ended. She was "soooo disappointed." The long boring ride through Georgia. She'd wanted to detour through Fernandina and see where pirates hung out. Stop on Ft. George island and walk through the ruins of a slave plantation. But the boys wouldn't stop. Finally they'd agreed to overnight in St. Augustine. You could drive on St. Augustine beaches so they'd sleep in the car on the beach. Save their money for the hotel in Daytona.

She'd written observations about the beach, and a loggerhead turtle that struggled ashore and laid eggs. Scotch-taped on the next page were fourteen shark's teeth, white and jagged. He crinkled the paper a little and poked his index finger against one of the teeth. Sharp as a knife tip. He wondered for a moment why the teeth were white? All of the shark's teeth he'd collected on the beach were black.

The third page ended "last night–EF on the beach was the best ever. Tomorrow at the fort again same time." She'd drawn a heart around the initials EF. On the fourth page she'd written the initials EF a half-dozen times with a question mark behind each set. He flipped through the notebook. And that was it. No other writing. He set the book aside.

Next was the copy of the murder book. A legal size folder, hole punched and bound at the top with metal clasps. As thick as a deck of cards. Not much paper for twenty-five years of investigation. Four tabs were glued to various sheets down one side. One tab read "Physical Evidence" and he turned to that page. Detective Richard Sharp had written "Diary" at the top of one sheet of paper and then the names: Kevin, Tony, Trey and the initials EF. Next to EF he'd noted "sex on the beach EF = killer?" Under that he'd written the numbers 2-4.

Winch thought about that. 2-4. Twenty-four. 2 bar four. A cattle brand? Two dash four, numbers squared? Then there should have been a sixteen. Two dash four, what did that mean?

One of the other tabs read "Statements" and those would be the interviews and signed statements of the three boys she'd traveled with. He'd get to those later.

Right now he needed to package Lisa Chambers' underwear, drive them to the DNA lab in Jacksonville. And Sarah's as well. Even though he had no DNA to compare it to, he might in the future.

He laid out the three pair of underwear from Lisa Chambers. On the waistband he numbered them in permanent marker: LC1, LC2, LC3. He placed each in a small brown paper bag and labeled it. No plastic baggies for body fluids. To preserve the DNA in blood and other body fluids, the samples needed to dry cleanly and not mildew.

The Styrofoam cup he labeled VR1 and placed that in a plastic bag. Hopefully it would contain cheek or lip cells from Vincent Renfro, proving him to be the donor on Lisa Chambers' underwear.

Next he labeled Sarah Fox's panties, SF1. But before he stowed them in a brown bag he wanted to test them. He pulled a blue cardboard cylinder the size of a telephone handset out of the drawer. He fished out two Q-tip cotton swabs, one yellow, the other blue. A small dropper bottle of saline solution and an even smaller bottle of reagent.

His office door burst open. Rudy Chambers, a plastic bag with a pair of nude colored panties in one hand, a briefcase in the other. Rudy stood half-a-head shorter than Winch's six feet. He wore khaki pants and a blue open-necked polo shirt stretched across his belly. The top of Rudy's head exhibited a circle of bald scalp the size of a CD giving him a Friar Tuck look, except for the pencil thick gold chain around his neck.

"I found these in the hamper this morning, Winchester." He tossed the plastic bag onto the table.

Winch lifted the bag gingerly with two fingers, dangled it in the air and examined it. He recognized them right off as La Perla hipster nude panties. Sheesh, he was way too familiar with women's underwear. "Has your wife questioned her missing underwear?"

"She thinks the babysitter is stealing them."

Winch took the nude hipsters out of the plastic bag and held them up.

Rudy plopped down into a chair. Crossed one leg over the other, flashing a fist width of a pale ankle between the pants cuffs and burgundy loafers. Penny loafers and no socks. Some people never grow up.

Winch labeled, dated, and initialed the La Perla, and slipped them in a brown paper bag.

Rudy stood and paced around Winch's desk then picked up the photo of Sarah and her siblings. "Family? Cute girls."

"Clients."

Winch took the photo out of Rudy's hand and set it back on the desk. "Don't even be thinking what you're thinking."

Rudy stepped over to the workbench. "You insult me, Winchester." He pawed through the bags there. Held up the bag marked SF1. "And who is Ms. SF one?"

"Put it down Rudy. She's too old for you." He spread Sarah's underwear and exposed the crotch. "I'm testing it."

He dropped some saline onto the stain and waited 30 seconds. Then he rolled the yellow ended Q-tip over the stain. "If this stain is what I think it is, the chemical on this swab will react with the zinc." He looked up at Rudy. "Eat more cabbage. It's loaded with zinc and increases testosterone."

"I don't like coleslaw," Rudy said, eyeing the Q-tip. "I don't see anything."

Neither did Winch. "It should turn pink."

"That's fitting," Rudy said.

"Don't be gross."

Rudy scratched the bald spot on his head. "You're standing there playing with five pair of women's dirty underwear, and you're calling me gross?"

Winch took the blue tipped cotton swab and rolled it around in the stain. Checked his watch. "This one takes three minutes."

Rudy plopped back into the chair. "How soon can you get the results back from the lab?"

"Four pair of panties and the cup. You're going to owe me thirty-five hundred. Plus." Winch eyed the calendar on the wall. "Let's see, today's the fifteenth, if you want the results before the weekend, the rush will cost you another hundred-fifty a test. Seven-fifty more."

"Forty-two hundred dollars on top of the five grand I already paid you?"

"Forty-two-fifty."

Rudy pulled an envelope as thick as a paperback copy of *War and Peace* out of his briefcase and counted out forty-three one hundred dollar bills. Slapping each one on the desk. "What is it with us? Why are we always chasing after women."

Winch looked at his watch. Squeezed a single drop of reagent onto the blue-tipped swab. "Should get some green streaks on this one. Nothing. No change. Crap. He'd been sure there should have been some DNA there. Why didn't the tests react?

He reached into the drawer, pulled out a sheet of instructions. He'd used these tests a hundred times over the last few years. You could buy them on the Internet but he bought them directly from a lab in New York. There. In the fine print he read, "the presence of zinc and acid phosphatase in dry stains are detectable as much as 2 months after deposition." This was 25 years, not two months. Maybe this test wouldn't give him the results he looked for but he knew that DNA on dried samples of body fluids would be recoverable for a hundred years. He packaged Sarah's underwear and sat at his desk.

"Rudy, you're a good looking guy." Okay, so he lied to his clients. Rudy was a dumpy looking guy. No wonder his wife played around on him. Nevertheless he'd make Rudy feel better. He did the same thing with his female clients. Told them how smart and attractive they were, and how after the divorce, guys would be chasing them all over town. His clients' checkbooks came out from their purses easier and objections to his retainer were fewer with a few ego strokes. "Why don't you just divorce Lisa and get on with your life? You'll do fine without her. You don't need to know who the other guy is. Isn't it enough to just know that there is another man?"

"Revenge, Winchester. Make him pay."

He'd had this discussion a hundred times with clients. "You're not going to do something stupid? Shoot him?"

"Heaven's no, I'll get him fired, or his house foreclosed on."

Winch thought about women and men and sex. Women all had the same basic parts. Look at their faces. Most of the women he knew had two eyes, one nose, two ears and one mouth. Yet they all looked different. Sex with women was similar or so he'd been told by his buddies. His own sex life had been pretty limited. He'd had sex with Tracy and that was about it. Still he'd dated and made out with lots of women and with each it was the same, but different. The smell would be different. They'd moved differently. One would moan or grunt. The other might be totally quiet. Other women, he knew, would be different also. One might squeal. With another it wouldn't be verbal. It would be through other senses that you could tell they were excited. Their lips or the tips of their nose might go cold. Or the middle of their back would sweat. And that's why men cheated. Not women so much. Women cheated for other reasons. But men cheated to experience the difference.

"Hey, Winchester, where did you go buddy? I wasn't kidding you know?"

Winch raised his eyes and met Rudy's. He looked at the pot-bellied, balding man and actually felt some sympathy for Rudy's wife. But this was his client, and he'd do his job.

Rudy scratched his knee. "Like I said last night, about the meeting with the licensing board. You'd better have something good here." Rudy gestured toward the brown bags. "I'm not going to pay you ten grand and then just walk away. I want results."

Winch was sure about the underwear. He'd tested that himself. But how sure was he that Renfro was the DNA donor? "I told you what I saw at the mall. I can only report what I see. I don't make things up. I think Renfro's a good lead. But I don't know where Renfro was last night. So he could be the donor," he nodded his head toward the La Perla, or he might not be."

"There's something else you need to know, Rudy."

Rudy gave him a questioning look.

"Somehow, Lisa knew about the surveillance–"

"You blew it."

"No, I don't think so. But when I was leaving the mall Renfro corralled me. Accused me of stalking Lisa. I don't know how she knew. I know she never saw me following her."

Rudy's head drooped, and he shook it from side to side. Winch thought Rudy was about to fire him. But instead he said, "It might have been my fault. When I left town, I told her she'd better behave herself. I'd hired a private investigator, and I'd know if she was fooling around."

"You dumb idiot. You told her?"

"Yeah, but I didn't think she'd believe me. I bluff a lot, and she knows it."

So when he'd picked up their cups at the food court, she must have figured this time Rudy wasn't bluffing.

"We'll know soon enough if it's Renfro. It could be someone else."

"You've got anybody in mind?"

Winch shrugged. "What about the jock? The babysitter's boyfriend. Any chance he's involved with your wife too?"

"You think I should try and score a pair of the babysitter's underwear? Bring them in for testing."

Winch shook his head. He didn't even want to encourage Rudy in that direction. Not that Rudy needed any encouragement. In another month after she turned eighteen he wouldn't be surprised if Rudy did just that.

"How much time have you got before you hit that big score you were talking about?"

"Less than a week. I'm going to make a million in the market, and I'm not going to split it with her. My attorney has the papers ready to file. Once we file, what I make after that is mine. But it also puts her on notice and she'll probably stop until we're separated. And I want to know who she's seeing before I file. After that, I don't care."

Winch folded the forty-three one hundred dollar bills and stuffed them into a front pocket on his jeans. He looked at his watch. If he hurried he could still make it to the DNA lab in Jacksonville before it closed.

Just as Rudy shut the door a little harder than was necessary, the telephone rang. The caller ID read Lambert & Gilbert, New York City. Parker Lambert, Carla Fox's literary agent calling him. Even *he* knew that in the publishing business, bad news comes by mail, good news comes in a phone call.

The phone rang again.

He looked at his watch, the phone, and then at Sarah's photo on the desk.

NINETEEN

Winch stepped into his office. Driving down from Jacksonville in rush-hour traffic he'd strategized on the Sarah Fox case. Where to go next? It'd been one of those languid summer afternoons where a quick passing shower steamed off the asphalt in rising curtains. Maintaining concentration on the case proved difficult because his mind wandered to the fantasy of selling his book. Did the literary agent, Parker Lambert leave him a message? Walking away from the ringing telephone, knowing that one of the top New York agents was calling him, had been even more difficult than leaving Tracy and her gold waist chain yesterday. He stepped to his desk and hit line one. Heard a stuttered dial tone. He had a message.

"Mr. Young, this is Parker Lambert's assistant, Jennifer, from Lambert and Gilbert Literary Services in New York. Mr. Lambert was hoping to speak with you. Would you be so kind as to give us a call back at . . ."

He looked at his watch. Six pm. Not likely he'd still be in, but why not? He dialed the number and a man answered.

"Parker Lambert."

"Mr. Lambert, this is Winchester Young in Florida. Your assistant Jennifer left me a message."

"Ah, Mr. Young. Carla Fox faxed me the first three chapters of your novel today, *Murder at the Conch House*. Excellent Mr. Young."

"Winch. Call me Winch."

"Winch then. And call me Parker. Carla indicated you may be looking for representation."

"Well, I have sent out a few queries and have had some interesting responses." Like a shredded manuscript and juvenile insults.

"Have you submitted the manuscript to any publishers?"

He wasn't sure how to respond to this. True, some publishers, despite the belief to the contrary will still buy un-agented material. But he didn't know what answer Lambert was looking for. Surely Carla would have told him that he didn't have an agent, much less a publisher. So he said nothing and let the silence hang for a second figuring that Lambert would fill the void.

"We find some unrepresented authors submit directly to publishers," Lambert said, "and once it's been rejected by one editor at a house, then it's usually considered to have been rejected by the entire house and we cannot resubmit. Even if it went to the wrong editor."

Might as well be truthful. "There is one agent that has asked for the manuscript, but I haven't sent it. No publishers have seen it."

He could almost hear Parker Lambert thinking. Lambert had been doing a favor for Carla, but now, maybe he had a hot one. Agents must all have the fantasy of acquiring the next *Da Vinci Code*. And now Lambert had to be thinking that if some other agent had an interest in the book he'd better grab it first. Winch had learned in the PI business that fear of loss is a greater motivator than desire for reward. Fear of loss, a more common motive for violence, than hope for gain.

"I'd like to read the manuscript" Lambert said. "But if I'm going to invest the time in going through it, I'd want an exclusive."

Winch thought about this. What did that other literary agent say? They wanted six months to review it? "For how long?"

"Four weeks," Lambert said.

That didn't seem unreasonable. He could send it to Lambert and forget about it and concentrate on Sarah's case. Forget about it? Not likely. He'd be reading his emails, checking his messages hourly. Any time the phone rang he'd look at the caller ID to see if it originated from New York. And then there was the question of how deeply he'd be indebted to Carla? What was the downside of sending

Lambert the complete manuscript? Another rejection letter. Whoop-dee-doo.

"Okay, Parker. I'll get it in the mail to you tomorrow."

"Better," Lambert said, "if you email it to me."

Lambert gave him his email address and they said their goodbyes. Winch leaned back in his chair. Maybe his fantasy was about to come true. He wished he could proofread the 430 page manuscript once more. With every reading he found typos and errors. But he didn't have time for another go-through now.

He composed an email to Lambert, attached the manuscript to it, and hit send. *Murder at the Conch House* would have to stand on its own.

* * * *

Detective Richard Sharp and the three boys who traveled with Sarah. Those would be Winch's next two steps. It bothered him that Sharp, the lead detective, had been shot a year into the case. The Sheriff's office hadn't made any connection between the two cases. Renfro seemed touchy about the issue. Had to wonder why. Sharp's death could have been an isolated freak thing, or it could have been related to something else Sharp was working. Winch had no idea about Sharp's cases twenty-five years ago and no way of making any sort of connection there. Or maybe he could. Just maybe he could track down Sharp's widow and see what she had to say.

And then there was EF. The person Sarah had apparently had met on the beach the night before she disappeared. Maybe he'd get some idea of EF's identity by talking to the boys. But Sharp had interviewed the boys, and they all denied knowing the mysterious EF. If Sharp had any clues as to EF's identity he hadn't put it in the murder book.

That was it then. He'd track down the boys. The murder book identified the boys by name, dates of birth, and their addresses. In '86, the social security number wasn't the popular identifier it is now. No identity theft back then. No Internet to speak of either. The old addresses probably wouldn't do him any good. But, he'd be one poor investigator if he couldn't find them with the info he had.

First he'd find Sharp's widow. Tomorrow morning he'd go back to the Sheriff's office. See if Patti in Records could pull anything on

Sharp out of the dust. Sharp's widow might prove difficult to locate. Women change their last names more often than he changed the oil in his Jeep. Maybe, just maybe, the ex-wife would know something, some crumb of information the detective had confided to her but had never written into the murder book. A hunch Sharp had. Or a lead he was going to work and never did. Something like that. And maybe she could tell him what Sharp's "two dash four" might mean.

TWENTY

Two larger-than-life-sized carved pelicans guarded the entrance to the Conch House Marina. Winch walked across the marled parking lot to the smell of conch fritters in a deep fry and fish on the grill. Reggae music boomed down the concrete dock. A trio played under the darkening sky across from the thatched roof bar. He smelled fresh catch and salt spray from the fish cleaning station. A half-dozen laughing gulls swooped and fought over flesh tossed by the charter boat mates filleting king mackerel, knives flashing faster than any sushi chef's. Woody Copeland had called him as he left the office and wanted to meet. "Something important," he'd said. Plus he'd met with Valene, the hooker.

Brandy, behind the bar, filled a glass with ice and what he knew would be Diet Coke. Waved it at him. He was tired. He had so much going on in his brain: the Lisa Chambers DNA case, Sarah Fox, and now an agent reading his book. A little decompression time before getting to some of the chores on his 'boat list' would be good.

Tiki torches surrounded the bar. Their flames produced a not unpleasant smell of orange-misted citronella, which drifted in the air and kept the mosquitoes at bay.

The bar wasn't crowded for an early Wednesday night. Half a dozen men and two women were trying their best to have fun. Four of the men were only occasional boaters from the look of their sunburned faces. The other two, with tans like burnt toast, were regulars he recognized and nodded to.

He pulled a stool out from the bar where Brandy had set his drink. "Thanks," he said.

Brandy sported a V-necked white tank top, printed with two fist-sized strategically placed navel oranges, each overlaid with a man's hand, below which read, 'Squeeze Florida Oranges.'

"How it's going, skipper?" she said.

One of the regulars held up an empty glass. She turned from Winch and filled a glass with beer from the tap with an inch of foam head. "Seen Woody?"

Brandy stepped around the end of the bar carrying the beer. She leaned forward more than necessary to set the glasses on the men's table. Better tips that way.

When Brandy resumed her place behind the bar, she turned to him, "He's in the head."

Winch raised his eyebrows.

"Haven't seen your client around today. She fire you already?"

"She's at her hotel working on the galleys of her new book."

Woody walked in. His gray-streaked hair to mid-shoulders, not in the ponytail he usually favored. He wore a gray striped baseball shirt. Then he shrugged out of it as he walked to the bar. In college Woody held the fastball speed record for a couple of years until he was expelled for some behavior that he'd never owned up to. Now he coached Little League.

"Team shaping up, Tonto?"

"Screw you, Winch."

Brandy eyed the two of them. "Why do you taunt him so, Winch? He's your one loyal friend." She set a glass of beer in front of Woody and moved a couple of steps away, then added, "Besides me, that is."

Was that all he had in the world after thirty-five years of life? Two friends, which he regularly insulted, and a derelict boat? He used to think Tracy was his friend, but a real friend wouldn't try to use him the way Tracy had. How many times had Woody told him that his ex-wife was not his friend? That she was not in love with him. Yet still he persisted. He knew the spark, no, the fire was still there.

"Anything new on the Lisa Chambers case?" Woody said.

A man and a woman in their mid-twenties sat at a table. Brandy walked over to them and he could see the man's eyes travel her length, admiring the goods. His date noticed and she looked at Winch and rolled her eyes.

"Did you see her at the mall again today?" Winch said.

Woody shook his head.

"She was with somebody last night. I took her underwear to the lab in Jacksonville. The DNA results will be back on Friday."

"And the Sarah Fox case?" Woody said.

"You tell me. What did Valene say?"

Brandy leaned in to listen. "She's young," Woody said. "I hate to see someone that young working the streets."

"And . . ." Winch said.

"She remembers the guy, for sure. How many one-legged men does a hooker see? Strange thing was, she knew the guy. Use to trick with him in Atlanta. Doesn't know his real name but she's certain she'd popped him a few times up there. She had a falling out with her pimp and he ended up dead. She moved south. Now this guy shows up again. Says he looked her up. He drove a Lexus. Ex-military type. Lost his leg in Afghanistan."

"Description?"

"One leg and a short . . . well, you know."

"Oh, that's a big help."

Brandy grinned. "You guys all have complexes about your parts. I wish plastic surgeons would come up with silicone implants. Then you could get on with the rest of your life and stop worrying about size. You know what I mean?"

"I don't need an implant," Woody said.

"Transplant for you," she said. "Get your brain out of your pants and into your skull."

If he could just run Georgia tags. Maybe it'd help if he talked the case out. He might see something from a different perspective. "I got the entire murder book from the Sheriff. They also had some of Sarah's clothes and a journal she kept for the trip. Seems she met some guy on the beach the night before she disappeared. She was supposed to meet this mysterious lover the next night."

Woody took small sips of his beer.

Three women entered the bar and all of the men's heads swiveled. He could see their minds evaluating. Brandy moved from behind the bar and took their orders. A few more customers and she'd stop taking table orders. She'd told him before that the tips were better when she worked the floor. Behind the bar she flowed like a dancer in a well choreographed ballet, from the cooler to the sink to the tap, bumping closed the refrigerator door with a hip and reaching for two wine glasses from the overhead rack at the same time.

Winch leaned closer to Woody, "I found a pair of her underwear in her bag."

Woody raised his glass and with a grin said, "To the underwear king."

"This is serious, Woody."

"I take women's underwear very seriously when I get to them. Whose underwear are we talking about?"

"Sarah Fox's. They were stained, and I ran them up to the lab for DNA. The Sheriff's office never tested them."

"The DNA will still be there after twenty years?"

"I just have to find the donor match, and I may find her killer."

Woody sputtered beer and choked.

"So what's up with you?" Winch said.

"I've got the big plans." Woody wiped his mouth. "I'm going to keep those developers from flooding our heritage."

"What you're going to do is get run over by a bulldozer."

"I'm going to kick those guy's butts."

"Dozers are big bucks, Woody. That'll be a felony. Is this worth it?"

"I can't let them strip thirty thousand acres of trees and flood out a half-dozen Timucuan mounds that have been there for a thousand years. Those are my relatives."

"Not really." Winch took a drink of Diet Coke. "You Seminoles are descended from the Creeks, not the Timucuan."

"We moved in when the Timucuans were still here. We intermarried. I have Timucuan blood in me. My great grandfather, Running Black Bear, told me so."

"It's private land, they can do what they want. Unless they find human remains."

"You think they're going to stop the big Cats for a few bones. If you think they care, then you can wait for the Easter Bunny to turn chocolate." He held up a small white garbage bag.

"Yeah," Brandy said.

"We take these bags. Push a couple down the fuel fills on the Cats. They float. But when the engines start the fuel pump will suck them down to the strainer, block the fuel flow. The engine dies. In a minute they float off and the engine cranks again. And then dies."

"Some of you will be arrested, for sure."

Woody made a frown. "That's why I called you." He reached into his hip pocket and pulled out a cashier's check. "You'll need to bail me out. I know you don't have a nickel. Here's five large."

Winch reached for the check unfolded it. Made out to him for five thousand dollars. "The guard business pays better than I thought."

"You've seen my truck. I keep my expenses low."

"You may spend a few days in jail."

"It's for my brothers, man. What else can I do? They're counting on me."

"Your dead brothers." He folded the check and put it in his shirt pocket.

"You Mormons," Woody said, "Don't you bless the grave site when you bury somebody? Something like that?"

"Consecrate, Woody. We consecrate the grave. Ask for it to be protected from scavengers and wild animals, that sort of thing."

"And land developers?" Woody said

"I guess we'll have to add that one."

"Our ancestors' grave sites are holy too. We may say different words than you, but it's the same thing."

"Surely the Department of Natural Resources sampled the mounds before the developers received their permits."

"This is Florida. Developers are king."

"I can't be with you—"

"Don't need you to be, Winch."

"I have to be someplace else, but I'll back your play. If they put you in a cell I'll have you out the next morning."

"You know what really takes my scalp?"

Winch knew. It bothered him too. "The name?"

"The worst case of double-speak I've ever heard. They're calling it the Timucuan Preservation. As if there's going to be anything Timucuan left. The tips of some of those mounds will be above the water level of the manmade lake. White men will be hitting seven irons on the graves of my ancestors. You know what would happen to me if I bulldozed down a white man's cemetery?"

He wouldn't put it past Woody to steal a big bladed machine and do just that. He supposed the bail would not be more than five grand. Winch looked at Brandy, and in a second she stepped over. Leaned across the bar toward him. He smelled the sweet scent she liked to wear. Her forehead had a faint sheen of sweat.

Winch's cell phone rang. Carla. "Hang on," he said to her. He turned to Woody as he left. "They got it wrong you know. They should have named it not the Timucuan Preservation, but the Timucuan Desecration."

* * * *

When the time on Winch's laptop read midnight he saved the files he'd been reading about the Timucuan Indians and powered down. Saving the Timucuan land was Woody's quest, and he should have learned more about it before. Been more supportive of his friend.

He stepped outside and walked the boat's deck, checking each dock line. Satisfied, he prepared for bed. Stripped down, used the head, brushed his teeth, left one light on because Carla said she might want to come over. When the boat rocked at 1:45, he woke and listened. The sliding glass door to the aft deck squeaked on its rollers. "Carla?"

"Did I wake you?" Her voice husky.

"I'm glad you're here." He pulled back the covers putting his feet on the floor when the light he'd left on in the main cabin went out.

"Don't get up," she said. Her silhouetted figure appeared next to his bed. "Can I crash here tonight? I didn't want be alone in the hotel." And with that she unbuttoned her silk blouse, slipped off her shorts, shoved him back on the bed, and pushed him until she had room.

"Carla, I really don't think we –"

She put the fingers of one hand over his lips. "Shush. I really am tired. I thought maybe we could . . . you know . . . just sleep. Okay?"

When she took her fingers off his lips the scent of hand lotion lingered. "Sure," he said. "That would be fine." Very fine, for sure.

She turned her back to him, and he spooned against her. Inhaling her scent. Some cigarette smoke caught in her hair, and a hint of something alcoholic on her breath.

The best part of being married, the part he missed the most, maybe the part that kept him going back was something like this. Her warm flesh against his. His arm over hers. The boat-calluses on his palms, hard as barnacles, lingering over her goose-down skin. His knee, nestled into the curve of her leg. This intimacy, better than anything.

As his hand played over the rounded softness of her shoulder, she said, “Hey, watch it buster.” After a few minutes he wondered if she were asleep. Their two bodies generated more heat than was comfortable, and he rolled onto his back.

She trailed the fingers of one hand down his chest. “No guts, no glory, Winchester.”

TWENTY-ONE

DAY THREE

Winch was thumbing through the murder book when Brandy brought her cheery smile into the office. She was wearing blue jeans, sandals, and a T-shirt that read *Conch House Ba*r on the front, and the back, *I'll Fry Your Fritters.* She bent over, picked a paperclip off the floor. Skin peeked through a hole the size of a half-dollar, just below the left rear pocket on her jeans.

"What do you know about cattle brands?" he said.

"Cowboys heat branding irons over campfires and torture the poor animals. Ought to be a law. You know what I mean?"

He turned the murder book around so she could see the handwritten note by Sharp. "See, two bar four. I'm thinking it might be a brand."

"Maybe he was building a shed or something and wrote himself a note to buy some two-by-fours."

He flipped three pages. "Here it is again." He flipped a couple of more pages. "Looks like a doodle but it's written in here five times. Two bar four."

"Looks like two dash four."

"Could be." Winch ran his hand over his face. He'd just shaved an hour ago but it already felt rough. His razor needed a new blade. "My grandfather in Arizona ran cattle. His brand was this." He wrote on a sheet of paper the figure A1"

"What's that, A1 sauce with an underline?"

"That was his brand, it's pronounced A. One. Bar. The bar makes it hard for cattle rustlers to forge the brand."

"Do you really think cattle have something to do with Sarah's disappearance?"

"Florida's the second largest cattle producer in the country."

"I don't eat red meat. It sticks to your intestines and rots."

"Thanks for that image. Do you know who owns the largest cattle ranch in the state?"

"Cow toots create the methane that promotes global warming."

"I'll have to remember not to light a match next time I'm around a cattle pen."

Brandy gave him a smile, then surprised him when she said, "The Mormon Church owns the largest cattle ranch in Florida."

"How did you—?"

"How quickly you men forget. MBA. Big business." She rapped her own head with her knuckles. "Yoo-hoo. Not all of us chicks have cow paddies for brains. You know what I mean?"

He'd give her that one. She was pretty bright. At least he thought so until she said, "You think the Mormon Church's cows tooted Sarah to death?"

He raised his eyes toward the ceiling. "That's not their brand. I want you to research cattle brands and see if you can find a two bar four brand anywhere."

"Maybe I should poke around their ranch. Look for cows with singed tails. You think?"

"There's a computer and a phone. Poke around there."

Brandy busied herself on one of the computers and Winch began his search for Sarah's three traveling companions. If he had been a paperback novel PI he would have called some computer wizard friend who'd have mysteriously hacked into the Social Security database and come up with their current whereabouts, their jobs, bank accounts, and credit card numbers. Paperback private investigators do that because paperbacks are written by writers who don't know squat about how real private investigators work. No surprise there. So the writers make it up. And that's why it's called fiction.

He had names and dates of birth. Not their Socials. Using the SSN is certainly the fastest way to get a fix on a skip. But *not* by using data from the Social Security office. In the late 1980's a half-dozen private investigators did some federal time for bribing a social security staffer and reselling the data.

"Come here," Winch said. "Let me show you how we find people."

She rolled her chair next to his.

"This is the way it works. We have access to what we call the Pizza databases." He showed her how to log in. "They have better info than the Social Security office. Consider this, many people have unlisted phone numbers and no government agency might have it. Or a cell number. But who do you give phone numbers to without a thought? Dominos, Pizza Hut, and Papa John's."

She looked at him with amazement. "They're selling phone numbers? And I thought they only sold stuffed pizza crusts and breadsticks."

"This is the information age, my dear. It's a product. Another revenue stream for the pizza companies." He pointed to the interviews of the three boys. Kevin Lawrence, Tony Hudson, and Trey Ellis. "See, we have their names and dates of birth but not their socials. We need their socials because that is the only unique identifier in the United States. Criminal justice databases run off of name and date of birth. Almost everything else in the US keys off of socials."

Brandy edged a little closer. He smelled soap and shampoo. Apricot maybe. Nice.

"Soooo, let's see," Brandy said. "We need the complete social and their current addresses and hopefully phone numbers. What do we do?

"The 'pizza databases' take names, addresses, and phone numbers, and combine them with what we call 'credit header' information. That's information from the credit bureaus, but it's not technically credit information. It's the top part of a credit report that contains the name, address, date of birth, and social security number.

"You really do know what you're doing, don't' you?"

"When it comes to locating people, yeah. But I'm pretty much in the dark in most other fields."

"Like with women?"

"Especially there."

He shoved her chair, sending her rolling toward the other desk. "Work on locating those guys. I've got a call to make."

He picked up the phone and called the Sheriff's office records section. "Patti, this is Winchester Young."

"You're pushing it, Winch. What do you need this time?"

"Sheriff's office trivia."

"Winch, I'm busy." There was some background chatter.

"I need some help."

"You're just now realizing that?"

"Very funny. I need to find Detective Richard Sharp's widow." He heard an intake of breath and the background chatter muffled like she'd put her hand over the mouthpiece. He waited. Nothing. "Patti? You still there?"

"I'm always here, Winch."

"Sharp's case is still open."

He glanced at Brandy, who was making no effort to hide her eavesdropping. "They working it as hard as Sarah Fox's?"

"You have a way of irritating your friends, don't you?"

"I need this."

Patti sighed. "I doubt even *you* have a client in the Sharp murder."

"I'm not trying to solve *that* murder. You know he had the ticket on Sarah Fox. I need to find his widow. Do you remember where she went after he was killed?"

"Personnel is upstairs in the other building."

"No way personnel will give me a peek. Do you have a friend that works –"

"No, and don't ask. Sometimes even these conversations are recorded."

"There must have been some talk about what happened to her. Something. Anything."

"For your own sake, Winch, leave her alone."

He placed the phone on the cradle, picked his car keys off the desk, and headed for the door.

Brandy waved two sheets of printout at him. "Wait, look at this."

The first sheet was the printout on Kevin Lawrence. Last known address was in Kansas. Next to the address in all caps DECEASED.

The second sheet contained the bio info on Tony Hudson. Last address was St. Augustine, Florida. DECEASED. Crap, what was going on?

"What about Ellis," he said.

She shook her head. "Can't find him."

"Trey is sometimes a nickname for 'the third.'"

"Like, junior, senior, and then the third?"

"Exactly. So try searching by last name, Ellis the third, and his DOB but leave the first name empty." He reached over her shoulder and typed, *Ellis III*, and then the birth date.

After about thirty seconds, Ellsworth Van Ellis III popped up with a dozen entries. The database showed Trey's most recent address as West Palm Beach, Florida.

"Crud," Brandy said. "If I had a name like that, I'd use Trey as well."

He jingled his car keys. "Run the address for phone numbers, too. And check the Palm Beach county property appraiser's website for the current value of Mr. Ellis's home. What he paid for it and when he bought it. Check the clerk's office down there for mortgages and give me a rough idea of how much equity he has in the house. I'd like to know if he needs money or not before I talk to him."

As for Sharp, he could look for Sharp's obit and find his wife's name in the death notice. But he thought he'd probably locate the information he needed quicker at the courthouse. "I'm going to the courthouse to track down Sharp's widow." For *his* own sake, Patti said, leave her alone. What was that about?

TWENTY-TWO

A street-smart PI has numerous ways to find information. In fact, information is what a PI really sells. The information from the PI is just gathered and packaged differently than say, Google, or Bing, or the encyclopedia. It's packaged as photographs, or a tape or surveillance DVD, and is usually accompanied with a written report, and of course, the invoice.

If Winch couldn't find anything on Detective Sharp's widow at the courthouse, then he'd drive to Jacksonville and pay a visit to the main office of the Florida State's Bureau of Vital Records. Get a copy of the death certificate, which would give him the widow's name. Or go to the St. Augustine Historical Society and peruse through the microfilm of the *St. Augustine Record* for the death notice. One way or another, he'd talk to her. He had to ask her what the two dash four meant.

A summer storm cloud, black as an asphalt lot, was building from the west. Raindrops fat as grapes splattered on the concrete curb. He hustled passed the bougainvillea arbor where he and Tracy were married, stepped past the courthouse doors, passed through the metal detectors at the entrance, and walked into the St. Johns County Courthouse.

The Clerk of the Court occupied the bottom floor. The criminal section files were located behind doors which require a pass card to enter. He wondered if they were locking files in, afraid they might escape. In the probate section he ran a search in the index from 1984 to 1990. No probate file on Richard Sharp. More populous counties might have had several probates on a Richard Sharp, but in the eighties, St. Johns County was sparsely populated. If developments like the Timucuan Preservation continued, soon the county would double its 1980 size.

Smaller estates in Florida are not probated, and Sharp, a deputy Sheriff, probably didn't have a substantial one.

Since probate washed out, his next move was to Official Records. Probably a good chance that Sharp and his wife owned a house. The deed and mortgage would have been recorded when they bought the house, and also when the lonely widow sold it.

Bingo. July, 1985. About a year before Sharp was murdered in Molasses Junction Lot 16 in Lake Travis Estate was purchased by Richard H. and Meredith M. Sharp, who paid $92,000. It was a single family house with title as Joint Tenants with right of survivorship. Now he refined his search just to Meredith M. Sharp. There she was again. In 1991, Meredith sold the home.

The nice thing about Official Records in many counties in Florida is that a single search in a county by the right name will net everything recorded in that county on the person. Deeds, mortgages, foreclosures, judgments, tax liens, and marriage licenses. His eye glanced further down the page then abruptly stopped. He couldn't believe what he saw. A marriage license issued to Meredith M. Sharp and Vincent Renfro on August 26, 1988. Sheesh! Just two years after Sharp was murdered.

He had to think this through. So Sharp was killed in 1986. His widow remarried in 1988, which probably means that Renfro moved into the dead man's home with the dead man's widow. Huh.

No wonder Patti had told him to leave her alone. And Renfro himself had warned him about investigating the detective's murder. How close *were* Renfro and Meredith before her husband was killed? When did the romance begin? Here was a definite motive for Sharp's murder. Winch sat there stunned.

He still needed to talk to the widow, the new Mrs. Renfro. For that he'd need Renfro's address. The detective would certainly have an unlisted phone number if he had a landline at all. Maybe just a cell phone. If he had a landline Winch was pretty good at breaking non-pub numbers. It always amazed people when he'd call them on their non-pub line. They'd yell, threaten to sue the phone company for giving out their number, and on and on. What most people don't realize is that a private investigator doesn't break a non-pub by getting it from the phone company. People will go to great lengths to keep their phone number secret, yet they willingly give it to the electric company, water company, cable company, etc.

Renfro certainly had a driver's license and his address would be with DMV. In Florida, driver's license information is considered confidential, but there is an exemption for licensed private investigators. However, because of Renfro's status as a law enforcement officer, his information might be protected from disclosure. But property records are public.

A quick search popped Renfro's mortgage, deed, and legal description of the property. The appraiser's records gave him the street address. Everything he needed except for a "get out of jail free card."

He had to orchestrate the interview of Mrs. Renfro, to make the contact with her when her detective husband wasn't home. Certainly she'd tell him later about the visit, but the last place he wanted to be was at Renfro's house when the detective drove up.

As he walked toward his car, he thought, surely whoever was investigating Sharp's murder would have looked at Renfro and checked his alibi. Right? Unless, of course, the case had been assigned to Renfro.

Well, he needed to stay focused on Sarah Fox's case. Sharp's murder wasn't supposed to be his problem. But Renfro's fingerprints were all over both of them.

TWENTY-THREE

A summer-fueled southwest wind blew briskly through the afternoon. Boats in the harbor lay taut on their anchor rodes, bows steady into the wind. Wavelets rushed past the hulls, pushed by the conjunction of tide and wind. Winch thought of it as a friendly wind because a southwest breeze made for an easy crossing of the Gulf Stream to the Bahamas. But he wasn't on his dreamboat, the Island Packet 48. Instead, he sat in his office, planning strategy with Brandy and Woody.

"I don't want Renfro showing up and surprising me," Winch said.

"The best way to prevent that, Bro, is to not go to Renfro's at all." Woody shook his head. "Forget her. What's she going to remember?"

"You've had two run-ins already, Winch." Brandy rolled a red Sharpie between her fingers. "If he catches you around his wife he'll toss your butt in the slammer quicker than he can say ten-four. And he'll probably jack you up a bit too. You know what I mean?"

Woody was nodding. "Why even bother? Stay away from that dude. Stay away from his wife. Hell, keep a snake's length away from him or you'll get bit."

"Don't you think it strange that Sharp, the lead detective on the Sarah Fox case, was murdered, and then the case is reassigned to the guy who later marries his widow?"

"You think Renfro murdered Sharp to get the Fox case assigned to him? That's dumber than dumb. Knock some dude off so the boss can add his work load to yours."

"I'm not saying Renfro murdered Sharp." Winch stroked his chin. "But there's a connection between Sharp's death and the case. Maybe she knows what it is. Men talk to their wives, right?"

Brandy and Woody looked at each other and shook their heads.

"Like she's really going to tell you," Brandy said. "A total stranger who knocks on her door."

"You got his address?" Woody said.

"It's just across the Bridge of Lions. Not far from the marina. Not a gated community." Earlier he'd stopped and soaked in the neighborhood. It was about where Oglethorpe had set camp during his siege of Saint Augustine in 1740. Across the bay and out of range of the fort's cannon. But where his own cannon could guard the harbor and prevent re-supply of the fort. After a month of trying to starve the Spanish out, his soldiers began calling it the "Mosquito War."

"Brandy, you'll be posted just off A1A where Renfro will have to pass you on his way in. Have me on speed-dial. If Renfro drives by let me know." He faced Woody. "You'll park up the street from their house." He handed Woody a video camera bag. "Renfro shows up while I'm still there, you shoot video. I want to document everything. Don't let anyone take that video away from you. That's my only protection."

"I don't like this, Winch," Brandy said. "Let's track down the one boy still alive and talk to him."

Winch shook his head. "She's here and he's not. "

"What color?" Woody said.

Winch rolled his eyes. Brandy squinted at Woody, a furrow on her forehead.

"Flowers at your funeral," Woody said. "Need to be prepared for every eventuality."

* * * *

Winch sensed movement behind the door. The front porch was wide, planked with yellow painted two by sixes. Two wooden armchairs with cushions sat on one end of the porch. A small white wrought-iron table between them. A beanbag ashtray sat on the table, full of cigarette butts, lipstick on the filter ends. He knocked.

A female voice, "What do you want?"

"Mrs. Renfro. I'd like to talk to you about your former husband, Richard Sharp."

"Dick? He's dead."

"I'm an investigator, Mrs. Renfro."

"Just a minute."

He waited. The door opened and Meredith Renfro stepped onto the porch. Even though it was nearly ninety degrees she wore a long sleeved cotton shirt, buttoned top to bottom. She rolled down the sleeves as she stepped across the threshold but he caught a glimpse of bruising on her wrists and forearms as she buttoned the cuffs. She looked older than Winch by at least five years with broom-straw hair and half-moon wrinkles, like sets of parentheses spread at corners of her mouth. She had a lit cigarette in her hand and put it to her mouth.

"Vinnie didn't say anything to me about this."

"I'm a private investigator, Mrs. Renfro–"

"Meredith."

"I'm investigating an old case Richard worked before–"

"Before some son-of-a-bitch shot him? But Vinnie–"

"Vincent doesn't know I'm here."

"He's got the neighbors spying." She looked down the street. "He doesn't like strangers coming around."

"Yes, ma'am, I'll be quick. I just have a couple of questions."

She inhaled the cigarette and then blew a long puff of gray smoke out of the corner of her mouth. "Make'em short. It's your life if he finds you here."

"Did Richard—"

"Dick."

"Did Dick ever talk to you about the Sarah Fox case? The seventeen-year-old–"

"Sure. But, that was so long ago. Too many cigarettes and too much Tequila. Not likely I'll remember much about *that* case."

Winch pulled a sheet of paper out of his hip pocket. Showed her a page from the murder book. "You see this notation at the bottom. The two dash four. Is that your husband's hand-writing?" He turned it so she could see.

"That looks like Dick's. I'd have to say it probably was."

"Do you have any idea what that meant?" He followed her eyes as they roamed up and down the road. A curtain moved in the blue house across the street.

"You see that?" she said. "We're busted."

"I'm sorry if our conversation causes you any trouble." He pointed again to the 2 dash 4 on the paper. "But this—"

"Of course." She inhaled on the cigarette and scowled at him. "What sort of detective are you? It means a two-fer. Dick always said, when he solved that case he was going to get a two-fer. You know, two for one."

He didn't want to appear stupid but he didn't understand. "A two for one what?"

She flicked the ash off her cigarette. "People really pay you?" She glanced down the street. "Solve two cases. Two murders, one investigation."

"Dick was working two homicides?"

She gave him a disgusted look. "You charge how much an hour?"

It was bad enough to be insulted by Renfro, now his wife too? "What was the other one?"

"The other what," she said.

"The other half of the two-fer? The other homicide?"

"I have no idea." She shook her head. "I don't think it was a real homicide. I mean it was, but not officially, you understand?"

He didn't understand. What was this woman telling him? "I'm confused," he said.

She gave him a look like she wasn't surprised. "He was pretty secretive about all that." She waved her hand. "This is St. Johns County, you know. We don't have many homicides and back then almost none. I mean, you think about it, even the Sarah Fox case was classified as a runaway. Not a homicide."

"So this was somebody he thought had been murdered but the murder hadn't been reported?"

She nodded vigorously, smoke pouring from her nostrils. "Yeah, now you're catching on. It's an FBI thing."

She'd done it again. What was she talking about? She must have seen a quizzical look on his face.

"The FBI, they keep statistics. It's all a game. The Sheriff lists Sarah Fox as a disappearance and Miami keeps its title as murder capital of Florida. Saint Augustine isn't even in the running."

His cell phone rang. Brandy. "Excuse me." He half turned away.

Brandy said, "He just came past. Driving ninety at least. I didn't think he was going to make the corner."

"Call Woody." He closed the phone. Crap. Exactly what he didn't want. He folded the paper and stuffed it back in his pocket. He faced Meredith. "So this two-fer? Any way to figure out who the other half might be?"

"Hey, you're the detective." She thumped his chest with the two fingers holding the cigarette. Ash fell onto his shirt. "Sorry," she said as she brushed it with her other hand. I just marry the jerks. I can't read their minds."

"Meredith, I think your husband will be here any second."

"That lazy lady across the street who's got nothing better to do than peep at me. Now we're both in for it."

That's what he thought too but he didn't say it. Had to remain calm. Cool. Not let this escalate. He handed her his card and she looked around and then slid it into the pocket of her jeans. "If you remember anything else Dick might have said about the investigation, please call me."

"Vinnie wouldn't like it."

"I know that Vincent can be," he hesitated, didn't know whether to even broach this subject. "A bit aggressive. If you ever need help," he nodded toward her long sleeves, "I'd be glad to do whatever. You know, if you're in a bad situation or something, I know people who can . . . places you can go."

She stared off toward the sky for a moment. "That's none of your business and I don't know what you're talking about."

"Yes, ma'am." He knew he only had a few more seconds. "Do you think Dick's death had anything to do with the Sarah Fox case?"

She laughed a throaty laugh and then coughed. "Hell no. If it wasn't some freak on drugs then it was probably some jealous husband getting even."

Renfro's undercover car screeched to a halt.

"Now you've gone and done it," Meredith said, turning her back and slamming the door as she went through.

Renfro was out of the car, an extendable black steel baton capable of breaking bones, in one hand. “Get down on your knees, Young. Hands behind your head.”

He did as he was told. Renfro walked up the sidewalk. He slapped the baton against his leg like a rolled Newsweek ready for the dog’s butt. Winch’s cell phone rang. He pulled it out. The Casa Monica Hotel.

“Don’t,” Renfro yelled. He pointed the baton at Winch. “Set it on the ground. Hands up.”

“Winchester Young?” the voice came from the cell phone.

Winch pushed a button setting the phone on to speaker. “Yes,” he turned his mouth toward the phone as he laid it on the ground.

“Carla Fox asked us to contact you with messages if she wasn’t in her room.”

“Yes,” he said, Renfro closing.

“There’s a message here from someone named Charon.”

“I’ll have to get it later. I think I’m about to get arrested.”

“Who’s that?” Renfro said, standing over him.

He looked up at Renfro.

“Mr. Young?” There was a pause. “Would you like us to call an attorney for you?”

“No,” Renfro said and stomped his heel onto the phone.

TWENTY-FOUR

Winch knelt on the concrete stoop of Renfro's house wondering how he was going to get out of this. Sand on the stoop ground into his knees. His face and armpits sweated. In a house across the street a face peered out from behind a curtain.

Renfro waved the short handled baton the size of a single nunjuck. An asp, a replacement for the old wooden batons. He flicked his wrist and the steel asp baton telescoped out like a striking snake. His pistol holstered on his hip, he circled around Winch, slapping the asp against his thigh like a Gestapo Captain.

"Why?" Renfro said. "What right do you have coming to my house?"

"I suppose it's just a coincidence that the lead detective on Sarah's case is murdered, you take over the case, and marry Sharp's widow?" Winch said.

Slap. The asp whacked his collarbone. Winch's left arm went numb and his collarbone lit on fire. Renfro paced.

From down the street Woody, video camera in hand yelled, "Hey, you can't do that man."

"Oh yeah, Copeland? Watch me." Renfro turned whacked his right rib cage. "You think I can't take that camera away from your red-necked Indian?"

At that moment a Sheriff's cruiser, blue lights flashing, pulled to the curb. A green uniformed deputy, as thick as the stump of a hundred-year-old water oak, barreled out of the cruiser and stepped onto the curb. "Vinnie, what's up my man?"

Renfro pointed to Woody. “I don’t think we want this on video.”

Brandy pulled her car to the curb, and stepped out. The deputy eyed her as she stepped out. Pointed to her. “You stay right there, ma’am.”

The deputy walked toward Woody, hand out. His bulk thickened by the bulletproof vest under his uniform. “Come on, fella. Give it up.”

“I’m on a public street, man,” Woody said. “I’m not breaking any law.”

“Give me the camera. That’s an order.”

Woody backed a couple of feet.

“Hey,” Brandy said. “Don’t you hurt him.” She stood just the other side of the cruiser, her cell phone pointed toward them. “I’m getting all this on video.” Winch knew she didn’t have a video camera in her cell phone. But they didn’t.

“Let’s talk about this, Renfro,” Winch said. “You don’t need this. We both want the same thing.”

“No we don’t,” Renfro said. He pointed the end of the asp at him but he didn’t strike.

The front door to Renfro’s home opened silently. Renfro, his back to the door, didn’t see Meredith standing on the threshold, hands on her hips.

“Did you kill Dick Sharp?” Winch said. “Kill him to get Meredith?”

Meredith’s hand went to her mouth and she cocked her head.

“You’re crazy. I love Meredith. I might kill for her, but I didn’t kill Dick Sharp.”

Then Meredith smiled a genuine bright smile.

Renfro spoke still unaware his wife stood behind him. “She is the best thing that ever happened to me. I watch out for her.”

Winch began to stand. Renfro turned toward him, cuffed the heel of his hand on his sore collarbone. The pain forced him to his knees. “Darn it, Renfro.”

“Stay there.”

Winch looked around. The tableau frozen. The patrol deputy eyed the play on the porch. Brandy, swung her cell phone first at him and then to Woody. Meredith stood stock still in the doorway.

“A bimbo bartender,” Renfro said, “a boat bum, and a Seminole Indian that needs a haircut.” He circled the air with his index finger. “Quite the little P.I. agency you’ve got there, Young.”

“I’m going to stand up now,” Winch said and lifted to a crouch.

Renfro raised the asp baton.

“Leave him be,” Meredith said.

Whack, the baton struck his shin.

“Stop that.” Winch rubbed his shin, grabbed the short railing and pulled himself to his feet.

Meredith reached forward, put her hand on Renfro’s shoulder. “Calm down, Vinnie.”

Renfro stepped toward Winch, his hand on his holstered gun. “I told you to stay down.”

“I’m doing you a favor. Beating the crap out of me is a federal crime.”

“What I’m doing is stopping someone from harassing my wife.”

“Violation of my civil rights under color of law,” Winch said.

“You an attorney now?”

“Ten years in a federal pen for what we have on that tape.”

“You’re under arrest for trespassing.” Renfro reached behind his back and came out with a pair of handcuffs.

“You can’t—”

“Ferguson,” Renfro shouted at the deputy still in the street. “Help me hook this guy up.”

Ferguson took a few steps toward the porch where they stood. “He been warned yet, Vinnie?”

Winch knew in Florida they’d have to write him a citation, warning him of trespassing before he could be arrested.

“You with him or me?” Renfro said.

Ferguson pulled on his chin. “I don’t like what I see, Vinnie.”

“Then hightail it, and you won’t be a witness.”

Ferguson stepped back to his patrol car, leaned against it, but didn’t make any move to leave.

“Mrs. Renfro? Did you ever consider that Vinnie killed your husband?”

“Shut the hell up.” Renfro waved his baton but didn’t strike. “Tell him, Mere. Tell him the truth.”

“Vinnie and I,” she said. “We never even met each other until after Dick was killed.” Meredith ran both hands through her short hair, pulling her scalp back. “I wasn’t good enough for Dick. I didn’t clean well enough. I burned his dinner. Any excuse for him to get mad and storm out. Dick came home late after our fights. I smelled perfume on him. Made me feel more worthless than a head of cabbage. And everything was all my fault.” She threw Renfro a glance. “I’m glad Dick’s dead and I hope whoever shot him gets away with it. He died better than he deserved. Gunshot was too quick for him.”

Renfro pointed his finger at Winch. “Now you stay away from me and my family.”

Winch knew abused women often transitioned from one abusive relationship to another. He wanted to rescue her but there was nothing he could do. “You beat your wife, Renfro, behind closed doors—”

“None of your business what we do in our house, Young.”

“That’s still a crime. Every bruise you,” he nodded toward Meredith in the open doorway, “you put on your wife there. It’s called battery. You either get help or I’ll find a way to nail you.”

“You care what I do, why?”

“You need to leave, Mr. Young.” Meredith said. “I think you boys have said enough.”

“He’s not going until I get that tape.” Renfro turned toward Woody. “Copeland, bring me that camera.”

Woody gave Winch a ‘what-do-you-want-me-to-do’ look?’

“Mrs. Renfro—”

“Meredith,” she said.

“Meredith, would you like me to photograph your arms. Have some documentation for when you file a complaint.”

“My arms are fine, Mr. Young.” Her glance went from him to Renfro.

He wondered why she stayed with him. Married a little more than 20 years. Certainly the beatings, the philandering had been going on for a while. Still she protected him. She must be terrified of him. Afraid if she left, he’d do something even worse to her than the bruises he’d seen. Or maybe she’s afraid no one would have her. His heart went out to her. He wanted to do something. Pull her out of her quagmire, but he knew if he tried, she’d resist and resent him. He felt impotent. He had no control, no influence.

“If you need. . . .” he said.

She patted the right front pocket of her pants, where she'd slid his card. They locked eyes and she nodded. "If I need to," she said. "Vinnie sometimes just doesn't know his own strength. Isn't that right sweetheart?"

Meredith studied him. "I did remember one thing," she said, "that might be of some help in your investigation."

"Oh?"

"I don't know." She waved her hand. "It's probably nothing."

"What?" Both he and Renfro said at the same time and looked at each other.

"You understand the term," she looked at Winch, "quid pro quo?" Then she nodded toward Woody and the video camera.

"Okay," he said. "Bring it up, Woody."

Woody removed the memory card from the camera, and handed it to Winch, ignoring Renfro's outstretched hand.

Meredith put her hand out.

Winch gave the card to Meredith, his arm heavy and numb from Renfro's blows. "Quid pro," he said.

"Quo," she said. "Dick was looking at using cadaver dogs."

"So he knew where to look?" he said.

"I heard him talking to one trainer about old corpses and recent corpses. He wanted to know, could the dog tell the difference. He didn't want to dig up acres of dirt."

"But where?" Winch said.

"You never told me that, Meredith," Renfro said.

"I don't know where." She laid a hand on Renfro's shoulder. "Come on in, Vinnie. And bring your deputy friend. Looks like he could use a cold soda." She turned to Winch. "You and your folks, run on along now."

Renfro put his arm around her waist and they went in.

Brandy put her arm around him and although he didn't need the help, her body against his felt comforting. As they walked toward his car he said, "Brandy. Do me a favor. Call Enterprise car rental and have them deliver a car to me at the marina. Say four pm. I don't want to drive the Jeep all the way to West Palm."

"You're going to interview Trey Ellis?" she asked.

He nodded but his mind had returned to the scene on Renfro's front porch. How did Renfro know Woody. He'd called Woody by name. And that day at the mall Woody also knew Renfro. Had said he was a major hound. How had he known that?

TWENTY-FIVE

Winch, heavy on the pedal, maneuvered his Jeep through the tourist traffic, across the Bridge of Lions toward downtown St. Augustine. Brandy had to open the Conch House Bar early and Woody had preparations for his Timucuan protest, so he was alone. But before they'd left he'd picked up the pieces of his cell phone from Renfro's front stoop. Not that he cared about the phone, but he didn't want Renfro to have access to the Sim card. No reason to let Renfro see his text messages or whom he'd been calling. None of which was any of Renfro's business.

The guts of his broken phone lay in his passenger seat. He'd used Brandy's phone to call the Casa Monica. Charon's message, short and pointed: Wire a good faith offer of $10,000 to a Barclay's Bank account in the Bahamas. Charon had left *his* good faith offer in an envelope taped beneath the mail drop box on the corner of Woods and Riberia Streets.

As he passed the post office he gave a thought to stopping to see if any new rejections from agents had arrived, but he needed to get to the drop before someone else accidentally found whatever it was Charon had left. He didn't thunder down Riberia like he wanted to. Instead he approached from an oblique angle. He knew the corner with the mailbox. The northeast corner of a one-block park. Boat docks and the Satilla River on the west side. On the east, hundred-year old shotgun houses that a few years ago went for twenty grand now sold for $300,000.

He stopped a block away and waited in the shade cast by a magnolia tree wide as a house. A trim white lady, mid thirties, hair the color of shelled pecans, in shorts, sandals and a halter-top, walked a golden retriever. As she passed the mailbox the dog sniffed the concrete slab, raised his leg and peed. She looked around, unleashed the dog and threw a yellow tennis ball for it to fetch. He didn't know who Charon was so he pulled out his Canon digital camera. Bayoneted on the 300 millimeter zoom and clicked off half a dozen photos of the girl. And for fun, a couple of the dog leaping for the ball.

He waited, noting passing cars. Looking for anybody that might have the mailbox staked out. He raised his pant leg and examined his shin. No blood, but a nasty welt like a whip mark. The skin raised into a bump the color and texture of a Plant City strawberry.

In a few minutes the retriever did his business and he and his mistress walked down the block out of sight.

He waited thirty minutes then walked to the mailbox. Dropped to his hands and knees. The odor of dog urine filled his nose. Taped to the bottom was a ten by fourteen inch envelope. He stood and opened it. Should have thought to wear gloves. He pulled his shirt tail out from his pants, used it to grasp the edge of a photograph and slid an 8 by 10 glossy half-way out. It was a photo of Sarah. Wearing the same ball cap she'd had on the day she left Athens. But in this photo she held a shovel. Stood in some outdoor location surrounded by palmetto thickets and slash pines.

The photo looked like a Polaroid that had been scanned and printed on a color laser printer. Not worth $10,000 but they needed to keep Charon in the game. He'd call Carla and suggest she wire the $10,000 in good faith. Charon would call again looking for more.

He sat in his car and studied the photo. No rocks on the ground around Sarah. What he did see were sand spurs and dollar weeds. Looked like North Florida territory to him. Behind her was a slight rise, a hummock perhaps. Clumps of razor-edged sawgrass and a creek with water and mudflats off to one side. Since the sawgrass blades were green, the photo was taken in the spring or summer, definitely not in the winter when they would have been the color of dried caramel.

So he had a new photo of Sarah, but was no closer to figuring out who Charon was or where Sarah was buried. Not much to show for the aches in his shin and collarbone. Or the $10,000 they were sending out of the country.

The hot tub at his old house, well, Tracy's house, no his house too, beckoned him. The house was still half his, the hot tub too. He'd used it before, calling first, and Tracy had always been accommodating. As he passed over the Intracoastal Waterway he wondered. Was it the hot tub beckoning him or the hope that Tracy would be there?

TWENTY-SIX

Winch turned on the gas to heat the hot tub. Green corrosion on the valve cracked around his fingertips and he made a mental note to change it out. He waited for the water to warm, wondering what kind of reception he'd receive if Tracy came home. He resisted the temptation to rifle through her personal stuff. He being in the hot tub, she'd understand. She'd let him keep a key to their house for that very purpose. She usually found an errand to run and wasn't there. He understood that message. Poking through her stuff would cross the boundary they'd set by default.

The late afternoon sun cast streaks of red and orange across the western sky. As the land cooled, the ocean across the highway kicked up a sea breeze keeping the mosquitoes grounded. The smell of salt, sea oats, and beach life blew through the screened patio. He pulled a pair of gym shorts out of his workout bag. Slipped into them and then into the caldron of bubbling water. Chlorine leached the beach smell away. The hot water stung his tender shin but it eased the pain in his ribs and shoulder.

Head back and eyes shut he rolled his neck, held his breath, and submerged into the cocoon of warmth. He could drift off to sleep and understood how people drowned in their own hot tubs. Too much alcohol and this warm womb-like comfort. Floating without cares in a safe environment. The good times he and Tracy experienced here flooded through his mind. He could almost smell her.

An iron claw clamped his hair and pushed his head down. Another hand grasped the base of his neck and shoved downward. He struggled, surprised. Not desperate for air yet his mind whirled. Had Charon followed him from the park and now wanted to take him out? He braced his feet against the bench, shoved off hard and twisted his body. He broke free of the hands that held him and in the process rammed his back against the wall of the hot-tub, scraping his skin on the roughed out non-skid concrete.

"Jeez," he sputtered, staring at Tracy whose blouse plastered wet against her skin.

"Scared ya, huh?" She pulled the fabric away from her chest. "I checked the caller ID. You didn't call."

"My cell is broken."

He stood. "I'll leave." Water bubbled against his navel.

"We're alone." She stepped out of her sandals and dropped the shorts she was wearing. "Stay."

She unbuttoned the blouse and tossed it over a chair. Like Eve in the garden, except for the gold chain around her waist. She stepped awkwardly over the edge of the tub, then the water swallowed her neck-high.

"I've been thinking," he said.

"Me too."

"About us."

Her feet touched his, the soles of her feet running over the tops of his. "You first," she said.

"I know you have strong feelings for me," he said.

"Of course. Wasn't it just yesterday that I tried to seduce you, and you huffed out of here?"

"You were trying to make babies, not seduce me."

"Same difference."

"If the roles were reversed and I tried to get into your pants, you'd want a commitment out of me. Something more than a quickie."

"Right now a quickie sounds good."

"I want a commitment." He pulled his feet away from hers.

"Your feminine side is showing, Winchester." She wiped perspiration off her forehead.

"Seriously, will you think about that?" he said. "A commitment."

"We've been married and divorced twice, Winch. And you want to go for three?"

"I know you love me. And I love you. We ought to be able to make it work."

"I'm hot." She stood and scooted on to the concrete edge of the spa, knees together.

They were both silent for a moment. Just looking at her made his heart race. He wanted her in the worst way. He wanted to wrap her in his arms, envelope her, let her being meld into his so they would be one. He wanted to marry her in the temple where marriage is not until "death do you part," but for "time and all eternity." But as soon as he thought that, he realized that was the barrier between them. Despite being married twice and having the Mormon missionary discussions multiple times, Tracy chose Starbucks over eternal marriage.

"You're right about one thing." She ran her fingers through her hair and slid back into the tub. "We do love each other. But can we live with each other? Sometimes, Winchester, I think you live in a different world than me."

"Than I."

"See. You're uptight about things that don't make any difference. What's wrong with 'me'?"

He didn't want to spark an argument. "There's nothing wrong with you," he said. "You're about perfect."

"Only about?"

"You're perfect for my world."

He didn't have words to say how he felt. But if he wanted her back, he knew he'd have to try. He reached out and took both of her hands in his. Looked into her eyes that glinted with mischievousness. "Tracy. You're wild. Unpredictable. You've got that crazy chain soldered around your middle. You're unreliable—"

Her face turned red, and he wasn't sure it was from the hot water, "I'm not—"

He put four fingers over her lips. "Let me finish and then you can talk." Her lips pouted.

"You can't balance a check book." He held one finger up. "You get too many speeding tickets." Two fingers. "You want to have a baby and stay single." Three fingers. "Don't you get it? In a conventional sense, you're a mess.

"This is a Mormon telling me I'm a mess?"

"But when we're together the times are good. It works. You are the wind, and I am the chime. And sometimes, I am the shout and you are the echo. You're my other half." He pointed skyward. "Look."

Overhead a white seabird with black tipped wings and a long kite of a tail drifted effortlessly on the freshening breeze.

"There see? That's us."

"I'm a bird?"

"Not you, us. That's a red-billed tropicbird." The bird folded his wings, which spanned longer than a yardstick, and dove, and then opened them and stroked and rose into the air. Floated, facing the easterly breeze, rising and sinking on unseen currents.

Tracy's eyes followed the bird. "He's graceful. Beautiful really."

"Tropicbirds mate for life. But see, he has two wings. That's the way we are when we're together. We're each a single wing and together we soar, and dip, and float. We may be opposites but it's a good opposite. Separate us and we're like a tropicbird with a broken wing. Grounded on the beach. But together we can fly. And raise our kids, together."

She stepped across to him and hugged him. Her arms folded around his neck. He closed his eyes, and she kissed him. "I love you, too," she said. "Maybe we *should* give it another try."

"Ahem."

Tracy turned when she heard the word. He opened his eyes.

Patti Reynolds, in her green Sheriff's uniform, stood at the threshold to the pool area holding a bottle of wine and two glasses. "I heard the bubbles." She waved the bottle in their direction. "And isn't this just too cozy for words?"

TWENTY-SEVEN

Winch sat upright in the hot tub, trying to read Patti. Wondering if she would throw the bottle of wine at him. Moot point really since Tracy was on his lap. He slid out from under Tracy and stood, steam rising off his chest and belly. "I'll go."

Patti stared at him and he couldn't read her look. "I'll get another glass," Patti said.

"Don't bother. Winch doesn't drink wine," Tracy said.

"You don't need to go, Winch." Patti stepped from the patio door threshold to the hot tub. Set the glasses and the bottle down and unbuttoned the shirt of her uniform. "I understand you found her."

Tracy's eyes sought his, a slight smirk on her face. "Found who?" she said.

"I really need to go." Winch looked for a towel.

"Winch has been out detecting." Patti let her uniform shirt hang open.

"That's what I do," he said. How had she had known? Probably the other deputy spread it around.

Patti looked at Winch. "Richard Sharp's former wife." She shrugged out of her shirt. A beige camisole covered her upper body. "Stay Winch, let's talk. You've been wanting to talk ever since you found out I was divorced."

Tracy shot him an accusing look. "You've been coming on to my friend?"

He wasn't sure how to answer that without getting in trouble. Honesty would be the best approach, he guessed. "I thought she was cute." Why was Patty doing this? What did she want?

"But what about me?" Tracy said.

"You know I think you're cute too."

Patti unzipped her skirt and tossed it onto the chair that held Tracy's shirt.

"Tell me about it," Patti said and stepped into the hot tub. Turned her back to him and filled the two glasses of wine. She handed one glass to Tracy and sipped from the other.

"About what?" he said wondering what he was doing in a hot tub with two women, knowing he could have neither of them. His Bishop certainly wouldn't understand.

Sometimes he wished he were Catholic. Sin. Go to confession and be forgiven by a priest. Repentance and forgiveness were so much more complicated in Mormonism. He thought of Christianity as a guilt-based faith. And Mormonism as much or more than any other Christian denomination. He'd always thought the Mormon Church should have as their slogan, "Guilt to the Hilt."

"I saw the article in yesterday's paper," Tracy said. "You didn't get much print."

He nodded. "Carla Fox's name sells more papers."

Water bubbled around Patti's shoulders and when she raised one arm to set her wine glass on the concrete patio he noticed dark wavy hair under her armpit.

Tracy caught his stare. "She's my nature girl."

Surprisingly, the idea of a wildly abandoned musky, unshaven, nature-earth-mother woman had a sort of attraction. "Let me guess, barley greens, flax seed oil, and protein powder shakes for breakfast?" he said.

"You've been looking in Patti's cupboards, Winch?" Tracy said.

He shook his head. But he had to wonder why she would shave her legs and not her armpits. What kind of statement did that make?

"Tell us," Patti said. She had a hint of a smile on her face. "Have you solved the Sarah Fox case?"

"You think this is a joke?" he said.

"I think it's a twenty-five-year old homicide and it's unlikely you're going to solve it this week."

"Winch is a clever boy." Tracy turned to her. "I don't think you're giving him enough credit."

"So," Patti said, "tell us what you got, Winchester."

"Renfro wasn't happy catching me talking to his wife," he said. Tracy gave him a quizzical look. "Renfro married Dick Sharp's widow."

"You think the murders are connected?" Tracy said.

"It's all over the office," Patti said. "Renfro hitting you with his asp."

"Hit you with his what?" Tracy said.

He levered his leg above the water, showed them the plum size bruise on his shin. "And here," he pointed to his collar bone, "and there," he stood, showing them the welt on his rib cage.

"An asp," Patti said, "is a kind of steel telescoping baton."

"Hurt a lot," he said.

"You idiot," Patti said. "I told you to leave her alone."

"I had to talk to her." He wished he'd lifted a cold can of Diet Coke from Tracy's fridge. "What she gave me, I think, was worth the fuss."

Patti arched her eyebrows. "Oh yeah, and what was that?"

"I have a suspect."

Patti sat upright. "Who?"

"I don't know. Well, I have a name. Not a real name, but a name he calls himself."

She motioned with her hands to come on. "And?"

"This can't get back to the Sherriff's office. Okay?" Patti agreed. "Charon," he said. Waiting for a reaction.

"Renfro's wife gave you that name?" Patti said.

"No, but she did tell me Sharp was looking for cadaver dogs."

"He must have thought he was close," Tracy said, "if he was lining up dogs."

"Or wishful thinking." Patti took a sip of wine. "You got the murder book, Winch. Anything in there about dogs and where Sharp thought she might be buried?"

He shook his head.

"She tell you that before or after he whomped on you?" Patti reached for the bottle of wine, refilled the two glasses. "You know he beats her, don't you?" Patti said matter-of-factly.

“I saw her wrists,” he said. “She tried to hide them under a long sleeve shirt but I saw them. Her forearms looked like bruised bananas.”

“Why does the Sheriff put up with that?” Tracy said.

Patti shook her head. “Somebody ought to K-five him. Put both of them out their misery.”

“K-five?” Tracy said.

“Targets on the firing range,” Patti said, “are in the silhouette of men. K is kill zone. The head, center of the chest, they’re K-fives. The hands and wrists are K-twos.”

“Is that what happened to her first husband?” Winch said.

Patti leaned back, arms on the sides of the hot tub and closed her eyes. “I wouldn’t know anything about that.”

He did some calculations. “You were there. Working for the Sheriff.”

“Part time, after high school. Dispatch. I never met Sharp’s wife until long after she married Renfro.”

“She said something else to me. When she said it I thought she was joking. Now I’m not so sure.”

“Well, come on,” Tracy said.

“She said that she was sure that her husband’s death was not connected to the Sarah Fox case.”

Patti pointed a finger at him. “See.”

“That’s not it. She also said that if the murder of her husband at Molasses Junction wasn’t some random shooting, more likely than not he was shot by a jealous husband. Apparently he got around.”

He knew there were pieces of the puzzle in there somewhere but regardless of how he turned them in his mind they wouldn’t fit together. Some larger piece had to be missing.

TWENTY-EIGHT

Tracy scooted across the hot tub and pressed herself against him. She gave Winch an appraising look. Slurps of water splashed onto the concrete. Her thigh and hip slick against his. "You poor boy. All beat up. Such a rough day."

He didn't consider that he'd really been beat up but he'd take the sympathy where he could get it. If Patti hadn't been there he would have kissed Tracy again.

"Turn around," she said, "Let me make you feel better." She massaged his shoulders, scratched his head, worked his neck, and pounded on his back with her closed fist. The hot water bubbled around him, Tracy, the woman he loved, her hands on his body. He could have stayed there forever.

Patti opened her eyes. Seemed to evaluate the two of them, and closed them again.

"I'm going to find her," he said.

"Ancient history, Winchester," Patti said. "You ought not to go stirring up the spirits of the past. Leave them be."

He wondered why stirring up the past bothered her. "Patti?" She opened her eyes. "What is it exactly you're afraid I'm going to dig up?"

"You don't get it, Winch. You ought to just leave this whole case alone. No reason to dredge up this muck. Sarah Fox is dead and buried and whatever you do is not going to help another living soul.

"You're probably responsible for Meredith Renfro's husband using that asp on her again. And look at you, cut and bruised and no closer to solving your big mystery. Not any closer than anybody else has been. Call it quits before somebody gets killed. And if you don't and they do, it'll be your fault."

He wiped a splash of water out of his eyes. "How do you know she's dead and buried?"

"Figure of speech," Patti waved her hand. "What? You'd rather think of her body in the marsh, eaten by turkey vultures, possum, and fiddler crabs?"

"There's a murderer out there somewhere." He scooped a handful of bubbling water and let it run out between his fingers. "Doesn't Sarah Fox deserve justice?"

"Who cares?" Patti said.

"Maybe Sarah Fox isn't the only person he's killed. Maybe he's still killing."

Tracy stopped her massage and moved between him and Patti. "How many murders here in the last twenty years?"

"Only one or two unsolved homicides in St. Johns County that I know of," Patti said.

"Sarah Fox isn't listed as a homicide," he said. "How many other missing persons cases are actually homicides? Maybe that's this guy's M.O. He leaves no bodies. The people just disappear. And what about Richard Sharp? He was murdered."

"Different M.O." Patti said. "He was shot."

"How do you know Sarah Fox wasn't shot?"

"Geez," Patti said. "We just established that she disappeared."

"Yeah," he said, "but still, how do you know she wasn't kidnapped and then shot?"

"Didn't you tell me your step-mother disappeared?" Tracy said, squinting at Patti shielding her eyes from the bubbling spray, a hand over each eyebrow.

Patti shook her head in dismissal. "She was 'the wicked witch from the west.' Good riddance to her. She didn't disappear. She left a note telling me what a rotten kid I was. Packed her bags and left. Dad told me she was getting it on with another guy."

"What about *your* parents, Winch?" Tracy said.

He nodded, "Yeah, they ran off when I was ten. I was fortunate to have Uncle Benjamin."

"See," Patti said. "People disappear all the time. Doesn't mean they've been killed. You think the guy who killed Sarah Fox killed your parents too?"

She was right of course. He knew his parents' disappearance had nothing to do with Sarah Fox. Unrelated events in different universes.

"You're a hot shot skip tracer," Patti said. "Find your parents."

"They know where they left me. They can find me if they wish." He'd run their names through all of his database services. No hits. He maintained a file and when a new database came on line he searched them. But he never admitted to anybody that he'd looked. He wasn't sure why. Pride probably. If his parents didn't want him, then he didn't want them is what he told himself. But, the real him knew that wasn't true.

"Okay," Patti said. "Now we're getting somewhere. Let's compare notes. See how our parents messed us up."

"Yeah," Tracy said. "All parents screw up their kids. It's nature at maximum capacity."

"Your folks were Mormon?" Patti said. "I thought Mormons had that family-oriented kind of thing?

"My mom was raised Mormon. Dad was baptized when he was eight but I don't think his parents were ever active in the church."

"Jack Mormons, huh?" Patti said.

"You could call them that, I guess. I never liked that term but some people use it."

"Jacked up Jack Mormons. Jacked up their kid didn't they?" Patti said.

Tracy put her hand over Patti's mouth. "Be nice.

"I don't know," he said. "I hope they're dead somewhere. Killed in an accident or something."

"Well shut the door," Patti said and slapped her hand on the water. "Why would you say that?"

"Easier for me to picture them dead, than to think they didn't love me enough to take me with them. At least *you* got a note. I didn't even get that."

"It was my stepmom," Patti said. "Life was better after she left." She paused. "For me at least. I pitched in. Pretty much ran the house. My stepbrother took it real hard. The witch left him behind with my dad."

“Well doesn’t that just suck?” Tracy said. “Parents do the worst things to their kids.”

The three of them sat in silence, the water gurgling and spitting. Winch was hot and scooted up on the concrete edge. He needed to leave. Every man’s fantasy was to be in a hot tub with two women. But his commitments to the church, his sacred vows, wouldn’t permit him to linger here. He should have left earlier. But now he had the feeling that if he stayed there might be more temptation than he could resist.

He stood to leave, gazed into Tracy’s eyes and they exchanged unspoken words. She cast a sidelong glance at Patti who’d closed her eyes. Tracy mouthed the word “later” and waggled the fingers of one hand at him.

He shook his head and mouthed back “No,” but wasn’t sure she’d seen him. He climbed out of the spa, gathered his clothes and left. He went to the marina, picked up the rental car and headed south to interview Trey Ellis.

He drove down A1A. Along Anastasia Island the waves rolled relentlessly onto the shore. Something nagged at him. Something Patti had said in the hot tub. It was like fly fishing for bonefish. A sliver of silver shadow darting right and then left, just below the water’s surface, and he couldn’t quite make the fish rise to the lure.

TWENTY-NINE

John Forester parked his car in the marina lot, checked his watch, 5:50 pm. He always enjoyed his monthly home teaching visit with Winchester Young on his boat. No reason to think tonight's visit would be different.

He stood on the concrete bulkhead admiring the ambiance of boats in their slips. The slap-slap of water against fiberglass. The lighthouse he could see. The fresh ocean breeze, better than any manufactured laundry scent. From the lot he could see Brother Young's boat, the *Dos XX*, and somebody in coveralls carrying a small toolbox standing on the boat's rear deck. Aft deck, Winchester would have told him.

This person was not big enough to be Brother Young. Seemed sort of late for a repairman to be working. He thought Winchester had been doing the restoration work on the boat himself. And this was Florida in July. Six pm and 90 degrees. Awful hot to be in coveralls. The repairman stepped off the boat and disappeared from his view.

Walking the dock of the Conch House Marina, John felt out of place wearing wingtips, black socks, blue slacks, white shirt, and a red tie. A couple passed him, the blonde in her shorts and sandals, and her husband, in T-shirt and Top-Siders, looked so boaty carrying a monogrammed canvas bag that read "Wind Spirit."

John had some tennies he could have worn, had he thought about it. Still, shoes were shoes, and he needed to get his home teaching done before the end of the month. While he enjoyed home teaching Brother Winchester, usually when he departed, a slight twinge of dissatisfaction gnawed at him. Sometimes his wife called him grumpy after home teaching Winch. Not to say he didn't have a good life, or a good wife, for that matter. But Brother Young's life just seemed so, how could he quantify his feelings? So much larger than real. He straightened his tie and walked down the marina dock. The early evening restaurant smells of conch fritters frying and grouper on the grill made him wonder if perhaps Winchester had it right, and he'd missed out by staying steady. Monogamous. Maybe a little bored?

The church placed a heavy emphasis on its home teaching program. Monthly visits with a spiritual message by one member of the congregation to another. He and Winch were both in the Elders' quorum. Every active member of the quorum had a home teaching route of three or four families. John's wife often accompanied him on his home teaching visits, but tonight she wasn't feeling well, so here he was alone.

Okay, he'd admit it to himself, even though he would never, ever, admit it to his wife. Yes, he was envious of Winch's lifestyle. He'd been married for 22 years, the only woman he'd ever had sex with. Mentally, well that was something else. Sometimes, he'd be thinking of someone else. Winch, single, living on a boat in the marina, a private investigator for crying out loud. How much more exciting could a guy's life be? So yeah, he was jealous of Winch.

John passed the bar, the tinkle of ice on glass in the air, smokers, with pursed lips, blowing grey puffs away from each other. Some good looking bartender in a loose shirt mixing drinks. He could stop in and have a root beer, but he wouldn't feel comfortable in a bar. And if people saw him, they'd probably think he was a gone-astray-Mormon.

He turned his gaze to the boats that cost more than his house. And wasn't the purchase only the beginning? Every boat owner he knew complained about the maintenance cost.

As he walked down the ramp that connected the fixed dock to the floating docks, he passed the repairman he'd seen on Brother Winch's boat. A short fellow, head covered with a long bill fishing cap, the bill pulled low over his eyes. A small black tool box in his left gloved hand. He nodded to him, as you do with strangers, but the fellow wouldn't meet his gaze. Low self-esteem he guessed. A flash of wispy auburn hair on the back of the man's neck was all he could really see. Well, whatever the problem, John hoped he'd repaired it.

A small wave from a motorboat bounced the floating dock. He gripped one of the hip-high dock lights and held on until the swaying ceased. He gazed around, embarrassed, but nobody seemed to pay him any mind. Flip, just the dock moving was enough to send a queasy feeling from his brain to his stomach. He guessed he'd never be a yachtie. Too impractical anyway with a wife and three kids.

When he reached the *Dos XX*, he wondered why a good Mormon like Winch would name his boat after a beer. Winch denied it was named after the beer, but still. . . . He knew for certain that Winch was a "good" Mormon. In his calling as ward clerk he'd had occasion to see Winchester's membership records. Winch held a temple recommend, given only to those members that paid a full tithe, didn't drink or smoke, and would swear to the Bishop that they were honest with their fellow men in all of their dealings.

Winch had taught him proper boat etiquette. He walked down the finger-pier and knocked on the boat's hull. He waited. Nothing. He rapped again. Nothing. Well, since Winch's Jeep was parked in the lot he certainly should be here. Maybe he was in the shower. He'd wait. He opened the boarding door and took a seat in a deck chair.

Sea birds of some type dodged and chased each other, chattering and cawing. Winch had pointed out to him the difference between Bonaparte gulls and Laughing gulls, Sandpipers, and Storm petrels. He really couldn't tell them apart but Brother Young certainly knew his birds. A light breeze blew across the deck of the boat. A sound track of Faith Hill from another boat two docks away drifted on the wind. He loosened his tie and settled in. He'd take the tie off altogether but that would be too casual. He, as a home teacher, represented the Bishop, and he needed to look the part. He'd tighten it up when Winch walked down the dock.

* * * *

Tracy drove her Toyota hybrid into the Conch House parking lot. She eyed Winch's Jeep. Good. She'd sent Patti home after Winch left. She'd made a huge mistake leaving Winch this last time. She was restless, she knew that, but she could keep a commitment.

She was sure she could. She wanted a child and she wanted one with Winchester, regardless of the cost. Every time Winch left, some part of her went with him. She did love him. Everything about him. He was right. They were two wings on the same bird. Opposite, but together. Maybe if she'd reign herself in a little and he'd flex a little . . . then maybe they should try it one more time. They could get a marriage license tomorrow and have the clerk of the court marry them in that little outdoor gazebo. Wouldn't Winch be shocked when she told him?

She walked past the Conch House bar. That bartender friend of Winch's in a loose weightlifter's T-shirt, collar cut low and sleeves cut high, caught her eye. She stopped and considered going in to say something but, no, why bother? She'd see the wedding band on Winch's hand soon enough.

* * * *

Brandy eyed Winch's ex-wife Tracy walking toward the bar. It was time she told Tracy to leave Winch alone. Stop trolling her bait in his waters and let him move on without her. She caught Tracy's eye, held up her index finger, told the guys at the bar she'd be right back and stepped onto the dock.

"Don't do this to him," Brandy said.

"What Winch and I do…is none of your business."

"He's my friend." Brandy looked her over. Ribbed T-shirt. Slender but not really hard bodied. She looked every bit her thirty years or whatever she was. At that age she knew Tracy had to hear the biological clock counting down.

"Aren't you a little young for him?" Tracy cocked her head. "You know he's got some wear on his treads."

"I'm just his friend." She gave Tracy a look. "You've been run a few miles yourself. I hear a ticking under your hood, and it's not the engine block cooling."

A confused look crossed Tracy's face and then she understood. "You're awful rude for a bartender." She knew Winch liked spunk in a woman. But what did he see in this girl who let her boobs hang out to get better tips?

"Who are you to judge me? I work here until last call, two-o'clock in the morning, and my first class is at nine. I'm paying my own expenses. Working on my MBA. How far did you get in school? And who paid? Your daddy, I bet."

Tracy looked toward D dock thinking maybe she'd misjudged Brandy. Working her way through school while bartending couldn't be easy. "Winch here?"

"Leave him alone."

"We're getting married. He asked me earlier this afternoon."

Brandy looked to Tracy's left hand.

Tracy followed her eyes. "No long engagement. We'll get our license tomorrow."

Brandy fingered her own unadorned ring finger. "Well then, I guess there's nothing else to say."

"Sure there is." Tracy waved the back of her hand at her as she walked away. "Say 'best wishes.'"

"Right," Brandy said, not loud enough for Tracy to hear. "Best wishes to Winch anyway. He's going to need them."

* * * *

It had been a while since John Forrester had seen Sister Young. Since the Youngs' last divorce. Flip, didn't that sound funny? Winch had married and divorced her twice. What was that about? Were they going for round three? John had helped teach Tracy the missionary discussions, but she'd never accepted the Gospel. Still, she'd gone to church sometimes with Winch.

She approached, beachy looking, slender as a sea oat, with short brown fuzzy-cut hair, freckled face.

Tracy stopped at the boarding gate to the *Dos XX*. She hesitated, then recognized Winch's home teacher sitting on the aft deck. "He's not on board?" she asked.

Forrester shook his head. "Nice to see you, Sister Young."

"Did he know you were coming?"

"The air conditioner is running." He leaned over the side of the boat, pointing to the steady stream of water coming from a hole, no, a "thru-hull," Winch had called it, just above the water line.

"It always runs," she said. Her armpits felt damp and beads of sweat broke out on her face. "We can wait inside, where it's cooler. I have a key."

It wouldn't look right for him to be inside the boat with Sister Young. Him a married man alone, in this bachelor's boat, with a woman. "I don't mind it out here," he said. "This time of evening is very pleasant."

She turned eastward. Felt the breeze on her face. Inhaled the humid air. The halyards on the sailboat in the next slip clanged against the aluminum mast. The noise annoyed most boaters, but she found it comforting. She stepped to the sliding glass door and tried the key. Damn thing wouldn't go in. Must be rusted. She pulled on the door, nudging it a bit one way and then the other. Did Winch change the lock on her? No, finally the key went in, but now it wouldn't turn. She looked to the home teacher. "Do you mind? I can't seem to get it."

Forrester put his hand on the key, wiggled it a bit. Then he bent down to examine it. "Look at this," he said. The keyhole was all scratched and chewed. Shiny aluminum cuts glistened where the door met the frame. "I think somebody's pried this door. Here, see?" He applied more pressure to the key, not wanting to break it off in the lock. He wiggled it, jiggled it, and it finally turned. He slid the door open, reached in, feeling for the light switch.

Tracy, standing right behind him, smelled propane. Took her a second to recognize the smell. One second too long.

"No!" She yelled. Then she thought, I'm never going to have a baby.

Forrester flipped the light switch.

THIRTY

Winch thought over how best to approach Brian Ellis, aka Trey. Ellis and his two fraternity brothers were the last known people to have seen Sarah alive. Did the three of them, in fact, accidentally kill her and then set up an elaborate hoax to stage her disappearance?

The subdivision he drove into spread over the western edge of Palm Beach County and bordered the Everglades. This horse town, named "The Acreage," consisted mostly of unpaved streets which were favored by this equestrian community. The lots were all acre-plus-sized with barns and horse paddocks. Well pumps alongside the homes and septic tank drain fields disguised as grass-covered humps the size of dump truck beds told him this subdivision was beyond the city water and sewer systems. Water-filled drainage canals, a favorite disposal area for bodies in South Florida, crisscrossed the area.

He made the turn from one dirt road onto another, his headlights picking up red-eyed reflections on the canal bank. He stopped and stood next to the car staring at a seven-foot bull gator, which seemed to nonchalantly return his gaze. After a minute, the gator on stumpy legs scrambled into the water, submerging until just his eyes and his nostrils were above water.

Ellis's home was a one story brick, on a maybe two-acre parcel, fenced with white polyvinyl fencing. A horse barn and tack shed stood at the end of the driveway. A closed gate with an open padlock dangling from a chain blocked the drive. Lights lit the drive, spilled out of windows and illuminated the front porch of the house. A pickup truck and a Porsche Cayenne SUV were parked on the paved driveway. Brandy's research told him the vehicles were registered to Brian and Sharon Ellis.

He walked through the gate, closing it behind him, having learned from ranchers always to leave a gate the way it was found. He approached the door wondering what Ellis's reaction would be. Even old secrets can be embarrassing.

Ellis came to the door, a man Winch knew from his database report to be four years older than he was. He stood two inches shorter than Winch's five-eleven and wore a closely cropped beard with lots of grey in it. His head, mostly bald, glistened. The smell of sweaty horses, leather, and horse manure lingered in the air at the front porch.

Winch introduced himself, displaying his PI identification and handing him a business card. Ellis raised his eyebrows.

"You should have called first," Ellis said.

Right, so Ellis could make himself unavailable. No. Always better to catch them by surprise. Ellis probably had a guilty conscious about more than one thing in his life and he'd be figuring that Winch was about to expose something private that he didn't want exposed.

"Who is it, Brian?" a woman's voice called from inside.

Winch nodded toward the interior. "Your wife, Sharon?"

"What is this? A blackmail attempt?"

"Not yet."

"Rachel's husband hired you. That little prick. How did he figure it out?"

Winch shook his head.

"Who hired you then?" Ellis said.

Winch tilted his head toward the open door. "Why don't you show me your horses?"

"Someone about the saddle on Craig's List," Ellis called over his shoulder, shutting the door behind him.

They walked toward the tack shed, Ellis leading by a step. "You tell that prick he can't intimidate me by sending a PI to my house." He looked at the business card. "Mr. Young, just take that message with you and get out."

"I don't know Rachel. Nor her husband. I'm here about Sarah Fox." The horses heard them, stuck their heads over the stall doors and eyed their approach. One of them whinnied. The sweet smell of hay grew as they walked.

"Kevin Lawrence's widow called me yesterday. Told me Sarah's sister was reopening the investigation."

Kevin, frat boy number two. "You see his widow a lot?"

"We're both into horses. We see each other at shows." He rubbed the snout of a brown sorrel which snorted and tossed his head. "In fact this one, Peddler, I bought from Kevin a couple of years ago. The best barrel horse in Palm Beach County."

"How did Kevin die?"

"Got drunk. Drove his car into an irrigation ditch in Kansas." Ellis shrugged. "They didn't find him until the next morning."

"Couldn't swim?"

"Looked like he banged his head in the crash. Knocked himself out and drowned."

"Tony Hudson couldn't swim either?" Winch said.

Ellis dropped his hand from the horse. Even in the barn lights Winch could see his face whiten. "Tony is dead?"

"Last month in Guana River State Park. Just North of St. Augustine. Found him in a lagoon." Winch read the article in the *St. Augustine Record* but it wasn't significant to him at the time. "Contact bullet wound to the temple. Hard to swim with a hole in your head. Bother you does it, that your two friends both met violent deaths?"

"I didn't kill them." Ellis shrugged but Winch could see his hand tremble and he grabbed onto the stall door.

"Tell me about the day Sarah disappeared."

"You read the police reports? It's all there."

"No it's not. I think you, Kevin, and Tony Hudson deliberately omitted facts you didn't want to admit to the police."

"Well, screw you, Mr. Young. I'm not going to let some nickel-and-dime PI. come onto my property and call me a liar."

"Yes you are. Twenty-five years ago you were young. People forgive transgressions by young stupid men. But do you want your name associated with a murder investigation now? How would that go over down at the firm?"

Ellis looked to the horses. Took a minute to rub each of their foreheads. "You ask me what you want and I'll give it to you straight, but it doesn't go any further than you and me."

"If you're complicit in Sarah Fox's disappearance I can't promise you that."

"I had nothing to do with her taking a flyer. Truth is, I don't know how she did that. Nobody up there could figure it out."

Ellis gazed over the horse paddock and then back to Winch. "I was pumping gas. I saw her go into the restroom and I watched those two doors the whole time. She never came out."

"Watching her?"

"Okay, here's the messy part. We were college kids. Frat brothers. Like you said, stupid. We knew Sarah put out because, well, she had a bit of reputation. You know. Her boyfriend was in our fraternity and sometimes, at our parties, Sarah would get a little, hmm, frisky, I guess you could call it. Take her shirt off. That sort of thing."

"Jailbait, wasn't she?" Winch said.

"Age of consent in Georgia is sixteen. She was eighteen."

"And then there's the federal law, the Mann Act. Interstate transportation of a female for immoral purposes." Winch slapped a mosquito. "No statute of limitations on that." He didn't know if there was a federal statute of limitations or not.

Ellis held his hands low, palms out. "Where's the victim?"

Winch didn't have an answer to that. "So tell me what happened?"

"The night before she disappeared, we'd slept on the beach and she hooked up with some local dude. We weren't about to let her boogie out on us and spend spring break with someone we didn't know. We were responsible for her."

"Responsible? Each of you thought you might have a chance with her? Did she know that?"

"We didn't think she knew at the time, but later, you know, back at school, we recalled we'd joked a bit about it while she was sleeping. Maybe she wasn't really asleep."

"Why stop at that station?"

"We needed gas to go to Daytona."

"But why that gas station? Why not some other?"

"You haven't met Snake?"

Winch gave him a look.

"Luther Calderon. His dad owned that station. More like a bait and tackle, really. Luther lived behind, over the garage, of the big house where his dad and sister, no, his step-sister, lived."

"And Luther–"

"Luther was a frat brother. Sarah said if Luther were there he'd pump free gas for us. But he wasn't home yet from Athens. His dad, or step-dad, whatever, said he'd be in later that afternoon."

There it was. The connection he'd been looking for between Sarah, the fraternity brothers, and the gas station. It wasn't just some random stop. They knew they were going to stop there. "Did Sarah know you were stopping to see Luther?"

Ellis considered it. "That was a long time ago." He rubbed his hands on his jeans. "You, know. as I recall, it was her idea. Snake and her boyfriend Andy shared a room in the Frat house. It's probably why she thought the gas would be free, but I wouldn't know that for sure.

"We pulled into another gas station on the outskirts of St. Augustine, but Sarah said 'No, let's go on down to Snake's gas station.' And we did."

"And you call him Snake because. . .?"

"Snake's a golfer. At the university he was on the University golf team. He's the assistant pro up there now. At Sawgrass, where they play the TPC. You a golfer? You'd know him."

Winch shook his head.

"Well, Snake grew up back there in the woods, more a swamp really. To this day he keeps two three irons in his bag. He's honed the edge of one club down to a fine blade. While the rest of his foursome are looking for their balls in the rough, Snake pokes around the water hazards stirring up moccasins. He takes that iron, cuts a snake's head clean off and knocks it seventy-five yards down the fairway with one swing. Hell of a thing to see."

"He never gets bit?"

"Naw. He whiffed one once but that club is longer than a snake can strike. We all ran for the golf cart but he stood his ground and sliced the damn thing into pieces."

"You were watching the restroom doors—how did Sarah make her escape?"

"I don't think she did. I think she's walled up in there somewhere, you know, like that Poe story. Take one of those alternate light sources they use on CSI, shine it at an angle on the wall and you'll find her image coming through the plaster. Hell, I don't know. She went in and she didn't come out. That's all I know."

Winch had been in the restroom. No windows. Only a small hole the size of a dinner plate in the ceiling for a fan. "Any of you ever hear from her again. Promise not to tell her mother that she was still alive?"

Ellis shook his head. "Nothing like that."

The way she'd disappeared was still a mystery. There had to be an answer but Ellis didn't know it. "What about the guy she met on the beach the night before. What was his name?"

"He was local. Not a college boy. About her age. Worked at the old Spanish fort."

"Castillo de San Marcos?"

"Yeah, that's the one. Yard crew, maintenance, or something like that. I don't think I ever heard his name. Just some guy she picked up. We had a campfire, and he sat there with us for just a few minutes and then he and Sarah took her sleeping bag and hiked off into the dunes. In the morning he was gone and Sarah had come back with her bag and was sleeping next to us."

"He must have called himself something."

"A swarthy looking fellow. Mexican, Mestizo, maybe had some Indian blood in him because we joked about the pale face and Geronimo."

"He spoke English though?"

"No accent. I think maybe he was Indian. I recall he gave us one of those Indian names. 'Son of Running Bear' or 'Leaping Deer in the Springtime.' Some other stupid animal name."

"Stupid to you," Winch said.

A deep croak boomed out from the canal. Bull frog or an alligator. Hard to tell them apart. They both looked in the direction it came from and then back at each other.

"I'm done here," Ellis said. "You're a pain in the butt, and I don't need to talk to you." He flipped the light out in the stable and took a couple of steps toward the house.

"I'm not finished," Winch said.

"Too bad. Close the gate on your way out."

Winch shuffled one foot. He lifted his shoe and looked at the sole. Horse dung. A not altogether unpleasant smell of hay and horses. He scraped it on the stall gate. "I'm staying in West Palm tonight, Ellis."

Ellis gave him a wave with the back of his hand. "Have a nice sleep."

"I'll be back in the morning. Have a chat with your wife. Shall I ask her if she knows Rachel and the little prick husband? That'd be interesting."

Ellis stopped and turned. "You enjoy making other people's lives miserable?"

"I think you've done a pretty good job of that yourself. Now look, I only have a few more questions."

Ellis waved him on.

"This Indian. Where did he go?"

"Back to the reservation? Why should I know?"

"You guys didn't make him disappear?

"No man, nothing like that. Sarah was just a bimbo. You don't kill some guy over a twit."

Lots of men have been killed over twits. Women, greed, and fear of exposure. Probably in that order. "When Sarah went into the restroom . . . you actually saw her go in?"

"No question. She toted her bag with her. A small duffle with her stuff. Said she was going to "freshen up'.

"That the same bag the cops found on the beach a few days later?" Winch said.

"It was. Now isn't that strange?" Ellis rubbed his chin. "She and the bag disappear but the bag washes up on the beach. No body. Nothing."

Winch didn't correct him about the bag having been found in the dunes above the high water line and not washed up. Since Ellis had that detail wrong, it seemed likely that someone other than Ellis had planted the bag on the beach. He could also reason that Ellis and probably the other two boys were not part of a conspiracy to kidnap Sarah Fox. But they were both dead, and he wouldn't have the opportunity to question them. Someone else had snatched Sarah.

"You think she's dead?" Winch said.

"Got to be," Ellis said. "It's been years. The bag popped up within a few days." Ellis stroked his short beard. "What do you think?"

Winch thought he'd better go back and take another look at those restrooms, and check out Snake's alibi, but he didn't say that.

"You know what I think?" Winch said. "By the time you got to college you were a low-life cheating scumbag. Trying to make it with your buddy's girlfriend back then. Now, cheating on your wife. In the morning, take a good look in the mirror while you're shaving. Those are all accomplishments that I'm sure would make your mom proud."

"Screw you, Mr. Young."

"I think you'd better watch your back, Ellis."

"Twenty-five years after the fact, someone's carrying out a vendetta?" Ellis ran his hand over his baldhead. "You think I'm in danger?"

"Only if your wife doesn't kill you first."

THIRTY-ONE

Brandy felt a whump of steamed air that nearly knocked her off her feet. The pilings under the open air Conch House bar shook. She grasped onto the oak bar. Water sloshed onto the tile floor from the wash and rinse tubs. A fireball at the end of D dock blossomed like a scarlet and pink spinnaker. Her eyes fixed on the explosion. Within the plume of fire the deck and super structure of the *Dos XX* levitated as high as the first spreader on the sailboat in the next slip. It hovered a second and exploded outward into a thousand slivers. Oh no, Tracy and Winch were down there.

She ran out of the bar toward the *Dos XX*. The floating dock bucked under her feet. Boats at the docks rolled heavily toward her as if hit by a rogue wave. Their lines popped cleats and slung them into the night. Pieces of flaming wood rained from the sky, lighting the thatched covered huts and setting afire the canvas tops of some yachts.

A wave of heat hit her. Then a smell like scorched hair.

She had to find Winch. She ran shielding her head from flaming debris. She got as close as two boats away from the *Dos XX* but the heat from the fire melted the fiberglass on the next boat and the hair on her arms began to smoke and crinkle. She backed off.

She jumped onto a dock box and scanned the parking lot hoping that his car was gone. Oh no. Winch's Jeep was parked right where he'd left it.

A man she knew, a boat owner, Matt—Crown Royal and Seven on the rocks, stood next to her with one of the dock fire extinguishers. He looked at her, shook his head and set the extinguisher on the dock.

Winch gone. It felt like a hole opened in her belly and pulled her in. She buried her face in her hands and sank to her knees on the swaying dock.

THIRTY-TWO

DAY FOUR

Winch spent the night in a bed that didn't rock, no halyards clanging in the next slip, and no putt-putting of the early morning river shrimpers leaving the dock to wake him. So he'd slept late. He'd called Tracy from the motel. But Tracy's phone went right to voice mail, and her mailbox was full. Very unusual for her.

He stopped at the Verizon store and bought a new phone. As soon as he reached the Marina he'd call Enterprise and have the rental car picked up. Then to track down Snake, and have another look at old man Patch's gas station before the bulldozers leveled it.

On Interstate 95 northbound the landfill west of Vero Beach passed on his right, the gulls and crows scrabbling over edible trash. The smell of rotting garbage blew full force through the air conditioner. Great.

Mile markers rolled by, climbing higher. The drive gave him plenty of time to think about Tracy. He'd married her twice. What an idiot. He knew it wasn't rational to even consider a third time, but dog gone it, he loved her. Right, he loved her. But could he live with her?

He'd have to stop somewhere and buy a ring. What kind of ring do you buy for a woman that you've married twice before? A diamond solitaire didn't seem quite right. Like a new bride wearing a white dress when she was already pregnant.

Finally arriving at St. Augustine, he slid the rental into a parking space at the marina. Crushed white oyster shells snapped under the tires. St. Johns County Sheriff's cars, a crime scene van and three City of St. Augustine PD cars were parked in the lot. Three Sheriff's unmarked cruisers, and an unmarked SUV too. Very weird. Did somebody get murdered?

He checked his watch. Two pm. Back before the deadline. He'd only be charged for the one day rental. A crane on a barge floated at the end of D dock, anchored by pine-tree sized studs driven into the silt bottom. Clouds of gray diesel smoke rose in rhythmic belches from the black-rimmed smoke stack.

What the heck were they doing next to the *Dos XX*? A bevy of people, arms waving, gesticulating, giving each other directions, shifted around at the end of the dock. The acrid stench of burnt plastic and smoldering rubber, or maybe shorted electronics, was everywhere. Flocks of gulls circled the docks and dove into the water as if feeding off a school of baitfish.

He grabbed his duffle and walked through the parking lot. On the concrete bulkhead that prevented the parking lot from slipping into the water stood Sister Forrester, his home teacher's wife. She heard his approach. Turned toward him, arms wrapped around herself.

"Winch? I . . . I thought . . . . " she waved one arm toward the docks, then wrapped it back over her chest.

"Sister Forrester, what are you doing here?"

"John went home teaching last night. He never came back." She pointed to a silver Dodge Caravan in the lot, two stickers on the rear bumper. "Missionary Dad" and the other "CTR." Mormon shorthand for Choose The Right. "His car's here. But they said there were two dead. I thought you and him. But you're not dead. Is John?"

"Why would he be dead?"

"The boat."

"What do you mean, 'the boat?'" From where he stood on the bulkhead it was easy to see the *Dos XX*'s slip was empty. Well, not empty, filled with debris. What had happened? The sailboat in the slip next to his, steel hull and fiberglass top, looked like a melted wax candle. The wooden mast, before tall as a telephone pole, now it was burnt to a shoulder-high stub. Floating yellow barriers surrounded the entire D dock. A black oily sheen, with streaks of rainbow, spread on both sides of the barrier.

He dropped his duffle bag at her feet. Moved away. He had to get down there. But she grabbed his arm and held to him.

She motioned with her chin to his slip. "They won't let me through," she said. "I tried to tell them that was John's body down there. I wanted to see it. Someone said there wasn't enough left to identify. But I would know if it was John or not. You go down there and tell them that's John's body they have, not yours."

He shook his arm but she clung to him. "I don't know what's happened, but I'm sure—"

"You can't be sure of anything," she said. "John is dead and it should have been you. John worshiped your lifestyle. Your ex-wives. Your job. Everything you. He thought I didn't know, but I did. And now he's dead because of you. And you're not." She covered her face with her hands and sobbed.

Then she pushed him. "Get away. My kids don't know. Who's going to tell my children their father's dead?"

He ran down the dock. Two pelicans sitting on a piling eyed him but didn't move as he passed. No music, no raucous laughter from the scorched thatched-roof dock bar. He caught a glimpse of Brandy placing glasses on a shelf. Gave her a quick wave.

Footsteps pounded the dock behind him. Brandy yelled something he couldn't hear. A blue uniformed St. Augustine policeman stood inside a strip of yellow tape that crossed the dock.

He pointed toward the end of D dock. "That's my boat," he said.

The policeman cocked his head. "Doesn't make any difference which is yours buddy, you'll have to wait until they finish their crime scene before you can go aboard."

Brandy caught him by the shoulder, turned him around with a pull of her hand.

She leaped onto him, locking her legs around his waist, arms around his neck, kissed him feverously on his lips, cheeks, forehead, chin, nose and back to the lips. Finally got out, "Oh—my—gosh! It's really you. You're not dead."

The policemen and a small crowd of three men and a girl he knew from the docks stared at him. "Me? I don't think so. Are you seeing dead people?" Actually the question wasn't as rhetorical as it probably seemed to her. Mormons have a firm understanding of life after death. When the spirit and physical body are separated at death, the spirit goes to a place Mormons refer to as "the Spirit World." The same place where Christ visited after his crucifixion.

But Brandy's kisses told them both he wasn't a spirit.

She dropped her feet to the floor. Stepped back a foot. "Why didn't you call?"

He shrugged. "I didn't have a phone. I didn't have time to stop—"

"Your boat exploded last night. They found a man's body. They think it's you."

"A friend from church came to visit me last night." He pointed to Sister Forrester standing on the bulkhead. "That's his . . . widow."

"Ah, man," Brandy said. "They've been picking up pieces of him from as far away as B dock. At least the ones the gulls haven't gotten."

"Let me through," he said to the policeman. But he couldn't move. The enormity of it swallowed him. The *Dos XX*, gone. Brother Forrester dead. All of his earthly belongings. His first edition book collection. If he hadn't forgotten Brother Forrester's appointment he'd be alive. The boat wouldn't have blown if he'd been there. "I need to sit," he said, and dropped heavily onto a dock box.

"There's something else," Brandy said. Her eyes shifted away. "It's Tracy. She was there too. She's dead, Winch." She hugged him. "I'm so sorry."

"Tracy?" His Tracy, gone? It should have been him instead of Forrester. If he and Tracy had died together, that would have been okay. They'd be together in the Spirit World, and maybe, somehow, they could have still been sealed in a Temple and been together forever. But now? She'd gone on ahead of him. Leaving him here alone.

No it couldn't be. "They were wrong about me. Maybe it's somebody else, not Tracy."

"I saw her Winch. It was her."

His face grew cold and clammy, but perspiration dripped off his forehead like a breaking sweat. His legs were shaking, shivering, but this was Florida summer. No, no, no, not Tracy. His chest heaved and he wanted to cry out. He looked at his hands and saw that he was actually wringing them. He hadn't known he was, but there they were. One hand dry washing the other. He couldn't sit anymore. He had to lie. He slipped off the box and curled onto the dock that smelled like cigarette butts and fish. Hugged himself. Brandy bent over, stroking him. He heard himself moan. It just came out all by itself. It hurt so bad. He didn't want to live without her.

His face was wet, tears or perspiration, he wasn't sure. People gathered around him, and Brandy telling them to stand back. He was making a fool of himself, but he couldn't help it. He wasn't in control. He sobbed. His chest ached. His shoulders shook. Oh why? Why? She was dead and he was still here. He didn't want to be here. Where was his gun so he could end the hurt? He understood now, people damning God for taking away the ones they loved. It's easier to be the one taken, than to be the one left behind.

He held tight to himself and rocked. Finally some measure of control ebbed into his body. He ceased his rocking and pulled in deep breaths. He raised himself to his hands and knees. He turned one hand over. Grit and soot like mud. Brandy, above, her arms around his chest. He smelled her perfume, like Mandarin oranges. She spoke, her breath warm on his neck, but the words made no sense. His brain still numb. She pulled him upright and sat him back down on the dock box.

"The *Dos Equis*," he said, "what happened to her?"

"Propane," Brandy said. "A leak."

"No," he said. He'd installed the propane stove. Plumbed the copper line back to the sealed tank compartment. Installed the sniffer alarm in the bilge. Propane, heavier than air, would settle in the bilge. Someone must have disconnected the alarm. Some person had done this deliberately. He straightened and shook his head. This wasn't some act of God. "This was no accident."

Brandy gave him a quizzical look.

"Charon," he said.

He would find Charon and make him pay. Make him suffer. The thought hit him. That wasn't a very Christian like attitude. And he didn't care. If Charon had killed Sarah twenty-five years ago and killed Tracy last night, then maybe God had just called him to be the avenging angel.

THIRTY-THREE

Winch heard a shower of water. The black-brown stuff rivered over the charred rim of the *Dos XX*'s hull and streamed from cracks in her side, as a crane raised her out of the slip. Lift-straps wrapped her like a spider web. He pointed to the *Dos XX*. "That one," he said to the policemen.

A look of understanding came over the man's face. "I thought . . . well, never mind." The officer called down the dock. "Detective, you ought to come here." The patrolman asked him his name and scribbled it on a tablet.

Renfro and another man he didn't recognize walked toward him. Renfro stopped in mid-stride when he saw Winch, then continued walking.

"The instructions were to pick up any pieces larger than a dime," Renfro said. He pointed to a black body bag on the dock in front of *Dos XX*'s slip. "Since it's not you, who's in that bag down there, Young?"

"A man's body?"

Renfro nodded. "More or less."

"John Forrester." Winch looked at the soot on his hands from the dock. Soot blackened the side of his shirt and pants, his elbows and forearms. He sniffed his hand, expecting the smell of burnt flesh, but it smelled like campfire. He gestured with his head toward the parking lot bulkhead. "That's his wife. Somebody needs to talk to her."

Renfro spoke into his handi-talkie, gave instructions, turned his attention back to him. "You've created more excitement around here than I can stand." His eyes shifted to Brandy and back to him. "You know about your—?"

"Tracy," he said. "Yes. But how can you be sure?" The crane lifted the *Dos XX* clear of the slip. Brackish water poured over her sides behind the floating yellow environmental barrier.

"How much is your boat insured for, Young?"

"If Forrester is in pieces then maybe. . . ?"

"Did you have a life insurance policy on Tracy? You the beneficiary? How much, Young?"

The man beside Renfro extended his hand. "I'm Mitch Wright, the county medical examiner. I'm sorry about your wife, ex-wife. The body has been identified. She's at my office. Is there next of kin we can notify?"

Next of kin? He was her husband. Wouldn't that make him next of kin? No, it'd make him the ex-husband. How did this happen?

The medical examiner put his hand on Winch's shoulder. "You okay? We can talk about this later if you wish."

He shook his head. "Tell me what you know."

"Looks like she was standing directly behind your friend. His body shielded hers. Took the brunt of the explosion. Shredded him, really. Your wife was remarkably preserved. Her hair was singed. Some burning to her extremities. But her face, well, it was impacted by the back of your friend's head." The ME shook his head. "The blunt force of his body slamming into hers with such explosive force was cause of death."

Winch was horrified. Water filled his eyes and he wiped them with the back of his hand. He couldn't stand to think of what he'd just been told. He looked at Brandy to his side. She put an arm around his shoulders and wiped her eyes as well.

Renfro put his hand up. "That's enough, Doc. He can read the autopsy if he wants."

"Right, right. Sure. Of course." He nodded toward the other end of the dock. "I think my people are about done here." He handed a business card to Winch. "Call me when you're ready."

As the coroner walked away, water from the *Dos XX* slowed to a steady drip. The crane swung her over the empty barge, held in place by a tugboat. Engine at idle. The tug's prop barely churning.

"Where are you taking my boat?"

"The Oasis on Riberia Street," Renfro said. "FDLE will have a crime scene unit go over it tomorrow. Looks like an LPG explosion to us. The boat's in pretty good shape from the hull-deck joint on down. It didn't really burn. The deck and cabin flew all over the marina. When the top blew upward, the bottom was forced down. Buried it three feet deep in the mud, filled with water. Burned the crap out of the boats around her but everything below deck on the *Dos Equis* will be there. FDLE will figure out what happened."

The crane settled the hull of the *Dos XX* into a cradle on the barge where men chocked her to keep her upright. The tug's smokestack billowed black, and the barge moved backwards away from the dock. The barge and tug pivoted and chugged out of the marina.

His boat. It was nothing compared to losing Tracy, but still it numbed him. All the effort he'd put into rebuilding it. He bowed his head. "Somebody rigged it to blow. You know this was no accident?"

Renfro gave him an appraising look. "An informant says you and Tracy argued yesterday after you left my office."

"We had no argument."

"Tracy and I did," Brandy said. "Just before the explosion. I told her to leave Winch alone. She told me they were going to be married." She looked at Winch. "See, there was no bad blood between them."

"So it's true you saw her yesterday?"

"I'm not talking to you about this."

Renfro stroked his chin. "He also says Tracy told you she was coming over here last night. Awful lucky for you, your boat blowing up and you're not here."

The tug and barge passed the inlet to the ocean, made a sharp turn to west. Headed toward the river, he figured. "This the way you guys went about investigating the Sarah Fox case? Tunnel vision on one subject and then when he's not the right guy, you shrug it off and move on to the next case?"

"This has nothing to do with the Sarah Fox case, Young."

"I think you'd be surprised."

Renfro pointed to Sister Forrester standing beside her husband's car, talking with a plainclothes detective. "What it does have to do with is you blowing up your ex and her lover. What did they do? Come over to tell you that they were together and you could get lost?"

"You're an idiot," Winch turned to watch the barge and tug in the distance.

"And you're not the only one who knows how to check records at the clerk of the court."

Winch faced Renfro. "I've got no secrets."

"I had the property appraiser give me a quick approximation of the equity in your house there in Vilano. You know, the one across the street from the beach? Where your ex-wife lived."

"So?"

"We also looked at the deed. "Joint tenants with right of survivorship. Well guess who survived?

Winch shook his head.

"The way beach access property has jumped right out of its socket, we figure the house is worth maybe eight hundred K. Your mortgage is less than a hundred thou.

"That's seven hundred thousand motives," Renfro said. "Get yourself a good lawyer, Young. You're my number one for the murder of your Ex and that woman's husband. A double homicide will go down hard here in St. Johns County."

"Three-fifty," Winch said.

"Huh?" Renfro said.

"Only three hundred and fifty thousand motives. Half of the house was mine anyway." He turned away from Renfro and the empty slip. "Come on Brandy. There's nothing left here for me."

He had to find a way to out smart Charon. Make him pay.

THIRTY-FOUR

Winch and Brandy, arm and arm, walked away from the wreckage of the *Dos XX*, up the ramp to the main dock. Brandy gave him a little squeeze around his waist, rubbed her hand up and down his back. “Where’re you going to stay tonight, Winch?”

He turned, looked at his empty slip. The remainder of his home floating on a barge about to be autopsied. Tomorrow strangers would paw through his cherished possessions. Then he wondered if Tracy were still around here somewhere. While not often talked about outside of the church, there’s a prevalent thought in Mormonism that the veil between the Spirit World and mortality is particularly thin after a loved one’s death. And in fact, spirits in the Spirit World are on occasion allowed to be seen and to communicate with mortals. Mormon theological history is rife with anecdotal stories of spirits of deceased persons visiting living mortals on the earth, appearing for special purposes.

So he wondered, could Tracy see him now? Maybe tell him who her killer was. Some people tended to think that once you’ve passed through the veil you can see everything, past, present, and future. Winch didn’t believe so. Tracy probably didn’t have any better clues than he did. After all, he was the intended victim, not her.

He turned and faced Brandy. “You know I didn’t kill her, right?”

“Of course. I mean you were at Tracy’s yesterday like he said, but the rest of that. It’s just bull. Right?”

"I need to think," he said. "I'm going over to Tracy's. Our house. Well, mine now I guess. I'll spend the night there."

"You think it's good for you to be alone? I could come over after my shift ends at the bar."

"Alone is what I need." He put both his hands on her face."

"I could sleep on the couch," she said.

He shook his head. "Alone means alone."

* * * *

When Winch inserted the key into the Vilano Beach house, his house now, he almost expected Tracy to be inside. But of course she wasn't. He sniffed the air. Nothing unusual. No way to tell that the person who'd been residing there had died last night.

He collapsed on the bed. Their marital bed that Tracy had a carpenter build for their second anniversary from the second time they'd married each other. Was that really a second anniversary or a fifth? Didn't make any difference anymore.

He smothered his face into her pillow. Smelled her scent. He wished there was someway to preserve it. Bag and freeze the pillowcase maybe? Too weird. Still . . . he loved the smell of her. But her smell would fade and die just as surely as Tracy had.

He needed to analyze this situation. A paperback PI would have a drink in his hand. Probably single malt scotch. Watch the ice cubes melt, the condensation roll down the sides. Hold the short thick glass to eye level and admire the sunset through the hue of the golden liquid. Take the occasional sip and come to some startling revelation.

But this wasn't paperback fiction. This was real. He slipped off his boat shoes and padded over to Tracy's refrigerator. A quart of almond milk. Four single-serving cups of low-fat yogurt. Carrots and celery in the veggie drawer. Food to make her live longer. In the pantry he found a twelve pack of Diet Coke. He filled a plastic tumbler to the brim with ice, poured in three-quarters of the can and sat by the pool on a webbed chair. Inhaled the smell of chlorine and enjoyed the sea breeze from the ocean. He listened for waves pounding on the beach. The ocean surface was flat, but a good swell ran from tropical storm Florence still to the south. His life was a torrent. Shouldn't the ocean roar with empathy?

He shifted in the chair. Needed to think through this Sarah Fox case. First he had to decide who was the intended target of the *Dos XX* explosion. Surely neither Tracy nor Forrester. Nobody could have predicted that either one of them would be on board and cause the detonation. So he'd been the target, for sure.

Who had motive to kill him? Money, love, revenge, fear of exposure. The four most common motives for murder. Renfro's fear of exposure? Renfro might be angry with him for learning of the spousal abuse. But it wasn't likely that it would lead Renfro to murder. He wasn't the only person who knew of Renfro's abusiveness toward women. Even Woody knew about it.

But did Renfro fear the exposure of his relationship with Lisa Chambers, Rudy's wife. He hadn't really proved they had a relationship yet. And Renfro's fooling around apparently was known by more than just him. Patti had alluded to it at the Sheriff's office. Scratch that as a motive for murder.

Charon and money? He'd wired Charon $10,000 and Charon should know that Winch was the link to the rest of the $50,000. If Charon were sharp, he'd know that if he murdered Winch, it'd be unlikely he'd get any more money.

It could be that the explosion of the *Dos XX* was not linked to the Sarah Fox case but he didn't believe that. Sure he had some irate husbands and wives he'd caught cheating, but nothing that anyone would kill over.

He closed his eyes and listened to a diesel engine rumble past on the beach highway, laying out in his mind the facts he knew to be true.

Theorem number one: The attempt on his life, the murder of Tracy and Forrester as accidental victims was linked to the disappearance of Sarah Fox. The murderer fearing exposure.

Theorem number two: If Charon wanted his money he wouldn't kill Winch, who held the key to the bank so to speak. The cash could have been on the *Dos XX*. Not likely that Charon would blow the *Dos XX*, not knowing for certain where the money was.

Occam's razor says not to make more assumptions than the minimum needed. Shave away all of the extraneous notions, and the one left is probably the right answer.

If theorems one and two are true then it follows that Charon wanted him alive. Therefore Charon did not blow up the *Dos XX*, and Charon could not be Sarah Fox's murderer.

Wow, that spun him in a new direction. Perhaps he could deduce more from his two theorems. If Charon's motive wasn't fear of exposure, because he hadn't killed anyone, then it was money for himself. Occam's razor. He wanted $50,000 because he needed the money. How stupid had he been to think Charon's motive was anything besides money?

Charon didn't kill Sarah and Tracy, because Tracy's death would be the same as Winch's death, which is the antithesis of what Charon desires. But he certainly knew something about Sarah's death. Something more than the Sheriff for sure. He had the photograph of Sarah taken after her disappearance. So Charon while not the murderer, might be able to identify the real murderer.

It'd certainly be possible that more than one person had a motive to keep the identity of Sarah's murderer a secret. Or not. He didn't think he had enough facts to make that decision. Whoever it was, it certainly was not Charon because Charon wanted the money. Charon would want Winch and Carla in town until he got paid.

So he still needed to I.D. Charon, but he'd have to start looking for other suspects with a motive to kill Sarah. Where to start? Back to the beginning, he supposed. Tomorrow he'd run down to Patch's store for another look and talk to Patch about his stepson, Luther Calderon, aka Snake.

But first he needed Tracy. He wasn't ready to let her go. He called her name, "Trace." Looked around the room. Could she see him? Could she feel the pain he was in? Did she miss him as much as he missed her? What he'd give to be able to hold her one more time.

He curled up on her bed, buried his face in the pillow. Inhaled her scent and wept.

THIRTY-FIVE

Winch raised his head from the pillow when the cell phone on the nightstand rang. He caught a whiff of Tracy's perfume. It took him a second to get his bearings. The clock read 6 pm. He'd slept for three hours. He realized that it was his fault that Tracy had been murdered. The boat blowing up was meant for him. Tracy, the accidental victim. If only he could tell her how sorry he was. Tracy was dead and he was to blame for it. Could anything be worse than to lose the one person on the earth you love, and it's your own damn fault?

The phone's display read "Woody." He dropped his feet on the floor.

"Hey, Bro," Woody said. "Sorry I missed you at the marina earlier. You okay?"

"I'm staying at Tracy's."

"You want company?"

"Brandy already offered, thanks."

"Valene called."

"The hooker? You think I'd take her over Brandy?"

"No, not that. She said that john of hers from Atlanta wants to see her tonight."

The John that was maybe following Carla Fox? The one legged man.

"You there, Bro?" Woody said.

"What time?"

"He's going to pick her up at 8."

"Tell her to call you when they land somewhere. Motel, hotel, whatever. Use the GPS tracker. Pull the fender skirt back on the front bumper and stick it in there. If it won't separate from the bumper then put it somewhere on the chassis." His GPS tracker, the size of a matchbox race car, fit inside a waterproof Pelican case, with a fifty-pound pull-magnet. The whole setup was as large as a point-and-shoot camera. The bundle together cost him a thousand dollars. "Please duct tape it too. I don't want to lose it."

"You think he's Charon?"

"No, but he plays into this somehow. I want to see where he goes after he finishes with Valene."

"Is this legal? The tracker I mean."

"Maybe. Maybe not. There's really no civil case law on it in Florida. As long as we don't get sued, it doesn't make any difference. If he finds it I doubt this guy would sue."

He'd no sooner ended his call with Woody when the phone rang again. Carla Fox.

"Why didn't you call me, Winch? You poor dear."

"It's been a trying day, Carla."

"I just heard about your boat." She hesitated for a moment. "And your ex. Where are you? Want me to come over?"

"Tomorrow," he said. "I talked to Trey Ellis last night.

"You found him? Great."

"Someone's trying to kill me," he said.

"It wasn't an accident."

"Murder."

"You sure?" she said.

"Just the wrong parties dead."

As soon as he punched off from Carla his cell rang again. Sheesh, couldn't people just leave him alone. The calling number read "Private." Whoever it was had blocked his caller ID.

"Winchester Young," he said.

"You can call me Charon," a male voice whispered.

His cell phone number wasn't secret. He gave it to clients all of the time. Still, how had Charon gotten it? "How about I call you butt-face?"

"I didn't blow up your boat."

"I know. You want the rest of the money."

Silence. Then, "Do you have it?"

"I have cash. Where's Sarah?"

"I'll be in contact tomorrow." Another pause. "Do you think she'll sign a book for me?" A hoarse chuckle.

"Jerk," Winch closed the phone.

He needed to brush his teeth. In Tracy's bathroom he looked under the sink and found a new toothbrush and used it.

In the medicine cabinet was a prescription bottle of Xanax. He took water from the refrigerator back to bed, downed two pills and turned off his cell phone.

In the last half minute before he drifted into what he knew would be a numbing Xanax-induced sleep, he wondered if he could get special permission for what he needed. From who? It'd have to be the Bishop and then probably a General Authority of the church. Someone in Salt Lake. An apostle maybe. To have your spouse forever requires a Celestial Sealing performed in a Mormon temple. He'd been married to Tracy twice. She'd chosen not to join the church and hence could not enter the temple and be sealed to him. A year after her death he could have her baptized by proxy. But since they were divorced, could he have her sealed to him? Certainly not without special permission. Even if he could convince his Bishop, most likely the General Authorities would tell him that he'd have to wait until the resurrection, when all of those things would be worked out.

This brought up another problem peculiar to Mormon theology. Mormon heaven is divided into three major places. Those who reject the gospel on this earth but accept it in the Spirit World are sent to the middle level of heaven. Sealing for time and all eternity only has efficacy for those in the highest level. Tracy had been taught the missionary discussions several times but never asked to be baptized. But her life had been cut short. Who knows if she might have accepted it the next time? Was she lost to him forever? He couldn't bear the thought.

Then his mind turned to Sarah Fox and Patch's gas station. Somehow she'd disappeared from there without being seen.

He had all of the facts. All of the evidence he was likely to get. He just had to sift it. Scope it from a different angle than the Sheriff had. Look for the motive, and he'd find the subject. Tomorrow, he knew, he'd figure out how Sarah Fox disappeared. There had to an explanation. He'd find it. He scribbled on a pad of paper next to the bed, *Sarah Fox. Exact time of disappearance??* And hoped his subconscious came up with the solution before he was out.

THIRTY-SIX

Winch rolled his legs off the side of the bed, the soles of his feet hitting the cool tile floor. The ceiling fan blades turned silent lazy circles. He looked to his cell phone for the time. Off. He powered it up. The clock on the nightstand read 8:45 am. He'd slept thirteen hours.

His phone chirped. Three new messages.

The first voice mail was the medical examiner's office. It'd be a couple of days before they could release Tracy's body. He looked around the bedroom. Tracy's photos on the wall. The one of the two of them she'd put up just the day before lay at an angle against one wall. He had an odd thought. Had the gold chain around her waist melted in the explosion? Or left an impression on her skin? What was that about? Was he going nuts to be thinking those things? He reached over and leaned the photo or the two of them upright.

He wondered if he had slept with her the other day, would she still be alive? Would one act like that put a bleep in the time-space continuum and change everything that followed? Maybe she would have gone to West Palm with him. Of if he'd just confided in her his planned interview with Trey Ellis she wouldn't have gone to the boat. Answering a phone call on the way out the door can change your timing at a traffic accident. Let the phone ring and you're in the middle of the accident. Pick up the call and you're a rubbernecker watching it as you drive by. So yeah, he probably could have prevented her death by changing their relationship. If he could have prevented it, was her death then his fault? One way or the other, he figured, he was to blame.

The second message was Woody. He'd attached the GPS to the john's car. It was parked down the street from the Casa Monica.

Winch needed to get a look at this fellow but thought the Georgia tag Woody just gave him was the same as he'd written on his palm. At least the GPS hadn't fallen off during the night. One thing going right for a change.

The third message from Gene Peterson at the Oasis marina. Was he interested in selling the salvage of the *Dos XX*? Winch didn't know. He had to see her one last time and see if there was anything to salvage. His book collection maybe? Not likely. But maybe his tools. A little water wouldn't hurt most of them.

* * * *

The Oasis was a small marina that catered to do-it-yourselfers. To his right, an acre of rag-baggers, stink-potters, and floating house trailers sat on the hardpan in cradles and braces. A forty-four-foot express cruiser, stove in on its port side and sunk at the Conch House marina during the last hurricane sat on stilts waiting for the insurance company to sell her for salvage. The oiled-dirt parking lot of the marina was as jammed as a Saturday night at the county fair. Parked amidst the boats were a half-dozen St. Johns County Sheriff cars, two Florida Department of Law Enforcement crime scene vans, and several unmarked Crown Vics. In the lot were two news vans with extended boom dish antennae.

None of the normal boatyard sounds of sixty-grit sandpaper on fiberglass or the whine of table saws cutting teak. Although all of the work in the yard had ceased and a crowd gathered near the boat ramp the pungent smell of resin and wet sawdust lingered. A faded blue travel lift, a machine that looked like a giant grasshopper with droopy suspenders used to lift twenty-ton boats out of the water sat, motor humming quietly. The center of attention was the flat barge with the lifeless remains of the *Dos XX* listing to one side. A dark ooze spread out of her and he wondered for a moment if she felt pain.

Yellow crime scene tape cordoned the area near the barge and a makeshift ramp ran from the slipway's concrete bulkhead to the barge. A uniformed deputy stood behind the tape, keeping onlookers at a distance. Vincent Renfro and some suit in a blue shirt and a tie were standing on the barge. Two FDLE crime scene techs in gray jump suits were poking through the hull. Everything above deck level had blown off. Her bare ribs exposed like canine teeth in a snarl. The hull from the waterline down was in surprisingly good shape.

Winch stood with the rest of the crowd and watched. He felt as if he were standing in on the autopsy of a loved one. She lay there, fully exposed, while strangers poked and cut and examined her. After a while the crowd thinned and the whir of power tools, grinders, and saws started up. Renfro shot him a glance and then turned his back. No matter. He would have the last laugh because he had Renfro's DNA sample.

Renfro stepped off the barge and approached. "What do you think we're going to find, dummy? We're taking bets. Incrimination or exoneration?"

"You wouldn't recognize an innocent man if the angel Gabriel came down and pointed him out to you."

Renfro put his hands on his hips. "I know what they look like. Our jail is full of innocent men. Just ask them."

Renfro pushed one side of his nostril with his thumb and blew a wad of yellow and milky mucus to the ground. "You're not innocent, Young. You're guilty of something. I can feel it. I just don't know what, yet. I'm going to stay on you like chiggers on a dog's butt."

Winch had been married and divorced twice, so yeah, he was guilty of being a slow learner, maybe. But not murder. "How long are they going to be? I'd like to salvage my personal gear."

"You'll just have to wait your turn buddy. Oh, here." He handed him some sheets of paper. "Nobody messes with my crime scenes until I'm finished."

The heading on the three pages read: "Search Warrant-*Dos XX*. He flipped to the last page; it was signed by Judge Lance Faircloth. He'd appeared in Faircloth's courtroom a dozen times to testify in various hearings. The judge a competent jurist who favored father's rights. Now that the judge had issued a search warrant on his boat, would that skew the judge's opinion the next time he testified? He folded the papers and put them in his back pocket.

Renfro turned back to Winch. “Oh, is that your Jeep over there?”

“What, you want to impound it too?”

Renfro handed him another sheet of paper. “Search Warrant for 2001 Jeep Grand Cherokee.”

Winch read through it. The warrant listed his Jeep’s VIN and gave the Sheriff’s deputies the right to search for tools, explosive materials or any other material that might be used in the making of a bomb or improvised explosive device.

“My Jeep? You think it’s guilty of something?”

Renfro held out his hand. “Keys?”

He fished them out of his pocket. “Happy hunting.”

Renfro examined the key ring, held up a plastic fob on the ring the size of the car’s remote. “What’s this?”

“I misplace my keys sometimes. I have a little transmitter that makes them beep so I can find them.”

“Oh great,” Renfro shook his head. “A PI trying to find a body missing twenty-five years and can’t even find his own car keys.”

Another detective, two uniforms, and a crime scene tech took the keys and went to the Jeep.

The uniformed deputy at the crime scene tape eyed him closely. “That your boat?”

Winch nodded.

“Shame. What’s she worth?”

“Before, maybe eighty thou. Now I’ll be in the red about ten K for cleanup and disposal. No insurance either.”

The deputy shook his head. “Awful careless blowing your boat and not having it insured.”

“Right. Just plain stupid.”

After about an hour Renfro and the man in the suit walked to where he stood. It looked like the crime scene techs were wrapping up.

“I’ve got to advise you of your rights, Young,” Renfro said.

“I wasn’t even in town when the *Dos Equis* blew. You’re wasting your breath.”

“Convenient alibi, isn’t it?”

“Convenient for me. Otherwise I’d be dead.”

Renfro recited the standard Miranda warning. The suit, about forty-five, compact and thick-bodied with black hair going gray at the temples, extended his hand to Winch. "I'm Special Agent Pernell. ATF."

Winch shook his hand. "ATF? How come?"

"Any time a bomb goes it could be our jurisdiction," Pernell said.

"Am I being arrested?"

Pernell shook his head. "Vincent's just playing by the book. You know how it goes."

"Not really. I think Deputy Renfro writes his own playbook."

"You think you're clever, Young. We'll see," Renfro said.

The crime scene crew carried his toolbox from the boat and also his smaller toolbox from the Jeep. Gave him back his car keys. "What are they taking?"

"None of your damn business," Renfro said.

"That's my stuff."

"Not anymore. It's evidence and we're seizing it."

They loaded his tools into the back of the crime scene van. "I want a receipt for everything you're taking off the boat."

"Blow me," Renfro said.

"You're spending too much time with your prisoners," Winch said. He turned to Pernell. "You know the law. If you're taking evidence pursuant to a search warrant then you have to give me a list of what you've taken."

Pernell nodded to Renfro. "Vinnie, show him what they found."

Renfro made a face.

"He's right," Pernell said. "You've got to give him a list. Why not let him see it now. Maybe he can explain it."

"What the hell." Renfro called to the FDLE techs. "Bring that pipe over here, will you?"

In a minute one of the techs walked over, smelling like bilge, his jumpsuit black with sludge. In a plastic bag he had two lengths of copper tubing. "Your propane line," he said. "See here? It'd been snipped. Then here," he pointed to one end. "The snippers probably compressed the line. See? Tool marks where someone used a pair of pliers, maybe vise-grips, to widen it to full open." He rotated the copper tubing. The grip marks still shiny and fresh looking.

Winch reached for the pipe, to examine it more closely but the tech drew back. "Uh uh. It's ours now."

Tools like wire cutters and hammers left their own unique marks, much like shoe and tire prints. "If someone used my tools to do that, doesn't mean it was me."

"We'll just have to figure that out. Now won't we?" Renfro grinned. "Give him the list."

He read the list of evidential items seized from his boat and Jeep.

One length of copper tubing approximately 20 inches.

Two plastic toolboxes with assorted tools.

Crap. He hated to lose his tools. "That's it? Winch looked up at the tech. "You didn't find any igniter? No point of ignition?"

"The only reason we found this was because it was below the water line and protected by the stove."

"What about the propane sniffer in the bilge? Did you find it? Someone must have cut the leads to it. It should have been screaming like a rusted up bearing."

"We found what we think are pieces of it. The wiring was all burned."

Well didn't this just suck?

* * * *

Winch looked at the dust swirling in the air left by the departing FDLE crime scene van in a convoy with the Sheriff's cars. The lone uniformed deputy rolling the yellow tape into a large wad.

The *Dos XX*, one side blown out, lay lifeless and quiet. On the barge Winch stood in the thick grainy fluid. From a distance the muck looked like her lifeblood, but close up it was just gray bottom silt mixed with oil. It smelled rotten.

Another motorboat purred down the San Sebastian River, the occupants threw a friendly wave, then their hands fell to their sides and they stared reverently at the corpse, probably thinking it was hurricane damage. He reflected on the pleasure the *Dos XX* brought into his life. Sitting on the aft deck in the early evening with Tracy. If the wind died they'd escape the mosquitoes, slip inside, the air conditioner humming at full tilt and put the queen-sized bunk in the master stateroom to good use.

He grabbed a short stepladder and leaned it against her side. Climbed up and peered into her belly. The crime scene techs had drained the marina water from her. It took him a second to recognize her. The teak and holly cabin floorboards splintered and split. Slick with muck. All of his clothes, like car wash rags, were piled in one corner. His bookshelf of prized books had been beheaded, just as neatly as if someone had taken a Sawzall to it. The top half probably blew upward with the deck. The books scattered and charred. Soaked pages blown everywhere throughout the boat. He stooped and picked up a hardback. *Booked to Die*. Worthless now. Another, *Nobody Runs Forever* signed by Richard Stark, pen name for Donald Westlake. Westlake died in 2009. He might find another copy, but he'd never be able to get it signed. Tears gathered in the corner of his eyes. For his books. For his boat. Mostly for his loss of Tracy. He tossed the sullied copy of Westlake's book into the corner with his ruined clothes and climbed out. He stroked her side and ran his palm along the stainless steel drive shaft. Flicked at a stubborn barnacle with his fingernail.

This had been his and Tracy's boat. She'd stripped the teak and mahogany. Done a lot of the bright work. He wondered if she could see him now from the Spirit World and if she understood how his loss of the boat magnified his distress over her death.

Mormons believe they have a better understanding of the mechanics of the resurrection than most Christians because they don't rely solely on the Bible for understanding. They have modern day prophets who receive revelation and can expand on the Bible's teachings. And they also have other scriptures. Because of this, they know that all living creatures, both animals and humans are endowed with spirits and as such they all will resurrect. The Good, the Bad, and the Ugly. Animals will have fulfilled the nature of their creation and will be resurrected to the highest degree of heavendom. A righteous person can also inherit the highest degree and have his animals and pets, with him. Boats have their own personalities, and the *Dos XX* was cantankerous as any. But he knew, as much as he loved her, she would never float again. Neither in this life, nor in the life to come.

"The engine any good?" It was Gene Peterson, the marina owner.

He shook his head. "But the propane stove is practically brand new.

"I'll give you five hundred for the salvage and haul her to the dump when we're finished. You better take it. It's the best offer you'll get."

He felt it'd be more fitting to have the barge she lay on towed out to the warm clear waters of the Gulf Stream and let her slip overboard into a final deepwater rest, instead of buried in a smelly, rat infested landfill. She was a boat after all, not a land-based rusting hulk of iron on wheels "Twenty-five hundred."

"Fifteen and that's my final offer. I'm taking it in the shorts at that."

Peterson was shrewd. He wouldn't offer anything unless he could at least triple his profit. For starters Winch knew Peterson would salvage the three bladed bronze prop, six hundred dollars. "Give me a minute to think it over," Winch said.

Woody Copeland and Brandy stood next to his Jeep. They both wore jeans, but Brandy looked better in hers. She sported a loose fitting burgundy Everlast weight-training T-shirt with short sleeves and a ragged bottom edge that came to just below her ribs, leaving visible her lower stomach, tanned and bare.

"Thought maybe you'd need some moral support, Bro," Woody said.

"Gosh, she looks terrible," Brandy stared at the hull of the *Dos XX*. "I'm so sorry, Winch." She hugged him. Squeezed him tight. She smelled of fresh soap and a hint of lime.

"And Tracy," she said. "I don't know what to say."

Woody shifted his feet. "Anything we can do?"

Winch looked at Gene Peterson who stood in the marina office doorway.

Winch stepped over. Peterson handed him a check for fifteen hundred dollars, a bill of sale, and a pen. He felt like a cowboy who just put a 30-30 slug into his lame horse. Roy Rogers might have Trigger in the next life. He might have Tracy. But he'd never see the *Dos XX* again.

THIRTY-SEVEN

A blue Porsche 911 Carrera 4 slid into a parking spot outside of the fence. About $90,000 worth of zero to sixty in 4.8 seconds of car. Carla Fox stepped out.

After the police vehicles left, the screech of power saws ripping through lumber and electric sanders whisking fiberglass returned to the Oasis Boat Yard and Marina.

Carla Fox looked as sleek and molded as the Porsche Carrera she stepped out of wearing white linen slacks and a sleeveless teal blouse that shimmered like a heat wave off the engine cowling. Winch wondered how she knew where he'd be.

"She called me." Brandy looked at Winch and shrugged. "I told her the marina."

Winch rubbed his chin. "How'd she get your number?"

"Four-one-one?"

He nodded. Sometimes even the most seasoned investigators overlooked the obvious. He walked toward Carla who stood by her car. Over his shoulder he said to Woody, "Might be better not to mention anything to Carla about the GPS until we know more." He'd learned not to tell clients about promising leads until they'd played out.

As Winch approached, Carla opened her arms and rushed him. Kissed him full on the lips. He felt her open her mouth.

He pushed her back, one hand on each of her shoulders. "Not today, Carla. With Tracy," he waved his arm at the *Dos XX*, Peterson already pulling the bronze props, "and all of this." He shook his head. Over Carla's shoulder he saw Brandy roll her eyes and give Woody a look.

"Of course," she said. "I was so concerned about you." She put her arm around his waist. "Is there anything I can do?"

"I've taken care of disposing of the boat. I have to deal with the arrangements, you know, Tracy and the funeral, but they haven't released her body."

He needed to put his mind elsewhere. Solve Sarah's disappearance and he'd find Tracy's murderer too. By damn he'd do it. Better than sitting around wallowing in grief.

"Let's go to my office," he said. "Brandy, I want to go over that spreadsheet you made from the invoices and IOUs from Patch's gas station."

Carla flipped him the keys to the Porsche. "You drive."

It wasn't everyday he had the opportunity to drive a Porsche with a top speed of 175 mph. Why not? He tossed his keys to Woody. "Bring it to the office for me, please?"

He spun the Porsche's wheels on the gravel lot. "Great car. Not much good for surveillance though."

At the office, Carla, Brandy, and Woody gathered around the computer. He brought up Brandy's spreadsheet. "Give us a breakdown, Brandy, on what we've got here."

"What are we looking for Bro?" Woody said.

"Scroll down to the bottom," she said. "Remember, these recipts are from twenty-five years ago so they weren't all that easy to read. Sixty-four transactions. Forty-two cash. No names on those tickets. Twenty-one credit card receipts. Stapled to each transaction is a cash register receipt with time and date. And one IOU, eight dollars and change, with Patricia Patch's name at four-forty-seven pm. "

Patricia Patch. Old man Patch's daughter he supposed. His daughter put gas in her car two hours after Sarah's disappearance. He hadn't realized she'd been around the station that day. He needed to interview her. Maybe she'd been there earlier.

"I don't see where this is of any help," Carla said.

"Maybe not," he said. "Let's look for what's missing?"

They shrugged their shoulders and gave him blank looks. "Patch told me he let his kids and their friends buy gas at a discount on an IOU and then work it off."

"Like Patricia there," Brandy said.

"If you were in college, like Patch's step-son Snake, and were driving home from out of state and knew you could get free gas when you arrived, would you fill up before getting home?"

"Snake?" Carla had a pad of paper and a pen in her hand. Making notes.

"Coast in on the fumes," Woody said.

"So where is the IOU from Snake?" Winch said.

"Who's Snake?" Carla's brow furrowed.

He related how they'd tracked down Trey Ellis and his conversation with him. How he learned of Snake and his sharpened three-iron.

Carla looked at Winch. "Do you have Trey's address?"

"Forty-two fourteen, a hundred and seventh avenue, West Palm Beach." Carla wrote in a note pad. "It'll all be in my report."

Her pen stopped. "Maybe Snake, whoever he is, filled up the next day," she said.

"This was spring break. You think he sat home all night?" Winch said.

"No freaking way," Brandy said.

"Right, so why isn't there an IOU from Snake?" He looked at his team.

"Patch omitted it intentionally," Woody said.

"And. . . ." Winch waved him on with his hand.

"Because the time on the receipt would show that Snake actually arrived home before Sarah disappeared and not after."

"But you can't take that to court," Carla said. "That's just supposition and theory."

"Right, but I can take it to Patch and throw it in his lap."

Carla stood, waved her cell phone and stepped outside shutting the door.

"Who'd care if Snake arrived before or after Sarah?" Brandy said. "Why lie?"

"The only reason to lie," Winch said, "is if you have something to hide."

* * * *

Winch idled the Porsche out of the parking lot and weaved around the horse drawn sightseeing carriages plodding their way past the old fort. Most of the horses wore blinders and they all wore diaper bags, keeping the old city's streets clean.

If he sold his book, could he afford a Porsche? Actually, he'd rather have an Aston Martin, but that'd be three times the price of this car. Would he really spend a quarter of a million dollars for a car? Nah. For a boat? In a nanosecond. But he could never replace Tracy.

"Tell me about Snake," Carla said

He told her about his trip, his conversation with Trey who at first he couldn't find because his real name was Ellsworth Van Ellis III and how he found him by searching the Pizza database with last name and DOB, and the suffix III.

"And the other two boys?" She laid her hand on his forearm until he had to shift gears.

"Deceased. One of them here in St. Augustine. The other in Kansas."

"So Sarah knew Snake, too? You think he was involved in her disappearance?"

He nodded. "He not only knew her, he was roommates with Sarah's boyfriend, Andrew." Why hadn't the cops checked his alibi and found out when he left Athens?

Carla blanched. "Why would someone would want to kill her?"

It goes back to motive. Figure out the motive, and he'd find the killer. He didn't see any of the boys having a motive to kill Sarah. They wanted her around for a good time. Something else was at play here. Something he'd missed.

"It couldn't have been the boys." He pushed the accelerator full to the floor. Even though they were already going fifty the sudden acceleration snapped his head back. "They were at the gas station. And they called the police. Why would they do that if they were guilty?"

"I know those three had something to do with it," Carla said. "They must have. They brought her down here."

"Right, but not to kill her." He braked, cut the wheel, swerving the Porsche to a stop in front of the porch at Patch's gas station. "Spring break—party time."

The rocking chairs were empty but Patch's green Willis pickup was parked alongside the building.

In the store, Carla walked around the small interior, dragging her fingertips over the counter, then rubbing them on her slacks. Patch must have heard them and came out from the back room. "Oh great, a D-dock-Dick and a Calamity Jane, too."

Patch looked Carla up and down and glanced out the window at the Porsche. "What's a classy little hustle like you," he cocked his head toward Winch "doing with the likes of this scalawag?"

"You remember the girl that disappeared?"

"I may be old, but I'm not stupid." Patch moved over behind the register. "It was just four days ago that you were here trying to sniff her out of my john." He looked at Carla. "Did you know he was queer for johns?"

"This is Carla Fox, Sarah Fox's sister."

"All growed up, huh?" Patch's eyes lingered on her. "Older or younger?"

"Nice to meet you too, Mr. Patch. Younger."

Patch reached behind him, grabbed the key to ladies room and tossed it to Winch. "That's what you come for ain't it?"

"I have a few more questions, too. But, yes, thanks. We'll be right back."

He and Carla walked around the side of the building. She shielded her eyes from the sun with one hand. "Why didn't you ask him about Snake and the IOU.

"I wanted to take another look at the restroom first."

"We've only two days left. Any ideas you have better move this along."

He knew how many days before the deadline. But crap, his wife—ex-wife had been murdered yesterday. And here he was poking through restrooms again instead of making arrangements for her funeral.

Carla stood in front of the restrooms. Made a face at the two doors.

"Alligator heads," he said.

"I know what they are. But how are you suppose to know which one is the men's room and which the ladies?"

"Bull gator is a male."

"Right, I'm from Georgia. We have alligators too. But both males and females have tails. I'm surprised the old fart didn't write 'split-tail' on the one."

He put the key in the "Gator Tail" door and opened it. Carla stepped inside.

While he waited for her, he blanked his mind, heard a few cars whistling down the asphalt of US 1. A wasp-like mud dauber flew silently around a clump of mud in the corner of the window frame. If Carla wasn't sure which was the men's room. . . ?

He took the key to the women's room and tried it at the men's room. It opened. The inside was identical to the women's except the vanity was on the outside wall under a blacked out window. He unlocked the window and heaved upward. Locked in by years of paint. Wouldn't budge.

The sound of a single pair of clapping hands made him turn. Patch lowered his hands to his sides.

"You're the first," Patch said.

Winch stepped into the sunlight. "The first?"

"The first to figure out those two doors are keyed the same. Saves me a lot of aggravation when someone locks a key inside the john. Or runs off with it."

"Detective Sharp? Did you tell him?"

"Wouldn't had made no difference. She went in the ladies room."

He eyed one door and then the other. "How do you know?"

The old man scratched his chin. "She was a girl. He pointed to the "Gator Tail" door. "Wouldn't have no business going to the men's room."

In his mind's eye he could see the face of spunky Sarah Fox from the photograph. The crooked grin. The "laid-back have-a-good-time girl" going into the men's room. By mistake or on purpose, made no difference. Maybe the ladies room was occupied. Maybe someone . . . maybe Snake, told her to use the men's room. Escaping. Shoving the window up and climbing out the back. Disappearing into the brush. Meeting with Snake because she didn't want to spend spring break with the three boys she was with. But then what happened to her?

Carla had slipped silently out of the ladies room. "You son of a bitch. You knew all the time. What did you and your snake-head Putt-Putt-playing weirdo son do to her?"

"It's time you left," Patch said.

"I should kill you," Carla said. "Where's your gun, Winch?"

"He's dead in six months, Carla."

She raised her eyebrows.

"Liver cancer," Winch said.

"Not soon enough," she said.

Carla's cell phone rang. After she answered she said nothing except ending the call with, "Thank you very much." She turned to him. Whispered in his ear. "The hotel. There's an envelope for me. Return address reads 'Charon.'"

THIRTY-EIGHT

Winch headed the Porsche toward the Casa Monica and Charon's envelope. He pushed the car well past the speed limit on US 1. He wanted to redline the tach, but traffic was too heavy. A hundred and seventy-five might not be a good idea.

They crossed Moltire Creek, the tide higher than usual, pushed in from ocean swells by tropical storm Florence southeast of Florida. He felt a slight change in the air. Heavier. Carla turned on the radio. The weather report said storm watches were likely to be posted later for the northeast coast of Florida, Daytona to Jacksonville.

Carla grimaced. "You should have told me he called you last night."

He shrugged. "Wouldn't have made any difference."

"Today and tomorrow." Carla pulled down the visor and checked her face in the mirror. "That's all we have left."

"You haven't gotten much for the ten thousand you gave him. He knows the deadline. He's desperate."

"How can you be so confident?"

He didn't want to tell her what he thought. That Charon didn't know where Sarah's body was and this was just a scam to get fifty K from Carla. He didn't tell her that because she wouldn't want to hear it. "When it comes to human nature, I'm more jaundiced than you are."

"I thought you were sort of innocent."

"I may have clean hands and a pure heart." He raised one palm off the steering wheel. "But I'm not naïve." He still wondered what

Carla's agenda was. Was she really here just to throw money at Charon and reclaim her sister's body. He didn't think so but he hadn't figured it out yet.

* * * *

They picked up the letter and the $40,000 from the hotel safe. The typed note read:

Three pm. Prepare for Hades. Bring the coin. Proof will be provided before you transit.

Winch looked at his watch: 1:45

Brandy and Woody were waiting for them at the office. Winch took Woody aside, "Where's the GPS?"

Woody shook his head. "It's headed south."

"How far south?"

Woody looked at his watch. "Right about now he's passing through Daytona."

He needed the GPS tracker, and it was on that stupid John's car going who knew where. Winch looked around the office. He went to an equipment cabinet and rummaged through a box of electronics.

"Here," he said to Brandy, and tossed her a flat object about the size of a guitar pick. It had a flexible wire antenna as long as his middle finger. He pulled a silver box, the size of half a loaf of bread out of the cabinet. The box had dual antennae and multiple dials, knobs, and meters.

"A transmitter. Originally developed to track elk in Canada," he said. "Carla, give Brandy some of those hundred dollar bills." The bills were rubber banded into stacks of $10,000.

"Cut Ben Franklin's face out of one of the hundreds and glue it onto the transmitter. Then glue that onto another hundred. Stick it in the middle of a stack. It should pass the riffle test."

Woody was playing with the receiver box. "How does it work?"

"Turn it on. You'll hear a beep. The closer the receiver is to the transmitter the faster the beep becomes. It's good for short distances on the ground. We have to stay close."

Brandy was busy at the worktable with an Exacto knife and a ruler.

"You don't think he'll be looking for a tracking device," Carla said.

"He will," Winch said. "So we'll give him one. A decoy." Winch turned to Brandy. "Give me your cell phone."

She gave him a look. "Am I going to get it back?"

"Probably not. We'll buy you a new one later." Thinking about his encounter at Renfro's house he said, "Something that takes video."

"No," she said.

"You'll be riding with Carla. We'll buy you an I-Phone later."

"Promise?"

"Yes, I promise. Now?"

She gave him her phone and he tossed it to Woody. "I'll tell him to call me on that phone." "You can track that phone?" Carla said.

"No," Winch said. "But Charon doesn't know that."

Woody was smiling. "Pretty clever for a white man."

"I don't get it," Carla said.

"Charon knows we're not stupid—"

"Gives you more credit than you deserve," Brandy said.

"So he'll figure we're tracking the money somehow. Hopefully he'll think we're using the cell as a tracking device, toss it, and not look further."

"Are we going to give him all of the forty thousand now?" Carla said.

"It's your money. Your call," Winch said. "But I'd suggest we hold back twenty until we either have a face-to-face." He paused, thought about it. "Or a body."

"Money is not the issue," Carla said. "Sarah is."

"You give him the entire 40 K, the next time you hear from him will be a post card from Tobago."

"You're tracking the money. What could go wrong?"

"We could lose him. And your money."

"You told me surveillance is your specialty."

He didn't want to be responsible for losing $50,000 of a client's money. That's half a year's wages for him. "He could have us throw it off a bridge and get away in a boat. Any number of things could go bad."

Carla huffed. "Fine. Do it your way, but I'd rather lose the whole fifty and know I tried, than to have spent thirty and see Sarah slip away." She held up one finger. "Thirty plus the twenty-five I gave you."

Offer to return the retainer? Walk away from the case? With his boat gone. Funeral expenses for Tracy. He needed every penny. But in that moment, on the boat, when he took the case, he'd promised Sarah, wherever she was, in the Spirit World with Uncle Benjamin—he'd promised her he'd find her and set things right. Retainer or not, he'd follow through with the best skills he had.

"My case," he said. "We'll do it my way. If it doesn't work out—sue me."

Carla shook her head. "Your show."

"This is how we'll do it." He went on to explain that he assumed the phone call would come with another money drop and Charon would resist showing himself. He passed out walkie-talkies to Brandy and Woody. They'd each be in separate cars. Brandy would ride with Carla and operate the receiver. Woody would be in his truck. Winch in his Jeep. Communication by handi-talkie was quicker than cell phones, and the whole team could hear each transmission.

The money was packaged in two bundles. One with the transmitter. One without. Each a bundle of hundreds, $20,000 to a bundle. He dropped one bundle on a postage scale. Slightly less than half of a pound.

* * * *

The digital clock on Winch's desk read 2:59 pm. All four pair of eyes watched it roll over to three pm. Winch looked at his cell phone. Three pm.

The time on his cell phone read 3:02 pm when it rang. The phone face lit, and Winch let it ring.

"Answer the damn thing," Carla said.

"I will," he said. It rang a third time. He answered. Caller ID said Private. "You're late."

"Good thing it didn't go to voice mail," the hoarse whisper said. "I wouldn't have called back."

This was a lie. Charon wanted his money but there was nothing to be gained at this time by throwing that in Charon's face. "How'd you get my number?"

"Do you have the money?"

"Of course."

"The cops have a warrant for you. Don't let them pick you up until I have my money."

Winch was stunned. He let the hand with the phone drop to his lap. It could only be one thing. Renfro thought he'd blown up the *Dos XX* to murder Tracy.

"What?" Carla, Woody, and Brandy all said at exactly the same time. He put the phone to his ear.

"I hear voices. Who's there?"

"Carla. A couple of my people." He held his finger to his lips. "How do you want to do this?"

"I know you're wondering," Charon said. "I have a pipeline into the Sheriff's office."

Winch knew he didn't kill Tracy and he could prove it. Or could he? How do you prove a negative? He was out of town but he could have set the *Dos XX* to blow when he left. Tracy would have smelled the propane and not cut the lights on. He could make that argument, but that's all it was. Not proof. He'd have to deal with the Sherriff's Office later. Right now Charon was top on his list. But he couldn't catch Charon from behind bars.

"Just you, Winchester Young. Nobody else. If I see you with anybody, or you play any tricks then the deal is off."

"Where is she?"

"The fourth floor of Kenan Hall," Charon said. "Flagler College. In the middle of the hallway between rooms 408 and 410 you'll find a panel in the wall that slides to the right. Open it. Reach inside to your left, and you'll find proof of what I have. Follow the instructions there. You have thirty minutes from now, or it'll be gone. And so will she. The clock is running."

He stared at the phone. Disconnected. They all turned to him expectantly. "The Sheriff has a warrant for my arrest. Tracy's murder."

"I don't believe it," Woody said.

"Believe it," Winch said. He knew he didn't kill Tracey. He'd never do anything to have brought bodily harm to her. He loved her still. Was going to marry her again for the third time. Why on earth would they think he set the boat to blowup when she boarded. He didn't even know she was coming to the marina. The love of his life murdered on his boat. Murdered by his boat. He loved the Dos XX too. He'd pampered that boat. Worked on it to restore her to pristine condition. He'd never harm the boat or his love, Tracey. Anybody that knew him or the boat would know that. Incredible that the Sheriff's Office could think that. That darn Renfro stood behind this warrant for his arrest.

Carla gave him a look he couldn't decipher.

THIRTY-NINE

Winch would have preferred to pick the drop location himself, but he was dancing to Charon's music. Trapping Charon at Flagler College with its numerous pathways, exits and entrances would be like trying to catch a river eel barehanded. Even finding a freaking parking place by the school would be impossible. And he knew he'd have to outmaneuver campus security; he hardly looked like a student.

Flagler College was originally built as the Hotel Ponce De Leon by railroad magnate Henry Flagler in 1856. It was turned into the school in the 1960s. The college's main entrance, with its Spanish renaissance architecture, terracotta tile, and palm tree sized sundial sits directly across the street from the Casa Monica.

The main building's upper floors function as the girls' dormitory. At least he didn't have to sneak in there. Kenan Hall was north of Main and separated from it by the Moorish looking dome of the cafeteria/student lounge.

One problem would be Flagler's architects. When Flagler built the hotel, his guests were paying today's equivalent of $3,000 a night for a room. With those high rates, Flagler believed the guest should see the hotel staff only when necessary. The hotel architects honeycombed the building with secret passageways and suspended circular staircases, allowing the service people, chambermaids, and charwomen to perform their duties, slip between floors and transit buildings, all while out of view of the paying guests.

"We'll take my car," Carla had said before they'd left the office.

"Carla," Winch said, "your Porsche is too ostentatious for a surveillance vehicle. Drive Brandy's Maxima."

"The Porsche is a good car for surveillance. Quick, maneuverable—"

"And about as discreet as a boil on your forehead," Woody said.

Winch pointed to Carla, "You drive and Brandy will run the elk receiver." Brandy gave him a quizzical look. "It's not hard, look." He gave her a quick rundown on the equipment. "Practice on it as you follow me and the money to the college."

"Woody, you be the chase vehicle. Your truck will blend anywhere."

"Except Ponte Vedra," Woody said.

Ponte Vedra was full of beachfront homes and gated residential areas. Community gates posed problems for private investigators. Winch had former clients in most of the gated areas that would put him on the visitor's list allowing him access for several weeks at a time. If he needed to enter a development and had no satisfied clients who lived there, he'd use a magnetic sign with the Comcast cable name and logo. Comcast uses subcontractors for disconnects. Most of them put magnetic signs on their vehicles when they're on the job. "If he goes through a gate, we'll figure it out when we get there," he said.

They headed out of the office.

Fighting the clock now. Eight minutes to the drop deadline, Winch looked left, right, turned around, circled the plaza twice. No parking spots near Flagler. St. Augustine visitor season was in full bloom. Tourists in shorts with sunburned legs clogged the streets and sidewalks, thick as marijuana smoke at a Jimmy Buffet concert.

The only open parking spaces within two blocks of Kenan Hall were spaces on the campus lot reserved for Security and professors. He'd be inside only for a minute or two. The chances of being towed were remote. So Winch took a reserved spot and sprang from the Jeep.

Winch entered Kenan Hall. Elevator or stairs? To his right he saw a set of stairs and bounded up. They ended on the fourth floor. Winded, he checked his watch. Four minutes to spare. He looked both directions. Various opaque glass fronted doors probably opened to classrooms. Charon had not chosen this place by accident. Why here?

Twenty yards to his right he found room 408. He could see the room number of 410 a bit farther. Room 409, across the hall. Its windows would face the street.

Just as Charon had said, there was a wooden panel in the middle of the wall, the size of a square garbage can. He laid his hands flat on it and pushed sideways. Nothing. He pushed the other direction and it slid, not easily, on a metal track. He peered in. Dark. This had been a laundry chute when the building was a hotel. He looked around. Nobody in the hall.

On his walkie-talkie he said, "I'm on the fourth floor and found the panel. It's an old linen chute. Watch for somebody running out of the building on the first floor." Two "ten-fours" responded.

He slid his hand around the inside of the chute and found an envelope duct taped to the wall. A note and a Georgia driver's license with Sarah's name and photo. Expiration date, twenty-two years ago. The note read, "I'm watching you. When the bell rings, drop the money. I'll call with the location where you can find Sarah."

He looked up and down the hall. Nobody was watching him and he couldn't be seen from any outside window. He checked the time. 3:30. A bell rang and doors opened. Students clambered out of their rooms and into the hall, some giving him looks, and others paying him no heed.

He dropped the box down the chute, hearing it bounce once against a side wall before it hit bottom with a resounding thump, hoping it didn't burst open and scatter $20,000 in hundred dollar bills all over the floor down there. He headed for the stairs. Pushing students aside, running now. Kids yelling at him to "watch it." Down the stairs as fast as he could.

Breathless he got on the radio. "Classes are changing. He's got to be coming out. Watch for the box." But he knew trying to catch Charon, here in the school was fruitless. Too many students clogged the halls. On the first floor he stopped a girl, a book pack slung over one shoulder, a safety pin in her eyebrow and blond hair streaked with pink.

"Is there a basement?" he said.

She shrugged, then motioned with her chin to a door and said, "There's an old wine cellar over there."

He ran the ten steps to the door. Padlocked. The old linen chute must empty out into one of Flagler's hidden service hallways between the walls. Surely there was an exterior entrance. He started opening doors on the interior wall. Classrooms, a custodial closet—stringy mops hanging like rag dolls, and steel buckets on rollers. Other doors, more classrooms, doors labeled restrooms. And that was it.

The restrooms? Inside the men's room then. Nope, no doors other than stalls. The women's room? He'd probably get arrested. He flung open the ladies' restroom door. A girl coming out of a stall yelled "Hey" and retreated back in. The bolt slammed shut. His eyes flashed across the mirrors. Tampon vending machine. "Get out of here," came the wail from behind the stall door.

A redhead, hair straight to mid-back, green cargo-shorts and sandals, a book bag slung over one arm, walked in. "The boy's broken?" she said. There behind the exterior door, before the first mirror was a door. He tried the handle. It turned but didn't open. Above the handle there was a latch to a deadbolt. He turned the latch. The redhead checked her makeup in the mirror, and eyed him from aside. "It doesn't go anywhere," she said. "It's just an old hallway.

He put one foot on the door jam and leaned backwards, griping the knob with both hands, engaging the quads on his leg as he pulled. The door moaned and popped open, causing him to fall backwards on his butt.

"What's he doing out there?" the girl in the stall said peeking out the door.

He picked himself up and entered the darkness. It smelled heavy with dust. He imagined black mildew on the walls, though he couldn't see squat. About the length of the girl's restroom, the hallway Tee'd, and went right and left. He closed his eyes to let his pupils dilate. Open, he could see better in the dim light. He ran down the hallway until he came to the money box on the floor. Empty, of course. The cell phone lay in pieces next to it.

He doubted his walkie-talkie would penetrate the concrete and coquina walls. He sprinted down the tunnel-like hall passing three doors on his right. Charon could have gone through any of those. But a sliver of light played across the wall at the end. The door there barely ajar. Just as he reached for the knob, the door opened and slammed against the wall. He was blinded by daylight.

"Get your hands up and face the wall," a male voice said.

A different voice said, "We got you, you pervert."

From the other direction he heard footsteps echoing in the dark. Two lights making their way toward him.

FORTY

Winch stared at the two security guards blocking his escape out the tunnel door. Their faces, backlit by the tropical Florida sun, were impossible to see. Could he take them and make his run? He cast a glance at the two behind, making their way towards him in the tunnel. They stopped their advance. Unsure perhaps?

He might talk his way past campus security. But before they'd let him go they'd certainly run his name with the Sheriff's office. Then they'd see the murder warrant on him and he'd never get free. These guys would be heroes.

What choice did he have? The two in front held flashlights, not guns. On their hips, tasers hung in black holsters. He hoped the ones behind were similarly armed.

"Come on," one said. "Don't make this hard on yourself. There're four of us."

He couldn't stand here and let Charon get away with the $20,000 and nothing more than Sarah's twenty-five year old driver's license to show for it. He twisted on his heel and bolted back down the way he'd come. The two in the hallway squatted, hands reaching for their sides. No time to see if the others followed. Midway between the two sets of men was a door he'd passed earlier. He said a silent prayer. Please let it open.

He twisted the knob. Shoved, pumped by the fear of being tasered by yahoo security guards. The door flew open to a classroom. A professor stood in front of a chalkboard, a small clump of students standing next to him involved in some sort of discussion.

They all stared at him when he slammed the door and threw the deadbolt.

“Don’t open this door,” he huffed. “There are some crazy people out there. If they try to get in, call security.” He hustled out of the room and tore down the hallway toward the parking lot.

He had only a few minutes and security would lock down the campus. The St. Augustine police department perched on the corner of King and Malaga streets, across from the Sebastian Winery. Two blocks or maybe three minutes away. He ran to the lot where he’d parked the Jeep. What? Oh no. . . . A tow truck had hooked the Jeep and was maneuvering it out of its parking spot. Sheesh. Could he have any worse luck?

His walkie-talkie in his hip pocket was squawking but he didn’t have time. The other $20,000 was still in the Jeep. As much as he wanted to believe in mankind’s decency, that kind of money would be a one big temptation to a tow truck driver making a $100 popping cars.

FORTY-ONE

The tow truck looked like a scorpion with its rear stinger snagged in a prey. It jockeyed back and forth, extracting the Jeep from its parking slot.

Winch sprinted to the driver's side window. The man behind the wheel, a St. Nick's beard with mustard yellow stains around his mouth, looked at him and shook his head. The driver ignored him, checking his mirrors, maneuvering the truck, easing the Jeep forward without hitting the Mustang or the Sentra parked on either side.

When the truck backed, he ran to the passenger side, opened the door. A pit-bull, drool stringing from one lax corner of his mouth snarled. "Does he bite?"

The guy smiled.

Winch pulled out his money clip. Threw a hundred dollar bill onto the seat. "Now?"

"Yep."

A fifty this time. The man gave him a look, stopped the truck, put his hand on the dog and rubbed his neck. "Easy now Spike."

Winch pulled the walkie-talkie out of his hip pocket, jumped into the truck next to the dog. "Can he scoot over a bit?"

The driver pulled Spike close to him.

"Drive," Winch said. The truck cab smelled like an onion and mayonnaise sandwich. Spike eyed him.

"Where to?"

"That's my Jeep. Let's get out of here."

The truck went in gear and moved through the lot and out onto Cordova Street. Behind them, two security guards yelled.

The driver gave him a look. "A hundred bucks more, I can drop it right here if you want."

"Just go. Give me a minute."

He transmitted on the walkie-talkie. "Brandy, speak to me. What've you got?"

"Where have you been, Winch? We've been calling."

The driver, head forward, eyes slanted toward Winch said, "You some kind of cop?"

Winch nodded. "Private." He couldn't believe he'd said that. He'd been waiting eight years as a private investigator to use that line. He'd heard it, what, three hundred times in movies and read it that many more in PI novels? But he'd never had a chance to say it.

"I think we've lost him," Brandy said.

"We need an airplane," Carla said. He could envision Carla and Brandy tug-of-warring over the radio.

From an airplane, three thousand feet high, the line of sight elk transmitter signal could be picked up for twenty miles in any direction. On the ground? A mile, if you were lucky. "Where was the last time you got a signal?"

"We're near the carousel." Brandy had the radio. "We lost the signal but picked it up here. Then lost it."

"Did you ever see him?" Winch asked.

"Who knows?" Brandy said.

"Yeah, Bro," Woody said. "There's ten thousand tourists slowing traffic."

"Let me think," he said. Charon and the money were gone. The last signal they'd been able to receive was near the carousel. The carousel was a private little park, next to the county library on a corner as congested as a fire ant mound. He knew every blade of grass in that park. The park served as a neutral exchange ground for separated parents, trading their kids on visitation days. Document a father's behavior when he had the kids for the weekend? The carousel is where the surveillance began.

He could figure this out. He closed his eyes. What was he missing? He didn't have an airplane. St. Augustine had no tall buildings where they could take the receiver and pick up the signal. The highest spot in town was the bell tower of the Catholic

Cathedral on St. George's Street across from Flagler College. He couldn't go back.

"You okay, buddy?" said the tow driver.

"Head toward the carousel."

"I ain't no cabbie."

Winch reached into his pocket, dropped another fifty on the driver's lap and closed his eyes again. They had the signal. Picked it up at the freaking busy corner and then lost it. That was it. They picked it up, not because they'd gotten closer to Charon but because Charon had put himself where the signal would travel farther. Be stronger.

He was wrong. The bell tower wasn't the highest spot in the county. The Vilano Bridge. A car traveling over the bridge would be half again as high. Plus all of that metal superstructure might boost the signal like a gigantic antenna. Charon had driven over the bridge, the signal range increased up the bridge and then decreased as he went down the other side and disappeared altogether. He didn't need an airplane. He needed a bridge.

"Vilano bridge," he yelled into the radio. "Get to the top. Quick."

He looked at the driver.

"Yeah, I heard you." The driver reached up under the dashboard. There was a ripping sound and he pulled out a long barreled revolver in a brown leather holster with Velcro on one side. "Who we chasing?"

"Geez, we won't need that."

The driver gave him a look. "Don't you carry?" He pushed the gun back under the dash.

"We're not shooting anybody today."

"Got him," Brandy said. "The signal is strongest from the north. A1A."

"Push it," he said. "Over the bridge you'll lose the signal but there's only one way he can go. You can catch the sucker."

"Roger that," Woody said.

The truck driver and Winch were just going up the incline when Brandy said she'd picked up the signal. Lost it after she'd gotten off the bridge but picked it up heading north.

"Can you move this rig any faster?" Winch said. "I'll cover any tickets."

“I chase skips for a living,” he said. “Hold on.”

The gas pedal hit the floor, the diesel engine rattled, and the truck surged up the bridge, faster and faster, swerving around a pickup loaded with bales of hay. The Jeep’s rear bumper missed the pickup by scant inches. Winch had one hand on a handhold over the door. One foot on the dashboard. Spike was snarling, tail wagging, head bobbing back and forth.

Brandy’s voice came over the radio. “The signal’s stronger.”

Good, good, good. “You got your lights on?” Winch said.

The driver flipped a switch and yellow flashes reflected against the bridge.

They weaved through traffic. Irritated motorists flipped them off. They passed the Ocean Oats condos and he wondered if Lisa Chambers was there and with whom? Renfro?

“I think he’s behind us,” Brandy said. “The directional meter is pointing the other way.”

“I’m behind it then,” Woody said.

Winch thought he saw Woody’s truck a quarter mile up the road. One car between them and Woody. “Hit your brakes three times for me, Woody.”

Yes. Three flashes of red. “We’re one car behind you.” He turned to the driver, “South bound lane is clear.”

“Hang on.” The tow truck crossed the double yellow line and slowly gained on the Ford Explorer in front of them. The driver gave them an incredulous look as they passed.

“What kind of car?” Winch said.

“Green XKE,” Woody said.

“Ragtop?” They were close behind Woody and he could see for himself.

Snake’s Jaguar.

FORTY-TWO

The twelve cylinder '73 XKE cruised along highway A1A running through Guana River State Park. Heavy surf from tropical storm Florence pounded the shore. The storm devastated the low islands of the Turks and Caicos with her high winds and seas. Now she had Florida in her sights. The park on the west side of A1A consisted of a low scrubby area sandwiched between the coastal highway and the intracoastal waterway. Sure to flood when the storm hit.

Winch knew he should have figured Snake for Charon. Now it was obvious. Snake lived behind the gas station where Sarah disappeared. His stepfather lied about the timing of Snake's arrival home from college. How could he have not seen it before?

Now that he had Charon two cars ahead of him, what to do? He wasn't law enforcement. As a private investigator he had no arrest powers. A citizen's arrest? He wasn't sure of Florida law. Many states required that a felony be committed in your presence before a citizen's arrest could take place. He wasn't even sure any law had been violated. And if there were a violation of the law, wasn't he complicit? Wasn't he the one with $20,000 in cash in his car, ready to turn it over to Snake? He couldn't call the Sheriff's office, there was a warrant out for *his* arrest on Tracy's murder. And he couldn't let himself be throttled down in jail. Not until he knew who rigged the *Dos XXs* to blow.

He had to bring this to a head some way other than involving law enforcement. Snake had to either pony up Sarah's body or return the money. He pushed the transmit button on the walki-talkie. "I'm in the tow truck behind Woody. When the oncoming lane is clear we're going around Woody and we'll pull up alongside Snake. Then we all slow down together. Brandy stay right in front of Snake. We'll force him to the side and confront him."

When traffic cleared, Winch nodded to the tow truck driver. The truck swung into the oncoming lane and passed Woody's pickup. Winch leaned out the window and yelled at Snake. "Pull over."

Snake looked up, rolled down his window. "Need directions?"

He spoke into the walkie-talkie. "Okay, Brandy. Slow down and come to a stop."

As her brake lights brightened, the tow truck, dragging the Jeep, crept its right wheels over the line toward the Jaguar. Snake blared his horn. Winch leaned out the open window, waved his arms, motioned to pull over. He felt some movement under his chest. Spike stuck his head out the window and barked. Dog spittle flew into Winch's face.

All four vehicles slowed. The Jag pulled into the sand well off the road. Brandy and Carla were out of their car trotting over to Snake. The tow truck moved up ahead of Brandy's Maxima and pulled into the breakdown lane.

"I'm going to drop your car here, Buddy. Three hundred bucks only buys you so much." The driver looked back at the Jag, reached under the dash and pulled out his revolver. "Lessen you need me to stay?"

Winch pushed the revolver away. "Drop the Jeep. That will be enough." He gave the driver a twenty. "Buy Spike a steak on me." He reached over to pat Spike on the head but Spike snarled and bared his teeth.

"Ingrate." He jumped out of the tow truck and hustled to the Jag.

Carla stood with her hands on her hips. Brandy stood half-a-step behind and to Carla's right. Snake standing in the sand in front of them.

"Okay, Luther," Winch said. "Where's Sarah?"

"How did you find me?" Snake nodded toward the women. "They weren't behind me. I was watching."

"Where's the money?" Winch said. A small red YMCA gym bag sat on the passenger seat of the XKE.

"It's mine," Snake said.

"Tracking device," Winch said and walked around to the passenger side of the Jag.

Snake took a step toward Winch but Woody put his arm on him. The golf pro tried to shake him off. Woody's grip tightened until the teak colored flesh around Woody's fingertips turned white.

Winch unzipped the bag. Pulled out the bundles of hundreds. Looked at Brandy. "Which one?"

"Effen me if I can tell them apart," she said.

"Hey, I earned that," Snake said. "Give it back."

"Right," Winch said. He riffled through the bundles until he found the quarter sized elk transmitter. He flipped the rubber off from the bundle of hundreds and waved the single hundred in front of Snake. "Old school technology."

Snake shook his head. "Tell this guy to let go and I'll tell you everything."

Woody dropped his hand.

Winch held the bag with the money. "You've got maybe fifteen seconds and we're gone. Plus we'll come after you for the first ten thousand I gave you."

"You owe me twenty more."

"You owe us a body."

"Do you have the rest of the money?"

The tow truck swung a U-turn and honked as he passed.

"You haven't earned a nickel yet," Carla said. "But we have the money."

Snake opened the door to the Jag. "Bring the money. I'll take you to her."

FORTY-THREE

The convoy followed Snake south on A1A, past Guana State Park, low lying wax myrtles on the west side led to the Intracoastal waterway, and head-high sea oat topped sand dunes to the beach on the other side.

A mile south of where the park ended, Snake pulled his Jaguar into a beach access parking area, and everyone piled out. The ocean was an eerie sight. It's surface, painted blue by a cloudless sky, was smooth as bathroom tile. No ruffles of wind. But the water itself rolled shoreward, pounded the beach with swells high as houses, pushed from the ever-advancing tropical storm. Two shrimp trawlers, outriggers with nets fully deployed on both sides, made slow progress northward, rolling, dipping first the port outrigger in the water as the boat rolled to port and then the starboard, up and down, back and forth, with each swell. Hundreds of gulls and terns screeched and cawed, swirling in a vortex around the stern of the boats, diving for churned up baitfish or tossed out by-catch. Farther out to sea, a blunt-nosed high-topped car-carrier transport rode low on its waterline, carrying Japanese and Korean cars to the Blount Island terminal in Jacksonville.

Winch inhaled the ocean fresh air. Reminiscing for a second, already missing life aboard the *Dos XX*. "Where is she?"

Snake shook his head. "The money first."

"Give him the money," Carla said.

"I don't think so." Winch looked around. He recognized this location as being only a few hundred yards from where Sarah's duffle bag had been discovered.

"There," Winch pointed toward the ocean, a little south of where they stood. "That's where your sister's bag was found. If there'd been a fresh grave anywhere around here deputies would have found it then."

Snake opened his arms, palms out. "I'll take the money and show you where she is. If she's not there, I'll give the money back. You know who I am." He turned to Winch. "You're the detective. You can always find me if I skip out."

"I wouldn't do it, Carla," Winch said.

"It's my money. My sister. Give it to him."

He looked at Brandy and then tossed her the keys to the Jeep.

"I've got an inside trade going on in the market," Snake said. "On Monday, I'm turning your fifty thousand into six hundred thousand. It's a sure thing. Done deal."

"Rudy Chambers," Winch said.

Snake's mouth opened. Then closed. He said, "How did you know that?"

"You said it." Winch thumbed his own chest. "I'm the detective."

"Who's that?" Carla said. "I might want in."

"Rudy's the dean of the Business School at Flagler College," Winch said.

"I give him free golf lessons." Snake swung an imaginary club. "He gives me stock tips."

"Martha Stewart. Insider trading," Woody said. "I don't know about you, but I slept better knowing Martha was locked up."

Brandy returned carrying the shoebox with the twenty thousand dollars in hundred dollar bills. She gave Winch a look. He took the box from her. "Hey, that's mine," Snake said.

"You know the law of possession," Winch said. "Let's take a walk." He turned to the others, "You guys wait right here."

Holding the box, he led Snake a dozen yards away.

"What?" Snake said. "Let's get on with it, man."

He wondered about Snake. How a person could be so low as to ransom Sarah's burial place to her sister. "Did you sleep with her?"

"I never got the chance, man."

"I know she went out the back window of the restroom. And then where? Up to your room over the garage?"

"I helped her escape from those dweebs she was with. She left them a note but they never showed it to the Sheriff."

Winch waved him on with his hands.

"She saw my collection of potsherds and stuff from the Timucuan mounds. A copper mask even. I used to dig out there in my spare time. Figured those Spaniards might have paid those Indians in gold or something."

"No gold in Florida," Winch said. "More like slave labor."

"Whatever. The thing is, Sarah was really into that historical antiquity stuff. She wanted to dig there herself. So after the cops cleared out we went out back and I let her dig. Took her photo. She found a nice little cup with a dozen sharks teeth. She was stoked."

The shark's teeth in her diary were white instead of black. They came not from beach combing but were probably saved by some Timucuan after he'd eaten the shark. "You had her driver's license."

"I partied pretty hard that night and passed out. The next morning she was gone. I'd thought she'd left but her stuff was still at my place."

"And after a couple of days you got scared and brought it out here. But you kept a few souvenirs."

"You got it all figured. You don't need me."

"And the Charon thing?"

"Hey, I went to college." Snake rubbed his arm where Woody had grabbed him. "I thought it was apropos, you know?"

Winch wiped a drop of sweat that'd run into one eye. "Her body's not really here. Is it?"

"Of course it is, man. I wouldn't lie to you."

They both knew Sarah's body wasn't anywhere close to here. Snake probably didn't know where it was any more than he did, but Carla was determined to see it through.

He held the box out. Snake reached for it but Winch didn't release it. "One more thing," Winch said. "How do you know there's a warrant for my arrest?"

Snake shook his head. "You may think you know it all, Young, but you're clueless."

Winch waited.

"My sister, Patti, she works for the Sheriff. She clued me in."

"Patti Reynolds is your sister?"

"Step-sister, really. She told me about the hot tub, man. The other day. You lucky dog."

Winch's head reeled. Patti—oh my gosh is Patricia Patch old man Patch's daughter? He had to get his mind around this. Patti Reynolds and Patricia Patch are the same person? Why didn't he see it earlier?

"You okay?" Snake snatched the box from Winch's hand. "They'll be a BOLO out for you. You'd better get a good attorney. They've got solid evidence you blew up your boat and killed your ex. Shouldn't have done that, man. She was hot."

Winch grabbed Snake's arm. "Wait."

Snaked tugged but couldn't pull away.

"You've been having an affair with Rudy Chambers' wife?"

"She's a cute little thing. Brown hair, wide eyes." Snake shook his head. "Not me. I helped her with her swing in one lesson. She rubbed her little fanny all over me. But Rudy's given me other tips that worked real well. I'm not about to end that winning streak."

Snake opened the lid and then closed it. "Made my day." He pointed down the beach. "Follow me."

They all trudged a hundred yards north along the beach and then back just above the high water mark. "There." Snake pointed to where someone had spray painted a red rectangle on the sand. "I marked it earlier today."

The rectangle lay between two areas the size of sofa cushions that had been marked with foot high red stakes. Sun-faded pink tape strung between them.

"What's that?" Carla pointed to the tape.

"Sea turtle nests," Winch said. "Probably logger heads. Awful convenient spot to mark for the body. No way we can dig here until those eggs hatch. Next month or the month after at the earliest."

Snake shrugged. "I can't help where the turtles lay their eggs."

"How did my sister die?" Carla said.

"I'm sorry Ms. Fox. I'm told she drowned."

"But how did she get here? I don't understand."

Snake shook his head. "Look, the deal was I'd show you where she was. I haven't done anything illegal, and I'm not going to confess to anything. Not even improper disposal of a body. A deal is a deal. She's there, and that's all I can tell you."

"You're scum," Carla said. "Why didn't you show this spot to the authorities back then?"

Snake rubbed his hand along the top of the shoebox. "I understand you're angry."

Winch wanted to punch Snake, take him down, make him pay for whatever had been done to Sarah.

But Carla lost control first. She stepped up to Snake and shoved with both hands against his chest. The move surprised the golfer, and he stumbled backwards, a foot caught in a sea grape root, and he fell. Bundles of hundred dollar bills spilled onto the sand. Carla kicked him in the ribs. Again. And again. He put his hands over his head and curled.

Winch waited, letting Carla act as proxy for him. Pummeling Snake. Finally he put his hand on her shoulder and turned her to him. She buried her face in his chest. Heaving. Sobbing. Her body shaking. Heat rising off her. She looked up at him. Sweat poured off her forehead.

He rubbed her back. Pulled her close. He wanted to fold her into himself. Comfort her and make the hurt go away. Shove his own hurt away too.

She pulled away from Winch and faced Snake, who was getting to his feet.

"I can sue," Snake said. "Battery." He stooped to pick up the box. "Collect a lot more than this."

"You fell off your bicycle," Winch said. "Get the hell out of here."

Carla sniffled a little. "Can we sit for a moment."

He held up his Jeep keys. "Brandy, you and Woody take the other two vehicles. I'll give Carla a ride back."

They sat on the beach above the high tide line. Hip-high breakers burst on the beach, sending waves of white foam toward them.

He put his arm over her shoulders. "We'll come back in two months and dig."

Carla held his hand. "I guess it's over," she sighed.

"Not yet, it's not."

"You've earned your retainer. I don't want any back."

He nodded up toward the dunes. "She's not there, you know."

"You think?"

"There's someone else involved. Snake wanted the money, for sure. But he didn't kill Sarah. I'm not stopping until I know who did."

"Let it go, Winch. We know she's dead."

Sarah's photo flashed through his mind. And then an image of Tracy, the last time he'd seen her, in the hot tub, mouthing the words "later." If only he could go back in time and change how he'd left that afternoon. She'd still be alive. If he'd told her, there with Patti, that he and she were finished that there was no "later," then Trace would be alive. But the boat rigged to blow might have caught him instead, and he'd be dead. Tracy died in his place, his proxy in death.

"We knew she was dead," Winch said, "when you came to me on the boat that first day. But now Tracy is dead too, and we haven't put either one of them to rest. I'm not finished."

"I'm so sorry, Winch. I guess I'm responsible for Tracy's death. If you hadn't taken this case—"

He put two fingers over her mouth. "Don't say it." He stood up. Offered his hand and pulled her to his feet. He kissed her gently on the forehead. Maybe, just maybe when this was over, in a few months perhaps, Carla and he might have a future together.

"We can't change what happened." He brushed the sand off his pants. Turned her around and brushed off the seat of her jeans. "But sure as the devil I can bring to justice to the persons responsible for murdering Sarah and Tracy. I have to. You know that, right?"

"Winchester." Carla stroked the side of his face with the back of her hand. "There are times in every person's life, when they have to fulfill duties to loved ones or shirk their obligations. You'd be a lesser person if you failed to do what's required of you. Good for you."

Good for me, he thought. But not so good for whoever killed Sarah and Tracy.

FORTY-FOUR

Winch dropped Carla at the Casa Monica and drove to his office. Somewhere here he had the answer to who killed Sarah and Tracy. There were no more facts to find. Charon aka Snake aka Luther Calderon wasn't the killer. He didn't believe Trey Ellis was either.

He sat in the chair behind his desk and swiveled back and forth, back and forth. He opened a drawer and pulled out the photo of Sarah. In the credenza, he found his favorite photo of Tracy wearing a simple yellow strapless summer dress and sandals. One he'd taken in Freeport, Bahamas with her standing under a palm, clusters of green coconuts overhead. A few fallen to the ground. The boats behind rested easy in their slips. She looked as pretty as the summer morning on which it was taken. And now she was gone.

He spoke to her as if she were there. "Tell me, Trace. Who did this to you?" Of course, she wasn't there. But he had to wonder. Wasn't there some way for her to pierce the veil between this world and the Spirit World? Show him who'd killed her? Then he realized that maybe she wouldn't know who her murderer was. Just because she'd passed through the veil between life and death didn't mean she knew things she wouldn't ordinarily know. The boat was rigged to blow before she arrived so she probably didn't have any better idea then he did. But she could talk to Sarah. They were both in the Spirit World. And Sarah could tell her what happened twenty-five years ago. Where she was buried. "Come on, Trace. Help me out a bit here. I'm lost."

The fax machine beeped complaining it was out of paper and had faxes in memory. As soon as he inserted paper it began spilling printouts. The DNA report from the lab.

He scanned through it quickly not believing what he was reading. He went through it again more slowly.

DNA was found on all samples submitted. The DNA on Lisa Chambers' underwear samples LC1, LC2, LC3, did not match DNA from lip cells found on Styrofoam cup of Vincent Renfro, sample VR1. Renfro was not Lisa Chambers' lover.

Now for the weird part. The DNA found on the Lisa Chambers' samples matched the DNA found on Sarah Fox's panties. How could that be? The samples were more than twenty-five years apart in age. Cross contamination? He'd been very careful. Followed the right protocol.

He read the report over and over. Same results. Whoever was currently sleeping with Lisa Chambers had also slept with Sarah Fox before she died. He could kick himself. If he'd done his job better and found Lisa's lover he'd have another clue to Sarah's disappearance.

There was a knock on his office door. The cops coming to arrest him? He looked out the window that faced the street. Not the Sheriff.

He opened the door. Lisa Chambers stood there in navy blue shorts, sandals, and a light blue knit top. Her red hair was cut to just below her ears showing off emerald studs. The earrings matched an emerald on her right ring finger. No rings on the left.

"Can I come in or do I have to wait until you finish counting my fingers and toes?"

His eyes went to her feet. A gold toe-ring circled her left fourth toe.

"Of course." He fully opened the door, gesturing to the chair in front of his desk.

As she passed him, he caught a fragrance in the air he'd smelled previously. Where *was* that? Somewhere he couldn't remember, but it'd come to him.

"I owe you an apology," she said. She waved her hand. "You know, for the thingee at the mall."

"How did you know I—"

"I didn't see you follow me. I was looking, too. You must be very good."

Let her think what she would. He realized now there was one way she could have known her husband had hired him to follow her. Someone had told her. "Rudy told you."

"Rudy's an idiot."

He wouldn't argue that. "What can I do for you, Mrs. Chambers?"

She pulled out her checkbook. "How much did Rudy pay you?"

"I can't confirm he paid me anything."

"I thought you were smart. The fool told *me* he hired you."

He smelled her perfume again. Orange and vanilla. Fruity? He recognized it from where? He shrugged. "I have no control over what your husband says or does."

She laid the checkbook on his desk, wrote his name on the top check, and glanced up at him. "I've hired an attorney."

"Good move," he said. "I'm sure he told you Florida is a 'no fault' divorce state."

She told him which attorney she'd retained. This was going to be a very expensive divorce for the Chambers family.

"You've been in the PI business eight years, Mr. Young."

He nodded.

"Then despite the law, you know judges look askance at infidelity that occurs before separation?"

"While both parties are still in the marital home," he said. He did know that. "And there are children involved as well." Another factor where infidelity might shift the advantage from one party to another.

She pursed her lips. "I'm not going to lose my children because Rudy's a jerk."

"It's okay to have an affair if your husband's a jerk?"

She finished writing the check and turned it so he could see.

"Thirty-five thousand dollars. That's a lot," he said. No crap. The cleanup bill at the marina was $8,000 for an explosion he didn't create. Funeral expenses would be another ten grand easy.

"It's yours," she said. "I need your silence. You don't know who I've been seeing anyway. You think it's Vinnie Renfro."

Not after reading the DNA results. "I know it's not Vinnie." The air conditioner kicked on. The vent over her head wafted her perfume toward him. And then he remembered. He'd smelled it when he walked into the security office that day at the mall. And again in the food court when he'd taken their cups from them.

"Woody Copeland," he said. "In the security office at the mall." He shook his head. "Geez, couldn't the two of you at least paid for a room?"

"You're a better detective than I'd been lead to believe."

Oh, that was a real confidence builder.

She tore the check out of the checkbook and began writing again. She turned it again so he could read it. $50,000. "We have a lot at stake, Rudy and I."

Rudy didn't know it was Woody. If he told Rudy, he'd extract some sort of revenge. But obligation required he report the facts to his client.

He reached across the desk and took the check.

She stood, "Good, we have a deal. And I'd like my underwear back as well."

He studied the check. This was going to kill him. But what could he do? He folded the check, tore it in half and then in half again. He laid the pieces on the palm of his hand and extended it to her.

Her cheeks flushed. "You know what you are?"

Oh, here it comes again. Somebody calling him names. "Loyal?" he said.

"You're damn impossible."

Impossible wasn't too bad. He'd been called worse.

She turned and strode toward the door. As she opened it, he said, "You ought to try a different perfume. That one doesn't suit you. Too sweet. Maybe something a little more tart."

She flipped him off and slammed the door.

Okay, he had to think this through. Woody and Lisa Chambers were having an affair. Which meant that Woody had been with Sarah Fox just before she disappeared.

He stepped to the workbench and pulled out the spiral bound notebook where Sarah had begun her "spring break" diary. He laid it on the table and leafed through it. On the last page she'd written, "last night—EF on the beach was the best ever. Tomorrow at the fort again, same time." He flipped the paper. The next page was blank.

Woody. Woody Eagle Feather Copeland. The mysterious EF. That son-of-a-gun. Why hadn't he told him? Well, he clearly didn't want Rudy Chambers to know he was banging his wife, but he could have told him he'd known Sarah Fox. Why hide that?

The afternoon sun glared through the open blinds on the west side-facing window. A slant of light and shadow fell across the notebook. His eye caught something. What was that? He searched the blank page. Tilted it in the beam of sunlight. Rotated it. There. Indented writing. He examined the spiral spring-like binding. The indented writing on the blank page didn't seem to match what was written on the prior page. Someone had ripped a page out of the diary. Maybe Snake had before he dumped the duffle on the beach.

He stared out the window. Dark clouds had rolled up from the south. "Thank you Trace," he said. Maybe she was closer than he realized.

He called Woody on his cell and told him he needed him at the office.

Most people would have just run a lead pencil sideways over the writing to bring it out. That would be fine if it worked. If it didn't, then the evidence was ruined.

He pulled out his Canon digital SLR and photographed the "blank" page. He shined a goose-necked lamp on it, moving the light, throwing shadows on the paper from different angles. Snapping shots in Raw mode as opposed to Jpeg so as not to lose any of the picture to compression. Moving the camera around.

Next the CF card from the camera went into the computer. Using the Raw Image and Tone Curve adjustments, in a few minutes he had a clear picture of the indented writing.

Some of the fainter indents matched the writing on the previous page. But there were other words indented on the paper that weren't written on that page. He wasn't sure what to make of them.

SJ1805 *Snake* *Copper Masks* *Skulls*

He printed the photo and was studying it when Brandy and Woody walked in.

"You rang? We're here, Bro," Woody said.

Brandy ran one hand through her hair. "I can't believe Carla Fox just dumped that load of money on Snake without more proof."

"I guess she doesn't care about the money," Woody said.

Upon hearing what Woody just said, Winch paused his thoughts for a moment. Was there something there? Carla not caring about the money? If the money wasn't important to Carla, what was? The obvious answer, finding Sarah. Really? Or is there something else more important than either of those?

He printed another copy of the indented writing and handed one to each of them. "What do you make of this?"

While they studied it, he studied Woody. "Why didn't you tell me, Woody?"

Woody bounced the edge of the photo off his forehead. Probably trying to decide how much Winch knew.

"What—"

Winch held up his hand. "Don't Woody. Don't lie to me. If you don't want to tell me, okay. I understand. But don't lie to me."

Brandy gave him a hurt look. "Winch, Woody wouldn't lie to you. Me either."

"Withholding information is the same as lying," Winch said.

Brandy looked at the two of them but said nothing. Waiting.

"The DNA came back," Woody finally said. Not a question. A statement.

"You're darn right it came back and it puts you square in the middle of both of my cases."

Brandy stood. "I don't believe this, Winch. What are you saying?"

"It means Woody, not Vincent Renfro, has been having an affair with Lisa Chambers."

Brandy sat down, her face ashen. She looked at Woody. "How could you do that and not tell us? Winch risked his life to talk to Renfro's wife and you said nothing?"

Woody pulled the end of his ponytail over his shoulder and examined it. "Okay," he said. "Winch was going to talk to Renfro's wife whether I was having an affair with Lisa or not. What happened out there had nothing to do with me and Lisa."

"But that's how Renfro knew you, right?" Now Winch could see it. "And how you knew him. He's friends with Lisa and she's told him about the two of you."

"Just friends," Woody said. "They go way back. There's nothing between them, like," he shrugged, "you know."

“You’re freaking crazy,” Brandy said. “When are you going to learn to keep it in your pants and not troll where you work?”

“That’s only half of it,” Winch said. “Woody spent the night with Sarah Fox on the beach, twenty-five years ago. He’s the mysterious EF.”

Brandy reached over and, whack, slapped Woody hard on the cheek. “You dog. Why didn’t you tell us? We’ve been running around chasing our tails.”

Brandy extended her hand again but Woody caught her wrist. “Do not hit me,” he said. “I don’t like that. Once is enough.”

Brandy jerked her hand away from him. Woody laid his hands in his lap, relaxed and whack, she slapped him again.

Woody jumped. Backed away from the two of them and rubbed his cheek. His eyes watered and he wiped them with the back of his hand. “I’m Native American,” he said. “Back then, if I’d come forward, I probably never would have even made it to jail. Much less, ever gotten out. Things aren’t that much different now.”

He was probably right. Some public defender would have convinced him to plead to manslaughter and his life would have been effectively over. “Did you kill her?”

“I saw her that one night. We were supposed to meet the next night but she never showed. Then I heard the news. I faded away back to my people. No crime in that.”

Winch paced. “We’re no closer to who killed Sarah or to who killed Tracy than we were when we started.”

“The picture of Sarah with the shovel? You still got it?” Woody said.

He’d scanned the photo and sealed it in an envelope to preserve any useable prints. Of course now it probably didn’t make any difference because he knew that Snake was Charon. Still, instead of pulling out the original he printed a copy and handed it to Woody.

“I know where this was taken,” Woody said.

Winch motioned with his hands. Come on, say it.

“At SJ 1805,” Woody said. “Maybe she’s still there.”

FORTY-FIVE

Winch grabbed the outdoor photo of Sarah holding a shovel from Woody. "*You* know what SJ 1805 is? And where?"

Woody headed for the door. "I'll be right back."

"Wait," Winch said.

"Cool your jets, kemosabe."

Woody shut the door behind him but Winch opened it. A cool front was passing through and he could feel the drop in barometric pressure. The tropical storm approaching.

Through the window they watched him run down the outside staircase, open his truck, and come back up.

Winch recognized the map from the security office at the mall with the area of the Timucuan Preservation outlined in red marker. Woody spread it out on the workbench. Six locations were marked with yellow circles. Each was numbered SJ1800 through SJ 1805.

"There." Woody speared one of the yellow circles with his forefinger. "You know where that is?"

He examined the topo map. This was all west of US 1 and north of the Interstate. "Patch's gas station would be about there." Winch took a pencil and drew a triangle on the map.

"You got it, bro," Woody said. "Those are all Timucuan mounds. These here," Woody ran his finger in a circle on the map which encompassed three of the mounds including SJ 1805, "are on Patch's land. They'll be flooded tomorrow when those dozers start moving dirt."

"What's with the numbers?" Brandy said.

Woody looked her over. “I’m not talking to you.”

Brandy stepped toward him. Woody flinched. “I don’t want to hurt you, Brandy, but I’m not going to let you hit me again.”

“I’m really, really sorry,” Brandy said. “I shouldn’t have done that. I had no right—”

“Damn straight.” Woody took a deep breath and let it out. “I did have you running in circles. I’m sorry about that.” He looked at Winch and Brandy. “We okay?”

They both nodded.

“The DNR,” Woody said, “gives a number to each Timucuan mound reported to them. These are low numbers so they were probably reported a long time ago.”

“DNR?” Brandy said.

“Department of Natural Resources,” Woody said.

“Let’s brainstorm for a minute. Why bury her in an old Indian mound when you have 8000 other acres of land?”

“Why kill her in the first place?” Woody said.

“My question first.” Winch drummed a pencil on the desk. “Why there? There’s got to be a reason.”

Neither Brandy nor Woody had an answer. “Okay,” Winch said. “Think this through. If you want to hide, say, a special baseball, where’s the best place to hide it?”

“In a sack with other baseballs,” Woody said.

“So,” Brandy said. “You hide a body with other bodies.”

Winch stood up. “Right. Remember what Meredith Renfro said? Her husband was going to use cadaver dogs but wondered if they could tell the difference between ‘old’ cadavers and new?”

“So whoever killed her put her in there with my deceased ancestors to conceal the body,” Woody said. “Pretty clever, really.”

Brandy scrunched her forehead. “Tomorrow is the tenth day. You think Snake knows she’s there?”

“I don’t buy for a second that two loggerhead turtles just happened to lay their eggs on either side of her grave.” He bent over the map and took a long straight edge, marking the lines of longitude and latitude of SJ 1805 and wrote them down on a yellow pad.

“You have another map, Woody?”

Woody shook his head.

He went to his computer. Brought up Google Earth and found the acreage belonging to Patch. He ran his cursor over the map until he got the right lat and lon and printed the view. Backed it out a bit and printed a larger view. “This’ll do,” he said. “I can get to Patch’s property from the back side by going down Princess Road. Hike east a couple of hundred yards and be on his land.”

Out of the equipment cabinet he grabbed his handheld GPS, powered it up and waited for it to acquire the satellites. Then he punched in the lat and lon of SJ 1805, and it gave him the bearing and distance.

“You’re not going in there alone?” Brandy said. “Tonight?”

“As soon as the sun sets.”

“There’s a tropical storm coming through tonight,” Brandy said. “Look.” She pointed out the window where an avalanche of dark clouds was moving up from the south. As if on cue, a heavy torrent of rain pelted the window and blurred their vision. “See,” she said.”

“Tonight is my last chance to find Sarah,” Winch said. “Tomorrow the area around those mounds will be twelve feet deep. You’ll need a Zodiac to reach them.”

“You know,” Woody was shaking his head, “those mounds can be bigger than barns. You’re not going to find a twenty-five year-old grave walking around in the dark with a flashlight. Someone will have to show it to you.”

Woody was right. In fact, the Mormon chapel south of St. Augustine has a Timucuan mound on their property. He’d walked that mound several times. It was covered with native vegetation. Scrub palmettos, wax myrtles, mature slash pine, and water oaks. Any surface depression from a decaying body would have long ago been filled in by nature.

He sat down in his chair. He could figure this out. How to get someone to show him the grave? Somebody knew exactly where that body was buried. He just wasn’t sure who. If Sarah was there, then either Snake, his sister Patti, or old man Patch must have buried her. Their land. They had the access.

“I’ll call Patti,” Winch said. “Tell her I’m going out to have a look. Word will get to the guilty party and someone will show up to make sure I don’t find that grave.”

“No way,” Brandy said. “Using yourself for bait, alone, at night, in the middle of a storm doesn’t sound like the brightest idea to me. You know what I mean?”

“I’ll hide in the brush. See who shows. Take it from there.”

"You're an idiot." She turned her attention to Woody. "You go with him. You're the Indian. You know the woods."

Woody shook his head. "I've got my own thing tonight. I'm going to put a stop to those developers."

Winch checked his watch, picked up the phone and dialed Patti. Voice mail. "Patti. Winch. I know Sarah Fox is buried on your dad's property. SJ 1805. Meet me there at midnight tonight if you know where I'm talking about. I'll bring a shovel."

FORTY-SIX

Winch would either find Sarah's grave tonight, and in the process reveal Tracy's killer, or fail. He laid the small backpack on the hood of the Jeep and sifted through his gear. He'd programmed the coordinates of the Timucuan mound into his GPS. He punched in his current location so he could find his way back to the Jeep. He wondered who waited out there for him. Patti? Old man Patch? Snake? Someone he hadn't met? Maybe he'd wander alone through the Timucuan mounds searching for Sarah in the blackness and discover nothing.

The heavy fecund smell of compost in the tidal swamp filled the air. Fallen water oaks decayed into rough slivers and were eaten into sawdust by termites. Fiddler crabs scurried sideways between white oyster shells with edges sharp as broken porcelain. A misstep, a trip and fall into the oyster beds could cause lacerations serious as a shark bite. He swatted at a swarm of mosquitoes. Squeezed a good glob of 100 % Deet and lathered it on his exposed flesh. He pulled up his pant legs, rolled down his socks and rubbed the Deet around his ankles and calves in the hope that it would repel the chiggers and ticks. He lowered his pants and rubbed the Deet around his waistline, the area of tight clothing that the little buggers liked best.

Tropical storm reports indicated maybe an inch of rain per hour for the next twelve hours which would flood low-lying lands and swell creeks. He sniffed the air which was heavy with low pressure. Slogging though flooded wetlands in the dark, avoiding gators, water moccasins, and the Florida black bears that fed here was not his idea of fun. But he knew that Sarah waited for him out there. He was certain. He had to find her before the sun rose, the yellow earth movers cranked, and flooded the area.

He had a plan of sorts. He'd planted the seeds with Patti. Now to see what sprouted. He checked the rigging knife on his left hip and his 9mm Smith & Wesson on his right. He carefully looked beneath a felled slash pine for deadly coral snakes before he wedged his Jeep keys under the decaying bark. Red and yellow kill a fellow, played in his mind followed by, red and black a friend of Jack. Coral snake versus king snake.

He donned his blue foul-weather jacket and trudged off. He'd given thought to wearing rubber wading boots but even at low tide some of these tidal creeks could be belly deep. Stopping to pour water out of waders made no sense, so he opted for his hiking boots with Vibram soles.

Six pm. Summer darkness should have fallen in two more hours, but the storm clouds already cloaked the area in darkness. He planned on entering Patch's land and arriving at SJ 1805 just before dusk. Then he'd set up and wait to see who came to ambush him. He'd brought his shovel but it would be of little use on a mound the size of a barn. After twenty-five years, he'd need ground-penetrating radar to find a burial spot. Even if he had a cadaver dog, the flesh of any body not embalmed would be long consumed by night crawlers. He just hoped he didn't join Sarah.

The first rain of the tropical storm arrived, not in a drizzle, but with a slap to his face, driven sideways by a fifty mile-per-hour gust. Like being hit with a jet from a fire hose during crowd control. He cinched the hood of his foul weather jacket tight but water still found its way under the brim and ran down his neck, wetting his shirt. At least the wind and rain had driven the mosquitoes to ground. When the first frontal shower band lightened he checked the GPS which he kept in the waterproof pocket. Three point four miles. He had to admire the Spaniards who'd trekked this land five-hundred years earlier following Timucuan trails, or hacking paths through the sawgrass and palmetto thickets.

The rain slowed him. When the wind whipped rain became horizontal, visibility dropped to a few feet. He had to hunker down and wait for it to slacken. The wind stripped leaves from branches of dismembered trees peppered his face. He heard the occasional crack of pines breaking in two at head height with gusts now up to 60 knots or almost 70 mph. The tearing sound of uprooting oaks, heavily laden and felled by their own growth. The storm would also conceal his approach. Cover the sounds of his thrashing through thickets and stumbles over carpet vines.

He waded through a creek, careful to stroke the water ahead with the handle of his shovel to ward off water moccasins skimming the surface. Rattlesnakes, too, were good swimmers, unafraid of traversing waterways. The United States had four kinds of poisonous snakes and North Florida was "blessed" to have all of them.

The creek mud sucked at his boots, so each step was a major effort. His quads tired and he began to fear he might not actually make it. The rain never stopped but its intensity varied. At its lightest, he pushed himself, covering the ground rapidly. At its heaviest, he'd squat, huddle in the lee of a palm, back to the wind and wait, hunched like some aboriginal human. Probably not unlike the early Timucuans. This was their land after all.

After four hours of slopping through mud, cutting his hands on sawgrass, twisting his ankles on oyster beds, he was near exhaustion. He considered waiting out the storm or returning home, but then the GPS flashed his arrival. He was here. Now two questions: Was he alone? And where was Sarah?

Twenty yards ahead and to the right was a hillock. Covered in the low growth of rattlesnake weed and prickly pear cactus. He'd found it. This was SJ1805. Drag marks scoured the ground where the lumberjacks had used steel chokers to hall the trees and load them on trailers. The mound was probably 800 years old. Hard packed wheel ruts ran north-eastward where the logging trailers had been hauled to the staging site and hooked to semi-tractors like the one he'd seen coming out of Patch's land earlier in the week.

He was the hunter. He had to find cover, a hunting blind of sorts, and wait for his prey. The rain drummed the ground, a relentless cadence beating a tropical rhythm. Sticky green tree frogs chorused loud between bands of rain. If he hadn't known better he'd have thought he'd been transported to a Caribbean rainforest. Instead, he was squatting in the swamp-laden piney flatlands of north Florida.

He walked once around SJ1805 searching the ground for recent footprints but that was useless in the rain. Near the mound a tidal creek ran southward. Not surprising since most of these mounds were dumps of oyster and seashells where the Timucuans made their meals and tossed their trash. Hundreds of yearly cycles of plant growth and decay would add soil to the mounds.

Winch found a thicket of oak myrtle and saw palmetto. Saw palmetto was a favorite hiding place for pigmy rattlers. He scooted backwards into it hoping that any snakes would rather flee than fight. He could see three of the four sides of the mound. The unseen side backed onto the creek. He thought it unlikely that any visitors would approach through the creek.

He checked his watch. Ten p.m. He pulled his cell phone out of his pocket, shielded it from the rain. No bars. He turned it off.

He'd never been more miserable in his life. The rain never stopped. He wondered if the tidal creeks would flood and he'd have to abandon position for higher ground, sharing it with the snakes. If nobody arrived by midnight, he'd pick his way carefully over the mound to see anything that might indicate a grave.

He realized how ridiculous of an idea this was. Coming here in the dark, in the middle of a tropical storm. Had he had any stupider ideas in his lifetime?

At 11:45 he saw a pair of lights. Then a rumble of a diesel engine. Whatever it was splashed towards him. Finally, through the downpour, he made out a tractor. Bright beams streamed from above the cabin like a pair of landing lights. His little trap was about to spring.

The tractor stopped and the engine idled down. A hooded figure with a rain poncho stepped to the ground and walked into the lighted path in front.

"Winchester? You out here? You better be or I'll be pissed as hell at you."

Patti. Had she killed Sarah? What would be her motive? This made no sense. He'd expected Snake, or Patch.

He waited. Heard nothing else. Saw no one else. Five minutes passed. She climbed onto the backhoe. He could hear her swearing.

Ten minutes. The tractor edged forward and began a U-turn. Now, he thought. Winch pushed his way out of the thicket and ran into the lights so she could see him.

Patti idled back the engine and jumped to the ground. "You scared the bejesus out of me," she said.

"I didn't think you'd come. Expected your brother, maybe."

"I got lost. I've never been out here before."

This confused him. "Snake's been—"

"Oh yeah." She wiped water off her face. "Snake came out here all the time. Dug in these mounds. You've never been into his room." She motioned behind her with her head. "The things full of broken pottery, ceremonial masks. Bone tools, stuff like that. A regular anthropologist he is."

"Why are you here, Patti?"

"Going to dig up that mound with that shovel are you? Figured you'd have better luck with the backhoe. This place is going to flood in the morning." She looked around. "Maybe sooner with all of this rain."

"Your dad know you're here?"

"Daddy went into the hospital this morning."

"But why you?"

"You're an idiot and a jerk. But I liked Tracy a lot. So here I am."

"Turn the backhoe around. Light up the hill."

In a minute bright halogen beams illuminated most of the hill casting shadows from the foot-high stumps of the logged pines. He could see where trenches with steep sides had been dug. Not graves, but someone, probably, with a backhoe, hunting for Indian artifacts.

He trudged 30 yards across the lit side of the mound and was making his back toward the lights, Patti a few yards behind and uphill of him.

"You think I'm crazy, don't you Patti?"

"You're a fool."

"Harsh words."

A voice came out of the rain from behind him. "Not as harsh as this double aught buck's gonna feel iffin you don't stop right there." Patch.

He was an idiot. Patti was nothing but a decoy. Now he the hunter had become the prey. He turned toward Patti. "You said he was in the hospital."

"I lied."

"Raise your hands Mr. Private Dick." Patch moved into the light. He waved the business end of a 12-gauge pump shotgun at him. He held the long barreled weapon loosely at his waist. If he shot, the gun would likely kick up and jerk out of his grasp. Still, double-aught-buck, at this range would cut Winch in half.

"Tie him up," Patch said.

"Put your hands behind your back," Patti said.

Winch knew he could duck and roll. If Patch fired, he stood as good a chance of hitting Patti as shooting him. Especially in this weather. Still, Patch might hit the both of them. The odds weren't good. A band of rain swept over them. Patch raised one hand to shield his face.

"You know he's got a gun on him somewhere," Patti said.

"Cuff him first and the gun won't make no difference."

Winch looked over his shoulder. He flexed his knees, ready to grab her arm when she got close, pull her in front of him. Then use his Smith and take Patch out.

"Why don't you just shoot him, Daddy? Be done with it."

"I'm going to be dead within the year either way, honey. But you got a long ways to live. A month from now, his body a comes floating up on their new golf course full of bullet holes, they'd know it weren't no accident. This way he'll die nice and natural like. Wandering out here they'll think he got snake bit, or eat by a bear. You won't have no more detectives snooping around."

"You killed Detective Sharp, didn't you Patti?"

He needed to get her closer but she kept her distance.

"I've never killed anybody." She reached under her poncho and pulled out a plastic wire tie, much like the flex cuffs used for handcuffing prisoners.

"And Sarah? Did you kill her too?"

"I don't know who killed Sarah. That's the truth."

"And Tracy? You did that, didn't you?"

"You should have left it alone, Winch. You come out digging up the past. A wrongful death lawsuit by Carla Fox against Daddy's estate. Tie it up forever.

"Quit your jibber-jabbing, boy, and get down on your knees, or I'll shoot you right here."

Patch raised the barrel slightly.

"Okay. I'm going down to my knees."

"Cross your ankles," Patti said.

In that position. On his knees, ankles crossed, he knew he'd been rendered helpless.

Patch came closer, but not close enough for Winch to make a move for the shotgun. Patch's face, in a peculiar way looked shrunken, too small for his head. But the skin under his jaw flapped loose when he spoke. "Tie him up now."

"Patti," Winch said. "I know your father will die long before he gets on death row. You're young. Florida does execute women."

"Daddy?" Patti said. "I'm not sure –"

Patch was quick. He slapped the barrel of the shotgun against the side of Winch's head. The front sight ripped a gouge over his ear. He fell sideways onto his chest.

"Damn Indian mounds. Brought nothing but trouble to this land from the day we owned it."

Winch rolled, began to rise but Patch put the barrel against his head. "Don't move now, boy. Come on, Patti. Do your thing."

She grabbed his wrists and in a second they were bound behind his back.

Patch yanked on the collar of his jacket and pulled him to his feet. The old man's hand reached under his rain gear and found the Smith. "Well lookee here." His hand dug into Winch's pocket and came out with the GPS receiver. "And what's this? Some kind of tracking device?"

Patch placed the GPS on the ground and stomped on it.

"You wanted to find Sarah, Mr. PI? You'll be right next to her." Patch chuckled but it sounded like a cackle. "Say hello for me."

"She's here then?" Winch said.

"I told you, you weren't no good as a detective. Now your Uncle Benjamin, there was a fine man. But you," he shook his head. "One piss-poor excuse for a private cop."

Winch eyed the mound, wondering where she was.

"Now let's just go on over there and you can see for yourself. Move the backhoe, Honey. Let's get this over with and out of this rain. I'm feeling a bit chilled."

"You sure, daddy?"

"Ain't got no choice."

The shotgun prodded Winch in the back.

FORTY-SEVEN

DAY FIVE

The rain poured. Like standing under a spigot with no showerhead. Ruts on the logging trail filled and water streamed down the face of the Timucuan mounds. Winch couldn't tell where the dirt road had been. The puddles, quickly becoming pools, were deeper than the tops of his hiking boots. Patti drove the tractor-backhoe, wheels spinning and grabbing, spinning and grabbing, churning water, spraying him with mud, as he walked behind. Every few steps Patch prodded him between the shoulder blades with the shotgun. Too high for Winch to reach upward and grab the gun with his hands behind his back.

Winch's left foot caught in a hidden root, and he stumbled forward landing with a splat on his face. He laid there, head to the side so he wouldn't drown. This might be his last chance. Could he turn this to his advantage?

"Get up," Patch said.

Patti idled the tractor back, twisted to look at him.

"I can't," Winch said. "My freaking foot's caught."

Patch edged closer sliding his boots. "Can't see his damn feet." Patch's foot bumped Winch's left calf. Quicker than a snapping turtle, Winch scissored his legs, curled his left leg around Patch's and pulled the old man down into the deepening water. The shotgun splashed off to the side somewhere. He rolled onto Patch's back, and held the old man's head under the water with his chin. Finally something went his way.

"Get off the tractor. Cut these cuffs or I'll drown him."

Patch wrestled his mouth above the water and coughed. Winch scooted up his back and put his left knee on Patch's temple, forcing him under the water. "Now," he said. "Get down here."

"I don't think so," Patti said. "He's going to die in a few months anyway. None to soon for me."

The tractor engine roared and in a second she had it turned around, running toward him, the tractor's blade fifteen feet away. Wheels spinning, the John Deere bucked like a bronco with every bite of traction. Death by tractor.

With his hands behind his back he knew he couldn't outrun the tractor. The tractor spun, the loader blade caught him across his shoulder and the side of his head, and he was knocked off Patch.

Maybe he blacked out for a minute because he didn't know where he was. Like waking up in a hotel room and not recognizing your surroundings. But it came to him quickly. Patti stood over him with the shotgun. Patch on his knees coughed and spat.

"You stupid. . . ." Patti shook her head. "He was just going to kill you, but now he'll want to hurt you. Nothing I can do about it."

Winch struggled to his feet. Dizzy, he stumbled, but didn't go down. Patch, too, got to his feet and grabbed the shotgun from Patti. Patch swung the wooden stock of the weapon at his forehead and then he was out.

When Winch came to Patti was at the controls of the backhoe, digging his grave. His mouth was dry and gritty with sand. He had a headache the size of the Grand Canyon. He opened his mouth and caught enough rain to rinse the sand off his tongue.

Patch stood close by with the shotgun and gave him a look, "That's your new home boy. You're going to be well acquainted with it shortly. Nice and cozy." He turned toward Patti. "What're your thoughts darlin'? Deep enough?"

She pulled the tractor forward a bit. "Get in, Winch."

He shook his head.

"Just shoot him, Daddy."

"Naw, I've got other plans for him." Patch wiped water out of his eyes and swore at the tropical storm. "Either climb into that hole yourself, Sonny, or that front end loader will push you in. Probably snap your back. That what you want?"

Winch tried to stand but couldn't. "Where's Sarah?"

Patch pointed to a spot of ground next to the hole they'd just dug. "Right there. You and that girl can have long talks for the next few centuries. All y'all are next door neighbors. Ain't that just too cozy?"

All y'all? Did that include Snakes mother, Virginia? Was she buried next to Sarah? "Did you bury your step-mother out here too, Patti?"

"I told you, I've never dug out here" Patti stood next to the green tractor. The rain eased for a minute. Steam rose off the engine cowling. "Sarah spent the night with Snake. He told you that, right? I saw her leave early in the morning with a shovel. Daddy saw it too and followed her. Daddy came back by himself." She gestured toward her father with her chin. "He never really put it into so many words. I could always deny I knew anything about it."

"Not now," he said.

"Daddy will be dead soon." She gestured toward him. "You're going to die tonight. This is the end of it."

"Killing me won't finish it." He stood. "I have friends."

"I hope they're SCUBA divers."

He looked around. The tractor was on level ground and the hole she'd dug was only a few feet above level. The Timucuan mound rose another twenty feet above them.

"Yep," she nodded. "The top of this mound will be an island. Folks with picnic baskets will be fishing for bass, and you'll be feeding the bull rushes."

Not likely. "Bull rushes don't grow in deep water."

"Quit stalling and get your butt into that hole," Patch shouted, "or I'll blow your legs out from underneath you."

She'd piled the dirt into a small mound on the far side of the hole. Like most of north Florida it was mostly sand. Mixed in the sand were shards of white oyster shells and other broken orange and brick-red shells larger than his hands. Florida horse conchs. He stepped to the hole, sat awkwardly on the ledge and hopped in. The edge came to just above his knees, not quite mid-thigh. "Not deep enough," he said.

"You idiot," Patti said. "Sit down."

He squatted, wrists still fastened together with the plastic wire tie. Then dropped to his seat, stretching his legs out in front. His shoulders now, just a hair lower than the edge of the hole. "You ought to take this flex-cuff off first," Winch said.

"Now why'd I want to go and do that," Patch said.

"My body floats up, plastic doesn't deteriorate."

"Couple of days in the water. The skin on your hands will slough off. The wire tie too. Fill'er up," Patch said.

They were going to bury him, except for his head. He struggled, trying to get to his feet. Patch knocked the butt of the shotgun against his head. Even with the rain pouring he felt the warmth of blood running down the back of his neck, certain his scalp had been split.

He shook the fog out of his head. "I will get free," he yelled."

Patch shook his head. Pointed the shotgun at him "Not tonight you won't." He turned to Patti. "Go on darlin'. Fill'er up."

Patti climbed aboard the tractor, and moved it around so the front-end loader-blade was scooping the freshly dug mud toward him. He knew that most people buried alive suffocated, but not from the dirt over their faces, well that too, but mostly from the pressure of dirt not allowing their chests room to inhale and exhale.

The tractor's engine revved. Patti backed and then pushed dirt and shell into the hole. The first load covered his legs. The next filled the hole to his belly.

The tractor pushed another load and he bent forward the best he could to create a cavity in front of his chest.

"You're gonna die right here, son," Patch said.

"If I die, and I can somehow make your life miserable from the Spirit World, I promise you I will."

"You ever have the cancer boy? You think there's any way you can make me a more miserable son-of-a-bitch than I am?"

He pressed forward into the dirt, hoping he wasn't just compressing it, packing it, making it more dense then it would have been. Then he realized he really was going to die. He wasn't immortal. In a few hours, or by midmorning he'd pass into the Spirit World and be reunited with his uncle. Who else? Tracy for sure, and he looked forward to seeing her. He had to laugh to himself. Who'd ever thought that he'd be buried before she was?

The Spirit World is divided into two parts. The good people of the earth, the righteous, are assigned to paradise to await the resurrection. Those less diligent are sent to the other half, what Mormons call, “spirit prison,” where the gospel is taught and they have the chance to accept it. Maybe Tracy, whose spirit preceded him, had already sat down with the missionaries. Was she watching him? Waiting for him? He was pretty sure relatives in the Spirit World were notified when a loved one was close to passing through the veil. That wasn’t Mormon doctrine. but he believed it just the same.

The next load of dirt caught him by surprise and filled in the little wiggle room he’d made. Crap. He squirmed and tried to move his feet and knees but only got a little range of motion out of them. He wondered if Patti would run over the filled in dirt with the tractor, compacting it and perhaps crushing the life out of him.

In another minute she finished, and he managed to keep a little space, maybe an inch or less between the dirt and his chest. He hunched his shoulders forward so the two of them wouldn’t notice.

“Quit wiggling, boy.” Patch pulled out Winch’s 9mm, aimed and pulled the trigger. An oyster shell two feet in front of his face popped in two. The larger half flew into his cheek, slicing it, and dropped in front of him. Crap, that hurt. He supposed he didn’t need to worry about infection.

“You going to ride back with me, Pops?”

“Go on, honey. I’m going to have a little chat with our detective here.”

Patti spun the tractor around on one wheel and headed away. In the red glow of the taillights the backhoe attachment bounced like the head of a dragon.

Patch stood in four inches of water on what had been dry ground. Tropical storm Florence had dumped at least a foot of rain, and it was still pouring. When the dozers broke through the dikes, this place would flood faster than a Georgia basement with a broken water main.

Winch ran his tongue over the inside of his cheek, wondering if the shell had pierced it. He worked his jaw back and forth. “Where’d you put the missus, Patch?”

“She’s in family plot at the cemetery. What’s it to you?”

“Not her, the other one. Snake’s mother.”

"So you figured that out, did you?"

"She was having an affair with Detective Sharp. You killed her and buried her . . . let me see, must have been out here." He nodded westward the best he could. "I figure Sarah was digging with Snake, hmm, where, the next mound over, and somehow she wandered over here found a fresh grave. Is that about right?"

"You ain't half bad for a piss-ant detective."

"And Sarah's disappearance gave Sharp a reason to keep snooping around. You couldn't have Sharp bring cadaver dogs. He'd find not one but two. Sarah and your runaway wife, Virginia." Sharp's twofer, the 2-4 that Sharp had written on pages of the murder book. "Sharp had to go, so you set him up. Patti worked the radio room at the Sheriff's office back then. She dispatched him to the shed so you could ambush him. How'd I do?"

"If you're so damn smart, what are you doing sitting here looking like varmint bait?" Patch looked up to the black sky. "We got Florida black bears here. They'll come around when I leave. Probably get your ears and nose first. You'll still be alive for that. Once they get a taste, they'll go for the soft skin of your throat. You'll die pretty quick. Or not. Hope you suffer some, you little snot. Caused me more aggravation than any cop in the last twenty years."

"Eat me," Winch said.

"I'll leave that to the bears." Patch gave him a grin and walked off.

FORTY-EIGHT

Winch sat for he didn't know how long. No way to keep track of time. The rain beat continuously on his head. He tried to wiggle but had very little room. The small cavity he'd saved for breathing space had quickly filled with water. With each breath the water sloshed over the dirt, and with each exhale it ran back in. He splashed the water in and out in front of his chest. Hoping it would wash the dirt away. Instead, more washed in.

He knew he couldn't count on a rescue. Having his head eaten off by a bear had to be one miserable way to die. Sheesh.

Facing death didn't really worry him. Still, he had regrets. No children, for one. His unpublished novel, for another. Maybe it'd be published posthumously. He thought of the writer F. X. Toole, whose collection of short stories, *Rope Burns*, was sold to a New York publisher at the age of 69. The movie by Clint Eastwood, *Million Dollar Baby*, was made from the book. But Toole died before the movie deal. Fame found him too late. Winch's $250 signed first printing lay ruined in the muck-strewn wreckage of the *Dos XX*.

The only way to really achieve immortality on this earth was to write something that lasted throughout generations, like Shakespeare. Still relevant after 300 years. And look at himself. Buried to his neck in mud, about to face an ignominious fate.

He bowed his head and prayed. Not a short little prayer. But a lengthy one, where he ran through his shortcomings, knowing he'd face a "preliminary judgment" when he died. Not the final judgment, but at death he'd be assigned to either Paradise or Spirit Prison, to wait until the second coming. How that judgment was made, and who made it, he wasn't sure.

He finished his prayer as lightening forks flashed illuminating his grave. Slightly forward of his left shoulder was the oyster shell that had cut his cheek.

Just maybe he could dig his way out. One little scoop at a time.

He leaned his head to the left. Wiggling his left shoulder he touched the shell with his ear. With his earlobe, he dragged the white shell an inch toward him. Not too far. He didn't want it falling into the hole in front of his chest. He hunched forward, moved the shell another inch.

Instead of trying to rise out of the grave he scrunched down the best he could. Maybe down a half-inch. He tilted his face toward the shell and felt for the hard-edged bivalve with his tongue. Grit and sand. Almost there.

He maneuvered the half shell until he sucked the thing into his mouth and gripped it with his teeth. A musky sand taste flooded his mouth. He probably looked like some white-tongued devil in a horror movie.

He leaned forward, shell firmly held, and scooped the dirt in front of him. He moved maybe a thimble full, but the mud stuck to the shell. He gave a quick flick of his head. The mud didn't move. Crap.

He dipped the shell in the puddle of water under his chin, and yes, the mud dissolved. Of course, what he'd just done was put sand into the very spot from where he was trying to remove it.

Tree frogs croaked. Bull frogs chortled until another rain band swept through then pellets of rain stung his face. The frogs ceased singing during the rain. He closed his eyes. Somewhere, he heard a noise that wasn't rain splatting on leaves. This was a scuttle through water. Something with stubby legs splashing around. Not enough noise to be a bear. He could see some through the dimness. The moon wasn't visible through the storm's clouds but a faint reddish hue penetrated enough for his eyes, well accustomed now to the darkness, to see features.

He turned his head to the right, then left, the shell firmly in his teeth. He didn't see anything moving, but his visibility was limited by the forty-five degrees he could rotate his head either direction.

He was a smart guy. He could figure a way out of this mess. His head was uphill from his legs. Water ran down hill. No genius thinking there. If he could somehow channel the rain that poured over him, maybe he could get it to wash the dirt away. But all he had was this stupid shell in his mouth. He leaned his face forward and pushed another scoop of sand away from him. Then he waited and sure enough, in a minute the rain washed the shell clean. Great, now he'd moved a teaspoon of dirt. This wasn't going to work. If the bear didn't get him, and he didn't drown, he'd starve to death before he could get enough dirt moved to escape.

Again, something sloshed in the water. The noise of some critter walking behind him. He caught movement out of the corner of his left eye. A possum, less than a foot away, stared back. The possum, grey and black furred, with black pink-tipped ears, swished the water with its rat-like tail. "Git," he said, the shell still in his mouth.

The possum hissed. Bared a mouth full of teeth. Spittle hung from its jaws.

Winch cocked his head to the right and whipped it to the left, flinging the shell at it. The shell went all of about six inches and plopped onto sand. The thing didn't notice. It sidestepped up to Winch's head, hissed, sniffed his cheek and licked.

Friggin critter. Winch barked like a dog. The possum latched onto his ear. Teeth sharp as sea urchin quills. It leaned backed, hind feet scrabbling in the sand, and tried to rip the ear from his head. Pain ran from his ear right down his spine.

Winch flipped his head right, left, right, left, back and forth. Ear on fire. Possum nails gouged his neck, dug in and clamped to him with each throw, as the darn thing held on.

With the next throw to the left, he slammed the possum onto the ground, knocking his own head against it, in a head-butt. Squishing it between his head and the ground. Pound, pound, pounding the side of his head against the possum, crushing it between the ground and his own head. Finally he realized it had let loose and lay motionless.

The thing looked dead. Lying perfectly still on its side. Some blood mixed with mucus smeared the possum's face. Whose blood was it?

All right, this was it. He was pissed now. He was getting out of here somehow, and was going to get even with the Patches, before the possum came alive and wanted seconds.

But how? He still couldn't move. If he couldn't use his head, then he'd have to use his feet or hands. He tried moving his feet and found he could actually wiggle his toes in his boots, but that was it. Hands buried behind his back he couldn't see his watch but he figured he probably didn't have more than a couple of hours before he'd be underwater.

He could wiggle each finger a little. He leaned forward closing the gap he'd left between his chest and the sand, opening a small space at his back. He explored the little space behind him. His right thumb brushed something hard. He ran the tip of his thumb around the little projection. The edge of an oyster shell, hard and sharp. Maybe, just maybe.

He moved both thumbs and index fingers, curling and uncurling, again and again. And then his other fingers, scraping sand away from the thumbs. One thimble full at time. Moving it from his thumbs, outward toward the little fingers. In a few minutes he could maneuver the plastic tie that bound his wrists against the shell. Now he rubbed the plastic back and forth, back and forth. A quarter of an inch is all the movement he could make. Would it be enough?

He bore down on the edge of the shell with all of his might, all the time rubbing that quarter inch against the shell that had been hard-packed into this mound for maybe a thousand years. He rubbed. Back and forth. Pain told him he was peeling his own flesh with each movement. Survival is all that mattered. He kept an eye on the possum, but it didn't move. Maybe it really was dead.

After how long, he didn't know, the plastic flex cuff snapped, all at once with no warning. It didn't stretch. One second his wrists were bound and the next they weren't.

He said a quick thank you to the Lord for giving him the strength to ignore the pain, and to the Timucuans for leaving their oyster shells here. Now to dig his way out. He couldn't move his arms but he could move his hands. In what seemed like a forever slow movement, with his right hand, he dug upward, using his fingers to shift the dirt and mud from above his hand to below it. Like a freshly hatched turtle digging his way out of the buried clutch of eggs. It couldn't have been more than few minutes, but it could have easily been an hour as well, he wasn't sure, his right hand, dirty and bloody, like some reincarnated Zombie's member coming out of a grave, popped free of the sand. In another minute he worked his entire right arm into the air.

Now he knew he wasn't going to die. At least not in this grave. He reached over and grabbed the oyster shell he'd had in his mouth, and scraped the dirt away in earnest. One hundred scrapes, two hundred, he quit counting and his upper body and left arm were free. He abandoned the shell and pushed the dirt off his lower body until he could bend his legs and climb out.

He didn't know what Patch had done with his shovel. If he'd had it, he would have dug Sarah up right then. But Sarah would have to wait for another couple of hours. He stepped away from the mound, took off his foul weather jacket and shirt and undershirt, and extended his arms. Bare-chested, he let the rain wash the sand off his body. He glanced over his shoulder at the hole that would have been his grave. The possum was gone.

He could find Patch and Patti. But he had no weapons and he knew that would be a problem when it came time to even the score.

FORTY-NINE

Winch shielded his eyes from the relentless rain. He normally had a good sense of direction. But here in the dark, the rain, he didn't have a clue which way to go. He closed his eyes. Said a quick prayer this time, asking for help to get to the nearest house. That would be Patch's.

He couldn't see the stars or the moon. No help there. He could start off in the direction that Patti had driven the tractor, but in 8,000 acres, in the dark, in the rain, in the freaking middle of a tropical storm, he could easily be lost. And that wouldn't help Sarah. Or Tracy. Or him.

After walking a few hundred yards in what he took to be a generally northerly direction he stopped. The two Timucuan mounds he'd been on, SJ1805 and Sarah's burial mound were no longer visible. Somehow, some way he had to get a sense of direction.

He heard a roar. Louder and louder. A spawning tornado? Sheesh, just what he needed. No place to take cover. He thought of the hole he'd just dug himself out of. No way he was going back into *that* hole. Not in this lifetime.

He laid flat on the ground between two pine stumps, held his head above the slowly rising water, and curled both arms around one stump. Curled his legs the best he could around the other and waited as the ground trembled and the roar grew.

It a minute the noise was so loud it drowned out the rain. A whistle blew. A train. A freaking train. He knew the train tracks ran north and south.

He picked himself up and listened to the train's rumble recede. The only reason for the train to have blown its whistle was because the tracks crossed a road. In his mind's eye he saw the Google Earth printout and could picture the tracks running parallel to Patch's land, and a road crossing the tracks north of the Timucuan mounds. So it had been coming from the north. Now he knew his directions.

The rain pin-pricked his face. He licked his lips and tasted salt. The ocean lay less than a mile away so the wind was blowing from the east. He turned his face downward to lessen the bite of the stinging drops, and trudged northward.

If he kept the wind in the same relative position over his right shoulder he should walk more or less north. He wondered about people who, lost in the woods, walked in circles, and didn't have enough sense to hunker down and wait out the storm, conserve their body heat and supplies. But he had the wind as his guide and the railroad tracks to the east. Within an hour he heard another roaring and its whistle and he knew he was still on course.

Twenty minutes after the whistle, a glow lit the ground ahead. Lights. Had to be Patch's house. He patted his pockets. No weapons. And no doubts that if Patti or Patch saw him they would shoot him, and drag his carcass back to the grave.

The wind-driven rain continued to pound, slacken, and then return, more fierce than before. Patch's house with yellow light spilling out of ground level windows was to his right. Dead ahead was a garage and a shed. The door banged against the shed wall.

No vehicles that he could see. With empty hands he crept toward the buildings. Here there were trees not felled by the pulp mills. Some were water oaks, as big as a two-story house, their branches thicker than his thigh. Smaller twigs, blown off by the high winds, littered the ground. A century old branch, big as phone pole, ripped from the mother tree, lay in the yard. These water oaks, top heavy and stiff, blow over in hurricanes. He looked through the scattered branches. Nothing he could use for defense.

To his left was another tree he recognized. A black ironwood tree. It was rare to see them this far north, but close to the temperate water, the ocean and the Intra-coastal, they will grow. Maybe he could use that. The Black Ironwood produces the hardest, most dense wood of any tree in North America. So dense the wood will not float. Axe-breakers, the conquistadores called them. This one was not large, maybe twenty-feet high. Large enough though.

At head height, a branch, as thick as his wrist, sprouted from the tree. He jumped, caught it with both hands well above where it joined the trunk, and pulled. It bent, and bent, and he pulled and pulled, levering it down and back with all of his weight. Biceps and forearms straining. Finally, with a crack like a forty-five, it splintered from the trunk, forming a sharp, jagged point where it released. While the sound was loud to him, the wind would have carried it away from the house and shed. He snapped off the smaller branches until he had a shoulder high staff.

The water was calf deep now. He slogged as quietly as he could toward the shed. Dark as a cave inside but he could see the tractor Patti had driven. The wind whipped in and out of the outbuilding. He stepped inside the shed and closed the door. He stood in the total darkness, glad to be sheltered from the wind and rain. Heat emanated from the tractor's cowling and he lay across it to warm himself for a minute. Then he felt around the instrument panel and found the key still in the ignition. He was afraid if he sat, he'd not rise again. He had to finish this. Bring Sarah out of her grave. With great reluctance he shoved the shed door open. The wind wrung it out of his hands and slammed it with a bang against the side. From here he could see lights in the main house. A silhouette moved in front of a garage window. A rhythmic swinging motion followed by a thud. And then the same thing again. And again. Strange.

He stepped out into the storm.

In the driveway, in front of the garage, Snake had parked his XKE. In a flash of lightening it looked like someone was in the passenger seat. Patti? He couldn't tell. Winch, ironwood staff in hand, stayed to the shadows and made his way toward the car. When a heavy rain band swept over him he ran up to the passenger side and flung open the door, poised to lunge with his branch. Snake's golf bag sat belted in like a human in the seat. Otherwise the car was empty. He laid his hand on the hood. Warm but not steaming.

The roll-up garage door was shut but there was a light on over a side door. He tried the handle. It turned and opened. He stepped inside.

In the middle of the oil-stained concrete floor lay a body. Patch. His head nearly severed at the neck. Blood spatter had sprayed the walls and floor in a long crescent pattern. Snake stood near the far wall with a golf club. A piece of green artificial turf, a yard square was on the concrete in front of him. Ten golf balls in a line. A bucket of white balls spilled behind the grass. A dozen or so golf balls lay around the garage. Three sat in pooled blood next to Patch's body.

"Snake?"

"Why am I not surprised to see you, Winchester?" Snake held the club out toward him. "You want a turn?"

"What happened here?"

Snake waved his hand in a wide gesture. "This is all your fault." He turned his stance toward Winch and swung. "Fore."

Winch ducked and the ball flew threw a pane of glass and out into the storm.

"Stop it, Snake."

He shanked a second ball which sailed across the floor at knee height, ricocheted off the rear wall and skittered into Patch's body. "What happened to you?" Snake pointed at his head with his club and pulled another ball in front of club's face.

Winch raised his hand to his ear. Tender as crap. "Possum tried to eat me."

"Ewwe. Nasty critters. You're lucky though, you know?" He shifted his stance a bit and swung. This time the ball flew through the rear window, smashing the glass on its way out.

He couldn't see how getting eaten by a possum could be considered good luck.

"They're practically immune to rabies. Now if it'd been a raccoon, you'd be taking rabies shots for a month. A bear would have taken your whole head. And an armadillo, they carry leprosy you know.

"Hey, watch this." Snake turned away from Winch and swung. With a thwack, the golf ball hit one wall and then another and another until it finally rolled to a stop.

"Crap Snake. Cut it out."

"Too windy to practice outside." He edged another ball with the club. Took a stance.

"You killed your step-father?" Winch evaluated the angles. Was he a target or not?

Snake shook his head. "Nah, he was like that when I got here."

He took a step toward the golfer.

Snake held the three iron up. Shook it at him. “Don’t come any closer.”

“You just about cut his head off with your golf club.”

“Wasn’t me.”

“We need to call the police.”

“You think?”

“I know where Sarah is buried.”

Snake reached for the bucket of balls. “Bully for you.”

Before he could tee the next ball, Winch closed on him, stopping a little more than a club’s length away. This close he could see blood on the club’s shaft and face. “Drop the club.”

“Not a chance in hell, Winch.”

“This is not going away. You can’t just carry your father out into the swamp—”

“Step-father.”

“—and bury him out there. Let him disappear like Sarah, and your mother.”

“I’ll cut your head off.” Snake swung at him. He turned but not quick enough and the club edge ripped across his side. Slicing through his foul weather gear cutting deep enough that his flesh seared.

Snake cocked the club like a baseball bat. “Come on, big man. Think you can take me in?”

He stepped toward Snake, his side on fire, holding the ironwood staff in front, hands shoulder-width apart near the middle.

Snake swung. The club edge hit the ironwood and stuck. The blow caused Winch to stumble backwards. He pulled and Snake fell forward to his knees. The club still imbedded in the wood.

“You just had to get in the way, didn’t you, Winchester? Why couldn’t you have just left this all alone?”

“The fifty thousand you got with your lies to Carla—not enough for you?”

Snake jerked his chin toward Patch’s body. “The old man hated my guts. Never put me in his will.”

Winch pulled and the club came free.

Snake stood, poised to swing again. Winch threw up the staff. The metal shaft of the golf club struck the ironwood with a clang. Snake drew it back but before he could swing, Winch lunged with the branch and drove the sharp end into Snake's upper chest. Blood rose-budded on his shirt.

"You stuck me." He dropped the club.

He shoved harder and pinned Snake against the wall. Snake struggled to get both hands on the ironwood branch. Gave up and slithered down the wall, legs splayed. A trail of blood smeared the plaster.

It'd gone clear through. He gently lowered his end of the ironwood to the floor. "Hold it in with your hands."

Snake grabbed the wooden shaft. "It hurts."

"Where's your sister?"

"Patti?" He jutted his chin toward Patch's body. "Come and gone."

Winch wondered what other motives Patti might have had for killing her father. "Cell phone?"

Snake nodded toward his front pocket.

He took the cell phone from the man's trousers. His eye caught on Snake's watch. "Swiss Army?"

"I'm sitting here bleeding to death and you're asking me about my watch?"

"Easy now." Winch leaned in closer and unfastened the watch. Held it up. Examined the watch face. Pivoted. "It has a compass in it."

"Tissot," Snake hissed. "Swiss, not Swiss Army."

He had to do something about Snake's bleeding.

The garage was empty, nothing here he could use. He leaned over Snake. Grabbed his shirt at the point where the ironwood entered the shoulder and ripped the material. In a minute he had the shirt off and pushed it into the wound, tucking it between the branch and the flesh as best he could. Snake writhed and twisted, swearing. Sweat popped out on his face. Blood ran down his chest in a steady stream, pooling in the folds of his stomach, and overflowing onto the floor.

Winch wasn't sure Snake would make it. He'd never killed a man before and wondered how that would play out in his mind. The shedding of innocent blood and all that. Something to worry about later.

"Hold your hands on it." Winch flipped open the phone. "I'm going to call for help."

Snake, chest heaving, looked up at him. Breathed out the words, "You said, 'my mother?'" He jutted his chin toward the door. "You found her out there?"

"I think so."

"She didn't leave me? All this time I thought she didn't care." Snake dropped his chin to his chest. Closed his eyes. His chest rose and fell.

Winch knew how he felt. He thought about his own parents, and how lucky he was to be raised by a good man like his uncle and not somebody like Patch.

Snake's hands slipped from the wound. Winch placed them back on the makeshift bandage. "You have to keep the pressure on." But as soon as he removed his own hands, Snake's fell away. Crap.

He checked the time on the phone. 3:45 a.m. He dialed 911.

When the emergency operator answered he gave them Patch's address and said, "We have a dead man here. And another seriously wounded. We need EMTs ASAP."

The operator asked him what happened. "No time for that," he said. "He's got a through and through to his upper chest. Call Detective Renfro. Wake him up. Tell him that Winchester Young found Sarah Fox."

"What's your name, sir?"

He looked at Snake's phone in his hand. "Luther Calderon," he said. "Most people call me Snake."

"Units are on their way. Please stay on the line until they arrive."

"I've got to go." He flipped the phone closed and tossed it on to Snake's lap. Slipped the Tissot watch over his wrist.

He opened the door from the garage to the house. Flicked on a kitchen light. Kitchen cabinet doors stood open. Shelves barren. Drawers clean. Nothing left but some trash and worn carpet in the house.

Back in the garage. "Snake?"

Snake lifted his head. Glazed eyes peered at him. His golf tanned face, white as the belly of a water moccasin.

"Got a flashlight anywhere?"

He dropped his chin to his chest. "The boot." The words barely audible.

Snake wasn't wearing boots. He thought for a moment and then remembered. Jaguar. British car.

He stepped out into the storm, opened the driver's side door of the Jag and popped the trunk release. A light came on and he saw a mag light and a blanket. He depressed the on switch. A weak light beam filtered out from the flashlight. He rifled through the rest of the trunk but of course there were no new batteries. Better than nothing.

No telling the condition of Sarah's body. He'd need something to carry the bones in. The blanket would do. He headed for the tractor shed. Slid his hand under the rain gear to his side. The blood on his palm and fingertips maroon in the darkness.

FIFTY

DAY SIX—THE LAST DAY

The sides of the tin shed vibrated in sync with the howling wind. Winch sat on the tractor and felt for the key. Some tree branch overhead slap, slap, slapped the roof. It surprised him that the shed hadn't blown into a heap. He wondered if the *Dos XX* was chafing her lines at the Chonch House, then remembered she wasn't there. Instead she lay on her side on the barge at the Oasis Marina. Or was she already in a landfill? Now he was off to another landfill of sorts. Oyster shell, Florida horse conchs, and human bodies.

He'd driven a John Deere before as a kid on the Mormon Church ranch just north of Holopaw, Florida. Deseret Cattle and Citrus Ranch. But it didn't have a front-end loader on it. He knew the levers to his right would raise, lower, and tilt the scoop. Or maybe it was the ones on his left? Not sure. One set would control the scoop, the other, the backhoe on the power takeoff at the rear. He'd figure it out when the time came.

He put his foot on what he hoped was the brake. Did he really want to go out into the storm again? This was the only chance he'd have to find Sarah. No choice. He turned the key to start.

The still-warm engine roared to life. He eased his foot off the brake and the beast leapt forward putting a dent in the wall in front. Crap. He found the gear shift. Moved it backward and tried again. This time the tractor rolled rearward and in a second he was out in the wind and the rain. He fumbled around for the headlight switch.

The area in front of him lit up. Some branches and twigs scattered in the wind and others piled against trees.

He checked the compass on Snake's watch and headed the machine south. Over the drowning effects of the wind he thought he heard sirens. Yes. In another minute red and blue flashes reflected off the windows of Patch's house. He considered turning off the lights but gave the tractor a little more throttle. Unlikely the cops would even notice him driving away, much less follow in the foot deep water he was traveling through. However, tractors, he knew, weren't immune from getting stuck in the mud either.

The problem he had was that the tractor headlamp shown straight ahead. It widened out further away, but when a rain band passed he couldn't see more than the length of a fallen tree. It'd be possible to drive right between the two mounds and never see them. So he snaked the tractor right and left like a drunk weaving across the yellow line. The dirt track he'd walked in earlier was not visible. Still, he was making good time when the tractor lurched to a stop.

Behind him the right rear wheel spun, the left didn't budge. No limited slip differentials on tractors? He guessed not because this baby wasn't budging.

He climbed down and as he did a pain in his right side, where Snake had sliced him with the club, shot clear to his shoulder.

He stooped and peered under the tractor with the flashlight. The center underbelly rode firmly on a wide stump. High centered, crap. He shoved the tractor sideways with his shoulder. Wouldn't budge.

Back in the driver's seat he flicked on the rear lights. Pushed the hand throttle up to rev the engine and locked it in place. Using the rear controls, he brought the backhoe bucket down as close to the rear of the tractor as he could and kept pushing the down lever. The bucket couldn't go down any further so something had to give and in a second the rear wheels pushed off the ground. All of the tractor's weight now rested on the backhoe bucket.

With the lever he nudged the tractor to the right. Released the weight on the bucket and the tractor plopped down with a crack. Hoped he hadn't broken the backhoe. He could see the stump now, well to the left of center of the tractor. He raised the bucket and was off. This was sort of fun actually. Maybe he should have been a heavy equipment operator instead of a PI.

He figured that in the last twenty minutes he'd covered the ground that it took him more than an hour to walk. He slowed the tractor and made wider sweeping turns, using the headlights, searching.

Patch's house, the cop lights, and the sirens were all long gone. Out here it was just him and the wild animals gone to ground for the storm. And the ghosts of the ancient Timucuans. And Sarah and Snake's mother. So he guessed he wasn't really alone.

To his left he saw a mound. To his right where Sarah's should have been. Nothing. He headed toward the one he could see. He didn't recognize the north side of it. But then when he'd walked away from Sarah's mound he hadn't really looked at this side. When he'd left earlier he had no light. No way to see anything.

He drove around to the south side, and yes, there was the hole he'd been buried in.

Now he had a decision to make. Backhoe or front end loader? Using the front end loader would require him to move more dirt. Start at the bottom of the mound and work his way up. Patch had said Sarah was right next to him. So he'd start there first with the backhoe.

He backed the tractor and turned on the rear-facing lights on the roll-bar overhead. This wasn't a regular backhoe. It was a farm tractor with a rear power take-off. So it didn't have feet that could be planted to anchor it. He set the brake. Pivoted the seat. Then remembered to use the hand accelerator to set the engine speed higher. He commenced digging. Even in the heaviest of rain bands, the lights were strong enough to see reasonably clearly.

He didn't know how far away from his own grave Patch had buried Sarah, so he began a ditch perpendicular to where he'd been buried. He figured once he hit something he would dig deeper and more carefully. But time was running out. It was 4:30 and the dozers would start the flooding at six, unless Woody's plan to sabotage them actually worked. Go Woody!

Thirty minutes later, three feet down in the trench, he saw something darker than the surrounding sand and oyster shell soil. He stepped off the tractor and lowered himself to his knees. What was that? He lay on his stomach and reached for it with his hand, barely touching it with his fingertips. Something soft.

He commenced digging again and wished he had a shovel. Five o'clock. He had to get this done. No reason to be too delicate. In five minutes he had the whole bundle of whatever it was on the ground next to the tractor.

It was body length. He moved it with his hands and it began to unroll. Some sort of animal skin. Wrapped inside were skeletal remains. The hair was long and loose around the skull, all of the skin having deteriorated long ago. A handful of multicolored beads lay behind the skeleton's neck. This didn't seem right. The beads had probably been strung on a piece of gut or maybe a woven grass fiber of some sort.

He rolled the skeleton back into the hide and extended his trench. In just a few minutes he found a similar skeleton. Beads and all.

Timucuan. These had to be Timucuan burials. Not Sarah and not Virginia Patch. He idled the engine down so he could think this through. What had Dick Sharp's widow said? Sharp was looking into cadaver dogs. Patti worked at the Sheriff's office. She'd probably heard some talk and told Patch. Cagey old Patch had put Timucuan remains on top of Sarah and Virginia to fool the dogs.

Back to the trench he dug faster now. Checking his watch. Another foot of dirt and something glinted in the tractor's lights. He scraped the soil off. Off what, he wasn't sure, but it wasn't Timucuan.

When it was totally exposed he climbed down into the trench. A plastic drop-cloth wrapped with duct tape. He heaved it out of the trench. The plastic crunched and broke apart. No question there were human remains inside.

He started thinking crime scene, and the Sheriff's office would want to process it, but this area would be under water before any evidence technician-types could get here. And the murderer was already dead. He tore apart the plastic with a sound like crunching twigs. A skeleton with swaths of clothing, women's leather boots with rubber soles, was still pretty much intact. Definitely not Timucuan.

He played the flashlight over the bones. A glint of gold flashed at him from below the skull, pillowed on a mound of hair. There around her neck was a gold chain and the nugget that her father had given to her. The same he'd seen in the photograph. Welcome home, Sarah Fox.

He gathered her up and put her in the blanket. He looked into the stormy sky and wondered if her spirit was nearby, watching. Sorry Sarah. She deserved better but it was all he had. He slipped the nugget and chain into his pocket. Tampering with evidence? If he hadn't been out here "tampering" there would be no evidence. So shoot him. He didn't care.

He dragged the blanket a few feet to the side and commenced digging. Three feet to the left, at the same depth, he found another plastic bundle. He slid this one into the blanket also. It would be the missing Virginia Patch. Would Snake live to see his mother properly buried? He rolled them together and set them gingerly in the bucket of the front-end loader. Tilted it so they wouldn't fall out on the ride home. Ironic that Virginia Patch was going to the home she'd lived in and that her husband waited for her dead on the garage floor. He doubted that when Patch died earlier in the night, there was much of a reunion between the two of them in the Spirit World.

He returned the Native Americans to their graves. Scooped some dirt over them and headed north. If Native American remains are found at construction sites then they must be relocated or preserved in situ. Construction stops until the issue is resolved.

He doubted he could get to anybody with authority over the construction crew within the next hour. That's what it would take to keep them from flooding the area. Then an idea came to him as bright as any flash of lightning. He knew how to positively stop the bulldozers.

FIFTY-ONE

Winch figured he was less than half a mile from Patch's house when the tractor's engine coughed, raced, and died. He turned the key. The starter whined, but it wouldn't start. Headlights still worked but the fuel marker stood on empty. Crap.

The rain eased a bit. Flashes of red and blue bounced ahead. The cops were still there. Crap squared. But then he'd expected that. Snake would have told them that he'd tried to kill him. And maybe he had. If he approached the house he'd be arrested for Tracy's murder. But he couldn't leave Sarah and Virginia. Not when he was this close.

He took the gold chain and nugget out of his pocket and hung the chain around his neck. No better place to hide it than in plain sight. Then he grabbed the blanket with the two sets of bones from out of the frontend loader's bucket and trudged toward the light. Carried them in his arms like a child. With each step he felt the flesh pull on his side. His left ear burned from the possum's bite. The blanket was surprisingly light. Maybe twenty pounds total.

Eventually he saw flashlights waving about through the trees around the house. As he approached, a deputy noticed him. There was a quick huddle of men and then Renfro stepped forward. "You look like road-kill, Young. What's in there?"

He extended the blanket like an offering. "Sarah Fox and Virginia Patch. At least I think so."

"Bring'em into the light. Slowly."

He walked forward and stood next to a command vehicle like a large RV with the Sheriff's logo on the side. A generator hummed and lights illuminated the area as bright as a sunny day at the beach, only it was raining. The wind gusted to about 45 knots and the rain blew at an angle. They moved to the leeward side of the vehicle out of the wet onslaught.

Renfro took the blanket. Called a couple of crime-scene techs over. "Take it inside before you unroll it." He turned to Winch. "Which one is Sarah?"

Shrugged. "You guys can figure that out. Mitochondrial DNA from the bones. Sarah's and Carla's should be the same.

"Messed with my crime scene out there did you?"

"There are at least two more bodies. I'll show you where." He didn't have to tell Renfro that he figured them for Timucuan remains. Renfro probably wouldn't stop the flooding for that. He checked his watch, 5:45. "In fifteen minutes it's going to be underwater."

Renfro shone his light on Winch's ear. "Jesus, a piece of your ear is missing."

"Possum ate it." He unbuttoned his raincoat, lifted his shirt and looked at his side. "Snake."

"You stuck him pretty good. He may not make it. He said he didn't kill his old man."

"Patti Reynolds was out here earlier. She and the old man tried to kill me."

"You got any proof of that?"

He shook his head.

"Tell me about the bodies."

"Two of them. Right next to—" A small lie. He didn't want to tell him they were on top of Sarah and Virginia. "—where they buried me alive."

"Who would they be?"

Winch shook his head. "Like they spoke to me?" The tropical storm seemed to have hunkered down over North Florida. The sky normally would have been lighter this time of day. Instead the heavy cloud cover kept it dark.

"You can show me where they are?"

"We'll need some fuel for the tractor."

Renfro turned to one of the deputies. “Go find the construction foreman. Tell him they’re going to have stand down for a day. We have a crime scene out in the middle of the woods and we don’t want to swim out there and back.”

Winch could hardly hold back his smile. Yes. Yes. Yes!

Renfro turned to him. “You’re under arrest for the murder of Tracy Young, Winchester.” To another deputy he said, “Search him. Cuff him. Get him to an EMT and then let him cool his jets in the back seat of your car.” He nodded down the driveway. “With his Seminole buddy.”

The deputy had him do the spread, against the command RV. Frisked under his foul weather gear. Ran his hands up Winch’s legs. Fingered the gold nugget. “They’ll take that from you at the jail.”

At least he’d found Sarah. But he couldn’t sit in jail and wait for a jury to clear him of Tracy’s murder. It’d be months, maybe years before it ever went to trial. He knew a guy who sat in jail for seven years before he had a trial date. And there’s usually no bail on capital cases. He had to think of way out of this right now.

FIFTY-TWO

Rain pelted Winch's bare head. The deputy cuffed him, hands behind his back, and led him toward a patrol car, and who knew how many months or even years in jail? His business, his finances, pretty much everything in his life would be ruined. Mounting a legal defense in a murder case would cost several hundred thousand dollars. There goes the house. All for something he didn't do. Would never do. Maybe if he offered Renfro something he really wanted.

"Okay, you're so clever, Renfro," Winch said. "Tell me where I slipped up. How did you catch me?"

"You don't know, do you Young?"

"I'd know if I'd done it, but I didn't."

"The toolbox in the back of your Jeep. We found the wire snippers you used to cut the propane line. Tool marks were a match."

"My prints on them too?"

"Wiped clean. Thought you were smart, huh? But not smart enough."

His jeep hadn't been broken into. So whoever used his tools to rig the *Dos XX* must have either used a Slim-Jim or had a key. There was only one spare set and he always left them at Tracy's house.

Winch looked around. "You follow the ponies, Detective?"

Renfro scowled. "What are you talking about, Young?"

"The Triple Crown."

"What is this, Trivial Pursuit?" The detective turned to the deputy. "Take him away."

Winch called over his shoulder. "The Kentucky Derby, the Preakness. The Belmont."

"Yeah, yeah, whatever."

"Sarah Fox, Virginia Patch, and your wife's ex-husband, Dick Sharp."

He and the uniform took a few more steps when Renfro said, "Hold up, Deputy." He came around and faced him. "What about Sharp?"

"I already gave you Sarah and Virginia. I can give you Sharp's murderer too. I know how it went down."

Renfro waved him on with his hand. "Spill it."

"I need a favor first."

"We're booking you for murder. You're out of favors."

"An hour's all I need. You drive, I'll ride." He looked around. "Nothing you can do here until it gets light. And you need me to show you where the bodies are buried. This will make you a superstar. Not to mention the points it'll buy you with your wife."

"Uncuff him, Deputy. If you screw me over, Young. . . ."

"I need one more thing." He nodded toward Woody in the patrol car.

"We're charging him with malicious mischief. Trespassing on a construction site."

"Misdemeanors," Winch said. "I'm giving you a first degree murder conviction. Be smart."

"Oh hell, I'll probably regret this." He nodded to the deputy. "Cut him loose."

* * * *

Winch sat in the front seat of Renfro's undercover, Woody in the rear. The windshield wipers ran full speed but the rain fell so heavily visibility was next to zero.

"Tracy's house. Err, my house," Winch said. "I need to get some dry clothes." While that was true, it wasn't the reason he wanted to go to Tracy's. "But first, we need to drive to the back side of Patch's land. I left my Jeep parked there. We can pick it up and Woody can follow us."

"This is not a taxi service," Renfro said. But he followed Winch's directions and in a few minutes they were at the Jeep.

The sky was finally beginning to lighten. Even tropical storm Florence couldn't keep it dark forever.

In some respect he felt like he was violating Tracy's space. Inviting people into her home and she wasn't there. He went first to the kitchen and pointed to the key hook on the wall between the kitchen and the door to the garage. "They're not there."

Renfro gave him a look.

"The spare set of keys to my Jeep I kept on that hook. They're gone, and I know who took them."

Renfro shook his head. "You're going to tell me that someone broke in here? Took your keys? Got tools out of your toolbox? Rigged your boat to blow? Put the tools back in the Jeep, just to frame you?"

Winch nodded. "Very clever for a detective."

"And who exactly would that person have been?"

"Patti Reynolds, aka Patricia Patch. She rigged the Dos Equis. I can prove it."

"I'm listening."

He fumbled around in Tracy's top dresser drawer and came out with a small grey box about the size of computer thumb drive.

"What's that?" Renfro said.

"It's a key locator. I told you at the marina. I'm always misplacing my keys. So I keep a little receiver on the ring. And I can press this button. . . ." He pressed it and a chirp, chirp, chirp, emitted from his key ring on the dresser. "And find them. Range is about 50 feet. I keep a spare here. One on the boat, and one in my office."

"And this is going to prove who killed Richard Sharp exactly how?"

Winch told him how. A bluff, but it might actually work.

FIFTY-THREE

Renfro cut Woody loose and he and Winch drove toward Patti Reynolds' house, wipers slapping full speed. Winch was just glad to be in a dry place, out of the storm. If this gamble didn't work, he could count on a dry bunk in jail.

Patti lived in the Lincolnville area of old St. Augustine, not far from Flagler College. A block from the Oasis Marina where the *Dos XX* had been disemboweled. Slaves, freed by the Civil War, with nowhere else to go, settled the area.

The traffic lights were all dark. Power outage.

"I had a phone call about you last night, from the West Palm Beach Sheriff's office," Renfro said.

He couldn't fathom why the Sheriff's office down there would be calling about him. "And?"

"Seems they had a drive-by shooting last night."

Winch fingered the butterfly bandages on his cheek. EMTs said he'd need stitches. "You know I was on Patch's property all night."

"The victim's wife said he'd had a mysterious visitor a few days before. They found your card in his billfold."

"Ellsworth Van Ellis the third," Winch said. "He cheated on his wife and thought I'd come to blackmail him. "Trey Ellis was the name he used. You, of all people should recognize that name."

Renfro nodded. "They ran NCIC on you and came up with your murder capias. They thought maybe you were a hired gun. I told them I'd bring you in today and they could question you."

"Am I under arrest again? "Winch said.

"Turns out it wasn't really a drive-by. Somebody shot him from across a canal while he was tossing hay to his horses. Why were you there?"

"Ellis was one of the three boys with Sarah Fox."

They sat in silence, until Renfro said, "Nah, twenty-five years later someone is trying to cover up Fox's disappearance? Patch killed her, right? And he's dead. You found her body. We've got it back there. Forensics will tell us it's her. So what is there to cover up?"

"Nothing," Winch said. "Absolutely nothing left to hide. Probably the jealous husband shot him. Clue them into that angle." But something nagged at the back of his mind. Slippery as a large mouth bass on the hook. If you didn't get your fingers into the gills before you removed the hook, the darn fish would slip right out of your grasp.

"You know," Renfro said. "It's too bad Patch isn't still alive so we could charge him—"

Winch raised his hand. "I had nothing to do with Patch's death."

"What you did out there tonight was pretty damn good, Winchester Young. That was you that made the 911 call from Snake's phone, right?"

Winch nodded.

"Thought so. When the office woke me up, I told my wife, Meredith, that you'd found Sarah Fox. She said she wasn't surprised. Said she would have laid money on you. You seemed pretty determined."

"Maybe you and I got off to a bad start," Winch said. "Tell your wife I appreciate the vote of confidence."

They pulled up in front of Patti's residence, a renovated "shotgun" house, a frame building on pilings of concrete blocks. "You sure about this, Young?"

Tropical storm Florence poured rain by the buckets full. Winch nodded. A band of wind blew the rain sideways. Orange trees in front of Patti's house leaned. Leaves, ripped from their branches, pelted the house next door. The citrus would have uprooted completely except someone had tied lines to metal stakes driven at angles into the ground. Heavier palm fronds and water oak branches littered the short strip of concrete walkway from street to house.

Renfro said. "Let's see what she has to say for herself."

Winch checked the time. Seven a.m. A faint light flickered through a glass panel in the front door. Candles?

He wondered, maybe Renfro should have some backup. Even though Patti wasn't a sworn LEO, she might have a gun in the house.

He suggested it to Renfro who just said, "Patti? She's worked for the Sherriff for twenty years. She's harmless."

The Patti he knew was anything but harmless.

"If she sees me, she'll think you're here to arrest her. By yourself, she'll think you're here to inform her of Patch's death

"You're assuming," Renfro opened the car door, "that Snake didn't kill the old man and Patti did."

"If Patti didn't do it, then she'll be totally shocked. Stands to inherit eight million dollars."

Renfro gave him a look. "Sounds like a motive. Let's go."

A pine tree across the street cracked like the discharge of a twelve gauge. The top of the tree crashed down, splitting a fence. The trunk landed parallel to the gutter, its branches tumbling into the street, blocking half the road.

"Sheesh," Winch said, looking at where they might have parked.

They hustled from the car to the covered front porch. Renfro opened the screen door but before knocking pointed to the side of the house. "Wait there until she opens. Then come up."

In a second Winch saw the front curtains pull aside, a faint light spilling across the windowsill. "She's home."

Renfro nodded.

The door opened. "Vinnie, what are you doing here?"

Renfro slid one shoe over the threshold, braced himself against the doorframe. "We need to talk. May I come in?"

"Can't this wait until we get to the office?

He shook his head. "Now."

She opened the door wider.

"I brought someone with me. Winchester."

She took a step back. Her hand went to her mouth, but she recovered quickly. "Why isn't he in cuffs?"

Renfro was all the way inside now, Winch behind him. Patti, dressed in the white uniform blouse and green trousers of the Sheriff office clerks, gestured to a burgundy leather sofa and matching chair. The house smelled of sea-scented candles.

A coil of line lay on the hardwood floor next to the couch. It looked like half-inch braided nylon. The ends hadn't been whipped, but burned and melted to keep them from unraveling. Patti caught his glance. "I was out last night staking the orange trees. Didn't want them blowing over."

"Was that before or after you and your father tried to kill me?"

She turned to Renfro. "Why is he here, Vinnie? I don't want him in my house."

"Sit down, Patti," Renfro said.

"I don't want to sit." Patti backed until she leaned against a mahogany antique secretary.

Winch stood, back to the door, watching her reaction.

"Your father's dead, Patti."

"You're mistaken. I was there last night. He was fine."

"Your brother—"

"Half-brother—"

"–found the body. It looked like he'd been chopped to death with Snake's three iron."

She turned away. Heaved a sob. Her hands went to her eyes, but they didn't seem wet to Winch. "Then he must have done it," she said still facing away.

"I understand you're inheriting your father's entire estate. Eight million reasons to kill someone."

"You're right. I'll inherit everything. Dad had liver cancer. Three or four more months, and it would have been all mine anyway. This is ridiculous. I had no reason to kill my own father."

"I'm booking Winchester, and then I want you to come to my office and give me a statement."

"Sure." She gave Winch a satisfied grin and a slight nod of her head.

"There's just one more thing, Patti."

She gave him a questioning look.

"Winchester thinks you killed Tracy. Rigged his boat to blow. And says he can prove it."

"Me?" Her hand went to her chest. "Tracy was my friend." Her eyes flicked between him and Renfro. "The tools? You found the tools he used, right? He had them in his possession the whole time. Your affidavit said so."

Renfro opened his arms. “There’s a problem. He wasn’t in town and can prove it.”

Her hands fell to her side, clenched into fists. “He rigged it before he left. Knew she was coming over later. I heard them make the arrangements with my own ears. I told you that.”

Renfro ran his hand through his wet hair. Wiped it on his trousers. “Anybody else in the house.”

She shook her head. “Now, Vinnie, why are you really here?”

“It’s Winchester,” he said. “You see, he has this theory that you took the spare set of keys for his Jeep from Tracy’s and used them to get the tools to cut the propane line in his boat. Snipped the wires to the sniffer alarm in the bilge. Shorted the light switch by the—” He turned to Winch. “What do you call that?”

“The companionway.”

“Right. The light switch and that’s all you’d need to do. Put the tools back in Winch’s car, and he looks guilty.”

She shook her head. “Ridiculous. I’ve been to Tracy’s house. I was there with Winch. He knows that. But I don’t know anything about his keys.”

Renfro nodded. “I told him it was a crazy theory. Save it for the jury, right?”

Now it was Patti’s turn to nod.

“Only seems,” Renfro continued. “That Winch here has a bad habit of misplacing his keys. So he’s got a little wireless key finder remote on each set.”

Winch pulled out the transmitter and pushed the button. In less than a second a staccato beep-beep, beep-beep, beep-beep played out of the secretary that Patti was standing next to. Her eyes darted between the two of them and the desk.

Renfro took a step forward. “Let me have a look.”

She turned her back to them. “No. I’ll get them. But there must be some mistake. I wouldn’t know,” she opened the desk drawer and the beep was significantly louder, “how these got in here.” She whirled around and in the same motion, pulled the trigger on Winch’s Smith 9mm, hitting Renfro dead center in the chest. Renfro pulled his own gun part way out of the holster but was too late. He stumbled backwards, landing with an oomph on the hardwood floor, rolling onto his side.

Winch dove behind the couch. Renfro's gun well out of his reach.

"You might as well stand up, Winch. You're next. This time I'll make sure the job is done right."

Winch grabbed the coil of line, holding the bitter end in his right hand. With a twist of his wrist he flopped the bitter end around the line and in half a second had a bowline and a loop about an arm's length wide.

Patti must have seen the line disappear behind the couch. She had to be wondering if Renfro would have let him keep a gun. He hadn't been handcuffed, so she couldn't know for sure.

"What do you think, Winch? Your nine or the rope? Which do you think will win?"

They both knew the answer to that question. Unless he could distract her somehow. But how? "I don't want to shoot you, Patti. Why don't you just leave? Walk out the door and we both can live. Otherwise we both die and Snake inherits your father's money. Is that what you want?"

"No way he's taking that money."

"Would have made more sense if you'd killed him instead of your father."

"Not really," she said. She edged toward Renfro.

"He changed his will, right?"

"You missed it again, Winchester. He was changing it today. Couldn't have that."

If he kept stalling, he'd be shot. He had to act now.

"You and Tracy can be together," Patti said. "Buried in the same grave even."

He slipped off his shoe. Hurled it at her voice, leapt to his feet and threw the loop. Her gun hand was near her face, barrel upward, fending off the shoe. The bowline and its loop fell over her head and the upraised arm. He yanked as hard as he could.

Off balance, Patti flew across the couch. The gun sailed backwards over her head, sliding under the antique furniture.

He leaped for Renfro's weapon. Had it pointed at Patti's back as she ran. He could have shot her. There was no religious reason not to. But she posed no danger running away. Renfro's life was his immediate concern. Patti would be the Sheriff's problem now. Her car in the drive started and backed with a short yelp of rubber on wet concrete.

He ripped Renfro's shirt open. No Kevlar vest. Red bubbles gurgled from a hole in his chest. In and out. A sucking chest wound.

Renfro, shot with Winch's own gun. If Renfro died, it'd be Patti's word against his.

FIFTY-FOUR

Winch waited in the hospital hallway. At Patti's he'd held his hand over Renfro's chest wound, sealing it the best he could. With the other he grabbed a cell and called 911. In a few minutes paramedics and deputies filled the house.

The Sheriff was in his office when Winch's call came, and he made it to Patti's house in seven minutes, accompanied by Sergeant Hardwick, chief of the detective division. Renfro was being carried to the ambulance right then. The winds were too fierce to life-flight him.

The Sheriff bent close to Renfro. Renfro's lips moved. Winch being detained by a uniform couldn't hear what was said. After the ambulance departed, the Sheriff approached him.

To Hardwick who had cuffed him he said, "Let him go. I'm having the warrant withdrawn." To Winch he said, "I made a mistake, Young. Vinnie said that Patti rigged the boat to blow and you had proof. She shot him too."

Winch rubbed the cuff marks on his wrists.

The Sheriff drew a deep breath and turned to Hardwick. "Make sure we get someone from the State Attorney's office. Have them get a warrant to search this place. Winch can give them all of the PC they need. Put a BOLO out on Reynolds. I want her caught. I'm going to the hospital. Call me when you need to."

* * * *

Meredith Renfro paced up and down the hospital hall, head jerking up anytime the operating room doors opened. After several hours a doctor emerged. The Sheriff rose from a chair. Meredith edged closer. Winch hung back. feeling guilty and responsible.

"I've done what I can," he said. "He's critical. I expect he'll come around in about an hour. You can see him then. You need to be prepared. This is a very serious wound and he may not make it. I know it sounds trite, but we're doing all we can. Any questions?"

Meredith pulled a handkerchief out of her raincoat pocket and dabbed her eyes. "Someone will let us know when I can go in?"

The doctor nodded. "As soon as he's conscious. If his vitals worsen, they'll bring you in anyway."

Meredith nodded, her shoulders sagged, and she leaned against a wall. Then she slid down and sat on the floor, drew her knees up, buried her face in her hands and sobbed, great heaving sobs.

The Sheriff went to her, offered his hand but she shook free. "No," she said. "It's not fair. First Richard and now Vinnie. I hate this. I told Vinnie I'd kill him if he got shot and died like Richard. I didn't mean it. I didn't mean it, but here I am."

The Sheriff shuffled back to his chair. Winch sat on the floor next to Meredith. Waited for the sobs to subside.

"I'm sorry Meredith. I feel like it's my fault. If it weren't for me, we wouldn't be here."

"You didn't shoot him, Winchester." She turned her face sideways to look at him. "That bitch Patti Reynolds shot him. They tell me, if he lives, then you saved his life. If you hadn't been there he would be dead already."

Winch wiped his eyes. He needed sleep. "Vinnie is a good man. On the way over to Patti's this morning, I think we finally came to appreciate each other's talents."

"I know what people said." Another sob. "But none of it was true. She rolled up one sleeve. Large bruises covered portions of her forearm. "People thought he beat me. You too, didn't you?"

He gestured to her arm.

She shook her head. "What appears obvious in this life isn't always so clear. This isn't what you thought. I'm on blood thinner and it's hard to control. Overdose a little and the tissues bleed. I bruise easily. Vinnie never would have laid a hand on me."

He just nodded. Thinking. What you see isn't always as it appears. He rose, suddenly realizing what he'd been missing. He laid his hand on her shoulder. "I've got to go. I'll keep Vinnie in my prayers."

"Are you religious, Winch? Do you pray everyday?"

In addition to a strong belief in prayer, Mormons believe in gifts of the spirit. Healing the sick is one of those gifts. He wanted to offer her that. "I could have some Elders come over and give him a blessing, if you wish."

"What church?"

"The Mormon church," he said.

"I never believed much in that kind of stuff," she said. "After Richard was shot, I was mad at God. Do you know how that feels?"

He'd had those same feelings two days ago when he'd learned of Tracy's death. "I do. But I also know that God didn't shoot Vinnie."

"Send your Elders over," she said. "It can't hurt."

Just then a nurse came through the doors. "Mrs. Renfro? Sheriff? I think you'd better come in. He's slipping quickly. There's not much time. I'm sorry."

As he walked past the Sheriff caught his arm. Meredith already passing through the doors. "Where're you going, Young?"

"It's not finished yet, Sheriff. One more knot to tie."

FIFTY-FIVE

The wind calmed to a flutter of leaves. Great waves of birds flew, swaying and sweeping through the sky, searching for food after two days on the ground. Winch stepped out of the hospital into partial sunshine. Above his head, clouds covered the sky, but in the east, the overcast ended in an abrupt black line on a blue chalkboard. On the other side the sun shone forth.

He wished it were an omen, but he knew he stood right in the center of his own storm. He didn't like being duplicitous. But a nest of snakes remained in this case and he'd have to conjure up his best acting skills to entice them out of their hole and cut their heads off.

It'd been a heck of a night. Buried alive, arrested twice, shot at, a possum snacked on his ear, Patch hacked to death, and him a witness to Renfro's murder. All in the last 12 hours. He was tired, but he had to push on. Then maybe he could get some sleep. He took out his iPhone and logged in to the GPS software site. The black Lexus driven by the hooker's friend with the tracking device still attached was stationary. It appeared to be near Interstate 95 and State Road 16. His first thought was that it was at the Outlet Mall. But no, when switching to street view he could see it parked at the Hampton Inn across from the mall.

He climbed into his Jeep and headed to the office to pick up his 35mm Canon. He needed proof and a photo of the John might do it.

* * * *

AM

9:50	Depart offices in route to vicinity of Outlet Malls.
10: 10	The black Lexus with Georgia tags was located in the Hampton Inn parking lot. He parked in a KFC, giving him a pretty good view of the Lexus through a chain-linked fence. He bayoneted on the 300 mm lens and changed the focus from auto to manual. As good as the electronics were, his natural eyes were better. An autofocus would almost certainly zero in on the fence as opposed to his subject a 100 feet the other side. He'd miss his shot, going home with a perfectly focused photo of the fence. Been there, done that. So he zoomed in on the car and waited. The humidity must have been close to 100 percent. In the aftermath of the storm, water pooled in ditches, spilled across roadways, and flooded parking lots. Every insect native to North Florida buzzed about. Finally he'd had enough of swatting flies, bees, and even mud daubers. With all of this standing water, in ten days, mosquitoes would rule. He turned on the Jeep, rolled up the windows and cranked on the air.
11:32	A KFC employee, trying to appear nonchalant, walked the perimeter of the lot. As he passed behind the Jeep, he wrote Winch's tag on piece of paper. Winch gave him a slight wave. Crap. It probably wouldn't be long before some Deputy would roll up behind him, whelp his siren, and turn on his flashers. He considered talking to the manager, show him his ID, ask if he minded if he sat in the lot a while longer. But sure as heck if he left his position for a minute his subject would come out and he'd miss the shot. No, better to stay put. If forced to leave he could find another spot or pick the guy up later. The tracker on the car should have several days of battery life left.

11:40 A slender man with buzz cut red hair, in his upper thirties, and very fit looking, stepped out of the hotel's front door and walked to the Lexus. He was wearing green cargo pants, tennis shoes, and a black t-shirt hugging a gym hardened body. He carried a blue duffle bag in his right hand. He'd probably checked out. Winch had his finger on the shutter, the Canon snapping pictures faster than a person could count.

There was something odd about the way the man walked, so he pulled the zoom back to shoot the entire body, and not just the face. He had a clear view through the fence of the driver's side and he continued to shoot until the car pulled out. Now to see where he goes. If the Lexus headed north toward Georgia, he and Woody would take a trip up there tomorrow and pull the GPS off the car.

11:43 He put the Jeep in gear and followed. In short order they were driving past the carousal from, jeez, what was it, just yesterday? He caught a red light in front of Ripley's Believe It or Not, but the Lexus made it through on the yellow. One of the red sightseeing trolleys zipped in front and blocked him from the Lexus. Come on trolley, get out of the way.

He proceeded past the fort, Castillo de San Marcos. In front of the fort were half-a-dozen horses and buggies waiting for customers. A tour group crossed the wide expanse of grass, following a woman in a long frontier-style blue dress. The slow moving trolley finally made a right and sure enough the Lexus was gone. At the corner where the Bridge of Lions crossed the harbor Winch drove past the old slave market. There on his right he spotted the car. The red headed man pointed his key fob and it honked and flashed its parking lights.

PM

12:01 The red-headed man, walking with a slight limp, crossed the street to the restaurant, O.C. White's, looked at his watch, and then sat at an outdoor table. Winch slid the jeep into a parking spot further up Marine Street where he still had a view. Camera at the ready he waited.

12:06 Carla Fox came around the corner from the direction of the Casa Monica hotel. The man didn't rise. Carla sat. He snapped off a dozen or more shots of the two of them talking. They didn't look romantic, but it wasn't all business either. There were smiles and laughter and once over lunch she poked him on his bicep with her fist. He'd seen enough. Whoever he was, Carla and he were connected. Somehow, he wasn't surprised, just disappointed.

12:15 Surveillance discontinued.

At the office he removed the compact flash card from the camera and slid it into the receiver on his computer. In a second he was scrolling through the photos. He picked a couple of good face shots, imported the time and date of the shots onto the bottom edge of the photos, and printed them with the color laser on 28 pound paper. A pretty good photo surveillance if he did say so himself.

He blew up one of the shots of the man getting into the car. The fellow's pants leg was raised slightly and darn if he didn't have a prosthetic left leg, constructed out of some sort of burgundy colored tubing, just like Valene had said. Could have been an accident. Could have been a war injury from Afghanistan or Iraq, which might explain some things.

He took the photo of Sarah Fox out of his drawer. There was Sarah, her little sister Carla, and her brother, Rusty. He compared the photos from today with that one from twenty-five years ago. Rusty had red hair. He and the driver of the Lexus could be the same person. Hard to tell for sure but there was nothing in today's shots that would preclude this man from being Carla's brother.

He printed off the GPS report on the Lexus's travel over the last three days. The tracker reported in every 5 minutes. The program kept a log in a spreadsheet of latitude and longitude each time the vehicle reported. It also gave him a "parking report" when the vehicle is stationary.

Renfro hadn't told him what time Trey Ellis was killed. But it only took a minute looking at the map on the computer to figure it out. The Lexus's route with speed and direction was clearly shown. At 6:20 am Rusty had parked on the north side of the canal next to Ellis's pasture. He recalled the lots there being heavily wooded. The pines and oak myrtles covered in air potato vines. Nearly impossible to see through.

He could envision this guy, Rusty Fox, ex-military, recently returned wounded warrior, crawling through the woods, waiting patiently until Ellis came from the house to toss hay to his horses and boom, shooting him from across the canal. There was no question in his mind that this was Trey Ellis's killer. And probably he'd killed Kevin Lawrence and Tony Hudson. Hudson's murder here in St. Johns County was still unsolved.

But now he had another problem. He may have broken the law by putting the GPS tracker on the Lexus. If he went to the Sheriff with his printouts, he might be arrested yet again. He could lose his license and actually do some time in jail. No. There had to be another way.

Even though Meredith Renfro hadn't blamed him for Vinnie's death, he wondered if it was his fault? What had Patti said in the hot tub that day? "Quit the investigation before somebody gets killed. And if you don't and they do, then it'll be your fault." Maybe he *was* to blame. Tracy, Brother Forrester, Philip Patch, Trey Ellis, and now Vincent Renfro—all dead because he was too stupid to realize he'd been a fool from the beginning. He was just his own walking hurricane, a swath of death and destruction from St. Augustine south to West Palm Beach and back.

But then wasn't Carla Fox really the root of this evil? Patch the Genesis of it twenty-five years ago. He'd brought Sarah Fox out of the wilderness by himself, hadn't he? He would end this today.

Alone.

FIFTY-SIX

The rain ceased dripping off the rooflines. The streaks of water on the office windows had dried. Winch brought up the GPS tracking website. The Lexus had traveled north on Interstate 95 and stopped just over the Georgia line. When Winch finished with Carla, he'd work a deal with the law, and they could arrest Rusty. Carla was the big fish. And he had the right bait.

Even though he would end it today, he'd need one person's help. Someone with an agenda toward Carla and someone she wouldn't recognize. He dialed Woody.

Woody's cell phone rang. Lisa Chambers, lying next to him, gave him the 'you're not really going to answer that are you?' look.

Woody picked up the phone. "It's Winch. My boy needs something. Got to answer it." He flicked open the phone. "Whoa, Winch, what's up?"

"Can you put me in touch with Lisa Chambers?"

Woody looked at Lisa and gave her a wink. "I'm kind of working on that right now. You know what I mean?"

"She's there? Ask her if she's free this afternoon."

"She's not licensed."

Winch knew that the Division of Licensing would give him a multi-thousand dollar fine for using an unlicensed employee. He'd take that chance.

Winch heard Lisa say, "I thought you and I were spending the afternoon together."

"Tell her," he said, "she's doing it for her friend, Vinnie Renfro."

Next he called Carla. "I have Sarah's remains."

"You . . . you do? You actually found her?"

"Can we meet in a couple of hours?" He fingered the gold chain and nugget in his pocket. "I have something to give you."

"You want to come to my room?"

"I'd rather do it someplace else."

There was silence for a minute and then, "I had a phone call from my agent today about your book."

"Good." He said. "We need to talk about Rusty." But he was wondering what her agent had said.

"What on earth could you have to tell me about my brother? Do you even know him?"

"Red hair. Prosthetic left leg. Saw Trey Ellis yesterday."

"Where?" she said.

"Three thirty. Along the river." He imagined the site in his mind. Played back the layout of the benches. "Along the walkway to the fort there are some benches. Meet me there. You can walk from the hotel."

"Three-thirty," she said.

"And Carla," he said. "Bring your checkbook. This will cost you."

"I'm surprised at you Winch."

He hung up. The checkbook she'd understand.

* * * *

Rusty Fox took the St. Mary's Georgia exit and filled the tank on the Lexus. As he sat in the Starbucks drive-thru he punched off his phone call from Carla. If this punk PI thought he could blackmail Carla and get a free ride, this guy seriously underestimated him. No way he would allow that.

When Charon's fax showed up, Carla dismissed it. But he'd seen it as a perfect ruse. It was his idea to use a PI to find Trey Ellis. The other two guys were easy locates. But he could not find Trey Ellis anywhere. Winchester Young, the fool, had located Ellis and gave him up to his sister. He'd taken care of the rest. Three up. Three down. Mission accomplished.

Except, how had Young put him at the kill-site. Young had never even seen him. He'd obscured his Georgia tag with mud before he'd driven to Ellis's subdivision. No way anybody in the neighborhood could have ID'd him. After the mission was over he'd washed the mud off with a bottle of water. He didn't want to get stopped by the cops for an obscured license plate but somehow this PI made the connection.

He thought while sipping on his coffee grande with two sugars. He'd overlooked something. No way this dweeb PI followed him down to West Palm without him noticing. And why would he even be suspicious? Unless that hooker Valene was a friend of his. But that didn't compute. The guy was a Mormon. Not likely that he'd have a hooker for a friend. Besides he knew the PI wasn't down in West Palm. Carla had said the PI was in St. Augustine getting his butt kicked by the tropical storm.

He'd wondered about Sara for a long time. What had really happened to her. He wouldn't mind being at her funeral. He'd missed his sister ever since she disappeared.

He set his coffee in a cup holder, pulled himself out of the Lexus. Paced around the car. "Damn." He lay on his side and scooted under the front bumper. The undercarriage emanated a hot oil smell. It was too dark to see so he turned on his side. Not an easy maneuver with his prosthetic leg. He felt along the entire length of the bumper. It was covered with a fiberboard sheet. Nothing seem disturbed.

Next he went to the rear and began there. No fiberboard covering on this one. Most of the bumper was plastic, but there were metal struts and it had a metal framework. He ran his hand around each inch of the bumper. Near the corner of the passenger side he found a plastic box with duct tape over it. He ripped it off and pulled on the box. With a pop, it freed.

The black plastic case was a bit larger than a pack of cigarettes. It had a snap on lid and a heavy magnet on the other side. Inside was a GPS transmitter. Two LEDs glowed red and green. He pulled the back off the transmitter/receiver. A Sprint sim card. This was one damn clever little tracking device. It received its location from the GPS satellites and then broadcasts its lat and lon using cell towers. The unit was powered by a bank of six double A rechargeable batteries banded together. Why would that piss-ant PI even think to put a tracker on his car? Lesson learned. Next time before a mission he'd check his ride thoroughly.

Well, now he had to drive back to St. Augustine and cut this wild hair right off at the root. Then he and Carla could get on with the rest of their lives. But first he had to put a little hurt on that smartass PI.

At the truck stop he saw a Chevy Suburban with North Carolina plates. A load of kids piled out, two of them wearing Disney World T-shirts. The adults trailed them inside. Perfect.

He awkwardly knelt behind the Chevy's steel rear bumper and stuffed the little GPS box into the crook of the bumper where it grabbed with a slap. Powerful damn magnet. In his car he followed the Chevy to the on ramp of Interstate 95 and watched it head north. The next stop for the GPS would probably be the hills of Boone. Better than perfect. Let that PI think he's still headed north. He entered I-95 southbound. The next stop for him would be the mop-up in St. Augustine.

* * * *

Brandy arrived at Winch's office about the same time as Woody and Lisa. He briefed them on last night's activities. Vincent Renfro's shooting death was all over the news.

"You poor baby." Brandy touched lightly the butterfly bandages on his forehead. Then put a hand to his bandaged ear. "Rabies?"

He shook his head. "Tetanus shot should do it."

Woody thumbed through the photos Winch had taken of Rusty.

Lisa Chambers had a self-assured look about her. Confident. Sassy even. A women who'd just satisfied her man kind of look. "And you need me, exactly why?"

He flipped the computer screen giving them a view of the GPS track. "Here, an hour ago, Rusty Fox was in St. Mary's Georgia." He pointed to the locations where the car had been. "He stopped for gas." He brought up a satellite view of the area. "See, gas pumps. Currently he's headed north at 74 miles per hour."

"Adios to the GPS," Woody said. "But at least he's out of our hair."

"Right. I've set up a meet with Carla," he checked his watch. "In an hour, on the benches in front of the fort. She'll think we're alone. I'm going to try and get her to admit what she and her brother have done."

"If she shoots you, I guess the cops can always arrest her for that," Brandy said.

"She won't shoot me in the open."

"Why didn't you put one of those trackers on my car?" Lisa said.

"I can't talk about your case with you."

"You cop an attitude and still want a favor?" She grimaced. "Why am I helping you?"

"Because you're a decent human being?"

"That's so untrue. I've committed adultery for a year and a half. You know I'm not decent."

"Amen," Woody said. "I can testify to that."

She shot him a look.

"Because you like Woody, and he's my friend?"

"What you did for my husband is going to cost me a bucket-full of money."

"For Vinnie. He's dead because Carla Fox duped us all."

"Duped you," Lisa said.

She was right, of course. He was the idiot. Every one else just followed his lead.

"Now Lisa, I want you on the next bench over from where I'll be." He showed her how to boot up his MacBook Pro. "Right here is a built in camera. I want you to keep this pointed toward Carla Fox."

"Why don't I just use my cell phone? It takes video."

"Because of this." He laid his Bluetooth earpiece on the desk. "This will sync with the Mac, and we'll get both video and audio. If the computer asks for the sync code, it's zero, zero, zero, zero. Got it?"

"That'll do," she said. They played with the laptop and the Bluetooth until she was comfortable.

"The Bluetooth should be good for 30 feet or so. But you'll be, maybe, ten feet away." He pointed to Brandy and Woody. "You two stay away. If Carla sees either one of you, she'll know this not a real blackmail attempt. We need her to think I need the money. Don't be anywhere near the fort."

“I respect your talents, Winch,” Woody said. “But why are you doing this? You did your job. You found the missing girl. You got paid. End of story. Close the case, and let the Sheriff do his thing.”

“It’s nothing to you what happens to Carla Fox,” Brandy said.

That’s where they were wrong. It was everything to him. Carla used him and caused Tracy’s death. This was too personal. Way too close to just let it slide. “The Sheriff has nothing on Carla. She’ll walk unless I can shut the door on her.”

Woody shook his head. “Is your life worth that?”

Well then, he’d be with Tracy. Maybe he could teach her about the church while they were both in the Spirit World.

“Sounds pretty sketchy to me,” Lisa said. “Any number of things could go wrong.”

“I’ll get her to talk. All you have to do is sit on the bench. The electronics will take care of everything else.”

“What if something goes wrong?” Brandy said. “What if Rusty U-turns and makes an appearance?”

He’d catch Carla and turn the evidence over to the Sheriff. Then he’d be done with it. “He’s north bound. He couldn’t get back in time if he wanted to. You two stay away. That’s an order.”

Brandy and Woody looked at each other. “I need to keep an eye on my woman,” Woody said.

“I’ll watch her,” Winch said. “I’m serious. I don’t want you anywhere near us.”

Winch refreshed the GPS screen one more time. Rusty was still driving north on I-95, slightly above the speed limit. He knew he was rolling the dice with Carla. The best odds in the casino are found on the come out roll at the craps table, an 8 to 4 chance of winning over crapping out. He doubted his odds were that good.

FIFTY-SEVEN

Winchester had to get solid evidence on Carla Fox or she'd walk. Paying blackmail to protect her little brother would be nothing for her.

Winch always set up early for surveillances. He checked the tracking site on his iPhone. Yep, the GPS tracker was still headed north. On the concrete path to the Spanish fort, Castillo de San Marcos, he'd sat Lisa Chambers with the MacBook on a bench. He took the bench, two over.

After the passing of tropical storm Florence the summer season returned to full bloom in the historic district of St. Augustine. The air as humid as a hydroponic garden. Tourists springing up like weeds.

The tender at the Bridge of Lion's blew the horn and in a minute a north bound ketch passed under. It seemed to him Spanish forts and the shedding of blood were synonymous. A tour leader with a group of teenagers walked across the grass and stopped at the ranger's booth. Along the curb three carriages with horses and drivers waited to be rented for a circuit of the old town. The sidewalks packed with people. A half-dozen boats were anchored short distances from the seawall, their sterns toward the inlet, anchor rodes taut, pulled by the current. He looked at his watch. 3:10 pm. In another half-hour a sea breeze would kick in, freshen the air, and lift the oppressive humidity.

He had to wonder how Carla would take the news she'd killed the wrong men. He understood the desire for revenge building in her for twenty-five years. Hadn't *he* spent last night and this morning avenging Tracy's death? Were they that much different?

* * * *

Rusty Fox knew he had to out smart this PI. The guy was no dummy. Before he'd lost his leg, hadn't he moved through throngs at the marketplace in Jalalabad wearing his long-sleeved wool chupan, watching his target for the right moment, buyers and sellers none the wiser? Nailed his man and drifted off never seen. This should be easier. He didn't have to darken his complexion, wear any disguise. He just had to get close enough for a good shot.

He passed through the two stone pillars on US 1 with the bronze statutes of Spanish conquistadores, swords raised, ready to charge. Sort of the way he felt. He parked in a closed car dealership and pulled out his customized .45 caliber target pistol. Checked the load. He added the frame mounted optical sight. He'd rather use his less bulky .22 but he'd only get one shot and it had to be enough to put this guy down permanently. He couldn't count on a long distance .22 shot to do that. At 50 yards this baby would put that PI down and he'd never get up.

Rusty knew if he could set up in the fort before 3:30 pm. he'd put this problem to rest. He parked a block north of the fort and walked. Less traffic would make for a quicker getaway. If he'd had time he would have arranged a boat, run it across to Anastasia Island near the Conch House Marina for his escape.

* * * *

Brandy and Woody left Winch's office. Looked at each other. They stopped at Woody's truck and he removed a camera and put it around his neck.

"Want to look like a tourist," Woody said. He slid his sunglasses off his forehead over his eyes. "We can hoof it the four blocks to the fort."

"He asked us to stay away." Brandy licked her lips. She wore a T-shirt printed across her chest: *Legal Yes—Available No*

"I'm covering his back," Woody said. "He's my bud. I don't care what he says."

"I don't think you even know how to follow instructions," Brandy said, "You know what I mean?"

"Okay, fine. You walk to Flagler College. Sit on your butt there. Call me when Carla leaves the hotel. I want to make sure she's alone."

Twenty minutes later, Brandy sitting on a bench next to the sundial with a clear view of the Casa Monica, dialed Woody. "On her way. Alone." She wanted to say, "alone, asshole" but felt bad about slapping Woody yesterday, so she let it go. "You see anything?"

Woody paced the upper-level gun-deck of the fort. A crowd had gathered near the cannon. In a few minutes, men dressed as Spaniards would fire the cannon. He had a clear view of Winch sitting on the bench. Lisa Chambers on another. He hadn't seen anyone else, if you didn't count the gazillon tourists walking from St. George Street and its Oldest Schoolhouse, the Oldest Apothecary, and the Oldest Jail. "Nothing. Nada. Zip."

"Told you so," Brandy said. Punched off. Stood to follow Carla from a distance.

Carla weaved through the tourist traffic that jammed King Street. As she approached, Winch stood.

"Hey, stranger," she said. She reached out to him. Hugged him. Her hands ran over his back. She cocked her head and examined his bandaged ear and his head. "What happened?" With an index finger she traced the white plastic covering the stitches on his cheek.

He flinched. The lidocain from the stitches this morning, long worn off. His ear throbbed too. "Lots to tell you. Let's sit." He positioned himself so he could see Lisa, Carla's back to her. He told Carla about Patch shooting the oyster shell, the shard cutting his cheek, the possum, and the grave, Patch's death, and Patti shooting Renfro.

"Hell of a night for you." She brushed his hair back with one hand. Looked at the bruise near his temple where Patch slammed the butt of the shotgun. "I'm truly sorry I've caused so much trouble, Winchester. Really, if I'd had any idea this would escalate the way it did I never would have come to you."

A shout from the fort:

¡REHASANSE! *Take your place!*

Carla looked around. "What's that?"

"Every hour on the half-hour they perform a cannon firing demonstration in the fort. That's the first of the commands. It takes about ten minutes. The slow procedure kept the inexperienced soldiers from wasting ammunition in battle."

"Hmm," she said.

He turned his focus back to Carla. "I know what you *really* wanted from me."

She gave him a look.

"Trey Ellis," he said. "His address."

"Your cell phone. It records? " She held out a hand.

He pulled out his iPhone.

She fumbled with the back of the device and handed it back. "Take out the battery."

"You really think I'd record this conversation?"

¡ATENCION! *Attention!*

Carla glanced toward the fort, then back to him.

"It's not safe to talk unless you remove the battery."

He handed the phone back to her. "You can't remove the battery on the iPhone without destroying the phone."

She took the phone. Stood. And heaved it into the bay.

"Good arm," he said.

"Girls softball in high school."

He took the Bluetooth off his ear and laid it on the bench. But he didn't turn it off. "There. Satisfied?"

"No. Standup. Pull your shirt out."

"You're going to frisk me and buy me a new phone?"

"I have to be careful."

So far, so good. He stood. She put her arms around him, ran her hands under his shirt, up his back. All the while her lips next to his. Her breath hot on his face. A hint of Vodka Collins. She ran her hands over his chest and snaked one hand into his crotch.

"Sit," she said. "I brought cash."

¡BENDIGAS SANTA BARBARA! *Bless us St. Barbara!*

"You really think I want to blackmail you?" he said.

"What I thought was that you and I. . . ." Carla waved her hand. "Well, you know. We have a connection. Don't we?"

It was true. He'd felt the heat, that spark of reciprocal interest that sometimes passes between two people when there's mutual attraction. That's what he and Carla had. Seven days of summer smoldering heat. Though it was more than a year since he and Tracy divorced, he still felt the guilt of her death. Tracy would be alive if he hadn't brought Carla into their lives. Now he'd extract Carla from *his* life.

He needed to get her talking. "I want an explanation," he said. She started to speak but he stopped her. "Not of what you did. You and your brother. I know what you did and I think I understand why."

"They stole our sister from us." She looked around. Nobody within easy hearing distance. "Because of them, my mom died. Rusty and I were left to . . . you ever live in a foster home? Those boys had to pay."

"*Those* boys didn't commit any crime. Old man Patch killed your sister. Murdered his wife, too and then claimed she'd run off. Sarah discovered the grave while she was pot hunting on that Timucuan mound. Patch couldn't let her live. And now he's dead."

"Wait. Patch killed Sarah?" She paused, held her hand over mouth. "He was a rotten man."

He couldn't disagree with that. The Sheriff's office would eventually figure out who killed Patch. Probably Patti. "And the other two? You and your brother killed them too."

Carla crossed her legs. Her top leg bouncing, her sandaled foot swinging. She closed her eyes, tilting her head back. "Oh my gosh. We killed the wrong people. And Rusty is . . . oh no."

"Rusty is what? Guilty of murder?" he said. But he didn't think that's what she'd meant. He'd missed something.

The air freshened. Sailboats swung on their anchors, caught halfway between the inlet's tidal current and the sea breeze. It'd be an uncomfortable anchorage until the tide turned.

"Why did you ask *me* to help?" Winch knew the answer but he wanted her to say it.

She shook her head. "This is all too much for me to absorb. And I don't want to hurt your feelings."

"Tracy is dead. My boat destroyed. My home teacher was blown to pieces. Renfro shot. I nearly killed Snake. Patch is dead. I got my freaking ear bit off. And you're worried about my feelings?"

"You just don't know how sorry I am," she said with a sigh. She placed one hand on his bare forearm. "You were the least experienced person I could find. About the only one that was not ex something: ex-cop, ex-FBI, ex-special forces. I wanted someone who was too stupid to figure out what I really wanted."

"Trey Ellis's address."

"Exactly," she said. "Only I underestimated you. We found the other two, no trouble. We couldn't locate Trey. When Snake's fax came in, you were the perfect patsy." She shrugged. "Only not so perfect, I guess."

¡ENTREN LA CUDHARA EN EL CANON! *Bring up the ladle!*

They both glanced at the fort then to each other.

"So it was never about Sarah," he said.

"No, you're wrong." She stood. Looked around. "It was always about Sarah. Just not the way you thought."

"You thought I was a fool."

Wasn't he? He'd fallen right into her trap and given her what she'd wanted.

"You're no fool, Winchester." She sat back down. "When I met you, I liked you. You're more clever than any man I've met."

"I have something for you." He reached into his pocket and withdrew the gold nugget and chain. Handed it to her.

"You—"

"Took it off Sarah last night." He offered it to her.

Tears filled her eyes. With the edges of her forefingers she wiped the corners. Fanned her face with one hand. Held the gold nugget and chain up. "I . . . I really don't know what to say."

He liked Carla and wanted to offer her hope. But here he was, establishing the evidence that would put her on death row. He said, "How about something like, I'm sorry I lied to you, used you. Had those innocent men killed."

¡RECONOZCAN SI ESTA CAREDO! *Check that the gun is clear!*

FIFTY-EIGHT

Woody spotted Rusty. At least he thought it was Rusty, but he was supposedly driving north through Georgia. Still, this guy wore cargo pants, a loose shirt, and had some sort of a heavy weight in the right thigh pocket of his pants. He concluded the man was Rusty Fox when the fellow raised his leg to examine the bottom of his shoe and he saw a flash of burgundy steel tubing, like a section of bicycle frame. Just as Winch described.

He eyed Rusty as he walked with a limped gait across the blue-green field of St. Augustine grass toward the fort. A group of thirty teenage boys jostled each other near the entrance. Their leader, a man in his forties spoke to them, gesturing with a broad wave toward the inlet to the ocean. Rusty slid past the group and into the fort. Somehow Woody had to warn Winch. He called Winch's cell. Voice mail. Damn. He speed dialed Lisa. She answered.

* * * *

Winch looked at Lisa on the next bench, his MacBook on her lap. Her screen angled so he could read. She'd typed in a 72-point font. *Rusty in the fort.* Crap.

¡RETIREN LA CUCHARA! *Lay aside the ladle!*

He scanned the seventeen-foot thick coquina walls of the fort. He'd wanted an open place with lots of people. On a busy tourist day, thirty-five hundred visitors might pass through the gates. He hadn't thought Rusty Fox would shoot him with three hundred witnesses. But he'd made a mistake.

If he ran now, surely Rusty would get him in his sites, lead him a bit, and shoot him like a running dog. Better to sit here and figure a way to outsmart him.

¡ENTREN LA LANADA Y TAPEN EL FOSEN! *Bring sponge & tend to vent!*

Carla shook her head. Little beads of sweat showed on her forehead. The wisps of hair in front of her ears were damp. "I don't know how to make it right."

"There's no way," he said. "You take someone's life. You can't give it back."

Her jaw line tightened. She gestured with her hand toward the gaggle of tourists. "There must be something I can do."

"Sacrifice your own life in exchange for someone else's." He shrugged. "That might bring you some forgiveness." He gestured toward the fort. "The walls, you know, are made of coquina. A composition of limestone and tiny shells." He nodded across the bay toward the lighthouse on Anastasia Island. "It only exists in north Florida and the coast of Africa."

¡PASEN LA LANADA EN EL CANON! *Sponge the gun*

Carla examined the gold nugget. Slid the chain through her fingers.

"No real stones in Florida suitable for constructing a fortress," he said. "So the discovery of the coquina was fortuitous."

From the east ramparts he heard the command.

¡RETIRENLA A SU LUGAR! *Lay aside the sponge*

He checked his watch 3:34 pm. Four minutes to firing. If Rusty had looked at the firing schedule. . . . He knew when Rusty would take his shot.

He brought his focus back to Carla. "Coquina is strong but not brittle. When attacking forces shot at the walls, instead of fracturing like brick, it simply absorbed the cannon balls. Swallowed them up. Cool stuff."

¡TOMEN EL BOTAFUEGO! *Take up the linstock*

Three more minutes. "I think there's a lesson there." He shot a glance at Lisa and the laptop. Nothing.

"Cut the bull," Carla said. "We're out of time. Let's go somewhere else."

"I think coquina teaches us that we can live a long and happy life by being flexible and giving." He took her hand. "We're fine here."

¡BOTAFUEGO AL CAÑON! *Position the linstock*

Two more. He had to be ready. His life depended upon it. He dropped her hand and wiped his palms on his trousers.

"I'm not here for history lessons, Winchester. I like you a lot but I don't need life lessons from a down and out PI chasing fornicators and liars."

"Speaking of down and out," he said. "Where's Rusty?"

She scratched her leg. The other hand's fingernails drummed on the wooden bench. "Does he need to be looking over his shoulder for the Sheriff?"

"I think they'll find him whether he's looking or not."

"You told them, didn't you?"

"Not yet, but I will."

"We can work this out." She reached into her purse. Pulled out her cell. Punched a number. "I have to stop him. He's going to kill you."

* * * *

Woody had to stop Rusty. More than five bus-loads of tourists mingled on the grounds. Another two loads were watching the show, waiting for the cannon to boom.

Rusty headed up the stairs leading to the upper ramparts two steps at a time, pushing through the slow moving tourists. The flat upper deck of the fort was wider than a basketball court and circled the fort. On one corner sat a bell tower. On the other three corners were sentry boxes like man-high chess board pawn pieces. Behind the seaward wall three replica cannons sat aimed toward the St. Augustine inlet.

As the crowd thickened Woody lost sight of Rusty. He scanned the upper deck. There were only two places of concealment that faced the benches where Winch and Carla sat. The sentry boxes on the southeast and southwest corners.

He knew the cannon firing routine. He'd worked in this fort twenty-five years ago and it hadn't changed. Two more commands until the big boom. When the command to fire, *Afuente* was shouted, the cannon would roar instantly.

He carefully approached the southwest sentry box. If Rusty were inside, he damn well didn't want to get shot himself. But from here, about half the distance from a pitcher's rubber to home plate, he could see the sentry's post was empty. Had to be in the other.

¡ALTO Y SOPLEN LA MECHA! *Halt, blow on the match!*

The angle of the sun was such that the inside of the other sentry box was cloaked in darkness. He didn't have a gun. What was he supposed to do? When he was within ten feet he heard a cell phone ring inside the lookout. Bingo.

The soldiers readied the big guns. He took the camera from around his neck and waited. As the costumed soldier bent to light the fuse Woody heaved the camera with his best fast pitch toward Rusty in the sentry box.

¡AFUENTE! *FIRE!*

He missed. The camera hit the edge of the sentry box. The lens shattered. Behind him, the cannons roared. A flash inside the sentry box backlit a man with a two-handed grip on his pistol.

FIFTY-NINE

The next to last command sang out from the fort. Winch had less than a minute until Rusty would kill him, using the blast of the cannon to mask the shot. That's what he would have done. He had to time his move perfectly or he'd be dead. Free to join Tracy in the Spirit World. Or worse. He could be wounded and paralyzed.

He should have told the cops about Rusty. Let them do their job. But it wasn't "their" Tracy who'd been killed. She'd been his. Both Patti and Brandy told him she was coming back to him. Would he have married her again? Absolutely.

¡ALTO Y SOPLEN LA MECHA! *Halt, blow on the match!*

Carla closed her cell phone. "No answer."

"He probably has me sited in," he said. "Made some allowance for the sea breeze."

"I tried to call him. I wanted to tell him that Patch killed Sarah. You have to leave, Winch. Right now!"

"Too late for that."

"I'm so, so sorry, Winch." She shook her head. "If I could stop him, I would. I don't know how."

¡AFUENTE! *Fire*

Winch rolled backwards off the bench, the cannon boomed, and at that exact second Carla thrust the palms of her hands against his chest and pushed, adding momentum to his roll. He scrambled toward an oak, knelt behind it, and looked to see if she followed.

She lay still on the ground, a red swath slashing through the back of her blouse.

He jumped back to her. “Carla?” Her breath came in shallow huffs. A thin red line trailed out of her nose. “Oh no.”

With a raspy voice she said, “Winchester Young, my hero.” She grasped his hand. “Tell the families it was a terrible mistake. I’m sorry.” Scarlet bubbles trickled through her lips. She took one breath. “Hurry now, he’ll come for you.”

He turned to Lisa Chambers on the next bench. He knew he had just a matter of seconds before Rusty would emerge from the fort with gun blazing. He grabbed the laptop from Lisa and pushed her. “Go. Go. Get away!”

* * * *

Rusty couldn’t believe what he saw. Carla lay on the ground, blood staining the back of her blouse. He didn’t have a clear shot anymore. His hand trembled. Even if he had a shot he couldn’t take it. He’d shot his sister. The plan was for the two of them to even the score, finally put Sarah to rest and have some peace. That murdering PI pulled Carla directly into his line of fire. He’d get him for this.

* * * *

Winch’s only chance was to get to Rusty before Rusty got to him. He sprinted the fifty yards to the fort, crossed the moat’s drawbridge and stood just inside the dark tunnel entrance. Rusty’s eyes wouldn’t have time to adjust. He panted as he stood, back to the cool coquina, MacBook raised. In just a second he caught a glint off a stainless barrel as Rusty ran full bore out of the sunlight toward him.

The man charged through the fort’s entrance, the .45 semi-auto in his hand, making no effort to hide the weapon. Winch swung the MacBook. He’d hoped to catch the running man full in the face, break his nose. But he miscalculated, like a batter swinging late on a fastball, he struck Rusty on the side of the head. It was enough to make him stumble, take three off balance lunges, and spill onto the bridge. The gun slid out of his hand and teetered on the edge of the drawbridge.

Normally the moat would be dry but with the tropical storm ankle-deep water collected. He threw himself at Rusty. The drawbridge bounced with their impact and the gun fell into the moat with a splash, followed by a heavier splash. The MacBook.

Rusty twisted under Winch, wrapped his legs around his back and squeezed. The prosthetic leg—an iron pipe crushing Winch's spine. He landed a punch on Winch under the eye socket. The stitches from this morning separated. Winch returned punches, right-left, right-left, pummeling Rusty's face. Slick with blood now, his punches sliding off the man's face. Winch levered the both of them so he was on his knees, Rusty still on his back. Rusty dropped his leg squeeze, pushed with the palms of his hands against Winch and then kicked Winch in the chest, sending him smashing back-first against the bridge railing. Rusty struggled to his feet.

Both men were breathing hard when Rusty threw himself at Winch. Their combined weight crashed through the hand railing and they fell into the moat, Rusty on top. Winch, the breath knocked out of him, sucked air but found water in his mouth instead.

He pushed Rusty off, on his hands and knees now. His stomach heaved retching out the foul water. Rusty pivoted on his prosthesis, roundhouse kicking Winch in the head. Knocking him to his back. But the prosthesis didn't pivot in the mud well and the kick that could have killed only stunned.

"You're dead now," Rusty said. He pulled up his pant's leg, ripped at Velcro straps, over-hand gripped the burgundy steel tube, on each end like a chin-up bar. One hop on his real leg and he fell on top of Winch with a splash.

Winch, head not yet clear, pushed Rusty with no effect. Rusty pressed the pipe against Winch's throat, shifting his weight, bringing it all to bear on Winch's windpipe.

Winch couldn't breathe. His nose and mouth were below the water in the moat. He boxed his hands against Rusty's ears. Tried kidney punching him with no results. He shifted his hands to the prosthetic leg, pushed upward, like bench-pressing two hundred pounds. He couldn't shift Rusty an inch. For the second time in twenty-four hours he realized he was about to die. His brain fogged but he wouldn't give up. He'd go to hell before he drowned in less than a foot of water.

He kicked and pushed, tried to maneuver Rusty off, but he couldn't. He heard Carla's voice, loving but stern, giving orders to a misbehaving eight year old. Was he hallucinating?

"Rusty," Carla said. "Enough."

At the sound of Carla's voice, Rusty straightened. The pipe came off Winch's throat just enough for him to swing a leg over Rusty's head and fling the one legged man onto his back.

Winch stood, the world swayed around him and finally settled. He grabbed the steel leg and held it over Rusty like a club. "Don't move," he gasped. "Or I will beat you to death as surely as I'm standing here."

Rusty pushed himself up. Got his good leg under him and rose. Winch swung, whacked him in the side and heard ribs crack. Rusty fell into the muck, rolled, struggled to his knees.

"Don't," Winch said. Rusty, once more, attempted to stand. Whack. He hit him on the other side and the man fell on to his back. Rested on his elbows, head above water. Moaning.

He stepped to the concreted side of the moat where a small crowd of onlookers stood. He couldn't see Carla. "Help me up," he said.

He passed up the leg. Several men gave him a hand and in a second he was pulled to dry ground.

Detective Sergeant Hardwick pushed to the edge of the moat, gun drawn. "Everybody back," he said. "Move now." He turned to Winch. "What kind of mess have you made here, Young?"

"He killed Trey Ellis in West Palm." He pointed to Rusty. "And Tony Hudson in Guana River."

"Hudson? That's my case." Hardwick shook his head. "I'll be damned." He pointed the gun at Rusty. "You down there. Don't move."

Winch ran back to the benches wondering how he and Rusty could have heard Carla calling. Lisa, covered in blood, held a shirt compressed against Carla's back. Woody bent over her body on the ground giving her mouth-to-mouth.

Woody looked up at him, took his mouth off of Carla. Began chest compressions. "You looked like you were doing okay in the moat. Thought she needed me here." Then he shook his head. "But she's gone, Bro. No pulse, nothing."

He knelt next to Carla. Held one hand and lifted some hair off her face. She had blood on her hands and he was surprised at how cool they were. From her open palm he took Sarah's nugget and gold chain. He wiped her face with the bottom of his wet shirt.

Siren's wailed. A rescue unit pulled over the curb and a park ranger directed them to the foot of the bridge.

Rescue was too late. Nothing could bring Carla back. He held the jewelry in his closed fist for a second, thought about heaving it into the bay, then slid it into his pocket.

Winch stepped back, looked overhead fully expecting to see Carla hovering in the air. A personage of spirit. She'd spoken to him and Rusty as she'd passed through the veil. Had she given her life for his? A blood atonement of sorts? But she wasn't there. Not visible to him, anyway. Was *he* visible to her? He didn't know.

"I've got no pulse," the EMT said.

One of the EMTs said to the other, "Get a large bore IV. Pump her with fluids."

The first EMT was on the phone, talking to the hospital. Giving Carla's vitals to a doctor. Turned to the other. "DRT," he said. "The doc called it."

"DRT?" Winch said.

The man lowered his head. "Sorry. Dead Right There."

In a minute St. Augustine PD cars arrived.

Amazing how the slightest shift in action, a fraction of a second of movement one way or the other could result in hugely different results. Had she not tried to push him out of Rusty's line of fire would she still be alive? He should have shoved her perhaps. But then he'd be dead instead of her. He hadn't shot her, but was in a way responsible for her death.

A human being, a human soul, is comprised of two parts. The body and the spirit. Now that Carla's body was dead, her spirit had departed. Who would meet her on the other side to usher her through the veil between the Spirit World and mortality? And as soon as he thought the question, he knew the answer. Sarah.

Police cars cordoned off the street. The horses harnessed to buggies, strained their reins, whinnied and shuffled hooves. A half-dozen green and white Sheriff's units arrived, screeched to a stop, sirens whelped, reds and blues blazed.

Carla's body was covered but not taken away. The rescue had turned into a crime scene. When he had a chance, he explained it all to Hardwick. Suggested they might want to fish the laptop and gun out of the moat. Carla's admissions would probably be recoverable and could be useful in Rusty's trial.

Since this was St. Augustine PD jurisdiction, Winch asked Hardwick, "Why are you here?"

"Check your bumper, Young. You're not the only person in town who has GPS trackers. The Sheriff told us you weren't finished yet. Said if you were anything, you were thorough. To stay on top of you."

"You used me for bait."

"You put yourself on the hook. We just played out the line."

Winch crossed under the yellow crime scene tape. Brandy put one arm over his shoulder, Lisa on his other side. In a second Woody stepped next to Lisa, placed his arm over her shoulder. The four of them walked down the riverfront, past the slave market, tourists lining the curb watching the police activity at the fort, beyond the Bridge of Lions, the A1A Ale Works, and walked the remaining two blocks to his office.

"You know, Winch" Brandy said. "The whole Carla Fox thingee. Would make one frigging hell of a book. You know what I mean?"

He put a hand to his freshly bandaged face and tapped the gauze over the butterfly bandages. He'd get the stitches redone later. "I don't do true crime."

SIXTY

FIVE DAYS LATER

Winch sat at his office desk watching dust float in a sunbeam of light. He buried Tracy this morning. A larger group turned out for the service than he'd expected. Woody, Brandy, some of Tracy's friends. Surprisingly, Meredith Renfro, the Sheriff, and Detective Sergeant Hardwick. He liked to think Hardwick attended because they'd developed a little bit of mutual admiration for each other's work. Also a bunch of people from church brought food to his house for a gathering after the burial. But nobody stayed very long. And he didn't really want nor need the company.

He consecrated Tracy's grave himself. Any worthy Priesthood holder in the Mormon Church, with permission, can perform that ordinance. He'd felt particularly inspired. First he dedicated and consecrated the burial plot as the resting place for Tracy's body of flesh and blood. Then he prayed, asking the Lord to watch over the site, to keep it hallowed and protected until the day of the resurrection, when Tracy would come forth from the grave in a perfect, glorified body of flesh and bone.

He prayed also that Tracy would be inspired to seek out the gospel while in the Spirit World. Understand the truthfulness of the restored teachings so that one day, they could be sealed, one to another, for time and all eternity. He wasn't sure if that part of the prayer had been inspired or came out of his own desires, but he said it anyway.

On his way to the office he stopped by the post office and picked up three letters from agents. He opened them immediately. If he learned anything from this case, it was life was too precarious to waste waiting. With the Jeep at idle, the air blowing full, he opened each. Three rejections.

An autopsy would be performed on Sarah and Patch's wife. But no one doubted that Patch had murdered both. Rusty was in custody.

The Florida Highway Patrol had picked up Patti at a rest stop on Interstate 10 near Pensacola, when she tried to steal another woman's purse for the ID and credit cards.

Renfro's funeral would be tomorrow, and he'd go.

The phone rang. Caller ID said Lambert & Gilbert. Carla's literary agent. Well, good news comes by phone.

"Mr. Young," Parker Lambert said. "You understand, don't you, that in view of recent events, there's no way we can represent you?"

"Killed the goose, did I?"

"Very funny, Mr. Young.

The phone went dead.

He opened the file he'd assembled on the Sarah Fox case. Took her photo out and looked at it one more time. The three of them, Sarah, Carla, and Rusty. He dropped the gold nugget and chain into an envelope and placed it all in its proper place in the file cabinet. Slid the drawer closed.

On the desk in front of him lay his manuscript, *Murder in the Conch House*. He hefted it. Three hundred and fifty pages. Not quite one ream of paper. He took two large rubber bands out of his desk drawer and slid them over the manuscript. He carried it to a file cabinet, opened the bottom drawer and dropped it in and shut the drawer with his foot. Maybe that book would make the grade to publication, maybe it wouldn't. Whichever way it went, his work on it was done.

Every successful author he'd ever spoken to had advised that while shopping the first manuscript, get to work on the next. So he would.

He had to think of a good title. He wrote on a legal pad: *Murder at the Castillo de San Marcos.* Too close to the truth. *Murder on the Timucuan Preservation.* Nope, nobody could pronounce Timucuan. *The Case of the Disappearing Spring Breaker.* Too long. Finally he hit on one he liked.

Next he'd need a pen name. If he were going to use the Carla Fox case as the basis for his novel he'd have to change the names of the characters, and his own. Nobody would hire him if they thought he'd write about their cases. Sort of took the meaning of "private" out of "private investigation." He'd need a name that was common. Something near the beginning of the alphabet so his books would be shelved next to the big names, like James Lee Burke and Dan Brown. He could use Black. Well, why not Brown. It'd put his book right next to Dan Brown's. Maybe someone would buy his by mistake. Increase sales. His last name Young would put him clear at the end of the mystery section. He thought a middle name, like Kerry, added a nice touch. Or he could use a first initial like *S. Kerry Brown* sort of like F. Scott Fitzgerald. Maybe a bit too pretentious.

He pulled up a blank document on his computer and typed:

REDEEMING THE DEAD
By
Steven Kerry Brown

The End

Acknowledgments

This book could not have been written without the honing of the craft of writing that I was taught by James N. Frey (How to Write A Damn Good Mystery) and Frank Green, The Bard Society, whose living room I occupied for over 20 years every Wednesday night listening to the difference between mediocre writing, good writing, and great craftsmanship.

Special thanks to my wife Melanie Tracey Brown who put up with my late night computer tasks.

Special thanks to my good friend, Jeffrey Philips (*Murder on Devil Ray Reef, Death at Obeah's Fire*). Jeffrey and I have attended many writing groups together. The Bard Society with Frank Green and multiple sessions with James N. Frey, here in Florida and California. We've dived and sailed together in the Bahamas. When I underwent a bone marrow transplant several years ago, after the first 30 days in the hospital I had to reside with a 24 hour caretaker for 100 days within ten minutes of Shands Cancer Center in Gainesville Florida. I rented an apartment and Jeffrey spent two weeks as my caretaker there. He's a very good writer and a special friend.

Thanks to my other critique partners: Jodi Sykes (*The House on Pancake Hill*), Joan North (*Secondary Colors*), Frank Linn, Brian Shea, the Queen of Lean—Nancy Pridgen, Mary Golly (Plane Life), Lorraine Haataia (DrLorraine.net), Bill Doughtery, Mike Walsh, Ken Overman (*A Lion in Spring*), Kathy Hynes, Joyce Nicholas, and Lori Thatcher.

The great cover art was provided by CrankShaft Marketing (crankshaftmarketing.com), my son Kerry Brown, Eric Nelson, and Will Pigg.

www.ingramcontent.com/pod-product-compliance
Lightning Source LLC
Chambersburg PA
CBHW030026180626
46810CB00001B/238